HIDDEN DOORS

KEITIKAT PARK

The brain is a fantastic thing. It controls everything that we do, say, think, and even remember. Some people can remember every detail of their life while others forget most of it. Their memories tucked behind the hidden doors in their mind. Some so precious that to remember them would cause us to waste away with longing. Some were so tragic and terrifying that remembering them would cause you to go insane. The mind's only choice is to lock them out to protect us from what lies behind them so that we can smile, laugh, and love those around us.

Table of Contents

CHAPTER 1

Discovering the beginning.

I am walking down this Stone Staircase. There are no handrails, only darkness on one side, and a stone wall on the other. The wall is lined with doors. Each one is different from pictures of faceless people in between. Some are shadowed by thick darkness and send spirals of cold and fear as I pass them. I want to turn back but cannot. When I turn to try all that is, there is a curtain of black, and it is like the staircase disappears into the shadows once I take a step forward. I know I have no choice but to continue. Suddenly I heard a voice in the darkness to pick a door and go in. My voice keeps telling me I am in a safe place and that nothing can harm me. Once I go through a door, it will be like watching a movie. But it will be a movie that I need to tell her every detail about. The light shines on a doorway, and I open.

I walk in, and I am standing at the bottom step of a porch in front of a large house. The house is so beautiful, all white with blue shutters, the tall pillars holding up a wraparound porch. I smell the roses that line both sides of the steps. I look up at the steps at the stained-glass door. I do not understand why I am so afraid to walk up to them. I feel like I have cement in my feet that I cannot take a step.

I hear the voice say, "it is ok taking your time.

Taking a deep breath, I start to walk up the steps to the porch.

The voice asks me "how old are you here?"

"I am 7 or 8 I think."

"Tell me what you are doing here?"

"I am here to pay our rent. My mom sent me so it wouldn't be late." I say to the voice.

As I walked on to the porch. I wave of fear washes over me. I hesitate to even raise my hand to knock on the door. I turned to walk away without knocking, I made the decision to lie and say that no one was home. I start to walk down the steps when the door opens, and I hear "oh good you're here. Come in and I will get your receipt." Says Dr Peterson

"that's ok. I can stay here." As I handed him the rent money.

"Your mommy said you had been sick so come in and I will check you out." He opens the door wider, and I know I cannot just Run home this time, or my mom will be mad at me again.

So, I put my head down and walked into the house. The house smells musty and if smoke. I can smell the whisky on the Drs breath. I hate that smell most. He is old and creepy. I get this uncomfortable feeling in the pit of my stomach like I want to vomit. I tried to tell him I am all better now, but he puts his hand on my forehead, and I know he can tell right away that I still have a fever.

"Come into the exam room so that I can see why you are caring a fever." he says as he is walking towards the door to that room. I hate coming here, it scares me more than anything. He leads me to the small room down the hall that he uses for patients. It has a tall exam table, one that I cannot climb up onto by myself.

I walk into the room and the first thing he does is pick me up and sit me at the exam table. He takes my temperature and feels my throat makes me open my mouth to look at it. Then he checks my ears. He pushes me down on my back. He then lifts my shirt and starts pressing on my belly. The pressure of his hands becomes lighter, and the bile rises in my throat as his hand goes to the waist of my pants. I keep my eyes closed so that I cannot see his face. He steps up onto the step at the base of the exam table the next sound I hear is his breathing it getting heavy I feel him up against my legs he pulls me back up to sitting and he is taking my hand and placing it on his naked male part I scream and bite his hand he yells and jerks away. Before he could grab me again, I ran away and out of the house.

I hear the voice again and she keeps reminding me that I am safe. That nothing and no one can hurt me here. When I calmed down, she asked me what happened next.

I run to Mrs. Kings barn and hide in the horse stall. I know I am going to be in trouble. I just hope I can hide till after my grandma comes. Then maybe I can go with her and not have to stay here.

I go to the stall with the horse that everyone is afraid of because no one will bother me there Mrs. King had the groom make a special ladder for me so. When I visit him, I can stand on it? This way I am tall enough to brush him and pat him. I brush his dark chestnut mane and talk to him while I get the tangles out. I do not know why no one likes him. He always stands still for me and is quiet. After brushing his mane, I braided it so that it would not re tangle. I put my arms around his neck and cried for a few moments. I sit on the clean hay by his door when I am done so anyone looking in will not be able to see me. The groom always has fresh hay piled up there for me just in case I visit, so I have a clean place. I always fall asleep there. A few hours pass, and I hear my mom's angry voice calling me as she is heading towards Mts. Kings, I know she will ask her to look in the barn. So, I slip out and run to the orchard and climb to the top branches of the largest cherry tree. Since my mom thinks I am afraid to climb trees she will not look for me there. I sat on the branch and pulled the book out of the small branch I had wedged in from last time. I sit and read till I see my grandma's car pulling in. I know it will be safe to go home now. I start to climb down and at the bottom there is a boy sitting. I look down and ask him "what are you doing in Mrs. Kings orchard." I find it odd because he has his head down and his long hair falls around his face.

He crosses his arms and says "I could ask you the same question. Why are you in one of my grandmother's trees and why did you hide in the barn earlier?" He asked.

I jump down and hold out my hand "hi I'm Katie. And your grandma lets me sit in this tree and lets me play with her horses."

He takes my hand and shakes it "it's nice to meet you. I want to know why you were crying in the barn?"

Just then I heard my mom calling me again. She sounds angry. I waved to him. I turn and run towards my house making sure that I cut through Mr. Johnson's yard so that my mom does not know where I was.

I get home and my mom and dad are throwing things into the back of the truck and screaming at each other. I see my Grandma Wilt and my Grandma Taylor also yelling at each other. I know I am in big trouble now. They turn and see me, and the first thing Grandma Taylor does is smack me across the face and screams at me that it is my fault that we must move away and that it is my fault that the landlord will not even return my dad's deposit back.

I held my cheek and started to cry. My Grandma Wilt walks over and slaps my Grandma Taylor and then wraps me in her arms. "How can you blame a 7-year-old when you don't even know what happen?" She asks.

"How is it anyone else's fault?" Grandma Taylor replied.

My grandma wipes my tears and tells me to go get some clothes. I am going home with her. I look at my mom and dad. My mom looks like she wants to beat me. My dad starts to walk over to me. I hide behind my grandma. "it's ok I just want you to tell me what happened, so I understand?"

I look at my dad and start to cry and I told him that the Dr smelled of whisky touched me in a way that made me afraid. He put his arms around me and told me it was ok. He looks at my mom and asks her "you know he scares her why did you send her?"

"She is just being silly, and I was fixing dinner and realized that the rent was going to be late, so I asked her to take it to him. I called him and told him she has been feverish for the last 3 days to please check her out when she brought the rent for me."

My dad smiles at me and tells me to go get my clothes so that I can stay at grandma wilts house for a few days. He dries my tears and hugs me. I smell the whisky on his breath. I see he stopped at the club before coming home again. I nodded to him and walked into the house.

My Grandma Taylor followed me and asked me to sit. She had something to say. I sit on the edge of her bed with my head bowed. She sits beside me "I don't understand you girl. Why are you such a worthless child because of you we now have no money and no place to live? I hope that You start to grow up just a little and soon." As she walked out, I heard her say under her breath that it would have been better if God had just let this mistake not been born. When she closed the door, I thought, well maybe everything would be ok if I were not around. I walked to the medicine cabinet and pulled out my Grandma Taylor pills she takes to sleep and sneak out the back door. I ran through the field towards Mrs. Kings. I stopped in the high grass behind the tractor, so no one can see me I pull out old man Johnson cooler he always has water in it and sit down on the ground. I open the bottle and start swallowing the pills one by one till all of them are gone. I lean against the tire and close my eyes. I started to feel sleepy and lay down. The cold from the ground washes over me and all the noise around begins to fade. I feel the darkness sweeping over me. It is cold so cold I feel like ice. I feel like I have no air. Suddenly I feel someone picking me up and shaking me. I look up, but everything is spinning, and I cannot make out who it is. I just smile at them and ask, "stay with me till the angel comes." And close my eyes again. The person holding me puts their fingers down my throat and makes me vomit until there is nothing left in my stomach. I hear yelling in the distance. I close my eyes again as I feel warm arms around me.

I hear the voice saying it is time to come back now.

I feel myself being separated from the child. I looked back and the door appeared again. So, I got up and walked to the door and started walking back up the staircase. I become less sleepy as I get closer to the top. The darkness of the stairway gets lighter as I get closer to the voice. You will awake when I snap my fingers 1 2 3, I hear her fingers snap and I am sitting in the Dr office on the couch I look at her and ask, "how did I do, do I remember anything?" She looks dumbfounded and asks me "what do you remember about the memory you just opened.

I shrug my shoulders and say not much only that I was a little girl.

She asks me again what I remember. I look at her puzzled "I did remember something didn't I? Why can't I remember now that I am awake?"

"I don't know but we will try something else next time. With your permission I would like to have a colleague. sit in next time who is an expert in forgotten memories. I already sent your chart to him to get his advice." She said.

"Ok anything to get the nightmares to go away." I replied.

"Ok I will call him." I got up and as I was leaving, I heard her on the phone. "Dr Park this is Dr Smith I just had a session with the patient we spoke about, and she has agreed to let you sit in with us."

As I make my way home, I have a very uneasy feeling, but I just try to shake it off since I must go pick up the kids. I pull into the school parking lot and wait in line for the kids to get out of school. I start trying to remember what happened in the Dr office, but I have a bad headache starting. The kids get in the car, and we head home. After dinner is done and the house is clean, I can finally go to sleep. I lay down and closed my eyes. It feels like I have only been asleep for a few moments, and I hear screaming. I try to get up and cannot seem to move as the fear washes over me .it feels like I have a heavy weight. sitting on me the screams are getting louder and I feel trapped. I start to push and scratch at the shadow that is pulling me in. I felt a sharp pain in my side like I was being stabbed. I push hard and roll away falling. I curl up in a ball and feel my entire body shaking. I begin to pray begging for the screaming and fear to go away. I feel someone put their arms around me and whisper its ok your safe. The shaking starts to subside, and the screams begin to become just whimpers and sniffles, finally there is just empty darkness.

When I wake up to get my husband Joe ready for work, he asks me "do you remember anything about the nightmare you had last night?"

"No, I only remember there was screaming and then someone holding me." I answered.

He turns toward me and for the first time I see his face. He has gashes on his face and on his arms. I gasp in horror "what happened?"

He gets a mean look on his face and replies "you did this in your sleep. You were screaming and thrashing about. When I tried to calm you, this is what happened. I do not know what is going on with you, but it better stop soon. I am tired of dealing with this weak-minded shit. If I had known how weak minded and worthless you where I would have left, you before we ever got married now, we got kids, and I am stuck." He grabs his lunch box and slams out of the house. I just stared after him with tears running down my face not knowing what to do.

I dry my tears and start to make the kids breakfast. I need to be as normal as possible around them. Things have been hard for them since my grandma and Dad died a few months back After getting them off to school. I start to clean the house lord knows I cannot have anything out of place when joe gets home. The day goes by in a blur as if I were an auto pilot. I do not really remember much about what I did today or who I spoke with. I even forgot to pick up the kids from school. Its days like today I wish I could keep the 5 of them home. Just so I could have distractions to keep me aware of what I am doing.

When Joe gets home, I have everything done and dinner on the table. After dinner and I get the kitchen cleaned I send the kids to bed. I go to get ready for bed and Joe tells me that unless I can guarantee that there will not be any nightmares I need to sleep elsewhere. I get the blanket and go sleep on the couch. And sleep there for the next 6 nights while he refuses to even speak to me except to remind me of what I do wrong. the week between my session with Dr smith seemed to be just one big blur I really do not remember much of anything that happened this week.

Today are the day Dr Smith wants someone to sit in with us. I am so anxious about this because it is hard for me to be open about myself about anything other than my family. Things about me personally I have a hard time with.

I walk into the Dr office, and I see a very handsome gentleman sitting in the chair. I feel like I have met him before, but I cannot remember where. I catch myself sneaking glances at him. He is so handsome. I cannot help but look at him, his dark hair falling just below his collar. The cologne he wears reminds me of someone I am so familiar with, but I cannot remember who wears it. He is Asian I am sure he is Korean but am afraid to ask. I would not want to offend him. His build is slender, but you can tell he is physically active and his suit fits. His tie is a little askew I fight the urge to walk over and fix it. He slouches forward, and I must bite my tongue to tell him not to slouch.

The secretary calls for Dr Park follow her back to Dr Smith office. She tells me she will be right back for me in a few minutes. I just smile and nod my head. A few moments later she told me I could go back now. I walk into the office and there is Dr Smith and the gentleman from the waiting room. He smiles at me and introduces himself. "Hi, I am Dr Park it's nice to meet you. As he reaches out his hand to me, I take his hand and shake it without even looking at him. His hand is warm, and I get an awfully familiar feeling from him.

"Kat, I want you to be relaxed and not to worry that Dr Park is here. if its ok with you I am going to let him guide you today through your session to see if you can remember anything after we wake up from the hypnosis." Dr Smith looks at me I just nod my head yes.

Dr Smith gets up and turns the light down to almost dark in the room. Dr Park takes a light pen out of his pocket and starts to sway it back and forth asking me to follow with my eyes telling me to relax. My eyes start to close, and I hear his voice "you are at the top of the staircase what do you see?"

"Doors and pictures of faceless people between them." I reply.

"Can you find the door from last time?" He asked.

I walked down the dark staircase and just like last time a light above a door came on I felt frightened and wanted to turn back. I do not want to go in.

I hear the Dr's voice telling me that there is nothing to fear that I am in a safe place, so I open the door and go in.

"What do you see around you?"

"I am in a hospital room, and I hear my father talking to my mother."

"What is he saying?"

"He is asking her why she would send me to that house knowing how scared I was of the Dr." "She is telling him that I am too afraid of things and need to learn to suck it up and grow up a little and that he babies me too much. "

He is looking at her as if she has two heads and gets up and walks out. I cry out "daddy wait." but he does not come back to my room. The Dr comes in and is wanting to examine me and I start screaming at trying to bite him. My mom walks across the room and slaps me across the face.

"Stop it right now don't you think you have caused enough trouble today now sit there and don't move unless the Dr tells you to." I start to cry, and she looks at me and says, "You make a sound I will give you a real reason to cry."

The Dr looks at my mom and says "Why did you slap her she is terrified and there must be a reason. You can't just disregard her fear as nothing I want you out of this room right now and send someone who will comfort her and not slap her in here." He tells the nurse to escort my mother out.

I look at him and ask, "can I have my pappy or my grandma wilt since my daddy left?"

The Dr asked my mom to send one of them in please.

My Grandma Wilt came in and held me while the Dr examined me. "She is ok everything is out of her stomach, and she is awake, so you can take her home any time." He looks at me and says, "now for your young lady no more taking pills unless you are told to by a grown up because you are sick do you understand?" I nod my head yes.

He asks me if I can tell him why I am so afraid of Drs especially the one today. I look at him and shake my head now.

"You know I cannot help you if you do not tell me what is happening. I know that you are not injured anywhere because I examined you. But I know you are very scared of Drs, and you should not be. We are here only to help you" he says gently.

I ask him "will you be my Dr always and only you?"

"Since I am your grandmother's Dr, I can be yours also. When you're sick just have her bring you to see me." He pats my hand to reassure me.

"Thank you."

"Is there anything you want to ask me.

"You don't have whisky in your breath. The other Dr had whisky on his breath. You did not breathe heavy or rub my chest like the other one." I look at him" why do Drs have big things sticking out of their pants and breathe heavy when they examine you." I ask.

He looked shocked "why you would ask that question?"

"The Dr I gave the rent money to. He always breathes heavily when he touches me, and he had that thing sticking out of his pants you know the part that makes him a boy. He tried to make me touch it that is why I bit him." My grandma gasps in shock, the Dr looks angry, and I hide my face in my grandma's shoulder. The Dr goes out and asks my mom to come back in. He asks me if I mind going with the nurse for a few minutes. The nurse takes me to a different room where there are toys and stays with me while he talks to my mom and grandma.

The nurse takes me to a small room that has toys in it. She sits with me and plays games with me.

I hear Dr parks voice softly say "it's time to leave here now you will never have to come back here again. Nothing in this room can hurt you anymore. You will not dream about here or even feel any pain if you think of his place. It has nothing to scare you with anymore. You can move on from this room and there will be no more nightmares because of here. When you leave this room, you will remember what happened and that it is just a memory and that it can't hurt you anymore" he then asked me to walk back up the stairway and wake up when he counts to 3. "1 2 3" and snaps his fingers he looks at me and asks what do you remember? "I look at him" I remember I was a little girl and that I was frightened of the Dr next door. I remember being in the hospital. I remember I took too many pills. I remember why I took pills.

"Ok that's all for today. I need to talk with Dr Smith I will see you next week."

I got up and walked out to go home and I could not get the feeling that I knew Dr Park from somewhere. As I Drove home, I felt at peace for the first time in an exceptionally long time. I was looking forward to the evening with my family.

I waited till Kat left the room to talk to Dr Smith. I need to find out if she will allow me to continue to treat her.

"There is something I need to tell you. I was not sure until I saw Kat in the waiting room. I know her personally and I know most everything that she has locked away behind the hidden doors of her mind." I look at her with dread wondering what she is going to say.

"Explain to me how you know her and why did you two pretend to not know each other?" she demanded.

"My brother is the one who saved her when she was 7. I did not meet her till she was 13. She became a part of my family and then a tragedy happened, and she was lost to us. As you know my uncle was an expert in hypnosis and he is the one who helped her to lock her memories away. Before you ask it was for the best at the time. We found that she could block some things on her own to where she would departmentalize them so that she could protect her mind. Some of her memories were too horrible and we became afraid for her very life. The problem is that I do not understand why she is having nightmares now and what triggered them. I need to keep my promise and to help her. Will you allow me to help treat her?" I asked her to hold my breath hoping she would say yes.

"I need some more questions answered first. Why were you afraid for her life?" she asked staring intently at me.

"She had been hurt badly after being patched up she tried to kill herself and almost succeeded. The only choices that we had was to take and help her lock her memories up or lose her to a permeant state of total mental shut down or death. Those were our options at the time. locking her memories away was the best way." I explained.

"I will allow you to help on one condition. That I sit in on every session, and I say when it is enough. If you can agree, then I will let you help. Personally, I am out of options on how to help her. Her family needs to agree as well. Since you know her, I cannot list you as her Dr because of conflict of interest."

"Thank you so much for allowing me this chance at helping my angel."

"Also, you can only use her real name in here you cannot use any pet names. Like you just did I cannot let your personal feeling come into this. Understand" Dr smith said very sternly I get the feeling that she has been having a hard time with keeping her distance from her as well. Kat has always had that effect on people, and I guess Dr Smith is not immune to it either.

I leave the office feeling overly optimistic about how to go about helping her and, in the process, getting the old Kat back.

My phone rings as I am walking into my office at the clinic. "Hello before you ask yes, it's her. The patient I told you about is her." The excitement in my brother's voice can be heard on the phone as well as the concern for her health. I begin to tell him about what I have learned about her so far and let him know that I will be meeting her every week for a while to help her recover her memories. Not just the ones that are terrifying to her but also the loving happy ones. "I must tell you she is nothing like we remember her right now. She is a shadow of herself now" my brother asked me to try and send him a picture of her. So, I told him next week I will try to get one of her without anyone noticing. I sit at my desk and smile at the thought of just spending time with her again. I just pray that I can help her and not cause her more pain. I open my desk drawer and pull out all the files my uncle had on her. I then picked up the phone to call Dr Smith.

"hello" I hear her say.

"Hello Dr Smith, its Dr Park I have some files on Kat that I think we should go over before her next secession it will give you more insight into who she is and why." I told her.

"Great can I come to your office tomorrow." She replied.

"I cleared my schedule in hopes that you would say that. So, I will see you in the morning." I hung up the phone and got ready to leave for the night. I said a little prayer of thanks on the way home.

CHAPTER 2

No place to go.

For the first time in months, I slept without feeling fear. I know there are other memories that I am afraid of knowing but at least hopefully I got some sleep last night. As Kat is going about her day Dr Park and Dr Smith are going over her records that Dr Park has

"Let me explain first how I got these records. My uncle was Kats grandmother's Dr for many years and when Kat would be sick my uncle was one of the few she trusted. My uncle was the one who first treated her when she was 7. He did it as a special favor to her grandmother. when he realized what happened he asked her grandmother to bring her to see him when she was sick since she agreed to trust him so that she would not be fearful to get treated when sick. He started keeping two sets of records on her when he realized she was being abused and she refused to tell him anything about who was doing it." I explained this to Dr Smith.

"Why two sets of records? Why not just report to the police the abuse?" She asked.

"Kat was adamant that if anyone found out that someone would die and that it would be her fault. So, he just kept quiet so that she would continue to come to him at least this way he could make sure she was getting proper treatment till she was ready." I explained.

"Ok I can see that but really how bad could the trauma be that she has blocked out all the memories of most of her life?" She asked as she started looking through the files, I watched her face as she read the files. I see tears form in her eyes and stream down her face. I knew now for sure that she was the person to help me help Kat. She has more than just professional motive now.

"Oh my God how could someone be so cruel and how could such a sweet gentle person survive all this and still be so loving and kind?" Dr Smiths sat there in bewilderment. Wondering how Kat survived such trauma. "I am not sure if her remembering all this will be good for her or not." Dry Smith said.

"Kat learned at an early age to block things that hurt her. My uncle says she disassociates from the things happening to her and she locks herself away so that she cannot feel or recognize what is happening. He said he found this out by accident one day when he was doing her female exam. He said the moment she touched her that she closed her eyes and lay there stiff and then a hazed look came over her eyes and it was not until he was done, and he had to talk to her some minutes before she even noticed that he was done. He used this disorder later to help her cope with the memories that would destroy who she was." I explained.

"So, the doors she told me she sees shrouded by darkness are her hidden memories that she is too scared to open. I guess the stress she has been under lately has caused some of those fears to come out even if she cannot remember the exact events. If we can open them and get her to face those memories, then she will not have anything else to fear and her nightmares will stop. We need to try to talk to her husband about this course of treatment because he is not the most supportive person when it comes to this, and he will give her a hard time over it." Dr Smith explained that

Kats husband thinks it is just that she is weak and just needs to grow up. That he feels that it does not matter what happened to her that it is in the past, and she should be over it already. She told me that he does not even like the Fact that she is seeking treatment. The only reason he is not given a choice is that she is here by court order. She was arrested for shoplifting but could not remember doing anything. She became so hysterical when she woke up in jail that they sent her for psych evaluation.

I feel saddened by this because I know Kat and she would never steal from anyone she would give everything to someone but never take. Kat loves people completely and for someone not to love her the same is just sad to me. I need to see who this man she married is like and try to get him to understand. I pray God can guide my steps in the right direction. After hours of going over my uncle's records and notes Dr Smith and I came up with a plan to help Kat get her life back. Tomorrow we will see if it works. I picked up the phone to call Kat's husband to see if he was willing to meet with us.

"Mr. Sanchez this is Dr Park I am helping Dr smith with your wife's care and would like to have a joint session with you and your wife to go over her treatment."

"Look I don't believe there is anything wrong with my wife except that she has a weak mind and lets things that are long over to still bother her. I think she lives in the past too much and needs to grow up and let it go." He spoke.

"If you believe that then why are you letting her get treatment at all. Why are you even still with her?" I asked, getting angry at how insensitive he seems.

"Despite what I sound like I love my wife I have since I first saw her. I know she has a lot of traumata I have heard about it from her mom, and I hear her screams in the night. I want her to learn to deal with everything I just do not know how. I can't help her with this because I don't understand how she feels in this I cannot relate to her." I could hear the sadness in his voice that he cared a lot more than what he showed.

"How about meeting with us on Saturday morning so that we can talk about what you can expect with this new course of treatment. This way you are not thrown off guard by anything and maybe since you will be forewarned then it may not upset you as much." I listen to a deadline for a few moments thinking he may have hung up but then I hear.

"Alright I will be there with her Saturday morning at 9."

"Thank you I look forward to meeting you on Saturday." I called Dr Smith and told her it is all set for Saturday now I just must read up on her current chart and see if I can help her husband to understand what is going to happen.

When joe gets home from work, he stands in the door watching Kat trying to see the bubbly happy girl he fell in love with. She seems unrecognizable to him. Her hair is stringy and dirty, she is still in her house coat. She has a sad look on her face that even though she is laughing at the kids that laughter does not reach her eyes anymore. She is so nervous and withdrawn she barely talks except to the kids. She does everything we all ask. She never asks for anything unless it is something the house needs. I wonder if it is partly since she just lost her dad and her grandma so close together. It is partly due to all the weight she has gained but she barely eats anything. All her clothes are too big for her despite her larger size. When did she become this person? When did I lose the woman, I fell in love with? As I think these things, she notices I am home. She rushes to the kitchen to make my plate and tells the kids to come and eat. I watch her as she hurries to make sure that everyone has a plate. I notice she does not fix one for herself. "Are you not eating?" I ask.

"My stomach is a little upset so no I'm not going to eat right now maybe later." She replied quietly. I then noticed that there was only enough food left for my lunch the next day. I wonder why she did not make enough for everyone. I decided to leave it, I do not want to upset her. Just then her sister walks in "wonderful I didn't miss dinner." She walks over and makes herself a plate and sits down. "Now Kat don't forget I need you to take Jonah to the Dr tomorrow and that the girls have practice after school. I can't pick them up, so I need you to do it." As soon as she finishes eating, she tells her kids to hurry, and they need to get home. "Did you give them their baths already?" She asked, "of course homework is done also." Kat replies as she gets up and starts cleaning the kitchen. She tells the kids to get ready for bed.

I sit there wondering if she just has too much going on. She is raising 5 kids, takes care of the house, works, and makes sure that everyone in both our families has all their needs met. Her problem is too much stress. Joe wonders as he goes to get ready to bathe for bed. He walks into the bathroom and Kat already has his bath run and his clothes waiting for him. She whispers good night as she walks past him to go to their room. "you're not done for the night so don't go to sleep yet." Joe states as he sinks into the tub. Kat walks into their bedroom and strips off her clothes and lays in bed waiting for joe to finish his bath. Joe walks into the room and climbs into the bed beside her and he pulls her into his arms.

"I know that I don't always show it, but I love you. If I did not, I would have left you a long time ago. I don't know what goes on in your mind all the time, but I just want you to remember that ok." He says as he leans down to take her lips with his. I softly kissed him back. I know that he loves me.

But if I cannot seem to find the emotions to respond in a way that shows him that I love him back. I go through the motions of making love with him with no feelings attached. When joe is spent, he rolls over and goes to sleep. I quietly get out of bed and go to shower. I cannot stand the feel of my body after it has been touched. When joe gets up in the morning, he knows she is not beside him. He gets ready for work. When he goes into the kitchen. She is there handing him a hot breakfast and his lunch packed. I walk over kisses his cheek "have a good day at work." And walks away and goes back to bed. Joe just looks at her and shakes his head. He then slams out of the house.

Saturday arrives, and I wake up early. I am a little anxious since Joe is going with me to meet Drs. He has always refused to come to even acknowledge that I even need help. I am worried about what is going to happen. We walk into the office and both Dr Smith and Dr Park greet us and invite us into the therapy room.

"Have a seat." Dr Smith motions us to sit down. "don't worry we are not going to have a session today. I wanted to go over our plan and what your family may see happen over the course of the next few weeks." Dr Smith explained.

"I will be helping Dr smith with your wife's hypnotherapy and hopefully we will be able to help her unlock the memories that are causing her such harm. Over the next month her nightmares could increase as well as her moods may become erratic. She may even withdraw even more than before." Explained Dr Park. He waited to see our reaction before going on. "My hope is that we can help her move, pass all the fear that she is experiencing and help stop her nightmares completely. What you need to understand is that she will be reliving these memories to work through her fear so that she can start to see herself as a person again. By doing this she will be able to move into the future." He waited to see what we were going to say. Joe speaks up first.

"Look if things get worse then she won't have a place to live. I have put up with her nightmares and her disappearance only to be a thousand miles away and cannot remember what she was doing there. I have put up with her erratic behavior and I am not doing it anymore she isn't going to be allowed to get treatment anymore not if she wants to live at home." He looks at me as he gets up to walk out of the room. I get up and mumble sorry and follow him out. We got to the car, and he looked at me. He has an incredibly angry look "do you think I'm stupid that I can't tell this is just an act so that you can behave anyway you want and blame it on this. I am not putting up with this anymore either you behave as you're supposed to, or you can get out. Stop being a worthless person and do your job." He yells, and he speeds out of the parking lot towards home. I sit their tears quietly streaming down my face asking God why am I even alive? Why can't I be the person everyone expects me to be?

Why can't he understand I have no control over what has happened and how I feel? Everything is empty and dark around me. All I think about is I want to die to end the pain. I have no emotions inside of me except anger and pain. I do not know how to see the light anymore or feel love anymore. What is worse is that I do not know why I feel this way. I cannot remember when it started or how to get back to the person that I was. When we arrive home, Joe calls my mom and asks if it's ok if the kids stay with her tonight that we have something to do. My mom says of course. He looks at me and says "just don't talk to me or even look at me right now. I must get out of here for a while. Take the time you have alone to figure out what you want." as he slams out the door.

I cried and waited for Joe to come home wondering what I was to do. I prayed most of the night for God's guidance and begged him to help me. It was about 4 in the morning when I finally heard Joe come in. He was completely wasted. He stumbled into the bedroom and got into bed. I could not stand the smell of alcohol, so I went to get up to sleep on the couch. He grabbed me and refused to let me go. "Your worthless except for a good lay occasionally so how about it." I pushed him aside and got up and went into the living room to sleep. In the morning I got up and did what I always did, fixed him breakfast and took it to his room. I sat it on the nightstand. I got dressed and decided I was going out for a while. I went out to get into the car and it was wrecked. It looked like he rolled it on his way home.

Furious I scream at the top of. My lungs

"What the hell do you think you are doing. Your stupid asshole. You wreck our only car just because you act stupid when you're drunk."

He wakes up startled "don't yell my head hurts."

"More than you head is going to hurt when I am dining with you." I yell back while throwing a pillow at his head. He catches it and starts across the room at me.

He grabs me by the throat and squeezes "I going to kill you if you don't shut up. I will do as I please and you will listen as always. Just because you have a new Dr does not mean things have changed. You will still do what I say and like it.

"I feel the air leaving my body I can't breathe. I really think he is going to kill me this time. I start to get dizzy and feel like I am about to fall, my head feels like it wants to explode. I suddenly feel myself being thrown to the floor. Joe walks over to the door and looks at me with anger" get this mess cleaned up before I get back. "He yells as he slams out. I hear him cursing and kicking the car as he waits for his cousin to come pick him up. After I hear him leave, I slowly leave the corner of the kitchen and start to clean up his mess. When I finished I went to shower and saw the horrible bruises on my neck. It's summertime, how am I supposed to cover them? I have a therapy session tomorrow. I need to call the clinic and ask if they can send the van to get me since the car is totaled. With a heavy sigh I will go to sleep in the kid's room tonight so maybe if he does not see me then he will not get angry.

Today is Kat's session. I am excited that I will get to see her. I promised my brother I would get a picture of her today. I hope I can make an excuse too. I pray as I drive to work. Dear lord, give me guidance and allow me to help my patients today. Allow me to give comfort and courage when and where needed. Amen. I smiled to myself thinking I pray several times a day because of her. She taught me that praying is more than just making a wish. It talks to the creator and that if you have faith it will happen. She also told me that sometimes just the act of praying gives us courage and comfort. I think about all the things that Kat taught my family when she was with us. It is truly breaking my heart to see her so lost right now. I went to the clinic and saw the great Dr Smith. She has a concerned look on her face. "We need to talk before you see Kat today." She says walking to her office. She motions for me to take a seat. "Kat called yesterday to request the van to pick her up. She does not do this unless something is wrong. I do not know what is going on, but you need to be prepared for anything today. The last time she needed to call for the van she destroyed my office in a fit of rage." I looked at her in shock, my angel would never lose her temper like that. I thought to myself.

"Before you think she has lost it. The anger was not at me or even herself. She was angry because she was in the middle of a psychotic break. Her uncle died, and her husband came home to her holding a gun in her hands. They played taps at his funeral, and it sent her into a tailspin. I didn't know why it upset her so much. Since I do not know what has happened, I just wanted you to know that you need to be ready for anything she is not always predictable."

Just then the day treatment therapist knocked on the door. "We are here, and Kat is with us. You need to come right away and bring a camera please." We leave Dr Smiths office and go to the day treatment room. When I walk in, I see her first. Her hair is dirty and does not look like it is being washed in days. She has a turtleneck sweater on and its summertime. I can see by her flushed cheeks that she is overheated. Terry looks at Kat and tells her "I am going to give you something cooler to change into and then we will talk ok." Kat just nods her head. Terry gets her a change of clothes. When she comes out of the restroom. I see why terry wanted a camera. Kat has bruised hand marks on the neck and her voice is horse. There are bruises on her arms, and I see a few on her legs as well. I cannot help myself. I walked over to her and put my arms around her. I cradle her head on my shoulder. The moment her head touches my shoulder tears begin to fall. Her cries here soft but heart breaking. Dr Smith and Terry looked at me in shock. I think to myself you have done it now. Dr smith is going to make you leave her. "Excuse me Dr Park let's take her to my office so that we can get to the bottom of this and not disturb the group activities." She motions for me to go to her office. Kat refuses to look up from my shoulder, so I walk with her pressed firmly at my side, her head down.

When we get to the office. Dr. Smith asks Kat "can I let Dr Park take pictures of your bruises please?" I whisper "ok but you can't report this please. It was my fault I knew he hated that I came here. I should not have let you talk to him. He does not understand that this is something I need to do to be a good mom and wife. He does not deal well with illness. He only sees weakness. I'm sorry that I have caused so many problems and made you concerned."

I can see by the looks on their faces that they are both overly concerned for my safety. When Dr Park speaks up "how is it your fault did you try to strangle yourself? Did you hit him first or threaten him? People handle their own actions and only theirs. You are not at fault. We will not report this under one condition. You allow us to admit you to the hospital for a few days even weeks to get you some intense therapy and keep you safe at the same time."

"But what about my kids?" I asked.

"I am sure your mom and sister will watch them. "Dr smith replied.

"Do we have a deal?" Dr Park asked.

The tears streamed down my face as I nodded my head yes. I am worried about what Joe is going to do or say. I watch as Dr Smith picks up the phone and calls my husband "Mr. Sanchez this is Dr Smith I am calling to inform you that we are admitting your wife to the hospital. I don't know how long she will be there it depends on how well she responds to treatment." I see the angry look on her face I wonder what he said to her.

She smiles when she gets off the phone and looks at me "I am going to have Terry take you to the hospital and there is going to be no visitors for the first 48 hrs. is there someone else I need to call?" she asks.

"My mom please." I ask her, she smiles and says ok as I am walking out of the office I pause outside the room when I hear her talking to my mom.

"Hello this is Dr smith I am your daughter's Dr we will be admitting her to the hospital effective at once. It is to the psych ward. No do get upset she did not try to kill herself again. Her husband tried to strangle her, and she is in a very delicate state. We need to see her to make sure she is not suicidal. How can you say that? How is it her fault that her husband tried to strangle her? that her husband lost his temper. You are her mother and should not be supporting her and concerned about your child, not about what she said or did to make him angry. I am sorry I do not understand this, you are telling me if I put her in the hospital that you are not even going to watch your grandchildren. This is ridiculous. oh, so you are helping your aunt who is on vacation. You are babysitting her kids that she watches for money. You feel that your daughter is making too big a deal of this. I am sorry, as her doctor I am telling you she needs this time if she is ever going to be healthy if you cannot understand that then I feel sorry for you. Report me I do not care because if it comes to that you can take me to court and there is no judge that will take your side when it comes to your child, I can have her deemed incompetent and have her put into hospital with no contact with anyone if that is what you want but that is not what's good for her or for her relationship with her children. your daughter will be admitted right now and no visitors for 48 hours the rest is between you and your son in law goodbye." Dr Smith hangs. Up the phone with a frustrated sigh.

Just then Terry comes to find me "you ready?" I nod yes. When we arrive at the hospital the first thing Terry tells the nurse is that I need a shower and to make sure my hair gets washed. She also tells her that I am going to need hospital clothes because I am coming in with nothing. The nurse informs her she has already been informed by Dr Park and that before my shower he ordered X-rays of my throat then a shower.

Chapter 3

Meeting Old Friends

*T*erry looks at me and takes my hand "it will be ok don't worry they will take care of you. I must get back, but I will see you in a few days." She waves goodbye and walks towards the doors. The nurse looks at me and says let us get started.

When I returned to my room after the test and X-rays there was a beautiful night gown lying on my bed, I called the nurse.

"Who is this for?" I asked.

"It's yours it was delivered while you were in the shower." She replied.

"Who is it from did my husband or sister bring it?" I asked.

"No one has come to visit since you are not allowed visitors. Dr Park said you had no other clothes and did not want you to be self-conscious in hospital gowns, so he sent it over. He also sent regular clothes for group sessions so that you would be more comfortable." I looked at her puzzled.

The nurse laughed at the look on my face "Dr Park had your case worker go shopping for you. He has done this before for patients who he feels need a little more care. Don't worry we are used to his actions."

I smiled and felt more at ease. I did not want to be considered pitiful by anyone. Before I got a chance to change, I notice a man standing at the nurse's station my heart gives a leap and all I can do is stare at him. My cheeks get warm and suddenly, I feel embarrassed. I cannot help but wonder who he is and why do I feel like I know him. I look at his beautiful face, how his thick eye lashes frame his dark almond shaped eyes. His perfect nose and chiseled chin. I look at his mouth, his lips are full, and I think to myself that it would feel like kissing them. Though he is not an exceptionally large man, but he has genuinely nice muscle definition in his arms, so he must work out his black hair is pulled back I notice a piece has come loose and it falls across his face. My head begins to hurt, and I get lightheaded. I feel myself sinking into darkness. Before I lose consciousness, I feel strong-arms catching me.

Sometime later I hear Dr Parks voice he is talking to someone. "Do you want us to get into trouble why did you come here today? Why did you buy the clothes?"

"I couldn't help it. I could not stand the thought of knowing she had nothing. I just wanted to see her. I didn't think she would faint." This deep soft voice spoke. Just hearing it made me feel safe and warm inside. I know this voice, but I cannot remember from were. I want to see his face not just his profile I need to try to remember. I look from beneath my lashes hoping they do not notice that I am awake. I see him he is the most beautiful man I have ever seen. I could stare at him all day. His shoulder length black hair with just the right amount of wave in it. I look up at him and just stare. I heard him say.

"Joesonghabnida," he bowed his head in apology.

I ask him "why are you sorry?"

He and Dr Park looked at me in surprise, "You understood what I said" he asked.

"Yes, you said you were sorry but why?" I replied.

"How do you know what I said?" He just looked at me waiting for me to answer.

"My aunt is from Korea, and I have had to say it to her a lot when she first came to visit us. "You

Dr Park looks at me. "Kat how much Korean to you know."

"Not much but I have always been fond of anything Korean even before my uncle married my aunt. I am so jealous every time he goes, and my brother is too. Why do you ask." I look at the man beside him I cannot seem to take my eyes from his.

"You know that I am Korean then?" Asked Dr Park

"of course, I'm depressed not stupid booboo." I said without realizing what I called him I look at him and see the shock in his and the man beside him faces.

They are staring like I have just grown a second head or something. I look at him.

"I'm sorry Dr Park for being so much trouble to you if you get me the receipts for my clothes I will try to see if my mom or sister will let me borrow the money to pay you back and thank you for them, I really appreciate them, but you didn't have to buy me such pretty things I would have been happy with just sweatpants and tee shirts." The man standing beside Dr Park looks at me and smiles.

"It was nothing I can't let someone feel uncomfortable in my watch." I look at him confused. he laughs "I'm Jun Ki Park head of the hospital psych ward. I am Jacobs older brother." He reaches out his hand I take it an awfully familiar and warm feeling rushes through me.

 "I am Kat Sanchez its very nice to meet you and thank you." We looked at each other for what seemed forever with our hands clasped together.

I hear Jacob Park clear his throat "Kat you need to rest I will be here in the morning to check on you. we will have our session in the morning with Dr Smith." With this Jun Ki let go of my hand and they both left my room.

CHAPTER 4

Old nightmares

That night my sleep was disturbed with many broken images. I do not know if they were real or dreams, but I know I kept waking up with tears streaming down my face. At one point I heard screams that vibrated the walls then a soft voice was singing to me

"I stood upon the hill Stared up at the blue sky and drew a lovely person in my heart.

I want to fly up to the end of heaven.

Hug the breeze in the air and whisper with the winged angels. Sleep now my heart. Sleep quietly for I will be close by. Watching and protecting you. Sleep well my heart sleep now. "I think to myself where I have heard this before it's not English its Korean, but my aunt never sang to me. So why do I know these words so clearly? I drift into a deep sleep feeling like a baby being cradled in someone's strong arms.

I was awakened in the middle of the night. It was my brother calling "Jacob she is screaming its horrifying to hear. I am sorry I could not stand to hear her screams." I can hear the sadness in his voice "I didn't have a choice I couldn't bear to hear her crying and screaming."

"What did you do?" I asked.

"I rocked her and sang to her just like when she was younger. I am sorry but the moment I spoke to her she started calming down, so I just held her and rocked while singing till she went back to sleep. I sang her a lullaby. She is sleeping peacefully now. Don't be angry it was what was needed I did not want to sedate her."

"it's ok just you have to be careful I don't want her to be more traumatized because of us." Jacob sighed heavily he will need to have a conference with Dr Smith and his brother to make sure that she will still be ok with him treating her and that she will not mind Jun Ki being there as well. This is breaking so many rules. Nothing can be done tonight I will just deal with this in the morning.

Morning came, and Kat was up and dressed right after breakfast waiting in the great room. Dr Smith watched her from the door. Take note that she looks rested more than she has in the two years that I have been seeing her. The bruises on her still looked bad. She does not look like a person who spent the night locked in a nightmare though. I decided to talk to the charge nurse to make sure what I was told was the truth.

"Excuse me nurse Henderson can you tell me what happened with my patient last night?" Dr smith inquired.

"I'm not sure I should say anything, but Dr Park calmed her down without even waking her from her nightmare. She was wreathing in what looked like severe pain and screaming. She had tears streaming down her face and she never completely woke up. I thought we would need to tie her down and sedate her, but we did not. Dr Park heard her screams and softly spoke to her while he held her hand then she started crying and getting upset again. He put his arms around her and sang to her softly while rocking her like a child, she went to sleep and slept the rest of the night without a single sound. When she woke up this morning she was smiling and had been talking to us. It was strange to see but amazing at the change in her. Before he did that, we could not even get close to her without her biting, scratching and kicking." I noticed the bruise on the nurse's arm and the bite mark on her hand.

"Did she give you those?" I asked.

"Sure, did you would never guess how strong she is. I just hope we can help her because if her nightmares are any sign of her trauma, I feel like she has been to hell and back." I watched her as she walked away. I knew her nightmares were bad, but I could never have guessed how bad it was till now. I walk back to the great room to get Kat for her session, and I see Dr Park with another man walking towards me.

"Dr Smith let me introduce you to my older brother Jun Ki. He is the staff Dr on the ward."

"Ahhh so was it you who calmed my patient last night?" I asked, pointing at Jun Ki.

He bowed his head and said, "yes I am sorry if I over stepped, but I couldn't stand to hear angel in such a state." I just stared at him he called her angel just like Jacob.

 "I'm sorry but I must insist that you refrain from pet names with Mrs. Sanchez it's not professional and I can't have personal feelings involved." glaring at him.

"I understand, and I will try to remember but I will tell you that I have thought of her. As an angel since I was 14." Jun Ki glaring back at her as if he were defending his property.

"So, are you that boy the one she spoke about in our last session?" I asked Jacob.

"Yes, he is, and I didn't mention that he worked here because I truly didn't think we would have to admit her here." Jacob said looking like a kid with his hand in the cookie jar.

I just sigh "it's ok but remember she is fragile and I'm only allowing to be on her case because you are able to help. Shall we go see our patient now?"

"Yes please. I will see you this afternoon before your shift starts Ki get some sleep this morning." I hear him say as we go to meet Kat.

Chapter 5

Door 2

Dr smith and Dr Park come in and motion me to sit Dr Smith. dims the light so that I can concentrate on the pen light that Dr Park is slowly moving from side to side I feel my self-getting sleepy and hear his voice saying.

"you're at the top of the staircase walking slowly down the steps. Has you taken each step you're going deeper into your memories as you go deeper the darker the stairwell becomes until you come to a door with a small light on above it what does it look like."

"it's a red door and it has a wooden stick with thorns for a handle." I go to reach for it but hesitate. I do not want to get pricked by the thorns. I hear his soft voice. Saying it's ok you can open it; it will not hurt you.

I open the door. I am at my aunt's house on the carport I hear all the grownups laughing and I know they are drinking. I hear them laughing and cussing. "Kat whispers

"How old are you now?" The soft voice asks.

"I am 9 I know because my hair is cut off short. I wanted to look like a boy, so I cut it short with peaches scissors. "Kat tells her.

"I hide in the cellar hoping no one will find me. I hear the grownups fighting over their card game. I try to sneak into the house; I need to pee, and it hurts bad. I ran into the house and tried to get to the bathroom, but someone was in there, it is the only bathroom. I try to hold it, but I cannot. My dad notices me prancing outside the bathroom.

"You better hold it I don't want you pissing your pants." he yells I tell him I am trying. I bang on the door and ask whoever is in there to please hurry it hurts to hold it. My sister started laughing and calling me pissy pants and told my dad if I were not careful, I would pee in my pants just like I did in class yesterday when the teacher would not let me go. I looked at her and started to cry. My mom promised no one would tell. I heard her smack my sister and tell her to hush she said enough. I bang on the door again. But the person inside will not answer. I hear laughing as my uncle goes over to the kitchen sink and starts running water. Just to see if it will make me go. I cry please hurry it hurts. Then I feel warm liquid running down my legs and everyone laugh harder. I sink on the floor and bury my head in my hands and quietly cry. My dad walks over to me, I smell cigarettes and whisky in his breath. He picks me up and drags me outside. He cuts a switch from the peach tree its wet from the storm. He begins to hit me with it. I cover my face with my hands so that he cannot hit me in the face. I hear my uncle and granddad yell to give it to her good, so she does not do it again. While he is hitting me, I hear my aunt yell to my cousin, "you can come out of the bathroom now you are missing a good show. When my mom finally gets my dad to stop, I have bloody stripes covering most of my back and legs. My mom goes and gets a warm bowl of water and a soft towel to clean me up. She looks at my dad and tells him you should be ashamed of yourselves all of you. Your adults she is a child should I beat you till your bloody the next time your too drunk to make it to the bathroom. I looked at my cousin and I asked her why she did not let me in. She says she is sorry. My mom calls my grandma wilt to come get me.

"What happens next?" The voice asks.

"My grandma Wilt comes to get me, and she sees the cuts on me."

"What does she do" he asks.

"She grabs my mom and hits her in the face and asks who did it? My mom points to my dad. My grandmother picks up the nearest object and goes after him. She starts hitting him with a rolling pin. She is cursing at him. I yell at her not to hit my daddy to please just take me home with her. She takes my hand and walks me to her car. She looks at my father and tells him if he ever lays a hand on me again, she will kill him."

"Where are you going?" He asks.

"She is taking me to Dr P she wants him to clean me up and see why I hurt so much in my girl parts."

"Ok so I want you to tell me what happened when you see Dr P?"

"First Dr P and his nurse clean my cuts then he tells me he needs to examine my girl parts but that my grandma and his nurse will be with me. He pulls my pants down and looks at me he then tells me he is going to stick a tube inside where I pee. It hurts but he finishes quickly and sends me to get pictures of my stomach.

"What does he tell your grandma is wrong?"

"The opening is too small, and my bladder is not large enough. I have an infection because my bladder wont empty."

"What happens when she hears this?"

"Dr P gives me medicine and tells her to take me to see a different Dr. When we get home my dad and mom are at her house waiting. My grandma hits him in the face and yells at him. "You think your such a big man to try to teach her a lesson. Your child is sick she has a bladder infection she can't hold herself you stupid moron."

"I want you to leave this room now nothing here will bother you any more nothing can hurt you from here ever again when I count to 3 you will wake up. 1 2 3." I hear a snap and I feel embarrassed.

"Look at me and tell me how you feel?" I look at Dr smith.

"Feel embarrassed because I heard my cousins talking about this happening more than once and I always told them they were lying. I never thought my dad would have hurt me. I am also embarrassed at the memory itself."

"Do you know the difference between this memory and the last one?" She asked.

"No."

"You were afraid but calm in this one even though it was more painful in many ways than the last one. I think it is because you had heard stories of this memory even if you did not believe it. I also believe it is because it is a memory that no one can deny because they all were present to see it. I think the memories that are behind these locked doors are things you do not want to face or acknowledge. The ones that others know about are easier for you to open to. It is the ones that you do not want to know, or share are the ones that are going to be harder for you. They are what is causing your nightmares." Dr Smith told me she and Dr Park said I needed to go rest for a while so that I would see them later. I leave them I know they are going to talk about me, but I am too tired to listen at the door.

Dr Smith looks at me with a strange look on her face.

"This memory wasn't in your uncles. records."

"I know I wasn't expecting this, but did you notice that the door was red and had thorns stuck? We can get clues from her descriptions of the doors to know what kind of memory she is going to share. I also noticed that her tone was incredibly quiet and completely devoid of any emotions this time where last time you could hear the terror in her voice. Do you think this could be one of the memories she locked away that she disassociated during the event so that she did not feel pain or anger at her dad? The Kat I knew adored her father never said anything but loving kind things about him. She worshipped the ground her dad walked on. I cannot imagine that she could have been that way with him if she knew he hurt her this way. I will tell everyone to watch her carefully these next few days. To document any changes in her no matter how small." I do not know what to expect from her. I only pray she will not withdraw too much. We end our meeting I walk by Kats room she is curled up in a ball asleep. I see Ki is back for tonight shift I motion him to go to his office we meet there, and I tell him about today's session.

"I knew about this her grandma told me. She said it was the only time her dad ever corrected her and that after that he never touched her again with angry hands. She said it was one of the few times she ever saw him cry was when she explained what the Dr told her, and he was so ashamed of himself for how he behaved because he was drunk and angry." Ki explained.

"Why didn't you ever tell me? Is this why she was so worried every time she would be around people when they drank?" I asked him.

"Partly because when they would get drunk. She told me that the adults became belligerent towards each other, and then fights would break out" He explained.

"Thought I knew everything about her, but she still has secrets" Jacob said as he walks away.

CHAPTER 6

Family first visit

*I*ts. Saturday I am so excited my family is coming to visit. I picked an outfit that I had not worn yet. I hope I look ok. I look at myself in the mirror. I wonder why am I still alive? Why does God keep sparing me and having me stay here? I walk to the chapel I have not wanted to talk to him for such a long time. I cannot remember why I stopped talking to him. I just know that these last years I have only gone through the motions of being alive for my family sake. I wish my grandma wilt and daddy were still alive. At least when they were alive, I had someone who loved me just for me. I kneel at the altar and take a deep breath.

"Ok here goes. Heavenly Father, I know I have not talked to you in many years. For that I am sorry. Talking to you has always brought me such peace and comfort for that thank you. I do not really know what to say right now except. Thank you for Dr smith and the two Dr Parks. Bless them for the kindness and care they have given me these last few days and weeks. I feel like you are trying to get me to do something though I have no clue what it is. It is just to talk to you again. My family is coming today, and I am scared. I have missed my children so much and wonder how they would have managed without me. I know it is silly since they really do not need me. I hear Joe brought his mother here to take care of things, so I know I am not needed. She does everything perfectly while I do nothing right. Can I ask you for a favor? Can you help me to become a person that people can love and help me to unlock the love I know is buried inside of me? I feel nothing inside except fear and pain. I know it is going against who I am, but I do not know how to change it. I feel like a storm is coming and only I can control it, but I am terrified. Thank you, God, for listening to me. I promise I will talk to you again soon. I truly do miss talking to you amen." I got up and turned around to leave the chapel. I saw that my uncle Fred was standing there, I did not know he was coming. He motions me to sit.

"You know I have always told you that you have a special gift. Your gift is that you know what others need. And unselfishly give it. This fear you are feeling is not the work of God for in God there is no fear. You have things you need to confront and resolve but you cannot do it alone. God has put the people you need right here for you, and he has never left you. So, do not be afraid all will be all right. You are the strongest person I know, and you will win with Gods help just let him help." He gives me a hug, something he does not do very often. "Now let's go greet the rest of the family don't worry me and your aunt got your back." He says with a wink and a smile.

We walk to the great room and all my kids are there including Joes family I cannot believe he told them I was here. My cousin Donna walks over and hugs me. "I told them you were here not Joe they were concerned for you and wanted to make sure you were ok." I say hello to everyone. I look around and I see my kids, mom, my sister, my mom's brother, and his wife. My mom's sister and several of Joes family but I do not see Joe.

I look towards my mom, and she tell me that the Drs wanted to see him. I become worried. My sister looks at me and asks "So are you ready to end this charade and come back home. Don't you think you have shrugged your responsibilities long enough?"

My cousin Donna looks at her and smartly says "Why are you tired of taking care of yours already?"

They exchange hateful looks. I just look at my sister and whisper "I will leave when the Drs say I can.

Joe walks in and declares "She no longer has a home to come back to. I do not want her back right now so when she is released you all will need to find her a place to live. I will not allow you to see the children till you are back to your senses." He tells my children to give me a hug and to say goodbye to the fact that they are leaving. When he leaves his family leaves as well. My uncle and aunt stay to tell me not to worry their home is always open to me. I smile and say thank you. As I walk back to my room, I wonder what the Dr said to Joe to make him so angry.

CHAPTER 7

Unexpected turn

The next morning Dr smith informs me that I will have daily sessions with her and Dr Park so that I can go home sooner. As the purr session starts, I ask Dr Jacob what was said to Joe to make him angry.

"I told him that he needs to get help with his anger issues. That the only reason he is not in jail is because you asked and agreed to stay here till you have healed some. He became angry because he felt that I was telling him what to do. I am sorry, but we cannot release you if you are in danger of being hurt."

"I agree with Dr Park you do not need to be in more danger not until we are comfortable with your emotional state." Dr Smith said.

"Let's begin now please?" Dr Jacob as he dims the lights to begin.

As always, I am walking down a stairwell and I notice there are fewer doors than before. I walk towards a red door, and I hear the voice asking me to describe the door. "It's red and it has a heavy lock on the door handle I can't open it I don't understand why I can't open it."

"Go to another door and see if you can open it? "

"ok" I look around and I see a green door. I do not understand this door seems peaceful, but it also has a lock on it I cannot open it. "

"When I count to 3 you will wake up you will be calm and refreshed."

1 2 3 I hear the snap and I am looking at the two Drs. I am confused we did not learn anything new today.

"Why couldn't I open any of the doors." I as in confusion

"I think these doors are ones that we will need help opening." Dr Jacob went on to explain "If the memory is too traumatic and the brain cannot handle it sometimes it will bury the memory and lock it away until something triggers that memory. We must figure out what is the trigger for those memories. But behind these doors are also what is triggering your nightmares. So, we need to have you open them." He leans forward resting his chin on his hands. I smile because he looks like a little boy this way.

"Booboo don't slouch." I say off handedly he looks up at me and without thinking replies.

"I know you hate it but I'm thinking right now."

"Excuse me but Kat what did you just call Dr Park?" Dr Smith inquires.

I look at her in confusion "I just told him not to slouch."

"No, you called him by a name and you Dr Park answered her without thinking." Dr smith tells her. Jacob looked at her in surprise then looked at me.

"Your first day here you called me by the same name without thinking. Have you been having bits of your memory return?" He asked.

"Not that I know of but then I do not know I always feel l like I know you and Ki from somewhere, but I don't know from were. It feels natural to be around you and I feel safe with you. I am embarrassed to say this, but I feel like I belong with you two though I do not know how I must stop myself sometimes from fixing your tie or straighten your collars. And when I see your hair out of place, I want to brush it back into place." I lower my head, so he cannot see me blushing.

"You are right we do know each other very well in fact. I did not say anything because I Didn't know what effect it would have on you. I think if I can find the key to open the doors in your mind you will remember us." He smiled at me "let's stop here for today I will try to figure it out tomorrow ok."

I nodded to them and got up to go back to my room.

I run into Dr Ki in the hallway "yeobol." I say without thinking "yes" he answers without looking up from the document he is reading.

He then stops and looks up and straight at me "What did you just say?"

I look at him "hi" as I reach up to straighten his tie. I get flushed when I rest my hand on his chest and feel his heartbeat. I raise my eyes to his and just stare at him searching for answers in his eyes.

'Yeobol" I say again.

"Yes, my angel." he replies.

"Who are you to me." I ask.

"Anyone you want." he says staring back into my eyes.

Jacob and Dr smith are standing in the hallway watching the exchange. Jacob clears his throat and. says,

"Ki, we need to speak with you." The three of them go into the office to talk. I go back up to my room.

Ki excitedly looks at Jacob "She called me yeobol she is remembering."

"No, she isn't she called me booboo earlier and scolded me. She does not remember her subconscious recognizing the closeness we share but nothing else right now. I need to find the trigger that will unlock her memories." Jacob explained.

Dr Smith looks at the brothers "I need to ask. Are you helping Kat for yourselves or for her sake?"

Ki smiles "I'm selfish I want to see her be the old her not this person she is now. I want her to know me and remember me. I want to be able to love her again."

"Who exactly where you two to her in the past?" She asks.

They both answer at the same moment "Her husband."

Dr Smith is in shock. "How could that be she was a mere child when you knew her. "

"It's complicated." Jacob answers

"We need to find out what triggered the nightmares so maybe we can find the key." Dr smith says as she is writing notes in Kat's chart.

"I know the key." Ki states

Jacob and Dr Smith look at him.

"How do you know the key?" She asks.

"My uncle made me the key when Kat hurt herself After she said her goodbyes to me James and Kris. He said that he figured if I were the key and since I was so close to death and not likely to survive then Kat would never be able to unlock those memories. All I must do is recite the poem she wrote and kiss her." He informed us smiling broadly.

"She is a married woman, and I cannot allow you to kiss her and its very unprofessional." Dr Smith exclaimed.

"I agree besides if anyone gets to kiss her I am." Jacob replied sulking.

"We just need to find out what has re-triggered the nightmares." Dr smith shot back.

In my session the next morning. The Drs asked me.

"Can you tell me when did your nightmares start again?"

"They started around a year ago."

"Do you remember what was going on?" Dr smith asked.

"Joe was in the hospital recovering from being in a fire. He was hooked to machines and unable to breathe on his own. I remember feeling helpless and scared. I remember spending days sitting in the hospital and watching Iljame waiting for him to wake up. I could not watch anything else, seeing his face on the computer brought me peace and comfort. I remember I would close my eyes and I would be sitting on a rock in the middle of the river with his arms around me and hearing laughter all around me. Watching this drama and dreaming about the actor at night was the only thing that kept me sane. But then when Joe came home the nightmares began, his temper was short, and he started becoming violent" I'm sitting there wringing my hands. Wondering what they were thinking.

Jacob looks at Dr Smith and smiles "Dr smith is you up to watching a Korean Drama."

"Sure, if it will shed some light on things." Ok then this evening in the great room we are going to have a drama marathon everyone brings their pjs and I will bring snacks. See you guys tonight. "Jacob gets up and walks out the door. He sees Ki in the hallway." We are watching Iljame tonight in the great room with Kat bring some pjs and snacks it's a drama marathon."

Ki smiles "I will bring my sexiest pair" and winks as he walks away whistling.

CHAPTER 8

Movie Night

That night Kat goes to the great room, and everyone is there. All the staff and patients are in their pjs waiting for her. The only seat left is on the couch between the two Dr Parks. Shyly I walk over to sit between them. I am excited to watch this drama again. It is one of my favorites. I adore the actor who plays him. Nurse Henderson sets up the tv to start the drama. She lets everyone know that it is a Korean drama and that there are subtitles that patients can go to bed anytime they like if they let their nurses know and that the snack on the tables is for everyone. I sink down on the couch getting comfortable. By episode 4 several patients were getting sleepy and went to bed. I was so enthralled in the drama I did not even notice. I could not take my eyes off the lead actor he is so beautiful. I did not even realize that I had smuggled into Dr Ki and was being held in his arms. Jacob Ki and Dr Smith watched my expressions and reactions closely.

Nurse Henderson sucked in a gasp the first time she saw the lead actor. "Omg he looks like a younger version of Dr Ki when he lets his hair down. The 3 Drs look at each other and then back at the screen. Dr Smith says you know your right he does resemble him a lot."

Without taking my eyes from the tv I say "yeobol give me something to drink." Ki hands me a soda. I take it without even looking at him. "isn't he the most beautiful man. I miss him so much." I did not even realize I had spoken.

 Ki asks, "what do you miss about him?" "

"His quietness, his strong arms always protecting me, his easy smile. But mostly just having his love." I reply.

Jacob asks "You know that he is an actor playing. A part. Don't you.?"

"I know but he looks so much like the angel that visits me in my happy dreams. I feel like my other half is with me when I watch his dramas. Half I am missing. I know I sound crazy but the person I miss has the same face as his." I look at him with tears in my eyes "Dr Ki has the same face just a little older looking." I turn to face the tv again. I watched the whole night and into the next day without sleeping. When the end came and ijma had died I cried like a baby. I was sure that everyone thought I was crazy, but I did not care. My heart felt like it was being ripped out. The three Drs stood in the doorway of the great room watching me. Dr Smith motions for them to go to Ki office.

"Well, I have to say that was entertaining even if a strange way to get inside of a patient's head. I think that Kats husband is suffering from ptsd from the house fire and that is why he is so irrational and quick tempered. And the combination of him lying in the hospital on life support her subconscious brought her trauma from the past to the surface and since Dr Ki is part of her trauma seeing someone so Close to his likeness her hidden memories are surfacing in nightmares."

"I agree with you. How do we use this to help her though?" Jacob asks.

"For starters I want to see if I can talk her husband into getting help so that he can be stable, and they can repair their marriage. I also want you two to tell her who you are and how you know her. I think it is the only way to get her to understand why she feels so close to you and why in unguarded moments she is so casual and Close to you. I think the sooner the better." She looks at us intently wondering at our reactions.

Ki speaks up "I agree with everything except saving her marriage part. I can't send her back to an abusive relationship no matter the reason."

"How about we get both the help they need first then we can see what Kat wants when we are done." Jacob suggests.

"Sounds good to me" says Dr Smith.

CHAPTER 9

A Breakthrough.

Dr smith calls Joe to set up a meeting to talk to him he agrees reluctantly but he does agree they set it up for the next day. He thought for sure that she was going to tell him that his wife was going to be released soon and try to convince him to let her come home but instead she was talking to him about himself. She started telling him about his symptoms of PTSD. After talking to her he realized that she was right. He was venting all the anger inside of himself at his wife and treating her no better than an animal. Joe agrees to get help but not from her or the park brothers. She informs him that it would not be possible for her to treat him anyway. Since she is his wife's doctor. She refers him to a Dr that specializes in PTSD and anger issues. He asks her how his wife is doing. She just vaguely tells him better.

Confident that they are on the right track to help this family, the Drs go ahead with a plan to help uncover Kat's memories.

Kat is surprised that the next day all three Drs were waiting for her.

"Good morning, Kat. Dr Ki and Dr Jacob have something to tell you." Dr Smith says.

Jacob goes first. "Remember you said that you felt like you knew me the first time we met." I nod yes. "We met when you were 13 in this very hospital. In this very ward. I was here because of an accidental overdose."

As Jacob is talking, I cry with pain and hold my head why is it every time it hurts so much. I start to rock back and forth holding my head crying in pain. I hear Dr Smith asking me what is wrong? I feel myself falling into darkness. Ki jumps from his seat and puts his arms around me and starts talking softly.

"Before the darkness falls lift your eyes to the sky.

Let the wind off the sea lift you high.

As the cherry blossoms fall like snow

Let them kiss away all the memories that bring you low.

As they blow away let them lock all the memories away and take you spirit away to a waterfall far away to wash all the pain and sorrow away

When the time comes, I will kiss you awake. I promise never to forsake or cause you heartache.

I will love you beyond any measure of time if you will be mine. "Ki lowers his head and softly kisses Kats lips holding her tightly to him. Kat clings to him and shyly kisses him back. Jacob clears his throat to remind his brother that there are others in the room.

After some time when Kat had fully come too, and the pain had subsided. Kat looks at Ki with tears in her eyes when she touches his face. Her eyes memorize every feature. Ki asks" Are you ok now angel do you remember who I am.

"You're here. I can't believe you are here." She looks towards Jacob and squeals with delight jumps up and crosses the room "booboo bear." And gives him a big bear hug. Dr smith looks on in shock at the pure joy on Kat's face as she holds both their hands.

"Kat, I want to continue our session, but I need to know what you remember." She asks.

"I remember that this is Ki and Jacob they are my husbands. My mind is still fuzzy I can't remember a lot, but I recognize them and am incredibly happy to see them but a little ashamed as well." I reply.

"Why ashamed." Ki asked.

"I am ashamed because how could I forget my soulmate and my protector. How could I be with you all this time and not remember who you were." Kat looks at them with tears streaming down her face. Ki wipes the tears away.

"Because it's our fault you couldn't remember us. Your grandmother, my father and uncle decided that it was for your own good. At the time I was near death with no hope of surviving. You had nearly died several times in a matter of hours. Your state of mind was too fragile at the time. So, my uncle used hypnosis to lock those memories away forever. But with the situation with your husband and the stress those memories started to seep out into the form of nightmares. You were becoming unstable and suicidal. Jacob had no idea when Dr smith asked for his help that it was you until he met you that first time in her office. You need to unlock the hidden doors in your mind so that you can face the horror behind them, so they cannot hurt you anymore. I know how strong you are, and I know you can do this. Jacob and I with Dr Smith will be here to help you. I promise."

"You won't leave me either of you till I am better and able to go home." I asked.

"We won't leave you angel promise." Replied Jacob.

Dr Smith looks at me and asks if we are ready to unlock some doors. "

"No first I need to say something to these two. I am sorry for always causing so much trouble for you. I'm sorry for causing you to worry so much." I look at them knowing they will forgive me but needing to hear it anyway.

They both at the same time smack me in the back of head "no problem"

"So, when do I get to see my other two husbands when do James and Kris come to see me." I ask.

Dr Smith looks confused "Kris and James?"

"They were our older twin brothers they were also her husbands, but angel you won't get to see them the day that we were coming to get you there was an accident. Our car was hit by a drunk driver and Kris and James were killed that day it was the same day that you and Ki almost died as well." Jacob looked at me with pain in his eyes at the memory of his loss.

"Oh no it can't be how could I cause them to die. I loved them so much. I am so sorry it is my fault. If you were not coming to get me then they would still be here. You should be hating me and not taking care of me. I should be the one dead not them. They had so much to live for while I am a worthless person with nothing to offer how could God take them away and leave me here how?" I am crying and screaming at them. Dr Smith decided to just let me cry and not push trying to do any real therapy today. Ki puts his arms around me and lets me cry. Jacob tries to console me.

"Angel it's not your fault it is and always has been the drunk driver's fault. You were not at fault. for any of it. They loved you as much as anyone and I know they would be heartbroken if you blamed yourself or if you had died that day. My grandmother always believed that they gave you their life force to you that day so that you could live. Their very last words where I love you angel. How could God do anything else but grant their last wish and allow you to live."

"Dr Smith have you talked to my husband?" I ask.

"Which one you have them coming out of the woodwork it seems." She says joking trying to lighten the mood.

"I'm talking about Joe my legal husband. Does he know about them?"

"Oh, that one. Yes, I have talked with him I have put him in contact with a Dr to help him with his issues. He doesn't know about who these two are though that isn't my place to tell him its yours and theirs." She replies.

"I need to tell him. I cannot keep secrets like this from him. I just do not know how to go about doing it. He knows that he is not my only soulmate. I told him that my soulmate died when I was 16. At least that is what I thought. I am afraid to tell him since his temper is so unpredictable right now." I look at her wondering what she must be thinking of me right now.

"When both of you are in a more stable place you can explain to him what has happened." She pats my hand as she stands up. ". I think it has been a very emotional day for you. You should get some rest." She walks out of the office and leaves me with Ki and Jacob

I look at Jacob and Ki not knowing what to really say. I still do not have my memories back; I remember who they are but not exactly all the details. Jacob speaks first.

"We know without asking that your memories of us are not clear and that we still must go through the treatment process to unlock the doors in your mind. Do not stress or worry. We always took care of you and let you go at your pace. We are your Drs first right now. Is there anything you want to ask us? "Jacob looks at me with his big kind eyes.

"Where is James and Kris buried, I want to visit them?" I ask.

"They were cremated, and their ashes scattered at our spot." Ki replies

"Why did you kiss me just now?" I say as I look at Ki.

"My kissing you after reciting your poem is the key to unlocking the doors to your memories?"

"So, does that mean you have to kiss me now every time we have a session?" I look at him with a playful and mischievous look in my eye.

With an excessively big grin on his face "I can only hope."

Jacob clears his throat "Ya enough it's not fair."

I get up and walk over to Jacob and lean down softly kiss his cheek ". What is not fair remember I am a married woman with children I will not cheat on my husband ever so do not forget that either of you. I do not know what is going to happen or how I am going to feel, but I know I must do my best to never hurt him. He loved me and accepted even though I was broken and was willing to accept the fact that we may never have children. He has put up with a lot just because he loved me. I cannot hurt him. If you know me like you say you do, then you know I love for life." I look at the hurt in their eyes I want to cry because I feel that by loving me, they had a lot of pain in their life. I do not know what to say or what to do at this point.

Ki looks at me smiles "We know that angel and we would not want you to do anything that goes against who you are and for you to disregard your love for him would be the opposite of who you are, and I would be upset about that."

"Ok then I will see you tomorrow in my session." I walked back to my room. Close the door and sink to the floor. What is going on? How is it that all of this has happened? How had my life gotten so complicated? Eventually I fall asleep for the night.

CHAPTER 10

Getting to work.

The next morning, I go to the therapy room for my session and all three Drs. are there. I am excited and a little worried at the same time. I do not know how to act with them now. Dr. Smith is the first to speak "good morning, Kat let us get started as she dims the lights and takes out her pen light. As always, I am walking down the staircase and a I walk up to the door." Hear Jacob ask me to describe it. "" it is the same door from before its red with a knife as the handle the lock is hanging open now. I can open it. I walk inside the door.

"How old are you here do you know?"

"I am around 13 I think by the clothes I am wearing."

"I see our shabby trailer and the trailer next door I'm sitting on the grass between them. I am playing with a little girl. She is meowing like a cat and scratching at the ground. I heard our neighbor call for us to go at supper time. We get up and go into the trailer. We are sitting at the dinner table, and it is just me, Mary, Eve and her husband John. Eve is telling me that she must go somewhere, and she is going to leave me with John for a little while so I can be there when my parents call. After dinner I clean up the kitchen and go to sit on the couch. John comes in, he is only wearing his boxer shorts. I feel uncomfortable. I sit staring at the tv trying to ignore the Fact that he is sitting there only in his underwear. He puts his arm around my waist and tries to pull me over to him. I scoot over away from him. He gets upset and grabs me." Please don't touch me. I do not like for anyone to touch me. "I plead.

"Don't worry you will like this. I have wanted to do this since we moved in. Your so sexy I have had a hard time keeping my hands to myself. I have dreamed about this since you were 9." He puts his hands under my shirt and starts rubbing and squeezing my breast. I squirm trying to get away from him, but his muscular body is too heavy, and he is too strong. "Oh yeah baby I like it when you wiggle it makes it much more fun."

"Please let me go. "I cry with tears streaming down my face. He just smiles and puts his arm across my neck to hold me still as he strips my panties off. He licks his finger, looks at me and grins.

" You are going to love this I promise. "His fingers find my girl parts.

 I cry even harder afraid of what is going to happen. Praying that Eve and Mary would come soon. He puts his fingers inside me as his mouth finds my breast. I Close my eyes and pray that God would take me from here. I feel all the pain that he is causing with his hands lift way I hear a door click I look around. I do not see anyone I am sitting in front of a glass door I look through it. I see what is happening, but I cannot feel anything the man is hurting me, but I do not feel what he is doing. My eyes are fixed on the ceiling. I am not responding to him I cannot move as he strips off his underwear and his large manhood is sticking out; he sits on the couch and picks me up spreads my legs across him in a straddling position. He rams his manhood into my body I hear myself scream. He stops for a second to lift me up and runs his fingers across where our two bodies meet. There is blood on his fingers. With a smile he sucks the blood from them.

" I love virgins. If you're good, I promise it will not hurt next time. "He puts his hands on my hips and moves them in the rhythm he likes until he has spilled his seed. He then carries me to the bathroom sits me on the edge of the sink spreads my legs and licks the blood and Semen from my body. He then turns on the shower and cleans me and himself up. He looks at me and speaks.

" Do not tell anyone what happened you would not want your mom to mad at you for seducing her best friends' husband would you. "I go to the room they told me I would be sleeping in. I get dressed and get into bed. A little while later I heard Eve and Mary come in. I hear John and Eve in their room they are having very loud Sex. I put my hands over my ears, so I cannot hear them and cry. When they are done, I hear eve come in.

" Thank you because you were such a good girl for him tonight, I got to have amazing sex also maybe next time we can have him together. "When the house was quiet, I got out of bed and went to the kitchen. I open the drawer and get out the buck knife without even thinking I cut my wrist from one side to the other. I then do the same to the other one I drop the knife and watch my blood flow praying that God would forgive me, but I do not want there to be a next time. I sit on the floor watching and crying as the blood flows out of my body. I hear Eve scream I don't respond I am so cold, and the darkness is calling me."

I hear Jacob say it is time to come back now. Nothing from this room can ever hurt you again. You will wake up remembering what happened but will not remember any shame or pain 1 2 3 snap I wake up and look at them. Not knowing what to say I bow my head and ask?

"I don't want to see anyone right now can I go back to my room please?" Dr smith says "Ok, but we will need to talk about this, and I cannot let you sink deeper into yourself because of these memories we need to deal with them as they come up ok. "I nod ok and walk back to my room.

After Kat leaves the 3 Drs look at each other Dr smith speaks first. "She was raped at 13 I know I read you uncles files, but he never said anything like this in it."

"She described what happened through her dissociative self-that's why the terror in her voice became monotoned and quiet halfway through. She was unconscious and almost dead when my uncle fixed her up. She had already buried the pain and locked it away before she even tried to kill herself." Jacob said.

"I wonder if when she tried to kill herself if she was still in a dissociative state and was only herself again when she regained consciousness." Ki asked.

"There is so much more behind that door but first she needs to come to terms with what we have uncovered so far. I suggest that tomorrow's session be only about what we have found out and helping her to cope. Was it just me or did you two hear the emotionless tone in her voice when she left? Could she still be inside herself right now? I think we need to keep a close watch on her tonight." Dr smith said as she got up to leave and consult with the charge nurse. The two brothers just sat in silence then Ki spoke "you know that this is a memory connected to when she first met you Kris and James. Is she going to be, ok?"

A rough time.

"Yes, she is because I have an idea, but I need to go to mom and dad's place. Tell Dr Smith that I have some things that will help her to deal with this. But I must go home for few days."

"Ok I will but hurry Can't bear seeing her so withdrawn. "Ki gets up and walks out.

Over the next few days Kat barely speaks or even raises her head to look at others. She has not left her room except when the nurses make her. She refuses to shower or change her clothes. Dr Smith tries to Draw her out, but she only talks to her in an emotionless voice and does not say more than a word or two. She will not answer when her name is called to Get her attention Dr Smith and the nurses must tap her on the shoulder. Ki has kept his distance in fear of causing her more pain. He remembers that he saw her like this before when they were separated. He went to see her from a distance. She looked and acted the same then also. He hopes Jacob gets back soon it is killing him to see her like this.

Nurse Henderson stops Dr smith in the hallway. "Excuse me Dr but I need to talk to you. It is about Mrs. Sanchez. We have become extremely worried for her she has not eaten these last few days she does not speak to anybody she is refused to shower and just sits in the corner as if we have not spoken to her at all. She also has not had any medication she throws it up as soon as we give it to her. When we talk to her and address her as Mrs. Sanchez, she does not acknowledge us if we call her Kat, she bows her head but still will not answer us. You need to do something because the nurses are worried that she will become psychotic if this keeps up."

"Thank you nurse for your concern we have been giving her some space because we uncovered a traumatic event the other day." Dr smith goes to Kats room she is in shock when she sees her, she is in the same clothes that she was in 3 days before her hair matted and dirty vomit on her clothes. She is sitting in the corner of the room in a ball. She walks over to her and places her hand on her shoulder.

 Kat grabs her hand looks up at her "Touch me again and I will break your hand." Dr Smith takes her hand away and moves back from her.

"Kat why are you like this. "She asks.

" I do not know what you are talking about I am not like anything I just want to be left alone." Dr Smith can hear the anger in her voice, she knows this is not like Kat in all the time she has treated her even when she destroyed her office, she never heard this tone before.

"Kat, can we talk about why you are angry and who you are right now? "Kat looks at her with a mean look on her face.

" I am nobody, I am not who you think I am. I am not kind or sweet, I am just me. I hate everyone and everything, especially that bubbly and forgiving person that everyone thinks I am. I guess you want me to finish what started the other day. I do not want to like it when this part comes out because everyone leaves me alone and I do not have to deal with anyone or anything. I do not know why God lets such a worthless mixed-up creature as I live. I am no-good to anyone. "Kat gives a hateful look.

Dr smith looks at her and asks" What is your name?"

"I'm Dorothy why?" Kat looks at her confused.

"Yes, I know your legal name is Dorothy, but you have always insisted on being called Kat." Dr Smith now knows what has happened, Kat never came out of her dissociative state when they brought her back from her last hypnosis session. "I want you to shower and change your smell terrible, and I will see you again after that. If you do not, I will have the force the nurses to sedate you and give you one." She gets up and walks out to hunt for Dr Park.

Dr Smith finds Dr Ki "Do you know when Jacob is coming back?"

"He called and said he will be here in the morning. I think that Kat is still in a dissociative state. I think Jacob pulled her out to soon because the day that happened is the day that she met him, and I don't think he is ready relive his past any more than Kat is." Ki informed her.

"I know that he spent time in here when he was younger for accidental overdose. I know that he had issues before he finally decided to go back to school and finish med school. Dr smith replied.

"How do you know that?" Ki asked.

"He explained it to me vaguely when he explained how he knew Kat. But I agree with you I think we should have taken her last session farther and that the person she is now is a result of that trauma."

They heard a commotion in the hallway. It was Kat screaming at the nurse to get away from her. Anger crossed Ki face as he saw her. He walked over to her and put his arms around her. She struggles to get free, but he holds her tightly. He starts whispering to her in his native language. She began to calm down and laid her head on his shoulder and began to weep.

"I'm sorry. I am so sorry I do not know why I was so mean just now. Please forgive me. Please?" She bowed her head and sank to her knees begging everyone to forgive her. Several of the nurses had tears because she sounded too heartbroken that she had caused them problems. Dr Smith was wiping her eyes it was the most touching thing she had ever seen. Ki only saw Kat's pain and all he did was comfort her, but it is not their place to be this personal with a patient.

 Nurse Henderson knelt beside Kat. "Kitten it's not just your fault it's my fault as well. I knew you were having a hard time from your last session, and I had the nurses try to force you. I was at fault because I did not tell them to not touch you. For that I am sorry. But you need to shower and eat please it's for your own good." Kat looked at her and you could see by the look on her face that Kat knew here was not the angry person from the last few days. What did Dr Ki do to calm her and get her back? Nurse Henderson got up and helped Kat up and kept her arm on her shoulder as they walked back to her room to shower and change. What about these two? Are both Dr Ki and Nurse Henderson over compassionate to the patients? I walk back to my office wondering when Jacob is coming back.

After Kat showered and changed, I heard a knock on the office door. "Come in." I call. It's Nurse Henderson she asks if she can come in. "of course. What can I do for you?"

"Please do not think I am overstepping my bounds here, but I think I need to clarify a few things with you. I know you have not been on staff long and I know your approach is more hands off than the two Dr parks. I do not want you to think that just because they are gentle and compassionate that they are not good Drs. They are two of the best and if you watch them, you will learn something from them." She is much blunter than I expected. I just look at her and ask her just as frankly "your right I think they are far too close to my patient and that they are too touchy feely to make objective decisions at times."

"They are the way they are because of your patience. They were very cold and rational when growing up. It was her who taught them to feel. That is why it hurts them to see her ill like this. Dr Ki wanted to sit with her the first night she was here because he saw the pain, she was in. He kept his distance because of him being her Dr. Do not be hard on them they are hurting as much as she is right now, and I was here when she came the first time. The person you know is not who she really is. I want to see the person she really is come back. When that person comes back you will understand why everyone here treats her so delicately." With that she turned and walked out. I am at a loss for words at this point. The Kat they know is someone I want to meet now for sure. I turn out the light and get up to go home for the night.

C H A P T E R 12

Brothers reach an understanding.

*J*acob arrives at the hospital early in the morning hours. He brought a box with him from his parent's house. It is filled with letters and mementos that will help Kat. When he turns on the light Ki is lying on the couch asleep. Jacob just smiled and wondered if he ever went home while he was gone. He decides to go peak in on Kat he missed not seeing her these last few days. He sees Nurse Henderson on the way.

"Dr Jacob your back did you have a nice trip?" She asks.

"Yes, it was nice to be home for a few days. How were things here?" The look on her face at that question told him volumes but he waited to hear what she had to say.

"To be frank it was a challenge and one that may have been avoided to some extent. Kitten was more than a handful and Dr Ki blessed him was trying his best not to do anything that could cause problems because of it until things got out of hand. Dr Smith did not make things better by threatening kitten with sedation and looking down at her uppity nose at Dr Ki. Next time finish what you start and make sure things are in order before you disappear from me. I'm getting too old for this you know." She pats Jacob on the cheek as she walks away.

What happened while I was gone? He wonders as he walks towards Kats room. He quietly goes in and sits beside her bed. She is sleeping peacefully. As he looks at her his heart flutters like always. To him she is still his sweet angel. Her reddish-brown hair and creamy white skin. He reaches out to take her hand. It has been so long since he has been able to just hold her hand. When he hears.

"If you want to keep that hand you won't touch her?" He turns around and Ki is standing in the doorway. Jacob can feel his anger from there. Ki motions for him to follow him. Jacobs gets up and follows him back to the office. As soon as the door is closed. Ki grabs him by the Collar and slams him against the wall.

"What is wrong with you why are you so angry?" Jacob gasps as he is trying to get Ki hands from him.

"You left her in that nightmare of a state. You did not make sure it was her that came back. How could you be so stupid? For 3 days she was stuck there. She would not eat, would not bathe or change even when she vomited on herself. She was hateful and angry, no one could even get close to her and when they tried, she was ready to draw blood. That person you let out is not her. I did what you told me, I gave her space, I kept my distance, but she was not an angel, she was the girl I saw when we left her, and that bastard started to hurt her. I only saw her from a distance all those years ago. This time I had a front row seat, and it was hell. If you ever leave her in that state again, I will kill you. Do you understand?" He finally let me go. I look at him and cannot help but wonder what he was talking about.

"I know when I brought her out of hypnosis that she was withdrawn but she just remembered being raped as a child. Anyone would have reacted that way." I just looked at him.

"No, you brought her back in a dissolutive state she was more than withdrawn she was a completely different person. She was nothing like her core self she was psychotic, and it was your fault." Ki inform me. "The only way to calm her was to whisper the lullaby to her and hold her like when she was a child. With the whole world watching. When she finally calmed down and was herself, she knelt and begged for everyone's forgiveness. Because of you she had to kneel to people. People who do not even understand what that means. Only nurse Henderson understood and knelt with her and comforted her. She is better now but if you dare to do that again I will truly kill you. He sat down and held his head in his hands.

"I'm sorry I had no idea. You could have called me." Jacob gave his big brother a hug.

CHAPTER 13

Healing begins.

The next morning Jacob went to find Kat, but she was not in her room. He began to panic after what Ki and nurse Henderson told him.

He saw a young nurse and asked her "Have you seen Mrs. Sanchez?"

The Nurse smiled "Yes Kat is in the chapel. It is so nice to have her back to herself. She is much nicer this morning." The call button went off and the nurse smiled and went to check on the patient.

I make my way to the chapel there I see her. I am mesmerized by her as always with the sun shining through the window. The sunlight looks like a halo around her as she kneels to pray. I sit in a chair in the back of the room quietly and say a quick prayer. I wonder what she is saying to him.

"Dear heavenly Father it's me your burdensome child. Please forgive me for these last few days of anger and hatefulness. I thank you for all your blessings that you have bestowed upon me. Father, I am incredibly grateful that you have brought Jacob and Ki back into my life. I ask that you please keep my husband and my children safe and from harm. I ask father that you help me to become well soon so that I can be home with them and that I do not cause anyone more pain. Please bless them and keep them always. Amen "Kat stood up and turned around she saw Jacob praying. She stood there quietly until she was done.

" When did you get back? "She asked.

"Early hours this morning. Do you remember when we were last in this room together?" Kat shakes her head now.

"It was the day my brothers died. You were so heartbroken and begging God to take your life instead of theirs. Even in the pain you were in you were begging for their lives to be spared. Then my mother came in and was screaming at you that you killed them. That she never wanted to see you again. What you did not know was that when you were in surgery. Your heart stopped three times and right after each time one of my brother's hearts stopped as well. James and Kris's last words where angel stay does not leave Ki and Jacob, I love you angel always. Before Ki heart stopped his words were Jacob love angel let her know she is my heart. They put the 3 of them on life support till you were able to see them. Kris and James were brain dead, and Ki was barely holding on. The nurse brought you in to see them. The entire ICU could hear your sobs and begging God to bring them back. When they finally pried you from Ki and took you back to your room. A few minutes later Ki monitors started going off his vitals were coming back his brain function started improving. My mom ran to Kris and James but there was no change. We then hear the nurse call code Blue to your room. You had ripped open your stitches and were bleeding out; my uncle rushed you back to surgery. It was then that they decided while you were between conscious and unconscious that he would hypnotize you to forget us and forget that you knew us you would only remember that your brother-in-law raped you but no real details and that your boyfriend died in an accident. Those were the only details that he allowed you to keep in your memory. Ki continued to recover and now you know why they did what they did. I am sorry angel that we could not be with you all this time. And I'm sorry that I left you in that state the other day." Tears pool in Jacob's eyes

"Jacob, do you know that I used to look for you guys everywhere in every face I saw. I yearned for the 4 of you. I was so lonely. I knew something was missing. I just did not know what to do. I decided that I was going to go into the army so that I could look for what I was missing. Then everything with him happened and my family found out. So instead of me going into the army I got sent away to my dad's family. Do you remember what they were like?" he nodded yes. "My mom couldn't stand not having my sister and nephew around and if I were home my dad wouldn't allow them to be there since my sister believed her husband. My dad begged me not to go to the army. He was afraid I would be reckless with no family around and wind up dead. I think everyone would have been better off. The only thing I have ever done is hurt those I love. I cannot even be the one thing I wanted most even after God granted me a miracle. I cannot be a good mom. I have screwed up my kids just like my mom did us when she was institutionalized. I do not understand why my entire life people have only wanted to hurt me. Am I really that horrible of a person?" Jacob wiped the tears from Kat's cheeks as she looked up at him.

His heart breaking at the despair in her eyes. Neither of them noticed that Dr Smith was standing at the door listening to the two. She learned more from eavesdropping on this conversation than she had in two years of therapy with Kat. She turned and walked away wondering how it was that this person could survive being abused and rejected by her family even as a small child. Being told you are not worthy to be alive and to have been raped by not one but several men. Most of the rape victims she had treated were messed up after just one. Kat Sanchez is a lot stronger than people give her credit for.

"We better go meet Ki and Dr Smith for your session. Though I am enjoying not sharing you with anyone. Do you think that you can do like you used to? Talk to me when you're upset. Please." Jacob asked.

"Sure, booboo I can do that. Let us go before Ki sends out the national guard. looking for us." Kat stands up and holds out her hand for Jacob's.

"No need for that I knew where you were." Ki said from the doorway walking across the room he closes his arms around Kat closes his eyes and takes a deep breath. "Are you ready for what's next?" he asks as he looks down into her eyes. She smiles and moves his arms and takes his hand in hers and then takes Jacob's. hand "Will you two be with me at all times and promise to make sure that I'm, ok?" They both look at her and smile "promise" they say in unison.

CHAPTER 14

A different approach

When they get into the office Kat sees the box sitting on the table Jacob tells her that these are items that may help her with her memories and may help her be able to come to terms with some of the things that she will remember. Jacob tells her that though most of my memories not be very nice he promises that they will also be some good memories that will make the others better he also told her that in the box I special things from Chris and James his father his mother and grandmother that she will learn just how precious and loved she was as well as how precious she still is that as she remembers things he will have different things to give her that will help her remember and that will hopefully help her feel the love that she had lost but that is still there waiting for her if she wants it Kat can't wait to look into the box the Jacob won't let her he says that only he is allowed to give her the items in the box and he can only give them to her in the order that she opens the door so he will not give her anything that is not in tune with what she remembers because he wants to reinforce the memories and not have her misunderstand I'll be at set by memories that she hasn't yet to unlock

Dr Smith asks Kat if she is ready to start. With a nod they dim the lights. Dr Smith tells her that today she wants her to find the same door but wants her to try to see what happened next.

"I only feel cold and see darkness. I am so cold. I feel numb and empty. My breathing has slowed too, almost nothing. I am in total darkness I can barely hear anything everything is muffled. I feel someone picking me up, but I cannot respond. I'm dying I know my daddy is going to be mad my mom a little sad but at least her mistake will be gone."

I want you to try to see what happens when you get to the hospital. "Dr. Smith asks.

I am in this room I am still not awake, but I hear Dr P telling me to hang on. I hear him yell for more AB + blood stat. I open my eyes and I see him, but he is a little different. "

"Who do you see?" Dr Smith urges Kat to focus on who she sees.

"The boy from before he is smaller somehow but still beautiful, I reach my hand to him I see them covered in my own blood. He takes my hand. I breathe a sigh and smile at him."

"Why are you smiling?" She asks.

"He kept his promise he promised to stay with me till I died and now he was here again to hold my hand just like before I feel safe and warm now. He came back to me just like he said." Kat whispered.

"Kat what else are you seeing?" She asks.

I heard Dr P telling the boy to stay and hold my hand since it helped me as he stitched up my wrist and gave me blood. I feel how warm his hands felt against my cold ones. He is crying and telling me I needed to live. That he wants to see me in the morning. He held my hand all night. Every time I woke up, he was there holding my hand. He never left me. "

"Are you ready to come back now?" I hear Jacob ask.

"Not yet the boy is sleeping holding my hand. I am just staring at him. I realize he is not the same boy. They look so much alike, but he is different. I reach over and smooth his hair away from his face. He wakes up and smiles at me. He cups my face in his hands and kisses my cheek." Thank you for waking up. "He sighs.

I do not feel scared of him, I feel safe. I hear the nurse come in "Ah our little kitten is awake. You know you gave us quite a scare last night. Jacob your uncle is looking for you." She tells him he reluctantly let us go of my hand and leaves my room.

"I'm ready now to come back."

"When you leave this room. You will be yourself and calm, the memories of this room will no longer hurt you. You will no longer have any reason to be afraid. you will not be angry or hurt by these memories." 1 2 3 snaps.

I open my eyes and they are all looking at me waiting to see if I am ok. I smile at Jacob. "Thank you for staying with me that night and holding my hand."

"It was the first time I wanted to help anyone. You saved me as much as I did you. Thank you for coming to save me." He replied softly "now in the box I have letters that we all wrote after you left us. I will give them to you as you remember things so since you remember our first meeting, I will give you one of mine first." He gives me the letter and tells me I can read it when I am alone in my room.

I open the letter when I get to my room, I am anxious to see what bad things Jacob says about me.

Hey angel.

I am writing because you have left us, and I am missing you. We thought that by writing you letters when we miss you will help us not to miss you so much. I remember when I first met you. I had been parting with my friends for several days drinking and doing drugs. I had partied a little too much and had overdosed. I now think it was God who put me there, so I could meet you. I remember leaving my room and going to look for my uncle when I heard him yell "get me some AB + or O + blood. I ran to see what was going on. I never heard such panic in his voice usually he is very calm and cold when working. I investigate the door of the room he is un. There laying on the bed is this small girl's blood everywhere. Your reddish-brown hair spilling over the side of the bed, your skin pale as porcelain. I could not help myself, I had to touch you to see if you were real. When I touched your cold arm, you opened your eyes and looked at me. They were the biggest eyes I think I had ever seen I could not tell if they were blue or green. When you smiled at me, I was already lost. when you said that you're here as if you had been waiting for me. No one ever looked at me that way before I looked at my uncle and without knowing why tears were streaming down my face. I begged him to please save her. Please she is an angel. He looked at me with a very strange look on his face and then said if you stay here be useful to help keep her calm. I cannot risk sedating her till her pressure and heart rate comes up. I placed my hand on your head and whispered to you to stay with me. That I needed you to be here with me. I stayed with you through the night holding your hand. I could not bring myself to leave you. I called my brother Ki and told him I wanted the 3 of them to visit me the next day because I had something important for them. When you woke up. I could not believe the bright bubbly girl hurt herself so badly just the night before. You shyly asked me why I was here. I just looked at you and told you what happened. You gave me a very stern talk too and told me how ashamed I should be to give my family so much grief. I watched you throughout the day and only saw you smiling and laughing as if nothing happened. I went to see my uncle and asked him what happened, how could you try to end your life one day and be so happy the next? He told me that you had a unique gift you can block out when people do bad things to you that you tried only show people the happy side of you not damaged part. I saw you writing something when I walked into the great room and when you realized I was trying to see it you told me it was a surprise.

I am so thankful that God let me meet such a giving and loving angel as you.

I love you angel.

jae

I cried myself to sleep that night not out of anger or self-pity for what I had remembered, but because I felt the despair and loneliness but also the love in Jacob's letter. I wish I could take it away. I miss my children and my family, but I want to be a whole person before I see them again.

CHAPTER 15

A talk

The next morning, I go to the chapel I needed to talk to someone who was not a therapist, so I talk to God instead.

"Heavenly father above its me your burdensome child. Thank you for letting Jacob and Ki live. And for letting me meet them again. Thank you for allowing me to start to remember what I had forgotten. Thank you for it being in a safe place and in a way which will not hurt my family as much as it could have if I were at home not knowing why these things were happening. Thank you to my husband who has loved me even though I am broken and for keeping my children safe through it all. I know I am not worthy of anyone's love or kindness. I thank you for the nurses and for Dr Smith for helping me. Father, I have only one request. Please do not let my past hurt anyone or cause them pain. Amen." I get up and turn around; I see both Jacob and Ki kneeling in prayer. I do not want to disturb them, so I sit quietly with my head bowed till they have finished their silent prayers. I get in when they do.

"Good morning you two did you sleep well?" I asked as we walked out of the chapel not knowing that the chaplain had been watching me every morning as I pray and had noticed that the Drs were regular visitors as well. He smiles and goes about his business as we leave.

"Good morning, Kat how did you sleep?" They both asked at the same moment.

I laughed and told them fine. When we get to the therapy room Dr smith is already there waiting for us. "Good morning everyone are we ready to get started?"

"Yes of course." I answer.

The lights are dimmed, and I am looking at the pen light. I see the stairwell and begin to walk down. I hear the voice asking me to see if I can find the door from before. I look around and I see several doors this time then I see it I walk over to it and open it.

"I want you to think about what happened after you woke up and tell us what happened next."

"I am in the great room watching tv with Jacob we are talking. He asked me why I hurt myself. I told him it's nothing, I just do not want my mom to mad at me. We talk about why he is here, and I thank him for staying with me."

"Where are you parents?" Jacob asks.

"They are on their vacation to my aunt's house. I was staying with my mom's friend she is our neighbor. I do not like them much though.

Just then three gentlemen come in I stare at the one he is the most beautiful man I have met the other two are identical except one is clean shaven with short hair the other has longer hair. I know him. He stares back at me then crosses the room and puts his arms around me. "I found you I finally found you. I have been looking for you for 6 years. How come you're here?" He asks.

I smile up at him "how are you here I remember you were with me before you're the one who stayed with me before."

He smiles at me and kisses my forehead "yes I am I have been wanting to find you for so long."

Jacob clears his throat "hey that's my girl your holding Ki what do you think you're doing?"

Ki laughs "sorry little bro but this is my angel I've been looking for all this time and you can't have her."

Just then Eve and John walk in. John looks angry when he sees me surrounded by the four of them. He starts to walk over towards me "get your things we are taking you home now." He says in an angry voice I hide behind Jacob and Ki the other two gentleman one leaves the room the other stands in front of Jacob and Ki.

He asks, "Are you, her father?"

John answers "What does it matter if I am or not. I'm the one in charge of her."

Just then Dr P walks in with the other gentleman "Excuse me but she will not be going anywhere with you. I called her grandmother and placed a call to her parents. She is in my care now and will be staying here till they return."

John looks angry his fist is clinched "Who gave you permission to do that I am her guardian right now not her grandmother."

Dr P looks at him "I am and have been her Dr since she was 7 years old, I know what you did, and I know you put her here under someone else's name. I have not called the police yet only because I want to talk to her grandmother first. I do not know who you are, but I suggest that you leave before I do. Do not ever come near my patient again. Do you understand."

I look at Dr P, he looks at me and smiles. Just then John grabs Eve and they leave.

Dr P turns to the one who went to get him "Thanks Kris and you 3 thank you for protecting her."

 Ki looks at him" Hey uncle no problem she is my angel. "

Dr P looks at him in shock and tells me to go to my room where he needs to talk to his nephews.

I hear Dr Smith voice Kat it is time to leave here nothing can hurt you anymore. You will be calm and yourself when I count to 3 1 2 3 snaps.

I look up and I see the 3 of them are looking at me. Jacob smiles at me. "How do you feel?"

"I am fine I am happy I remembered James and Kris. I could see everyone clearly this time not like before I recognized everyone." I told them.

"So, Jacob do I get a prize today. You said I would get one as I remembered things."

Ki laughs at me "you're you this time that is good I'm happy."

Yes, you got a prize today but there is something I must ask. "He looks at me very seriously.

"What is it.?" I am afraid of what he is about to ask.

"Since it seems that we can let you choose the doors now that your memories are coming back more can we try to open a few happier one's next time I am concerned that you may become overwhelmed with such traumatic memories and that it may have an adverse effect."

I look at Dr Smith and Ki as well to see what they have to say, "I agree I don't want her to become too depressed or withdrawn." Dr Smith added "me to" states Ki.

"Ok we can try that next time." I say as I hold out my hands for my prize.

Jacob smiles at me as he hands me three envelopes.

I giggle and take them quickly before he changes his mind.

"Hey why does she get 3 this time?" Ki asks.

"She remembered our first meeting with all of us, so she gets to read a letter from you James and Kris." Jacob replies.

"Mumm, can I read them with you? We have never been allowed to read what each other wrote to you and I would really like to know what everyone wrote." Ki asks me.

"Hmmm I tell you what I will do I will read them in private first then the next session I will read them to you three if I want to share because some things, I may want to keep to myself ok." I look at them waiting for their answer.

"Ok we can do that because curiosity is killing me wanting to know what they say." Dr smith answers for everyone I go back to my room and start reading. I read the letters several times crying laughing while reading them I cannot wait to share them tomorrow.

CHAPTER 16

Letters of healing.

When I wake up the next morning, I cannot wait to see everyone share letters with them. So, I ran to the office right away and waited for them to arrive. Only to find that the three of them are waiting for me already. So, I decided to read Ki letter first.

Hello, my little angel blossom.

I miss you and am counting the days till I see you again. Jae has told all of us that to get over our sadness we need to write as if we are talking to you so here goes. I remember the very first time I saw you. You were running across my grandmother's field to the horse paddock, and I followed you because you were just a small kid and my grandmother's horses were big and did not let anyone near them except the trainers and riders. I was worried you would get hurt if you got too close. When I walked into the stall there you were cooing and talking to firefly as if she were a puppy instead of this mean and nasty horse that she was my grandmother never even would go near her. But you were sitting on the stool in her pen and feeding her an apple talking to her as if she understood everything you said. the other horses became restless because I was there but I was wanting to hear what you had to say so I slipped into the stall beside her pen so that I could listen to you .You had the sweetest voice it was so calming and soft it actually almost lulled me to sleep when you started to tell her about what was going on at school and home but when you started to sing to her I just closed my eyes and listened to me it sounded like an angel singing you had the cutest little voice and I wanted to see you closer but every time I tried the horses would start to get restless almost as if they did not want me near you before I knew it I was awakened by the groomsman who came to feed them and I did not get to see you that day I was so upset because I did not get a good look at you before and knew I just had to meet you .when I got back to the house I asked my grandmother who you were she just smiled and told me you were Katie the neighbors daughter and you would go to the paddock when you were sad or upset and feed the horses apples and talk out whatever was upsetting you with them. I asked her why didn't they behave the way they normally did around other people with you that all I had to do was walk in there and they become restless she told me she had no idea but as long as the horses were ok with it and you did not get hurt she has no objections I told her that you put me asleep with you talking she laughed at me because the groomsman says the same thing that your voice is calming and puts him to sleep I asked her if you rode and she said no that you were too afraid to get on any of them that you would only sit with them and talk to them but nothing more . I made a point of watching you over the next few days because I really wanted to see what you looked like because my heart skipped every time I saw you or even heard your voice but I would get a glimpse of you and you would be gone then one day I saw you racing thru the field again I remembered what my grandmother said that you went to the horse paddock when you were upset so I took off after you but before I got very far you were laying on the ground not moving I ran to you and picked you up and you opened those big eyes of yours and asked me to hold you till you passed I fell in love with you the second that I looked into your eyes I knew you were the one for me for the rest of my life that I never wanted to let you go that I needed to have you near me forever after I got your stomach emptied and you told me what happened

I realized that you were only 7 and that you would be gone the next day I could not let my angel leave me ever so I ran back to my grandmothers and told her we needed to find a way to keep you she told me to late that by the sounds of the yelling that you were already being taken away by your grandmother. I knew that I would find you again because you were my heart and you belonged to me I looked for you everywhere I made my mom check every girl named Katie in the county to see if it was you it took me six years to find my angel and this time I was not letting you go I f I could help it when I walked into the common room at the hospital to see Jae and I saw that long curly reddish brown hair my heart stopped and I held my breath but when I heard your voice I knew without you turning around that I found my angel but when you turned around and I looked into those big eyes and you smiled up at me I only had one thought to hold you and never let you go again I don't even remember crossing the room all I remember was having you in my arms and you smelling like cherry blossoms. Jae started fussing telling me to let go of his girl but there was no way you belonged to me you were mine and nothing was going to change that not even my brother I remember holding you and keeping you close to me every second that I could I remember watching you sleep and when you began to get upset in your sleep singing to you to calm you back to sleep and whispering to you about all the places I wanted to take you to see I knew that I would love you every second till I took my last breath. I love you with every breath and every beat of my heart. I cannot wait to have you in my arms again your eyes hold the stars, and your smile holds the sun your skin is as pale as the moon you lip as sweet as honey. I was so angry to find out why you were with him in the hospital but also grateful to have found you again. I was also very jealous of my brother. It took me forever to convince my uncle to allow me to stay at the hospital while you were there, I even used my brother as an excuse though I know he saw right through me. I am waiting for you always.

Love you forever.

Jun Ki

"I knew it. I knew you only used me. As an excuse. I was just grateful that James and Kris didn't want to stay it as well was bad enough having you around all the time." Jacob says laughingly as he threw a pillow at his brother's head.

"Hey, I told you right away she was my girl." Ki replies throwing the pillow back at him.

"Excuse me but please remember you are Drs, and we are here to help our patient not to play." Dr smith reminded them.

"Kat how are you feeling about what you read and what you have remembered we need to make sure you are moving forward from these memories." Dr smith turns to me.

"I don't want to think about the bad memories because I don't know what to do with them now. I still do not understand why these things happened to me and why my family never did anything about it. I saw my father and mother always taking up my sister and fighting over anything that anyone said or did to her that was bad but me they only wanted to hide what happened to me. My mom would say things like" I told you to not be nice or too friendly to people and look at what happened. I told you to keep your distance from them. She never told my dad about Dr or Jon and what they did to me. It was like if it was not acknowledged then it did not happen. My mom is still like that. She brushes things under the carpet a lot. My brother-in-law can talk harshly to my sister, and she gets angry, but joe can push me and leave bruises and it is just a tiff I need to get over. I have always been the one to give up everything I wanted for them, but they do not do anything if it means sacrificing anything for me. My mom thinks I am having a tantrum right now because I am here. She will not listen to anything about how I feel or what I need since I am not taking care of my responsibilities. I miss my kids and I hate to think about what they are telling them about me. "

"Do you think being here is helping you?" Dr Smith asks, looking at me very intently.

"Yes, I think that remembering the things I have and dealing with all the pent-up anger and hatred I have is helping me. At home I vent my anger at the kids at times and it frightens me. I worry that someday my anger will become more than I can control. If that happens, I worry I may hurt my kids, so I try to keep a very tight rein on my emotions when I am at home. I tell them if I am yelling, I am in control and if I stop yelling then they need to worry. When my anger takes control, I don't think I only react and that scares me more than anything." I tell them my voice is shaky from the emotions welling up. I want to cry just at the thought of the possibility of ever harming one of my kids. I am also a little embarrassed because Jacob and Ki do not know this about me. They only remember the nice girl from before not the person sitting here now. I wonder what they are thinking right now about me.

"I always tell you I want my angel back to who she was before. What I have not said is that I know you will not be here again exactly. Too much has happened to you, but I know that the person who taught us how to love and how to be a family is still there because if she were not, you would not worry about the things you do. Yes, I still love that girl and want you to remember who you were then. Only so that you can balance who you are now. I want you to be smiling and happy. I want you to be proud of how strong you are and to show that strength to your children, so they can see how amazing you are. All the negativity you are voicing against your family is your anger talking when you are more yourself you always are positive about everything. I think that the more you come to terms with the bad as well as the good that has happened to you that we will see more of the person we loved before just a more mature version of her." Ki explained to me I smiled at him. It seemed like before he knew what I was thinking without me even saying anything. I wonder what joe is going to think when he finds out about what I have been remembering and if he is ever going to forgive me for staying away so long. I wonder if he has found a new woman yet. I wonder if my children think I have abandoned. them. It has been a month since I have been here. I have only seen them for short periods. I really miss my family, but I am afraid they have given up on me now.

"Did you read Kris and James letters also?" Jacob inquired.

"Not yet I will let you know when I do ok." I look at him wondering if he already read them or not.

"I haven't read anyone's letters they are yours not mine." He lets me know right away I guess we are starting to be like old times where we know what the other is thinking.

A new ally

I ask Dr Smith how long I will need to stay here. The bruises on my neck have disappeared and I think I am doing better. Her only reply was soon. I am not doing as well as I thought. I am more relaxed, and I have remembered a lot. I know the more traumatic memories are still locked away. I can feel the fear in my throat overtime I wake up. These last few nights either Jacob Ki or Nurse Henderson have been beside me when I wake up. So even if I am not remembering that I am having a nightmare I am. I think I will ask today in my session. I got dressed today. I decided I am not wearing night clothes or hospital gowns and I am going to wear street clothes for the first time since being here. I look at the soft pink shirt that is in the closet. It is so pretty I feel like I have seen it before. I know it is not something I own. It was one of the outfits that Ki bought me. I put it on with a pair of black jeans that he also bought. I start to brush my hair when Ki walks in and takes the brush from me.

"Here let me do that. Your hair has not been brushed for days and is a rat's nest. Knowing you all you will do us pull it back into a band. If you do not let me, get the tangles out, you will have to cut them out. He pulls up the chair and pats the seat. As he sits behind it on the bed. He divides my hair into sections and starts combing from the ends up. Very gently he gets the comb through my hair.

"no one has brushed my hair since I was small except the beautician. It's nice to have someone else do it since it's gotten so long again." I told him.

"Every time you stayed with us; we would sit in the family room. Each of us would take turns brushing our hair till the curls were completely tangle free. Then mama would braid your hair so that you could sleep without it tangling again. Every time you would fall asleep by the time she was done. Then Jacob would carry you to the stairs and James would carry you up them and wait for Chris to take you and carry you to me then I would tuck you in. Grandmother put a bed in her room for you and she would always be waiting for me to bring you in to her. Papa always came out of his study when he would hear us on the stairs. He always came to kiss your cheek good night. My grandmother and mother would just smile at him when he did that. They said that he could not sleep if he did not when he knew you were in the house." Ki finished combing my hair and asked me "are you ready for today's session?"

"Yes, when do you think I can go home?" I look at him.

"Right now, your husband is still adamant about you not having a place to go. Your uncle says you can stay with them. Personally, I do not want you to go till we have unlocked all the doors. I am really worried about how you are going to react when the worst of your memories are revealed, so do not rush it. Dr smith is trying to get your family to come for another visit, so you can see your kids. Everything is going to work out don't worry ok." He reassured me he held out his hand to me waiting for me to get up from the chair.

"Do you mind if we stop by the chapel before we go" I asked him he nodded ok. We walk to the chapel and the chaplain is there, he smiles at me.

"Miss, do you remember me?" He asked.

"I don't think so. Should I know you?" I look at him intently trying to place his face. I look at Ki wondering if he knows him.

"He knows who I am, but he doesn't know how I know you if its ok with the 3 Drs I would like to sit and talk to the 4 of you today if that is, ok?" He looks at Ki.

"I think a change of pace could help sure I don't see why not come with us now and we can start and Kat if you feel like you want to pray, we can have a prayer in the room ok." Ki agrees with him, and we head to my secession.

When we get all settled. Ki takes the lead.

"Today we have an incredibly special request. The chaplain Reverend Cook asked if he could sit and talk to us today, so I agreed. I think a change of pace could give Kat a needed rest from the doors and give us a chance to have just a sit-down talk."

"I think that will be ok. Since we have unearthed so many traumatic events in her past. It will give her a breather today. Smiles Dr Smith replies

"Thank you, Drs., I have a story to tell MS Kat its one I know she doesn't remember and it's not one that anyone else knows. But it is something she needs to hear. It was about 13 years ago you were still a child just starting the 8th grade in middle school. My daughter was a person who liked to bully others and you were one of the girls she picked on. One day you saw a man who was old enough to be her father trying to convince her to get into his car. You ran over and started to talk to her and took her by the hand. You walked her away from him and back into the school. You stood in the door and watched as he pulled the car away. You told her to stay away from him, that he liked little girls and that he would hurt her if she went with him. She shoved you and told you to mind your own business. That night when she got home, she asked her mom what kind of stupid person stops someone who torments and beats them up from getting hurt. My wife told her to ask me. That night she asked me the same question. I asked her if she is the person who does the beating or is the one getting beat. She lowered her head and told me that she picks on this girl at school that she beats up regularly. today this handsome man was flirting with her and wanted to take her someplace special. She said the girl rushed over and acted like they were best friends and took her by the hand. She took me back inside the school and told me to stay away from that man that he hurts little girls. I asked her if I could take her to school the next day. I am sorry for what my daughter did to you, but I am also incredibly grateful to you because you saved her from getting hurt. When I contacted the police about a strange man hanging out at the school and that he tried to get my daughter into his car. They were able to start having a car at the school to watch out for john. Because of your kindness, who knows how many girls you saved from experiencing the pain you were given at his hands. I was also the chaplain that was called the night you were admitted here. I was asked to come and pray with your family. When I looked at you lay on the bed you were so small. I could not understand why you were here alone. Why were your parents not here? I found out from one of the nurses. She told me you had been raped but there was no evidence, but you were badly hurt in that area. She told me when you first arrived, they believed the people who admitted you were your parents. That was not till one of the Er nurses recognized you and called Dr P. They checked the chart and found that they listed you as self-paid and that you were brought up in under a different name than the nurse. Remembered. Dr p was in the hospital and rushed in to see you. He knew you would not let anyone examine you but him. I went to the waiting room to try to talk to your family. Only to find that they told the registration nurse that they would be back soon. They had something to do. Then when I saw you at my daughter's school. I knew what John did. I stayed in the background that night watching and praying my heart would not let me leave. I saw john drop off a woman at the door. I heard her ask about you and told the nurse she was your guardian. Thank you for living and for protecting those around you. Because of you John was not able to hurt any other girls. "His voice is very calming. He spoke in soft tones so as not to scare her. even though you could hear the emotion in his voice. You could hear the concern and compassion he felt for her.

"Your Charity's dad. You were the one I heard praying over me and Jacob that night asking God to protect me and to let me live. Why didn't you talk to me before?" I have been here for over 3 months, and you never said anything. "I asked him.

"I was ashamed. My daughter bullied and beat you up and yet you protected her. I was told you did not remember many things and that was why you were here. I do not know if you remembered what happened. Then you withdrew so much after you remembered and was in so much pain. I was afraid of making you worse. I heard your prayer last time and knew that I needed to talk to you. To tell you how grateful I was and to let you know that God is going to help you through this. You are a strong person." He was so sincere and looked so sad that I got up and walked over to him and gave him a big hug.

"Thank you for telling me about what you knew about me. Do not be sad or feel ashamed anymore. Your daughter and I became good friends in high school. After I blackened her eye that is. There was nothing you could have done to change what happened. Also, Charity was that way to me because she thought I liked the same boy she did. The boy she liked was my best friend since we had been babies, and we were awfully close and affectionate with each other. Though we thought we were acting like family most thought we were an item and that would have been just to ewe for us." I told him. "

The Drs listened to the two of us without interrupting till we were done. Dr Smith was the one who spoke first.

"Thank you, reverend Cook, for sharing this with us. I had no idea that you knew her. Kat are you ok with what you just learned?"

"Yes, I am. I am happy that I was able to keep someone from being hurt. Also, now that he has told me who he is I will feel more at ease talking to him. I had been worried that I was bothersome with how much time I spend in the chapel and rush out as soon as I see him." I replied smiling today I liked the session because I did not have to only remember something bad, but I got to hear that I did something right.

"There is something I don't understand why no one called the police?" Dr. Smith asked.

"I can answer that. The priority was to take care of her and to patch her up. It was not till the nurse saw how heavy she was bleeding from her private area that they thought to check her there. The only concern they had was her making it through. They did call the police and the police came and took the information. Then nothing happened. I later found out that because she was registered under a false name and because no physical evidence was found other than the damage she suffered. When the police came to follow up, she could not remember anything other than she was missing her mom and dad and thought if she were hurt then they would come home early. The police felt that there was no point in following up with it. Even though she could not remember she still knew that john liked little girls it was not till he got his foster daughter pregnant, and his wife told police officers some of the things he done that he was arrested." Reverend cook explained.

"I was not expecting that we would be talking about this night again today but in a way I'm glad because I wanted to give you a few things that belong to you." Jacob said as he pulled a small leather pouch from his neck. And pulled out a piece of paper "This is what you wrote me when we met, I have carried it with me every day since then.

"You wrote this for me when you were 13 years old to help me to remember to never give in to the darkness.

When in the face of darkness, you lose all sight.

 When the darkness takes you, there is no light.

When you embrace the darkness, you lose your soul.

When you accept the darkness, flows the life it stole releasing the pain and sorrow of tomorrow.

 when in the face of light there is hoped to borrow

When the light takes you, faith is being renewed.

When you embrace the light, the darkness is subdued.

 when you accept the light life begins anew"

He also pulls out this worn notebook and hands it to Dr Smith to look.

"This was the journal that my uncle had her write in while she was here. I did not have this one until I came back from my parent's house with the box of memories. You may want to read it before giving it to Kat if she does not mind. It will give you some insight on how she felt at that time as well as how you want us to proceed with these sessions, but I think we should let her rest for today if that is ok with everyone." Jacob asked.

"Kat is it ok if I read this before giving it back to you. I think that Jacob is right in this instance it would be beneficial for me to see firsthand what you were feeling then and maybe we can go over it next time." Dr smith was looking at me as if a little worried I would say no. I am wondering if she is afraid of what I wrote will cause me to withdraw again. So, I agree to let her read it first. I thank reverend cook for today as well. I am glad we did not open any new doors today. I am not ready to face anything else, yet I am still wondering what everyone thinks of me now and if it changes how they see me. I want my husband to talk to and have him just hold me, but I am very afraid that he does not want or love me anymore. Since it has been so long since we have seen each other. I wonder if he even misses me. Kat thinks to herself as she sits in the room waiting to go to sleep.

Later that night Dr Smith is looking at Kats journal wondering if it will really make much difference if she reads it. As I sit at my desk reading the journal that Jacob gave me.

CHAPTER 18

Pages from the past

June 24, 1979

Well the Dr is asking me to write how I felt today so that he can try to see how I feel and see things I have never really written anything before so I hope I can do this I don't know if I can because I really don't know what to say except that I hope no one finds out because if they do it truly would be better if the darkness really did take me away because my family will be so angry that I have said anything . It will have been better for all since I am worthless anyway. I cannot make anyone happy and cannot do anything right. I walk into a room and my mother frowns, and I wonder what I do now. I wish I were invisible so that no one can look at me or want to touch me. It makes my skin crawl every time anyone sees me. anyways I should already have been eaten by the worms by now but then my cousin said even if I died, they would rather starve then eat me, so I guess I am even no good to feed the worms. He wants to know why I cut my wrists open and wanted to die though he promised that the person who stitched me up would make sure that there will be only a tiny scar that will eventually fade so that I can wear pretty clothes as if right. I turn everything ugly not pretty I am the ugliest out of all the girls in my family and all the uncle try to make me feel better because they feel sorry for me my aunt said so .So since she is never wrong then I know it's true I am just a waste of space I don't know why that men always try to touch me it's not my fault I wear clothes that are three sizes to big so that

I look fat and I leave my hair dirty as much as possible so that it won't curl it will just hang over my ugly face so no one can see me I try to be useful so I do as much of the chores as possible so that they will be happy with me but I always do something wrong and they start asking me why am I so stupid to think that I can do anything right my uncle says that God doesn't make mistakes well he did when he made me so he needs to quit sending me back here and let the bugs eat so he can correct his mistake maybe I should have just used a gun instead of cutting my wrist because I know I can't miss with a gun I know that is one thing I am good at my dad tells me though not to let anyone know or they will make fun of me and try to beat me at it so that they can humiliate over it it's so dark and cold here inside I can't see any light anywhere so why doesn't it just take me away why did they find me too soon and why did the boy from my dreams have to come to me again and tell me to still be here why couldn't he just let me stay in the cold dark place so that no one has to see me and why did he save me the first time anyway didn't he know he save a worthless person I try to be good and take care of everyone I try to always smile and love everyone I know they tell me these things because they don't want me to hope that anyone could ever really love so that I don't get hurt my cousin said I might as well just go ahead and get used to being alone because no one could ever love such a person as me always smiling trying to be pretty when I am not why would my smile be pretty when the rest of me is not so maybe if I never smile again then men won't see me or bother me and boys wont stare at me and try to get me alone I really like the cold dark place I felt when my blood was leaving my body because no one could see me and I felt nothing my grand ma Julie says that God gave me a too big of heart filled with love and that it shines thru my eyes and smile and that is my special gift and when I learn what he wants me to do everything will be ok well he needs to take everything back and just leave my body to rot because it's not working I have no love or light that she keeps talking about if I did then wouldn't I be pretty and wouldn't people love me just like I do them but I guess it doesn't work that way I guess I am only supposed to love them it doesn't matter if they don't love me I guess It's okay I don't deserve it any way not until I can do something right and make them happy I just wish there was one thing I could do to make them happy but it doesn't work I only want them to be happy

I stop and wonder about Kat and how hard her life has been. Most think that she is spoiled and childish. Reading her journal makes me feel so sad. How could a child endure so much and only think about the happiness of others? It makes me almost afraid to read the other entries. I think about the last few months I wonder what is going to happen next. I wonder if I am doing the right thing allowing so many people to help with this case. I have taken such an unconventional path with her. Without thinking I picked up the phone and called my father.

"Hey dad can I ask you a few things?" I ask when he answers.

"Sure, what is going on?" he replies.

"In your career have you ever done something that you are not sure if it right?" I asked him.

"All the time psychiatry is not an easy field. Each person deals with things differently and has different stresses and issues. No two people are the same. Why do you ask?" After a short silence I answer him

"I have a patient who has severe major depression ptsd with borderline personality disorder suicidal tendencies and a dissociative disorder. I called a college in to consult with her and it turned out he knew my patient. They had not seen each other for years. And my patient had no memory of him. As it turns out I now have him his brother and the chaplain even came today to help with getting her memories back. I guess I am just worried that too many people are getting involved. Also, her husband has all but abandoned her." I wait to see what he is going to say.

"When it comes to lost memories, it never hurts to have several people helping, especially if the person doesn't have much support at home. Have these Drs interfered or done anything that you did not want them to? Have they made changes in her treatment plan that you did not approve?" He inquired.

"No nothing like that they have done nothing but be supportive of my decisions. We meet every day and discuss her family situation and how we should go ahead. They have shared everything they have from her past that they know. I guess it maybe because they are so kind and considerate to their patients more so with her that I wonder if it's the right thing maybe if they were more aloof, I would be more comfortable." I hear him tapping his pen which means he is considering what I just said.

"There are some Drs who treat patients with positivity and compassion. I am that way with many of my patients. I know so much about them that I have a fondness for them. But I would never put my fondness before what was best for them. If what you are doing is what is best for your patient, then it will be ok. I had a friend who was an amazing talented Dr. He was a master at hypnosis and psychiatry and could stitch up a wound better than a plastic surgeon. but he chose to be a general practitioner because that was where his heart was. He treated his patients like they were family, but he never hesitated to do what was right for his patient. He had one a little girl who did not trust Drs he was the only person who she would allow to treat her. It did not matter when she came in or even which hospital, she was in he would go to treat her. I remember one time she was in Texas visiting her uncle and she got hurt. They took her to the ER she became so frightened and hysterical they called him to see what was wrong with her. he asked to talk directly to her. He calmed her down, got her to agree to allow them to run the test and he stayed on the phone with her the entire time, he never left her. Most Drs, my self-included, would have told them to sedate her and treat her but not him. Only you can decide what kind of Dr you want to be to your patients and if you do no harm and you have your patient's permission it will be ok have faith." He reassured Me.

"Why does that word keep coming up?" Everyone, even my patient keeps telling me to have faith. "

"I used to think it was all me and that I had everything figured out. Till one night this young girl came in she was no more than a child. After watching my friend patch, her up. I thought for sure she was not going to make it and if she did, she would be in an institution for a long time. When I came in the next day, she had everyone laughing and playing games. The entire mood of the floor was lighter and brighter. I asked nurse Henderson what was going on. She told me God sent angel to brighten our day and to have faith that all would be ok. By the time the child I thought would be in an institution left the hospital I was a believer in faith. That child spread sunshine to every person she met, and I had several patients who I thought would be there longer go home early. After that I changed a lot in how I thought. I began treating my patients with more positive attitudes and my job became more than just listening and doling out prescriptions. I found I learn as much from them as they did from me."

"Thanks Dad I really needed this talk. I feel much better now. Would you come for lunch with me tomorrow? I'm sure nurse Henderson would love to see you." Dr smith asked her father.

"I would love to." he replied.

After hanging up I decide to read the next entry of her journal

June 25,1979

Today I got to see the boy who stayed with me last night. His name is Jacob, and it turns out he is not really a boy. He is already a man. He is not even in school anymore. He is exceedingly kind and funny. He reminds me of Aunt Chong. We had fun playing games in the group room. I hope he gets to go home soon. I wonder how mad Dr P is at me. He just keeps watching me and has not said much today. I told him I was sorry when he scolded me. I told him I did keep my promise. I did not take pills. He just gave me an incredibly angry look. I hate seeing that look, especially from him. He is always so kind and nice to me. I feel ashamed for causing him so much trouble. I wish I could change who I am. I really do not mean to keep causing so much trouble to everyone. I really do not understand why I am so useless and miserable. My mom is going to kill me if she finds out what has happened. Hopefully, I can be home before everyone gets back. Dr P said he talked to my grandmother, and she said she will keep everything quiet for now. She is worried about how this will affect me if it gets out about what happened she told him she will take care of things at home if he takes care of me. I am worried about what that means my grandmother is not the nicest person when you do something to make her angry, and I am not sure if she is angry with me or with the others. I guess I will find out when she picks me up in a few days.

I wonder what Kat's grandmother did exactly to keep things hidden and calm.

CHAPTER 19

Kat shows a different side.

The next day when. I walked onto the ward and all you could hear was laughter. The most delicious smell was coming from the occupational kitchen. I go in and the entire ward, including all the nurses are in the great room all laughing and playing games while cooking with patients. The day treatment therapist was beaming like a proud mother. The group leader was sitting at the table chopping veggies. I wonder what is going on.

"Good morning, everyone. What is happening? Why are you all not in your sessions?" I ask all the while taking in the festive atmosphere.

The day treatment therapist spoke up first.

"Kat told us that Feb 5 is Dr Jacobs birthday as well as the day his twin brothers died. And since we have only 3 patients in the ward today and noticed there was lot of food that will be expiring soon. We decided to have a therapy cooking session and have a birthday party for Dr Jacob. So, Kat is teaching us some Korean dishes."

"Really but you know he may not want to celebrate with us." I told them.

"Now I know Dr Jacob for years and anything we do for him he will appreciate and enjoy it why don't you come in and sit at the table with us and help out its really fun educational." Nurse Henderson urges me to come over to join them just then Kat walks in with some bags.

"My aunt just dropped off the rest of the ingredients I asked her to pick up from my house last night, so we are all set. Oh, Dr smith please join us I don't have a session today and I really would like it if you would come and rest you don't have to do anything but sit and I will make you a cup of tea please." Kat pleads with me. The happiness I see on her face is more than I can take so I agree. I go over and sit at the table. I am amazed at how well Kat seems like she belongs in a kitchen. She patently explains and shows everyone what she needs them to do. She has everyone eager to help. I find myself listening quite intently to what she is telling everyone about each dish we are making. Everyone is laughing and telling each other stories about themselves. It is amazing. After a couple of hours everything was done, I sat there for the entire morning watching and listening to everyone. It was the most relaxing time I have had in an exceptionally long time. Just as I was checking the time, I heard Kat squeal and run towards the doorway.

"Dr David is that you?" she asks as she gives my father an excessively big tight hug.

"Oh, my little Angelina Mia you have grown up." He smiles at her and his joy at seeing her is very clear.

"I have been having problems with nightmares and such so I am here to get help to cope. Did you come to celebrate Dr Jacobs birthday with us and have lunch." at asks still holding David's hand.

", I came to have lunch with my daughter. If she is joining, you then yes, I will be more than happy to stay." He turns to look at Dr smith as if asking her please can we stay.

"Oh, who is your daughter?" Kat asks.

Dr Smith stands up and walks over to her father and puts her arm through his.

"I am, and we will come back in time for Dry Jacobs party, but I would like to talk to my dad alone for a moment." She says as they leave the room when they are walking down the hallway David asks his daughter.

"Is Kat the patient you were asking about last night?"

"Yes, but I have never seen this side of her before in the past she has always been kind and sweet. But always reserved, like she was afraid to be too friendly. How do you know her? Was she one of your patents?"

"Yes, she is the child I was telling you about. I was very worried about letting another patient help her when she was here. The child was such a ray of sunshine you would never believe anything bad had happened to her until it was nighttime in the dead of night her screams would send chills down your spine. The only time she slept peacefully was if Jacob or his brother was holding her hand and humming at her. I only had her for a few days, but she made quite the impression on me. You know her aunt and sister work here in the hospital and she would send me cakes cookies and small handmade presents from time to time. She is a middle child and she learned early on how to hide her feelings through laughter and by just hiding away. She hid a lot from her family because when she did tell them things, they felt it was just to get attention because she was the one who was lost in the shuffle the most. Her father at the time I saw her was not around much and her mother had her hands full. Her mom had been institutionalized when Kat was young because she withdrew to the point that she did not know her children she thought they were her siblings. When she came home. I think Kat is the one who tried not to need anything because she was afraid her mom would leave again. So, she hid a lot to protect her mom. In the process she became neglected in away because her mother never felt needed by her." he explained to his daughter

"That explains so much. I thought her family just did not care. It is just that they do not know what they can do because she does not let them. Thank you, Dad, you helped me understand this contradiction if a person." Dr smith hugs her father.

"Dad, can I ask you something else? What did Kat's grandmother do to keep things quiet and calm all those years ago?" I look at him hoping he can tell me.

"She knew that Kats mother would not be able to handle what happened and her father just recently had gotten his life together. For the first time they had a home of their own. He was no longer in and out of jail or drunk somewhere and had a decent job. So, she met up with the couple who hurt her granddaughter and beat the living hell out of them. She deliberately crashed their car so that she could use it as an excuse for Kat being in the hospital and would explain their beating. She warned both that if anything else happened to her baby they would be dead, and their bodies would never be found. The only reason she let them off was because her granddaughter seemed not to remember exactly what happened and that she was afraid what would happen if she were forced to remember."

"let's go eat the food smells delicious." He pats her hand as they get up to join the party.

CHAPTER 20

Jacobs Birthday

When Jacob and Ki arrive at the hospital, they are bombarded with smells of food cooking. Not just any food but food that reminds them of their grandmother's kitchen. They head for the great room as they pass the nurse's station, they see Dr Smith with an older gentleman. It is not until they get closer that Jacob recognizes him.

"Dr David, how are you? How are you here today I was told you retired?" He asks as he gives him a big hug.

"My father came to have lunch with me today." Dr Smith informs him.

"Your father. Wow I would never have guessed. Though I am pleasantly surprised since your dad was an amazing Dr and mentor that means I am working with the best then." Jacob grins

They all laugh for a second and then Ki asks.

"Where is everyone and what is that amazing smell it reminds me of my grandmother's kitchen?"

"it's a surprise so let's go." Dr smith leads the way to the great room. When they arrive, everyone is waiting. On the table a variety of Korean foods is spread out there is seaweed soup, bulgogi, kimchi, bamboo, dumplings, jopchae, rice, scallion pancakes. The room has balloons on one side and a small table set up with fruit and a few other small dishes. The cake on the card table says Happy birthday Dr Jacob. Besides it is a small cake with James and Chris you missed. Jacob and Ki know that Kat made this happen.

"Wow this is amazing how did you know today was my birthday I have never celebrated it?" he asked as tears welled up in his eyes.

"It was kitten's idea she said that today was your birthday as well as the Memorial Day for your brothers. So, we all staff and patients worked together today with her help to make both birthday and Memorial Day food so that you could celebrate both." nurse Henderson told him.

"Wow I'm very touched that you would do this for me. Thank you all very much. Let us eat, I am starving. Jacob motions for everyone to sit. Jacob sits at the head of the table with Kat and. Dr smith on each side then Ki is sitting beside Kat David beside his daughter. Everyone is chatting and having fun, laughter is everywhere. Nurse Henderson hears the security buzzer ring as she gets up to answer the door. Its joe Kats husband she shows him to the great room. When he comes in, he sees everyone laughing and enjoying the party." is this what my wife does all day here. Party? "He asks. Nurse Henderson can hear the anger in his voice.

"Not normally its incredibly quiet and tense around here. Today is a special day. It is Dr Jacobs birthday. So, we are celebrating a little that is all." she holds her breath wondering if that will calm him down.

He walks over and takes his wife's arm. You can tell he is hurting her buy her face.

"Hi baby why didn't you tell me you were coming today. I would like to let you know we were having a special lunch. Did you eat yet your welcome to join us?" Kat says to him you can tell by her voice that he is hurting her, but she is trying to keep things as calm as possible.

"I came because mom told me your aunt came by the house to get some stuff and I was curious as to why you needed it. I can see now why. If you feel well enough to party, don't you think you should be well enough to do you duties as a wife?" He jerks her arm and drags her out of the room. The next thing we hear is Kat screaming and crying. The Drs rush out of the room. They see Joe standing over her. Her shirt is torn, and her mouth is bleeding. Nurse Henderson calls for security. Ki goes to grab him when David stops him. "Let my daughter handle it."

"Mr. Sanchez I'm sorry you are under a misunderstanding. The party today was part of a therapy class. We used the opportunity of Dr Jacobs birthday to help the patients. We usually use occupational and group activities to help patients to open and feel at ease so that they can share things easier in a group. I do not know why you are so angry with your wife when she was only doing what was expected of her to work on interacting with others. She has been extremely withdrawn and depressed since being here, barely leaving her room except for the therapy sessions and mandatory group discussions. This is the first time she has even spoken more than a few social words to any of the other patients." Dr smith explains as she slowly wakes towards him. She can feel his anger coming from his body. It's stifling. Just then security arrives.

"The police will be here momentarily. We saw him attack her on the camera and were on our way before nurse Henderson called. Sir we need to take your hand from the patient and come with us." The officer requests Joe.

"I'm not letting go of my wife. She is mine to do with as I want." Joe stares angrily at Kat like daring her to speak.

"Mr. Sanchez if you don't cooperate you will be arrested when the police arrive." Dr Smith informs him.

"Amor, you need to listen. You cannot get into trouble our children need one of us at home with them and I am not able to be there. I'm still having nightmares and there are things that I need to deal with before I can be a good wife and mom." at pleads with her husband.

"Shut up your worthless bitch you don't know anything. You are not even trying to come home. Why should you be here you are getting waited on at home you do everything. I am about ready to look for someone else to take care of your duties. I have never had to go this long before." He tells her.

"Oh, this is what this is about. You're horny because I have not been there to service you. If that all you need then ok come on." She takes him by the hand and drags him to her room, closes and locks it. Once inside the room Kat tells her husband "

"If all you need is to get laid the fine fund someone else, I am not going to be just your maid and whore anymore. I am your wife and if that is what you think a wife is then I want a divorce. I will not come home to you. I will come home to my children but not you. You can have till I am discharged from here to decide what you want. You will bring me my children to visit me, and you will apologies to those people outside. Its either that or go to jail for assault. "Kat tells him angrily.

"Your serious. I thought we came in here to do you know. Instead, you're giving me a hard time." he says as he pulls her into his arms. I pushed him away.

"That's not going to happen. You cannot really expect me to do that after you just hit me. I am not your punching bag or your quickie if you want our marriage to work you must stop being so angry and selfish." Just then a knock on the door

"Kat the police are here open the door.

"Before I come out you must promise that nothing will happen to my husband?" Kat insists.

David had taken Jacob and Ki aside when Kat took Joe to the room.

"Look I know you want to protect her and tear him apart. If you interfere my daughter will not have a choice but to remove, you from her case. Then you will have to stay away from her from now on. Do you want that? "David asked them.

"Not of course but how can he be that way?" Jacob replied.

"I don't understand him being abusive, but I can see his anger and jealousy. He has not seen his wife for a few minutes for a month. The first time he sees her, and she is laughing and smiling at another man. That is what he saw not what was happening. He did not notice anything else in the room, only her and the fact that the 3 of us were beside her. If she had been in a circle of women, he would not have even reacted beyond saying hello to everyone and ask her if she would talk to him." David pointed out.

Dr Smith spoke to the police officers and got them to agree to step back and just be close unless needed. "Ok Kat they have agreed to step back and do nothing."

I opened the door, and we went out. Joe looks at everyone.

"I'm sorry for ruining your lunch party. I was just so upset because I have missed my wife so much and to see her having fun was a bit too much for me. I thought she would be moping about and sad missing me also and she wasn't." Joe waited to see if everyone would forgive him.

"That's no excuse for you hitting her. She has done nothing wrong. She has only followed her program which is more than I can say for you. I think you going to jail would be a good thing to wake you up, but I do not think it will be good for your children to have both parents gone right now. I do not want you to come anywhere near your wife until I get a report from your Dr that you have completed the anger management program as well as come to terms with your own issues. This anger is of your own making, it has nothing to do with your wife. I imagine having the officers escort you out. Don't come back till I say its ok." Dr. Smith informed Joe the officers came and removed him from the ward. He looked so angry that I wanted to go and hide instead, I looked at everyone hoping they were not too angry.

"I am sorry everyone for my husband's disturbance. He has never had to take care of things at home. He is not used to doing anything but going to work and then home and once he is home his every need is taken care of. He must be struggling with everything. Please let us go back and eat before everything is cold." I turn and start to walk back to the great room hoping everyone will follow me.

"Kitten it's not your fault or your place to apologist. It is your husband's, none of us blame you or expect you to make things right for him. Come with me and let me look at you and make sure you're ok." Nurse Henderson takes me by the hand while everyone else goes to the great room she wipes the blood from my face. when she is done cleaning me up, she smiles at me "let's go and enjoy Dr Jacobs party."

Everyone was laughing and talking at the table when we went in, I went and put my chair between Ki and Jacob.

"Thank you so much for the dinner. It was delicious. Exactly like grandma cooking." Jacob looks very content and happy eating with everyone.

"Oh, but this isn't all we have real presents for you as well and a cake." Nurse Henderson lets him know.

"Oh, really I can't wait to open my presents." Jacob smiles excitedly as she brings his presents and Dr Smith gets the cake and ice cream.

I sit quietly as he opens his presents. I watch how happy he is as he receives each gift. I hold my breath when he is handed mine. I wonder if he will like it or not. It has been so long since I have done something like this.

As he pulls out the crochet angel, I see happiness on his face. "I know who made this without even looking at the tag. Kat, you made me one. Now I have a set. Thank you so much".

I look at him in confusion "you have one already. I am sorry I did not realize. I will make you something else then." I go to take the angel away, but he stops me.

"No, you can't take it away its mine. You promised me a set the last time we were together. You do not remember do you. You made me an angel ornament for our Christmas tree. It held a crystal in its hands. I asked you if you would make me another one so that I would have a pair, one for you and one for me. You told me for my birthday you would make one hold an amethyst so that way we could tell them apart." he holds up his angel and tied in its hands is a purple crystal "it is exactly what you promised me. Thank you so much if you will excuse me for just a moment, I have something to show everyone." Jacob gets up and walks down the hall to the office. A few moments later he comes back and, in his hand, is an angel ornament holding a crystal in its hands he holds them both up for everyone to see. "I now have my set after all this time."

I smile at him not knowing what to say. All the nurses look at his gift and ask if I will make them one. "

"Sorry ladies they are only for me. I have waited years for them to be complete." He informs them.

Dr David stands up "may I propose a toast to our host Angelina Mia thank you for a wonderful meal and a day filled with precious memories. As always you spread sunshine and warmth. Ever since you were a child you always had a way to make people feel happy and warm. I am so happy my daughter invited me to lunch today. So that I could see you again." He walks over and gives me a hug. I feel my cheeks get warm from embarrassment.

"Oh, Dr David I still cause more problems than happiness but thank you for making me feel better." I hugged him back and looked at Dr Smith.

"Thank you, Dr Smith, for everything. For not putting Joe in jail. For letting me share your dad today I have thought of him many times over the years. Thank you for letting us have this celebration today. I know you are more reserved and not as comfortable with all the touchy feelings sometimes. I know you think that to be aim you cannot get involved. You're right in many ways. anyway, thank you for being here today and for not giving up on me." I look at her and give her a weak smile hoping she understands what I am trying to say.

"Kat its ok I understand and now that I know who Angelina Mia I is no longer need to be jealous or worried about her." She smiles and winks at her dad.

"Do you know what it means?" Dr David asked his daughter.

"Yes, I know it means my angel In Italian I know because I asked the Italian priest at church after he made a reference to the word angel. Though I thought it was Spanish for the longest time and even took Spanish classes to find out." She explained.

I looked at her with surprise. "So, you understood when Joe would curse at me in Spanish?" I felt embarrassed at knowing this because I always felt a little comfort thinking she did not understand.

"it's ok I didn't want anyone to know. I was afraid that everyone would be cautious around me if they knew. Therefore, I never asked you to explain things because I already knew."

CHAPTER 21

Gossip is hurtful.

Sometime between cleaning up the great room and bedtime it begins to snow. I sit by the window of my room and think about everything that has happened. How the people from forgotten past without even knowing have relationships with those of my present. The fact that my current Dr is the daughter of my past doctor is amazing to me. I wonder if Dr Smith will ask Dr David about things from when I was his patient. It was so nice to see him today. I just wish I could have been able to make sure Joe was ok. I wish I could tell him everything that is going on so that he later does not think I lied to him about things. I will ask Dr Smith tomorrow if we should explain things to him or just let him be for now. I hope the kids get a snowy day from this storm. It would be nice for them to be able to relax and just have fun. If they do, I know Joe will have the day off and take them sledding or at least have snowball fights with them. I sit and watch the snow for a long time not even knowing how long. It is so peaceful and quiet tonight I am afraid to sleep. Afraid that the nightmare will visit if I close my eyes.

I hear voices when I look outside, and the sun is up. The ground and trees are covered in beautiful snow, everything is so beautiful. It takes my breath away. It is the housekeepers that I hear talking. I am sitting behind the curtain of the window sitting on the vent, they do not know I am here. I hear them saying my name, so I am very still, so they do not notice me.

"I hear she is sleeping with the two Dr parks and that yesterday she got caught by her husband. Then he hit her and to appease him she slept with him while the Drs were outside her room. The commotion was so bad they called the police."

"What a whore she is married and giving it to anyone who looks at her. I have not seen her yet, but I hear that she is not even that pretty. I also heard that she was raped and that she likes being abused that's why she was so eager to screw her husband after he hit her."

Hearing them talk made my skin crawl. The tears were streaming down my face. How could people say such things that are so untrue? I need to leave here. I cannot have people talking about Jacob and Ki this way. It will ruin their reputations as Drs and cause them problems if I stay. I slip out of the window cubby when they leave. I get my shoes on and put a couple of shirts on. I walk to the room next to the security door and wait for a chance to try to slip out. I hope that I do not get caught.

After a while nurse Henderson is asking the nurse behind the desk

"Have you seen kitten this morning she isn't in her room or anywhere in the common rooms."

"No, the only people I have seen this morning were the housekeepers. In fact, one of them asked me if she left because her bed had not been slept in. I told her no she was still here but that on her good days. She will make her own bed." she replied.

"I'm going to inform Dr Smith that we can't find her. Call the security officer and let him know that we can't seem to find her." nurse Henderson tells her as she starts walking down the hall towards the office.

It is so dark inside the closet. The fear rises in my throat. I do not want to stay here anymore. I do not want to have people think bad things about those I love. God why do I always cause everyone so much pain. My family would be so much better off without me. I close my eyes trying to calm my nerves. Eventually I fell asleep.

Nurse Henderson knocks on the door "come in" Dr smith calls.

"Excuse me Drs but we may have a problem. Kitten is missing." She informs them.

"What do you mean Kat is missing?" She asks.

"Well, no one has seen her since last night and her bed was not sleepy in. We haven't found her in any of the common rooms either." She lowers her head waiting for an outburst.

"Ki, you go to the security office and check the cameras. Jacob, you check her room for any clues and nurse Henderson call everyone to the conference room that has been on the floor since yesterday I mean every single person even if it's their day off." Dr smith calls the head of security and the hospital administrator she also calls Kat's family's departments to see if anyone has heard from or seen her in the last 24 hours.

Ki goes to the security office and tells them that he needs to see the security tapes from the ward. They start scrolling through them and he has them pause and play the tape from when Kat took Joe to her room. He hears what she says to him and smiles. So, she is not as afraid of him as she puts on. He copies that part to a disc along with everything that happened in the hallway. They begin to scroll the tapes again, and he has them stop when he sees the housekeepers in the room. "Play that part please I want to hear what they are saying." He hears the cruel thing they said. Ki swears under his breath. He then sees Kat slide out from behind the curtain. Omg she heard everything they said. He sees her wiping her face and take a pile of clothes to the bathroom to change. "Show the hallway. Why are the cameras in the other rooms off? The two patients were discharged today so the only room we need to keep watch on are the common rooms and your patient. He sees Kat slide behind the linen cart and then there is no sign of her after that they never see her go out of the door, so she must still be on the floor somewhere. "

Give me the discs that I asked you to record please?" Ki asks.

Ki heads back to the floor. Meanwhile Jacob has no idea where she is, only that she is not in her room and some clothes are missing. He heads to the conference room to see what anyone else has figured out.

Dr smith is addressing the staff and informing them that a patient is missing and that she needs everyone to cooperate.

"Ok we all know that yesterday there was an incident with Mrs. Sanchez husband and that things seemed ok last night after it was calmed down what I would like to now is why no one noticed she was not in her room."

"She was sitting in the window watching the snow when the lights were called. And her door never opened till the cleaning crew came in this morning. Since she has such difficulty getting a good night sleep, I didn't bother her I just listened to the monitor for any sounds of distress but there was none." the night nurse spoke up.

Just then Ki came in. "She is still on the floor somewhere, but she is very hurt. We have a problem and it's a big one." He looks at the hospital administrator. "We need legal here now to help take care of this or else there is going to be a very large lawsuit." He informs him. The man sitting beside the administrator looks at him "I am already here. As soon as I heard a patient was attacked yesterday and went missing, I tagged along."

"Good. Nurse Henderson, we need to find out who is spreading tales to other departments. And these two ladies he says pointing at the housekeepers your fired with no reference or severance pay unless you want to be arrested for slander and defamation of character."

"What who are you to say that?" The housekeeping head asks.

Ki hands the disc to Jacob "play this and you will see.

On the disc it shows that Kat had slipped behind the curtain during the night and did not appear until after the housekeepers left. When listening to the disc they were able to hear the entire conversation between the housekeepers. It showed them looking at the labels on her clothes and going through the closet. All the while barely cleaning the room. They then put the disc in that shows the day that Joe attacked Kat. On it shows him attacking her and her pretending to take him to her room to have sex. Once in her room they play what happened. it shows her standing up to him and trying to get him to understand how his behavior is not acceptable. The housekeeping supervisor is appalled at what she heard and saw.

"He is right collecting the things you're doing here. As you saw she only said and did what was needed to defuse the situation with her husband how could you say such things and how can you say that you cleaned that room you checked cleaned windows if you had you would have seen she fell asleep in the window. You spent the entire time riffling through her things and gossiping about things you know nothing about. Who told you those things who?" She demands.

The team leader speaks up "no one it's based on what we have overheard from morning reports from the last few months. As well as the fact everyone calls her pet names and is affectionate with her. Even nurse Henderson who is very stiff and all about regulations calls her kitten. We figured that it meant she was given special treatment because of who she is to the Drs even old Dr smith has a pet name for her."

"That is no excuse to cause someone harm and distress. Do you realize you have made statements that are untrue but if anyone but her have overheard them could cost the Drs and nurses their license as well as a large lawsuit against the hospital? Yes, she is a special patient because her first trip to this hospital ward was when as a 13-year-old child barely hanging on to life. But she was a loving-giving person so that despite what nightmare she was going through she thought of those around her not of herself. Nurse Henderson had just lost her child when she was here then, and she saw her sadness and she made a point to make her something special that still sits at the nurse's station to this day. The angel poem over the nurse's station she wrote to her and told her to not be sad that her little angel was with her still she just needed to become an angel to watch over her instead of being beside her on earth. Yes, Dr Parks knows her because she at one time was an excessively big part of their family, they are helping Dr Smith to recover her memories so that she can cope with the nightmares that torment her. They are not her Drs they are here as consultants and friends. Nothing more. You have caused a great deal of trouble to a lot of people, and I bet you have not even met her. And how do you think her family who works in other departments will feel if they hear people gossip about her." Dr David lectured them "I apologize I am here because I came for lunch yesterday and wanted to check on her today, I know I have no say in what goes on anymore."

"Oh no Dr David its fine you shed some light on why people are the way they are with her and that even though they are friendlier to her than most they have done nothing wrong. Not like these two. So, ladies I expect your resignations effective at once and if a single rumor starts by anyone about this patient or this situation those people will be fired on the spot with no explanations. Director, I think that a reminder to all employees in all departments is necessary to remind that patient confidentiality and respect of patient's privacy is our priority, and anyone found violating it will be fired on the spot." The attorney informed the staff of the two ladies responsible for apologizing to everyone and asked if they could be forgiven just this once.

Dr smith looked at them "we are not the ones who you have hurt its our patient and no you may not be forgiven. Anyone who talks about our patients in this award is never forgiven because unlike the regular floors here we deal with people who must bare their souls and face their nightmares and demons. Things that are not for everyday conversation or banter. When they come into these walls we call them by any name they like and we help them face them and find ways to cope so that when they are outside they can be confident that they deserve respect and can handle what may come many feel like they have very little left to live for and that they are undeserving of any kindness it is our jobs to help them know that they are deserving and that they are strong enough to cope with whatever comes On this ward the only way to protect them is keeping what is said within these walls here nothing goes beyond these doors . And you have violated that rule when patents leave here, they need to know they are safe from the world knowing their issues, so they can be treated like everyone else beyond these walls."

Now does anyone have any ideas where she is? The phone rings and Dr smith picks it up. Its Kats sister

"Hello, Shay, how are you. Yes, I did call, I do not know if you heard what happened yesterday with your brother-in-law or not. Well to be honest Kat has disappeared we cannot find her anywhere. But we know she has not left the ward. You are kidding really. I would have never thought of looking someplace like that. Oh yes, the Dr parks are here ok I will give you to one of them." She hands the phone to Jacob.

"Jacob, do you remember which room she slept in when she was here before. And what she would do during thunderstorms if you were not there. I bet you lunch she is hiding in a closet somewhere out of embarrassment over yesterday." Jacob looks ay Ki.

"Shay says to look in the closet of room 301 that's the room she was in years ago remember how she would hide in the closet during thunderstorms if I was not around. Hurry goes check?" Ki runs out of the room and into room 301 Dr smith is behind him. They quietly open the closet door and curled in a ball in the bottoms of the closet is Kat sound asleep. Ki reaches down and gently picks her up and carries her back to her room. He hears the housekeepers gasp when they see the bruises on her face. He just gives them a nasty look and continues to her room he settles her on the bed and leaves her with Dr smith.

"Shay, I owe you lunch thanks "Jacob informs Kat sister.

"Just bring me your birthday leftovers and we will call it even. "She laughs "tell her that I will be by tonight before I go home ok."

I will thank you for not freaking out on us. "

"It's nothing I'm used to having to pull her out of dark spaces you know I am partly to blame for what's been happening. Joe overheard me tell mom not to worry that Kat was in good hands because you two were taking care of her. My mom only remembers bits a piece about you guys, but she knew who Ki was right away and told me that she did not worry anymore that her baby's angel was watching over her. I do not think he understands completely but he may have an idea who you guys are now. I'm sorry I didn't think he was there." Shay tells him.

"don't worry about it we are not hiding it from him we just haven't filled him in on all the details yet. We were hoping he would make some progress on his own issues before adding more." Jacob tells her.

"Thanks for taking care of her and do not forget my lunch ok."

"You got it I will see you at lunch. "Shay teases

The attorney was listening to the conversation.

"I see that the family doesn't have any objection to you two working with Dr smith on her case. But hat the husband might. Why is that."

"it's because when she first arrived, she did not remember us, so we left things as they were, and he wasn't interested in her treatment plan."

"Then that will not cause a problem because he has met you, I assume, and you have tried to discuss her treatment with him and with his abusive behavior we can always argue if it came up that since he abandoned her and was abusive that he relinquished all rights to have a say in her treatment. "He explained" so do not worry just worry about helping your friend get back on her feet."

He shakes Jacob's hand and walks out. The hospital administrator looks at Jacob .and asks.

"This patient she is the one my father, your uncle. and Dr David took care of. she is that child we hid from those people isn't she."

"Yes, she is, and she has so much hell to still go through before she is done, I just hope we have the stomach to help her through it."

"I remember her my dad brought me in with him we were on our way to a game when dad got the call and now, I understand why you two are helping and why everyone is so attached you won't get any grief from bye me. I know because of her my dad changed the policies for this ward so that no one had to tell who they really were if they did not want. help her I would like to hear her laugh again." The administrator tells him.

"You should have come yesterday before her husband came you would have enjoyed hearing her laugh." Jacob tells him.

"Oh yes, would you like me to deliver Shay her food so that way I can get some to please." The administrator smiles hoping to get some lunch as well.

"Ok let us go you know there were only two servings of everything left and it was supposed to be mine. "Jacob grumbles

"Yes, but you owe me and Shay of course." He teases Jacob as they go and get the leftovers from the fridge.

The two of them head for the kitchen and see Ki coming out of Kats room. "How is she?" They ask.

"She is sleeping. By the sound of her breathing, I think she cried herself to sleep. I feel so bad for her she just cannot seem to catch a break. I wish I could just take her out of here for just few days away from everything." Ki tells them.

The hospital administrator asks, "why can't you?" I mean it is a Friday and there is about a foot of snow outside so there will not be any visitors this weekend. Why don't you ask Shay when she comes for a visit this afternoon and see what she says? "

"For starters, the argument her husband had with her yesterday was that he thinks she is on vacation here and wants her out of here. He thinks she is shrugging her responsibilities." Jacob reminds him.

"Ah but you can take her out for a treatment weekend. There is a special group for rape survivors this weekend in Charleston I could call and register her and you two and Dr Smith could go with her this way her husband cannot cause her any trouble and it will get her out of here for few days." He tells them he will make all the arrangements and talk to Shay for them.

Shay hears a knock on the edge of her desk. And sees a stack of small bowls placed in front of her. She looks up and instead of seeing one of the Dr Parks she sees the hospital admin standing there.

"Oh, hello I see Jacob sent you." She smiles.

"Actually, I volunteered I need to talk to you can you bring your lunch to my office please?" He says as he walks away from her desk. She looks at him and wonders what is up. Shay tells her supervisor she is going to lunch. When they get to his office, he motions for her to have a seat.

"There is a retreat for rape victims this weekend in Charleston. I think that your sister needs to go. I think that to be away from here for a few days away from the hospital will do her good. Since I do not think that sending her home where her husband can harm her like yesterday. I have suggested to the Drs to take her. I told them I would discuss it with you since you are the only person besides her husband that she has given us permission to talk to." He informs her.

"I can understand that. Though I think seeing the kids would be more helpful for her. Our children are everything to her." Shay looks at him wondering why he is getting involved with her sister's case.

"I know that, but I do not think trying to put a happy smile on a bruised-up face for her kids with no one to stop her husband from hurting her more is going to help her." he replies.

"Her face is bruised up then he really did hit her yesterday. Here in the hospital. I thought the rumors I heard were wrong." She puts her face in her hands covering it to hide anguish at the thought of her sister being hurt.

"There are rumors already?" I suggested this after what happened today so that she can get a break from this place and not have to worry about what people think. The three Drs will be going with her, and I will have my secretary make all the arrangements.

"I heard about the commotion with the police yesterday. The whole hospital has. I am sorry that my sister's family problems have interfered with the hospital. Though I know my sister and I know the two Dr Parks, I did not think anything about that part of the rumor. thank you for thinking of her but I know she can't afford this, and it's not covered by insurance." Shay informs him.

"Who told you this rumor? The hospital will be paying for it. It is the least we can do after what happened these last two days." He looks at Shay waiting for her reply.

"My supervisor pulled me aside to tell me that the police were called to the psych ward and that my brother in law's name was given as the person they were here to pick up. I agree it will help her, but she has nothing to wear." She tells him.

"Not a problem I have already sent my secretary to the store to buy a few things she will need. Shay, I do not want you to think that I am trying to get out of any liability the hospital has for what happened yesterday. Or today. You are going to find a memo from legal coming out to remind all staff that safety, privacy and respect for all our patients is our priority. As well as all her bills to date will be written off, we will only receive whatever the insurance covers for her care. Though the law says we are not responsible or liable for what happened. I still feel we should do something to help." He tells her.

"Thank you it will be appreciated. I was wondering how we were going to cover her bill." Shay excuses herself from his office telling him she needed to get back to work. After she leaves, he calls the retreat and makes the arrangements for them. He then calls Shay's supervisor and legal.

"I need you in my office immediately." He tells them.

I think to myself I hope this is not going to blow up in our faces.

When both parties arrive in the office.

"Ok Mrs. DeLaughter how did you know what happened yesterday in the psych ward?"

"I was coming back from lunch when I saw the police officers arrive. I heard them on the radio with their dispatch and heard that a man had hit his wife on hospital grounds in the physic ward and that they were on their way to assess the situation. I told Shay because I know her sister is there. And it has been for several months. I am the one in charge of billing for that department and noticed her name. I did not want Shay to hear it from anyone else." She explains.

The attorney asks, "have you discussed this with anyone else?"

She fidgets with her skirt.

"Well, I asked the housekeepers what they knew earlier today, and they told me that she is a little bit of a slut. And that her husband hit her because she is having an affair with someone in the ward. And there was a discussion about it in the employee lounge. Therefore, I told Shay about it." She is wringing her hands by the end of her explanation.

The attorney hands her a notebook and a pen "write the name of every person in that room. And then go clean out your desk you are fired for breach of contract every person when they are hired signs a confidentiality agreement and it plainly says that gossiping and discussion of patients and hospital events will not be tolerated." He walks over to the desk and tells the person in the hr. department that he needs to have every employee in the hospital in shifts in the conference room starting at once starting with the names on this list and that Sarah De Laughter is ended at once with no reference or severance pay. He looks back across the room at her and informs her.

"Before you state this isn't fair put yourself in the patient's place. How would you like it if strangers discussed your business? And untruths were being told about you. What you have done is commit a crime you have committed slander and defamation of character. You can either take your firing or be grateful that you are not going to jail. Or you can make a fuss and I will have you removed in handcuffs. The choice is yours." The attorney motions for her to get go. The phone on the desk rings it is the HR department she has called everyone on the list to the conference room they are waiting for them.

The attorney tells the hospital administrator to let him do the questioning and talking. When they arrive, they see several Drs 3 nurses and a few other employees from various departments.

"Good afternoon I'm sorry that we have interrupted your busy schedules, but we need to ask a few questions. I need you to write down what the discussion in the staff lounge was about today and every person you have discussed it with. Now remember there are cameras in there that picks up every conversation and I can pull the security tapes to find out who is lying." He informs them.

Having already called security to pull the last two days' tapes he wants to see who is going to be honest.

"The Dr from the Err raises his hand." I have a question. Does this have anything to do with the incident in the physics ward? I am asking because the 3 of us warned several people that to gossip about a patient is a breach of patient confidentiality. "

"Yes, it is. We need to stop false rumors and half-truths before people lose their license and jobs as well as patients and their family being hurt.

"Can anyone tell me who brought up the subject of the incident please?" The attorney inquires.

A kitchen staff member raises her hand "it was Mrs. DE laughter in billing she was talking about the police was in the hallway heading for the physic ward."

The hospital admin is closely watching everyone to see who is nervous and who is calm. Everyone seems to agree that she brought the subject up.

"What else was said?" He asks.

The nurse from pediatrics raises her hand ' she was saying that Shay's sister had caused some problems in the ward that her husband beat her up. And that she could not understand why she had been here for so long.

Normally patients only stay for a week or two, but she has been here for months. She was very hateful towards her. "

The Dr from the Er raised his hand "that is when I informed her that she was breaking patient confidentiality and that she could get into trouble. I also told her that it is not fair for shay to say such things about her family that it's hard enough for her already."

The secretary from radiology raised her hand "she was really pumping the two girls from housekeeping that work in the ward for information on Shay's sister. Most of us just listened but said nothing. None of us wanted to get into the middle of it but I had a hard time keeping my anger uncheck because this woman was talking about my family as if it was trash. I grabbed her after lunch and told her that she needed to keep her opinions to herself if she knew what was good for her .and that I had better not hear any rumors, or she would regret it. I thought that was why I was being called in here because she reported me for threatening her."

"What relation ate you to her?" the attorney asks.

"I'm her cousin but we were raised more like sisters. My cousin has had a lot of traumata in her life and does not need people talking about her when they know nothing about the hell she has been through. That woman is just lucky that I know the truth about my cousin or else you would have had to call the police officers on me. Only her and the two- housekeepers really said anything but all of us heard them. I don't know if anyone here spoke about it to anyone else, but I have been worried and listening for any mention all day."

The attorney looks at the group. "How many of you agree with what has been said so far? "

They all but one raised her hand he looks at her and asks her if she has anything to add.

"I work with Shay and Mrs. DE laughter took great pleasure in telling her that her sister and her husband caused such a scene yesterday. And that she should quit in embarrassment. Mrs. DE laughter does not like Shay because Shay must go in and fix everything behind her. Our department runs smoothly because Shay does everyone's clean up when they mess up. She does not like her sister because since she has been here Shay has not been able to stay late or come in early to fix things and she has been getting scolded for it. Mrs. DE laughter was up for a promotion and has been upset thinking that Shay would mess it up for her."

"Thank you for telling us this. I will be in touch after reviewing the security tapes of the conversations and if any hint of a rumor goes around about this conversation or the one from the staff lounge there will be consequences. you may go back to work." They all got up and left. The hospital admin looks at the attorney.

"So, what do you think are we going to have a mess, or do you think it's contained." he asks him.

"it's too soon to be sure but I am hoping for it contained. For the biggest part it looks like it was just the three of them, but we will see after we listen to those tapes.

They headed out to the security office. Back in the ward the 3 Drs. are getting things ready for their trip with Kat. The secretary has dropped off her new clothes and the Drs have stepped out to go home to pack. Nurse Henderson brings Kat a duffle bag that she had in her locker for Kat to pack her things in.

A secret comes to light.

"Here you go kitten. I want to chat with you for a moment please." She pats the side of the bed for me to sit.

"Listen to me. I do not want you to think about what those two said. They were just gossiping, not knowing anything about you. They have been reprimanded for their wrongdoing. You and the docs have done nothing wrong. Understand. I want you to take these few days at the retreat to really relax and to learn as much as you can so that when you get back, we can work on getting you home soon, a stronger, more capable person who can do anything. You know you saved me all those years ago. So, let us help you now please. I know that it has been hard for you to be here for so long. I know you will get back on your feet."

"Thank you nurse Henderson it's nice to know that you are rooting for me and believe in me. I promise I will make you proud." I smiled at her. I know she cares about me. I just worry that I will cause her pain without realizing it.

As I pack my things, I hear a knock on my door. It is my sister and my aunt. I give them a weak smile and hold my breath. I am worried about what they have to say to me.

My sister notices the look on my face.

"don't worry I didn't come to scold you. I was coming anyway after I got off." She gives me a hug and whispers in my ear "don't sweat the small stuff its ok."

My aunt just gives me a hug and tells me she loves me and that she knows I am doing what is best for everyone in the long run. I am a little scared because normally they are railing at me. Over the smallest thing. This was a big thing, and they are not saying anything. I wonder what is going on.

Just then I heard another knock on my door. This time it is my mom. She brought the kids to see me. All five of them rush in and give me hugs. I sit on my bed and have them around me. I ask each of them how is school .and if they are being good. They handed me their report cards to see and to read all the comments. As usual three of them made the honor roll and the other two just missed it as always. They brought me some handmade cards. I am so happy to have them there. My nephew looks at my throat and asks me.

"Why is it every time I see you anymore you have bruises on you. Did someone hurt you in here?"

"Well, you know how clumsy I am and that I bump into things a lot." I told him. I do not want them to know that my husband put them there. My daughter speaks up and asks.

"Did daddy do that again. I know he came to see you yesterday. He came home angry. I heard him talk to Mimi yesterday. I couldn't understand what they were saying but I heard your name a lot."

I looked at my mom. My aunt ushers the kids out and takes them to the great room. My mom tells me.

"He came home angry. He would not talk to me, but he had a lot to say to his mom. She refused to look at me and would only talk in Spanish. I know she is trying to get him to divorce you and take the kids back to Mexico away from you. She is against him getting help for his issues. She thinks that you are the only one with problems. I am telling you that I can't deal with her much longer I am going to explode if I hear any more negative things about you come out of her mouth."

Just then Dr Smith comes in.

"Hello. I could not help overhearing what you just said. Do not worry. If we need to, I have video of him attacking her unprovoked. And we have a police report. We also have pictures of when he choked on her. I can also call his Dr in to verify that he is violent. This is one of the reasons that I insisted that she come here for these months. To protect her from being killed and to get help in a controlled environment. Your son-in-law has no grounds to take the children once she is released or to file a divorce. It will be all on him if he does. He will lose if he does that. I checked with an attorney as well as child protective services after he choked her, and we admitted her. They told me what steps to take to protect her rights. I have been keeping incredibly detailed notes and they have been in touch with the school to ensure that they are ok. You need not worry. I would like it if you did not mention any of this to anyone. I would not like him to get angry and hurt your daughter again or pick up in the middle of the night with the intent to disappear with the Children." Dr Smith informs them.

I look at her. I am putting my faith in a woman that I cannot tell even if she really cares or is just putting on a front. I pray she is going to be behind her daughter this time.

"I won't say anything. I am only glad she is getting some help and is safe." She replies.

"Dr Smith can I talk to you. In private please?" Shay asks.

"Sure, let's let your mom and sister have some private time ok."

Shay and Dr smith walk out of the room and head for the office.

Dr smith motions fir shay to have a seat.

"I know to most that it looks like we don't care for my sister and don't really take care of her. It is my sister who holds all of us together. I do not know how far you have gotten in her sessions. My sister has every reason to hate us all and never speaks to us again. She is who keeps us going." Shay tells her.

"I'm not judging you. My only concern is for your sister. We have uncovered what happened when she was 13 and how she came to meet Jacob. We started unraveling her memories of them. We have not gotten to what happened to her as a teenager and she has already had an exceedingly difficult time. When she uncovered her memory of being here at 13, she withdrew completely and became quite a different person. So, we are taking things slow for her mental health.?" Dr Smith explained.

"Wait my sister was in here at 13. I do not. Remember her being in the hospital at 13." Shay looks at me very confused.

"Yes, your neighbor John raped her when she was 13 and she tried to kill herself."

Shay stood up looking very shocked. "I need to get my mom." She started to turn away.

When I picked up the phone. "Nurse, can you ask Kat's mom to come to my office please?"

"Please sit back down. We can ask your mom about it. I know your grandmother knew she was here because she is the one who signed the paperwork." I pulled out the copy of the discharge papers from her file.

When Kat's mom came in, I motioned her to sit. "I was just telling Shay about Kats progress when she informed me that she was not aware of an event that happened. Do you know about her time here when she was 13?" I noticed her mom fidgeting. She is nervous, so my guess is she does but may not want to knowledge it in front of her daughter.

"Yes, I know it was one of the things that. I kept from everyone. My husband went to his grave never knowing about what happened. We told her it was a nightmare and that it never happened. When she would wake up crying, I would remind her it was just a dream, and it didn't happen that she was confused and making up stories and to repeat them would only cause problems." I look at her not knowing what to say.

"How could you allow your child to be hurt and then tell her that it never happened. You made her believe she was a bad person and that she was unloved?" I pulled out the journal entry from the day that she was first admitted at 13 and handed it to her mother. "Read this and you will see what she felt after having her life torn apart by that person and just, so you know I believe the worst is yet to come." I leave them to read her entry so that I can leave with Kat and the other two Drs. I hope that this will help her and not set her back. I go and start to pack the car when I see Jacob and Ki.

"I don't know what to do I'm so frustrated with Kat's situation her family confuses me, and I just don't know what to do." I tell them.

"You talked to her mom I take it." Jacob looks at me and smiles. I nod my head "don't worry they are very confused, but they love her and think that they are doing what's best. I learned a long time ago that her mother is like an ostrich. She feels as if she ignores things long enough then they will go away or work themselves out. Shay is so used to Kat holding things together and taking care if things that she does not realize how sad she really is till something happens. Her Grandmother wanted to kill anyone who even looked at her wrong. She felt she was weak and a push over and, in many ways, she was because she thought about what would happen to those in her family before herself, so she just bottled things up she used to do the same to us she would do and be what she thought we wanted and hide anything that would upset us or cause us hurt or worry." He explained.

"That is why I believe at an early age she learned to hide things and later they would surface as Fantasy stories or nightmares but when she would tell people about them because to those people, they could not imagine such things happening. They thought she was only trying to get attention. She used to say she could feel a void and the next thing she would hear that someone died or would be hurt. I remember one time during the time we were at our grandmothers. She got up in the middle of the night. Told grandmother that she needed to get ready to leave. My grandmother looked at her confused because she had tears running down her face but was so calm almost like in a trance. About a half hour later her grandmother called and said that her great grandmother had passed and asked if we could bring her to meet her. When we dropped her off, she had finished crying and was fussing over her grandmother as if she was an adult. It was the first time we really got to see her interact with her family. People just assumed we knew the deceased, so we got the stay close for the next few days. She became like a little host before our eyes automatically serving food and checking on everyone making sure that the grownups were fed and doing ok while the other kids did what kids did, they were chatting and playing around. She watched over the smaller children and expected what others needed, not sleeping or talking much to anyone. That was when we saw for the first time how she could become invisible to those around her. It was heartbreaking to me to see because she was my light my soul and my angel." Ki told me in a very subdued voice as if he were reliving that moment in time, I could only look at him because that is all she has ever shown me in the time I have known her. I feel like since meeting the two Park brothers and their interactions with Kat, that I have been given a rare glimpse into the life of my patient. She is so much more complex than I ever thought. At first, I thought just like the Dr she saw when her father brought her in after she disappeared that she was playing a game to get around things that had happened. After these few months of seeing her interact with her family and these two Drs. Hearing her in session under hypnosis, hearing the pain and loneliness that she has been trapped in for so long. I find that she is not only a strong person but a very selfless one. I doubt that I could have survived even a small part of what she has and still be able to love anyone. Let alone forgive them. I am overwhelmed by the fact that we have only opened a few doors and have found so much pain and trauma and there is still so much more to go. I see Kat walking out with her family giving her kids one last hug and telling them to be good. I hear her remind Shay that the kids physicals are due that their appointments are next week. Also, not to forget that tryouts for baseball are coming up for them, that the boys need new cleats and that the girls will need new sports bras if they decide to play. Oh, that Vicki is going to need to see the dentist in two weeks for her cleaning. I do not know how she could remember that after not being home for these months. Just then a car pulled up and blocked our car. It was Joe, he got out and motions for the kids to get in the car. I realize I am holding my breath waiting for something to happen. Kat walks the kids to the car and tells them to be good that she is working hard on some things, so she can come home. To be a better mother to them. She looks at joe and asks him to please take good care of them.

"I will. I am sorry for being that way the other day. I have never been jealous before of you but knowing who they are and you not being home. I let my insecurity get the better of me." he said as he caressed her cheek. She smiles at him.

"I guess that means you don't hate me as much as you want everyone to believe including me then?" She asks him.

"Nope I don't in fact I love you as much now as before even more. I do miss you and even if I do not show it, I know that you have a lot going on. I'm just afraid that once you face everything and get passed everything you will change and not love me that you will go back to one of them." He told her before he gently kissed her cheek where he left the bruise on her face.

She didn't pull away, but she also didn't return his affection instead she looked up at him and informed him "I don't hate you, but you will never lay another hand on me in anger do you understand. I am not going to be anyone's punching bag, whore, or maid. I am a person and the things I do for you have never been done out of fear or obligation, it was always because I loved you and felt that you deserved to be treated good because of that and the fact that you work so hard for our family. Do not mistake my way of caring is the way that it will always be. I deserve respect and caring also. If you cannot fix your issues, then I cannot guarantee you anything. The only thing I can promise you is that I will always be a good mother to my children." He just looked at her as if she had slapped him. He nods his head at her. When she turns around you can see the tears in her eyes. Her mom walks over to her.

"Well, I can only tell you that it's time to suck it up buttercup because if you keep playing this game, you're going to lose the only man who ever looked at you or wanted you. He is a good father and provider if you lose him no one will ever want you again."

"Mom how can you say that when he hit her and has been so mean to her lately.?" Shay asks her mom.

"Oh, please it's not like she was never hit before, and worse. He is getting help with it. I'm not saying its ok that he has hit her, but she has put him thru hell these last few years she is lucky he has stuck around." Her mother pats her on the cheek and tells her to hurry up with her little farce and come home past is past no use crying over spilled milk.

Kat looked at her mom with so much anger and hurt on her face but said nothing, she just flipped her hood over her head and got into the car silently. Before the three Drs got in Dr Smith shook her head at all of them as if to say shame on you.

Ki could not keep quiet anymore "you call yourself her family. You all are a poor excuse for one. You have no idea what she has gone through just to protect you all. And FYI your wrong Kat is a beautiful loving person who has always had a line of guys waiting for her to give them the time of day. She just never felt that she was good enough for any of them. By the time we are done I plan on making sure she knows that she worth more than any of them and is more deserving than anyone else to have someone love her someone better than any of you." He turns and walks to the driver's side of the car and gets in.

Jacob crosses his arms across his chest "you know I really wish her grandmother was still alive because I would love to see her kick your butt and rip you apart for daring to lay a finger on her baby."

"Yeah, well her grandmother loved me." Joe replied.

"Yeah, maybe but not as much as him." He said pointing to Ki "I bet she never took her to meet up with you or stayed overnight somewhere just so that they could see each other. I bet she never threatens to beat someone up over you either. Think about it" with a smirk he turns and gets in the front seat beside his brother and waves goodbye as they pull out.

Kats family gets into the cars and head home. On the way Kats mom asks Shay "were they really that close and did my mom really like them that much?"

"Yes, she used to take her all the time to meet them for dinner drop her off at the movie. She would even cover for them when they would take her to their family's home to stay overnight or when they wanted to take her to concerts. She thought they would be together forever until the night of the accident. Then it all fell apart. I guess when she found Joe that she just wanted her to live again and to be loved again." Shay replied.

"Wait when did she do that?" Kat's mom asked.

"Every time she would supposedly take her with her to aunt Vinnie or Uncle Jay house."

"Oh, my, my mom must have really liked him then." She replied a little shocked.

CHAPTER 23

A revelation at home.

"Yeah, she did." We drove the rest of the way in silence until mom asked to be taken to Kat's house. When we. Arrived mom looked at me "let me do the telling you stay out of it ok." She said as we got out of the car. Shay braced herself not knowing what to expect. When they walked into the house. mom told the kids to go to their room she needed to talk to their dad and grandmother.

We waited until we heard the door close knowing, they would not be able to hear much. "

"We need to clear the air and you are going to sit and translate every word I say do you understand me son?" She says looking incredibly angry at my brother-in-law.

"Yes mama."

My mom looks at his mother and begins to talk to her.

"Now I want you to know I am incredibly angry with you. You have caused my daughter some major problems and its time that it stops." She waits for him to translate to his mom.

"She wants to know what you mean by that?" He tells mom.

"When you were lying in that bed in the drug induced coma your family brought her here not waiting for my daughter to do as you two had always talked about. They ignored her request, and they insisted that the Drs only talk to your mom once she arrived because your mom told the Drs that my daughter was the one who set the fire all because my daughter asked the Dr if you did not wake up was it because she left you some medicine to take for your headache that day. While you were sleeping, she constantly whispered in your ear when Kat would be out of the room and unable to hear what she was saying. I asked the nurse what she was saying and one day she told me that she was telling you it would be ok that she would make sure that your wife would not get another chance to hurt you. I never understood it. Since you have been home and have healed. You have been cruel and hateful to My daughter. I know it's her fault."

Joe turned and translated this to his mother. She became very pale and nervous then she started talking amazingly fast to him as if trying to explain to him what she said.

Joe gets up and screams at his mother and throws a chair across the room. The girls come out of yen bedroom "uncle joe I asked Aunt Maria what well said the last time aunt Kat took her to her house and she told she was just setting things straight with my aunt. That was the night aunt Kat took the extra pills." He looks at the girls and asks them "what else do you know?"

"I know that grandma told the ties to tell her that she needed to be a better wife and she needed to either love you and cater to you more to make up for trying to kill you that she should be ashamed for what she done instead of acting innocent and that you were too good for her and it would have been better if she had been in the house not you." Those were the words that we heard the aunts tell mommy if you do not believe us, you can ask them.

Joe turns to his mom again and asks her again what she has said to his wife and what she had said to him while he was sleeping in the hospital. He tells her what the girls told him and calls his cousins to ask them. When he gets off the phone, he is incredibly angry. His anger was directed right at his mother.

She explains that it is not exactly what she said she just wanted his wife to be a little sorry for what happened and that how could she love him when she wants even at the hospital when she arrived.

Joe takes a deep breath and explains to his mother that "she wasn't at the hospital because we always agreed that if anything happened that their children would be safe and comforted first and foremost because the person sick or injured would be in a place to be taken care of and their children would need the be taken care of and in a safe loving place. That was exactly what his wife was doing, and that the Dr had the number to call her for authorization for anything that needed done once she explained to the children that was happening and made sure they had all their needs met she never left my side. Also, she had every right to ask the Dr that question because I was welding that day and had a horrible headache I did not even want to eat. So, she placed her migraine medicine on the coffee table for me in case I needed it. She had no idea that the fire had started next to me and that I was overcome by the smoke, she knew nothing about any of the details of the fire. You wrongly have accused her and caused mistrust between us. I will send you home before she comes home, I need to make things right between us. I think you need to think about what you have done and try to get her to forgive both of us. I thought my nightmares in the hospital were just that I did not realize it was you putting those words in my head. I have been angry with her for nothing. "Joe places his head in his hands feeling shame at how he has behaved.

His mother looks at my mom "I'm sorry." Then she speaks again in her language "I did not understand that they already had a plan in place and when I heard what she asked and then her absence I thought that it was her fault. I truly am sorry, but everyone was whispering about how odd it we that she was not there more than a few hours the first night and then coming late the next day."

Joe translated what she said for us.

"You never asked. You only assumed. My daughter stayed till the Dr told her to go home the night of the fire he told her that he was stable and if he needed her, he would call. He knew she had two small, frightened children at home that needed to know that one of their parents was ok. She did what her husband expected her to do, she took care of her children while he was being taken care of. How could you think that someone who took such good care of your son would do something like that?" Mom explained.

"I did not know her that well and did not see her do anything but cry and make him angry. I'm sorry truly." His mother replied to Joe for him to explain she went over to the girls and hugged them tightly "I'm sorry. Tears ran down her face. You could hear the regret and sadness in her voice.

Mom looks at her and tells Joe "Become the man I always thought you were and make sure she apologizes to my child. Make sure you never lay another angry hand on her, or I will be the one to kill you myself. I always loved you like a son and never tried to interfere in your problems but if you don't want to lose your wife you better bend over backwards to correct this."! With that mom walks out the front door letting me know she is ready to go home she was done.

CHAPTER 24

Unexpected meeting.

eanwhile Kat is sound asleep in the car not knowing anything about what is going on. She is in such a deep sleep she does not even hear her three Drs conversation.

"Do you think that he will straighten up now that he thinks he has competition?" Jae asks Ki.

"Personally, I hope he does not, and he doesn't think he knows he does. I know the choice will be hers, but I would like a chance when she is better to make herself happy and have something of the life, we wanted those years ago. I know right now I cannot be anything but her Dr but later I would like the chance." Ki responded.

Dr smith was only half listening to them she was thinking of how strange things are in Kat's life. She has a mom who one minute supports her and then the next criticizes her to tears. It is so confusing for me I cannot imagine what it is like for her not knowing how her family will react next. I look at her as she sleeps. She looks so peaceful and young when she is sleeping. Ki looks in the rear-view mirror. "don't worry she always sleeps when the car is moving, and she is not the one driving." He tells her.

"We used to take turns holding her when we would take her places. Don't be surprised if sometime during the drive if she curled up beside you and puts her head in your shoulder or lap." Jae tells her.

"While she is asleep can you tell me about her from then.?" Dr smith requests

"Sure, what would you like to hear?" Jae asks her.

"Why did the four of you call yourselves her husbands?"

"It started when we decided to follow her to the vocational school. We told everyone that she was ours so that they would not mess with her. And since we were all over the legal age to date her, we told everyone that since she could not make up her mind who she liked most that she decided we would all be her husband till she chose one. We still had to share her with other guys her age." seeing the look on her face Jae busted out laughing "I do not mean like passing her around or anything like that. It was just she had a lot of male cousins who looked out for her. So, they were always around as well as her best friends who were guys, she also had a few that liked her that hung around. Since her father forbid her to date when we would meet her at the skating rink everyone would take turns skating with her so when her dad came to check up on her she was always with someone else on the floor, so he knew that they were nothing but friends, but everyone knew that we were there always watching and making sure that she was ok. They would even keep us informed when someone bothered her at her regular school." It was wonderful, and she was so carefree and happy. She never stopped laughing or smiling. "

Ki interrupted Jae "everyone knew that she was my girl and the three of them were like her big brothers. It became a joke when one teacher asked her what her relationship was with so many different guys so during lunch one day, she brought him to the table and started giving introductions. She let everyone choose how they wanted to introduce themselves. He was a little intimidated I think because her cousins asked him straight up why he wanted to know about their little cousin. There he was in the center of 6 big mountain boys, 4 of which were on the football team. Then two others stepped forward, one looked at him, look, I have been her best friend since we were in diapers. The other told him I am her adopted brother. He looked at us knowing we were not related. And James steps forward and informs him that we were her husbands and that anything he had to say could be addressed to us. He looked at all of us standing there waiting to take him apart and he just looked at us. His reply was that she was getting teased and talked about behind her back by a few of the students in her class and he wanted to put a stop to it. James smiled at him well since I have taken the time to get to know all the high school and middle school students, they know who we all are, so it must be the adult students in your class I got this. He walks over to their lunch table. So, who has a problem with our family hanging out during lunch? You see we all are her family if you do not believe me then here is her grandmother's phone number or you can ask any of those 6 guys over there for their home numbers and talk to her aunts. And right on cue her sister and a few of her friends walk in. She sees the commotion and they walk over. Shay looked at this one girl and she knew who was causing the problems. She looks at the teacher and asks if miss Perry was there that day. Yes, why can you just call her and ask her to come down. After a few minutes miss Perry comes down from the office. She asks what is going on. Shay looks at her miss Perry these adults have a problem with my sister hanging out with her friends and family on her lunch time they think she is something she is not because they all happen to be guys can you tell them how you know us. Miss Perry crosses her arms and looks at Kats teacher what you cannot handle your students from picking on a child. I am their aunts' best friends, and I am that one's Godmother. These guys are her cousins, if you think this is a lot you should see Sunday dinner at their grandmother's house. There are like over a hundred people on any given Sunday and that is still just a handful. I would not suggest you mess with her because they tend to hit first and ask questions after the only people allowed to mess with the family is family. The girl who started it all turned white as a sheet and started to apologize to everyone. turned out she had a crush on One of the cousins and could not get his attention because he was always hanging out with us. So, the nick name stuck we became the husbands."

"Does she really have that large of family?" Dr Smith asked.

"Yep, over half the county is most likely related to her in fact you already know a few of them they just don't go around announcing it but if you see them together you will know right away who they are." Jae told her.

"How would I know them?" She asked.

"I know at least 15 people works at the hospital in different departments. I bet if you look at the guest sign in and call logs you will recognize several names." Jae told her.

"In fact, I know you will meet a few this weekend they are from her father's side of the family. They work at the clinic we are going to attend one is the director the other is the coordinator. She doesn't know they will be there so don't say anything I want her to be relaxed for this drive please."

"Why would she have a problem with them they are family.?" She looked confused.

"One is her father's half-sister. Her father was born out of wedlock in the 40s and adopted by his grandmother because of her father's birth circumstances they never got close this will be the first time she will see her since her father's death. So, watch her closely you might see a completely different side of her this weekend." Ki informed both.

"You didn't think you tell us this before we left if I knew that I would have asked that we take her someplace else." Jacob scowled at his brother.

"Look the moment we check in and she sees her. Her aunt will call her other aunt that lives close to Shay or Kats mom. Once they know that she is there, and her aunt and uncle will be there also her husband nor anyone else can say anything about her trip with us." Ki smiled at them any problems that could arise from this retreat will be resolved without any issues because she will have family there. I know that the hospital administrator did not know about this when he suggested it, but I am relieved that they will be there. "

I feel a tap on my shoulder as we pull up to the retreat center. I look out the window and it is so beautiful, the old plantation house with the ground and trees covered in snow. I wonder what time it is. The sun is getting close to setting. I hope I get to stay in a balcony room so that I can watch the sun set. I sigh and get out of the car to get my bag out. I hear the clicking of high heels, I guess someone is coming to welcome us. I hear a voice of a woman greeting Dr Smith and the two Dr parks.

"Welcome to covenant house. How was your drive." The woman asks as she shakes each of their hands, I put the trunk down and gasp. Standing there is none other than my Aunt Rita. I try to turn away before she sees me and cover my head back up. To no avail she noticed me right away.

"Kat there is no use hiding I know it's you. I was waiting for you as soon as I saw the name on the registration." She walks around the car, stands in front of me, and takes my hood off. She starts fussing with my hair to make it look some semblance of order.

"Hi aunt Rita, how are you?" I ask quietly.

"I'm fine dear but I see you are having a hard time. Don't worry I have taken care of everything." She gives me a big hug and kisses my forehead.

"You didn't have to go to any trouble for me." I told her.

"Sugar it was no trouble. Now I have not told anyone that you're here. I cannot without your permission you know, but I would like to call your mom and let her know you are here and you're safe. Also, would you and the three Drs like to have dinner with the family tonight? You know it has been so long since I have seen you. I know the other aunts and uncles will be upset if they knew you were here, and they didn't get to see you."

I look at the three of them. Hoping that they can tell by my face to say no. Jacob as always speaks up. "I'm sure that will be fine. It's been a long trip how long would we have to drive to meet you all for dinner?"

"Oh, I will give Carlen a call and he will arrange everything. Just be ready by 7. Now Kat, do you have anything better to wear or do I need to have Jess send you something to wear? My gracious girl you don't even look like a girl in these clothes. I would think that you would have had better sense and pack at least a dress or two." She took my hand and pulled me behind her as if I was a naughty child. I am so embarrassed. Why is she being so nice for. She has never cared how I dressed in all the years that I have known her. What is going on? I look at the Drs and mouth "I'm sorry" to them Jacob is smiling almost laughing. Dr Smith gives me a smile. Ki is scowling. I wonder if he is like me worried about what is going on.

We went inside, and Aunt Rita took me to my room. It is the balcony room. "I remembered that you like to look outside at night, so I arranged for you to have a balcony." She puts my bag on the bed and opens it. She starts unpacking it when she sees the pretty shirt the secretary just bought for me along with the black dress pants. "This will do simply fine for tonight's dinner. Though you did not bring much. I will have jess or Gig go shopping for you a few more things."

"Aunt Rita that's not necessary I have plenty of clothes here I'm only going to be here for 3 days, and you don't have to be nice just because of the Drs." I interrupted her to tell her.

"Aiesh sugar I'm not being nice because of them. I have always had a soft spot for you but could never really show it much. You remember when you were small every time you came to visit, we aunts always tried to counteract the coldness of your grandfather and uncles. That is why I always had you stay with me every time you were home for a visit, I even came to pick you up a few times. I always felt you were neglected compared to your siblings. Besides this is my workplace and I am the one in charge here. I can spoil you a little and no one can say anything about it. So, let me take care of you this time especially since it's my job." she pats me on the cheek and notices Dr smith in the doorway.

"Oh, can I help you Dr Smith?" She inquires.

"Yes, I was wondering why my request to share a room with my patient was denied?" she asks looking closely at my aunt.

"Oh, that I thought maybe since she was going to be near family that she would be ok not having you close by, but if you want to share the room with her its fine." Aunt Rita explains.

"Yes, please she has had a rough time, and I will feel better knowing I'm in the same room with her." she answers my aunt.

"that's fine I will just have to change your room number in the computer you two will be sharing the adjoining sitting room with the two Dr parks. Their room is two doors down with the sitting room in the middle." She walks over to the door to unlock it and open it. You could see a very cozy sitting room with a fireplace next door. "I will get out of your hair for now so that you can shower, and change take a little rest before its time to go. If I know my niece I bet, she slept the entire trip and isn't tired anymore."

My face gets warm, I know I am blushing from embarrassment. I tell her thank you for everything. I just wonder what is going to happen at dinner.

As my aunt walks out of the room. I fidget with my bag hoping that Dr smith will not say anything. Why did the retreat have to be here of all places?

"Kat, you know you don't have to worry about anything that happens here. You have the three of us here with you to give you support and I'm not going to let anyone bully you." Dr smith tells me as she unpacks "that is why I asked to share your room. I did not want anyone to say anything about you or mistreat you in any way so don't be embarrassed or worry about what may happen ok."

I smiled at her and thanked her for her kindness and finished unpacking. I really hope things will go well this weekend. I hear a knock on the adjoining door. I go over to open it and its Ki "how are you ladies doing? I have finished unpacking and am going to go pick up our itineraries for the weekend is there anything you need?" He asks.

"No, we are fine just getting ready for Kats family dinner tonight. Are you and Jacob ready for this?" Dr smith asks.

"Yep, we are don't worry angel no one is going to bully you tonight you have the three of here to protect you. I promise ok." He replies with a thumbs up and a smile he turns and goes put through the sitting room as we finish getting ready. About an hour later there is a knock on the door. Aunt Rita's assistant came to let us know that it was time to leave for dinner and that my aunt was waiting for us.

CHAPTER 25

Night with family

When we got downstairs, I saw my cousins Gig and Jess. I felt a lot of excitement and happiness at seeing them but also some dread. Jess saw me first, she squealed in excitement and ran over and gave me the biggest, tightest hug. I hugged her back just as tight as it was when we would see each other as kids. I was so happy to see her. She looked at me with a mixture of happiness as well as sadness in her eyes.

"So, cuz why is it that I haven't heard from you since grandma died. You know that you could have called me anytime." Jess looked at me.

"Well, you are now the phone goes both ways you could have called me anytime as well. How are you, Jess? I asked her.

"I'm me like always. So, after the adults get done with this dinner how about me and you ditch the old folks and go to a party like we used to. Though we will have to get you something else to wear. Since when you dressed so old looking, we need to get you looking like you again." she noticed Jacob and Ki I could tell she was interested in them even though she is married. I hope she does not start hitting on them. I would not like having to put her in her place over them.

"So, who are these two sexy guys?" Making no secret that she is interested.

"Jess this is Jacob and Ki Park they are my Drs. As well as my friends the lady is Dr Sarah smith, she also is my dr." I look at them and introduce both Jess and Gig to them.

Gig looks at me "wait Jacob Park are you the same one who went to school with my brother Thomas?"

"Yes, I am I didn't realize you would remember me." Jacob replies

I look at Jacob and I feel a little hurt he knew my family and did not tell me. I look at him with misty eyes almost ready to cry thinking how much more he knows that he has not told me and how many of my family does he know.

Jacob notices Kat looking at him with confusion and hurt in her eyes. He does not know what to say to her, not in front of everyone. To do that would take too much explaining and cause more problems. Jacob looks at Ki and his brother gives him an incredibly angry look. He knows that Kat is going to have an awkward night already and it just got more complicated.

Rita comes out of the office and smiles "good everyone is ready let's go we are going to have dinner at your aunt bobs house ok."

We go out to get in the cars and Gig asks Jacob if he would ride with her and Jess. He tells her it is not necessary that he can ride in our car with his brother Kat and Dr smith.

"Oh, but Kat has to go with aunt Rita she can't ride with you guys' aunt Rita wants to talk to her alone that's why she had us come and meet you guys, so we could show you the way to the house while they stop somewhere first." Jess says with a little smirk.

Jacob looks at Gig and Jess "what do you mean by that. Where is she taking her? What is she going to talk to her about?"

"You will know when you see her at the house no need to worry Kat was always the favorite out of all the bastard's children no one will be to mean to her." Gig informs him.

Jacob turns and walks quickly to the car looking at the other two Drs. "did Rita take Kat already?"

"Yes, they just left, why?" Dr smith asked.

"What's going on Jacob?" Ki looks at him his displeasure showing.

"It seems Rita us taking her someplace before bringing her your dinner and that she wants to talk to her alone. I'm really worried now things don't feel right." He says as they get into the car to follow Jess and Gig to the house.

When Kat and Rita got on the road. Rita started the conversation.

"I want to take you to see your grandmother and grandfather before going to the house. I need to tell you about a few things before we get to the house."

"I can't go there I can't. Please don't make me please." Kat becomes very agitated and nervous.

"Why are you still so afraid to go to the graveyard. I mean as a younger child and into you teems you used to play pranks on Halloween with your cousins why now this fear." she asks while she pulls into the cemetery.

Rita parks the car in the section near the graves of Kats grandparents. She turns and looks at her. I know when your uncle died you sat in your room with a gun after hearing taps. Your mom told me. I also know you have never gone to your dad's grave or your other grandparents' either. Can you tell me why? "

"I don't know I only know that it terrifies me and makes me physically sick. I cannot explain it. I'm sorry I am such a disappointment to everyone, but I really can't go in there." Kat breaking out into a sweat and Rita can hear the fear in her voice. Rita pulls her across the car seat and into her arms holding her like a child whispering to her.

"it's ok baby girl its ok nothing or anyone is going to hurt you. I didn't bring you here to scare you or upset you I wanted to share a special moment with you is all I have something to read to you and I thought that reading it to you with your grandparents would give it more meaning but not if it's going to make you so afraid." She wipes Kats tears away and kisses her forehead.

"Truly you didn't do this to be mean or hurtful?" Kat looks at her aunt.

"Truly and I'm sorry that you would even ask that. I guess we have not been the best family we have. I know we have not and for that I am deeply sorry. Oh, and do not be upset with Jacob, he only has your best interest at heart always has. He did not know you would see me his brother Ki knew only because I mistook him for Jacob at a conference once and he asked me if I were the same aunt, he had met but he had no idea that I would insist on you are having dinner or that I would take you away from the center. Jacob went to school with Thomas, and we got to know him a little while he was in college. I knew he must have known you somehow because every time he would come around, he was always looking at your pictures when he thought no one was looking. I didn't think he knew when he became friends with Thomas that you were cousins. The first time he came to my house and saw your picture the shock was all over his face and the sadness in his eyes when he looked at it, I knew he knew you, but I never asked. He is a good man and I know from reading the notes in your chart that you are dealing with a lot, and I am sorry that I as an aunt and as a Dr I have not been able to help you in any way." Kat could tell she was sincere.

"Even though I can't bring myself to see their graves I did love them a lot. I asked dad one time how he could love me after I hurt so many people. He told me that after he got his life together, he understood why his mom gave him to his grandmother to raise. That it was her love for him was greater than her need to keep him with her. That with his grandmother he could have some peace away from his stepdad and brothers. You know my dad loved his brothers and sisters so much he yearned to have a good relationship with them, not one tainted by the fact that he was a bastard. He even loved and respected grandpa a little but it never happened my uncles never could see past the fact that their father was not his and never could accept his love and that makes me not only sad but angry because my dad would have given everything for them just once let him be a part of the family. He only wanted to be accepted and wanted his children to be accepted." I told her.

"I know, and I have told your uncle that he missed having a wonderful brother. They will never believe that they were wrong though. That is not why I brought you here though. When we cleaned out your grandmother's things from the nursing home, we found this addressed to you." She handed me an envelope and a box.

I look at it and wonder what it could say. I opened the envelope and there was a letter.

Katydid

I am sorry that I could never tell you this in person. I could never forgive your grandmother for her betrayal in having your father with my best friend. Even though it was before we deployed to go to war, and I had not done more than show a little interest in her. I thought she understood my feelings. Your grandmother and I loved each other completely but I still could never get passed the fact that your father was not mine. So that meant that you were not mine either. That last summer you came to stay with us I saw a different girl than the usually talkative smiling child that always followed me around annoying me with stories and questions. I did not mind that much, and you always gave me such a laugh trying to help with the chores. That summer you barely spoke, and you seemed so jittery. At first, I thought you might have gotten into drugs, but Rita assured me that it wasn't that. Then the nightmares started, and I could hear you in your room crying in your sleep. I called your dad for the first time in my life to ask him what happened to you. Your mom answered and said that nothing was wrong but if you were bothering me, I could send you to your other grandmother's house. I didn't like her tone. So, I called your dad at work. He told me that you had been molested by your sister's husband and that you could not be at home right now because your sister was not allowed around if you were home and your mom thought you needed time away to get your head together. I asked him if he beat the bastard that hurt you. He said no he grabbed him up but that your mom stopped him because it was not what a minister does. He asked me if I was ok. I told him the truth and I told him if he could not protect my granddaughter then I would. I spoke to your uncles and that summer we all agreed to keep a close watch on you. I know that was the first summer I ever let myself really get close to you and truly get to know who you were. You were so happy just because I was spending time with you. I was happy just to see you smile, that is until I came home one day, and your brother was there instead of you. I was so upset that you did not say goodbye to me. Your grandmother told me later that you left with your aunt because your brother came and was making hateful comments about you and taking up for your sister and her husband. Then all I heard the rest of the summer was how your drama was destroying your family every time, he opened his mouth I had to leave to keep from hitting him. I am sorry I was not able to protect you anymore than your dad was. I am also sorry that I was too stubborn and hateful to show you that I cared for you.

Your grandfather

I looked up at Rita. "He really did like me a little. I always cherished the fact that he called me his granddaughter even if it was only the one time."

"We all love you but sometimes life is complicated and once there is hurt and pain it's hard to say you're sorry or ask for forgiveness. I know it was hard for you when people did not believe you until he was arrested. I believed you and so did the others wait for you back at the house. We noticed the change in you that summer. I wanted to tell you that even though the uncles won't show it they do care for you and will be happy to see you." She turned the car back on and we drove towards the house. I wonder if the others are already there.

Jacob was agitated that Kat was not at the farmhouse yet. Where did Rita take her? Though he was happy to see the family that he got to know when he was in med school with Thomas. When they got out of the car Thomas came over. "Jacob how have you been. It is good to see you again?"

"I'm good Thomas how about you. I was sorry to hear about your grandmother passing." Jacob said as they shook hands. "This is my brother Ki and Dr smith." He introduces everyone.

Ki asks, "where did Rita take Kat, and will it take long?"

"Rita took her to visit her grandparents' graves. She wanted to talk to her about a few things before dinner. Do not worry, no harm will come to my niece. They will be here soon. "One of Kats uncle's chimes in.

"Kat hasn't been here since my mother died. We just wanted to visit with her is all nothing bad is going to happen." another chimed in

"After dinner Thomas I told katydid we were going to take her out for some fun it's been too long since we got to party together." Jess told him.

"Now Jess you know she is on medication so you can't take her drinking. I will go also to make sure you two don't get arrested like last time." Thomas's brother jumps in the conversation.

"What do you mean arrested?" Dr smith asks.

"Well, when she was 17, she came for a visit and this guy came on too strong and she broke a bottle and tried to slice his throat open. Though the judge considered it self-defense she left him with a permanent scar." Bryan lets them know.

"What that's do not like her what did he do to warrant her to do that." Ki inquired.

Before anyone could answer Rita walked in. "he refused to take no for an answer. And pinned her against the wall and would not let her go. He deserved it."

Jacob hears Kat suck in her breath." Really, I did that? "

"You sure did and. I still have the scar to show for it." Jeffery stepped out from behind Kat's aunt Bob. On the left side of his face and neck was a faint scar.

Rita gasps "who invited him!!!!!" She shows her irritation looking around the room.

"don't get your panties in a bunch Rita I'm not here to cause problems. I came to apologize to her I didn't do it at grams funeral because her husband looked like he was ready to fight anyone who spoke out of turn with her." Jeffery explained.

"I should be asking you to forgive me. You're the one who had to live with that scar not me." Kat replied.

"No, I was drunk and angry because I had a crush on you since the first summer, I met you. It was the first time that I even had a chance at getting you alone and your grandfather warned me to keep my distance from you since back then I was a troublemaker. You were so quiet and withdrawn I thought you were just ignoring me and trying to blow me off. I got angry and tried to force a kiss on you. I was not expecting this little thing to cut me like that. It was not till you left that I heard your brother telling my brother and Jess that a neighbor girl told your parents that she saw your brother-in-law hurt you in a bad way but that no one believed you when you told them what happened because your sister took her husband's side. If I had known I would have stayed sober and just sat and talked to you that night instead of trying something so no I deserved what I got, and can you forgive me?" He asked.

"Since I don't remember anything of course I can." Kat replies.

"Ok no more talking let's eat and enjoy dinner and have some fun." Aunt Bob speaks up. Rich says grace to bless the food and for the next several hours all you hear in the house is laughter and singing. It was a night filled with embarrassing stories of Kat as a child and playful banter. Dr smith was amazed at how playful and full of life Kat was. Playing with her cousins and her uncles and aunts teasing her over the smallest thing. She also got to see her interact with the park brothers in a relaxed setting. She could see how close they were and how easily they fit in together. She gave everyone attention for the first time. I believe I am seeing the Kat everyone has described to me. She is truly a wonderful, complicated person. I can see why so many men in her life love her. Rita and Bob came over to sit with me "our little angel is something else isn't she." Bob asked Dr Smith.

"You call her angel also I thought only the Dr parks called her that."

"No everyone who has met her has called her angel. You know I met the four of them once. I was at an American legion meeting in Kats town and saw them having dinner in the hotel restaurant. I just watched to make sure that she was ok and not going to a room with any of them. I had not let anyone know I was there. They were so sweet with her, and she beamed with happiness being with them even more than usual. She saw me and ran over, not caring that I was surrounded by other people and gave me a big hug and kiss on the cheek. She never cared where she was if she loved you. Everyone around knew it. I knew who Jacob was when Thomas brought him home the first time. I never gave him away because her other grandmother told me what truly had happened to her. I knew he did not know Thomas was her cousin, but he recognized me right away. I felt that for his sake it was needed for him to still be connected to her somehow." Bob explained "I never told any of the others what happened to her how much she lost or suffered. If my dad had known the full truth, he would have killed someone he was a hard man, but he had a soft spot for her. She kept a lot bottled up and hidden so that no one would feel sorry for her. Also, so that no one would think she was not worth having around. To her since those things happened, she felt she should have been cast aside not worthy of friends or love. And in some ways my sister-in-law did just that when she sent her here instead of getting her help and taking her side over her sisters. As always though Kat forgave all and made sure that her sister and her children were taken care of and that she was there for them. I don't know anyone who could have done that. "Aunt Bob told her.

Dr Smith looked at the two ladies. "Thank you for showing me this side of my patient. I have only seen a kind but withdrawn scared woman these past two years. But since meeting the park brothers and her family I have gotten to see just how complicated she is."

"She isn't complicated she is just a loving forgiving person who tries to take care of others but not herself." Rita told her "This is who she really is right now loving a family that rejected and belittled her at every turn because they were afraid to really love her. There was so much anger and hatred between her father, grandfather and uncles. That it tainted everything. No matter how hurt she was she never stopped trying to be apart she never gave up on us." Titan looked at Dr Smith and asked, "I have one favor to ask of you."

"What is it?" Dr smith holding her breath just a little

"don't make her give up those two too soon. She needs them right now a lot to find her way back. Also, I only put her in sessions that would not press her for any real details. I do not think it would be good for her to have an issue while here. I would like her to have the most pleasant visit. She has been through a lot lately and the worst is to come." Rita patted my hand as she got up to go over and join the others.

"I agree with her on that one. Let her enjoy this weekend and don't push her too much." Bob agreed with Rita.

After the group arrived back at the center, they parted ways at the sitting room door. Kat thanks them for spending the evening with her family.

Weekend away

The next two days was a series of group events designed to help come to terms with ptsd and learn to deal with some of the fears associated with the trauma of being raped. As Rita promised Kat was only assigned classes that explained the different aspects of ptsd and treatments. After dinner in the evenings various family members came to hang out. On the second night Thomas and his girlfriend came to watch a movie with the 4 of them and to reminisce with Jacob. They had a great time laughing and playing around. Dr smith asked Jacob on the last night to sit with her after everyone left. "Why were you so afraid of Kat being with her family they are very nice and seem to be more caring than the ones I have met so far a lot less confusing as well."

"You think they are not usually this nice. They are usually very hateful to her. You should ask Ki what her family is like also he had some experience with them when Kat was a small child. You remember the door we opened when she was 7 the grandmother who hit her was her great-grandmother, her father's adoptive mother. Ki had classes with one of her older cousins and they are very prejudiced against anyone who is not white. That is why she has never brought her husband around this side of the family very much. I am happy for her that they were supportive and loving this weekend but if it were more than a few days the worthless and blaming her for everything would start. I believe that like always when she was a child, they tried to give her happy memories and care, but they could never get passed her father's birth and the fact that to them she is not good enough. You will see once we get back home, she will not hear from them again and if she calls it will be just pleasant conversation. At least she had this weekend to remember and if anyone says anything about her being here, they all can verify that she spent all her time in class or with family." Jacob explained.

"I always thought that she was anti-social and introverted but seeing glimpses of who she is when she opens is like night and day. Her aunts told me that she is the most forgiving and loving person and never gives up trying. I honestly thought the opposite of her." Dr smith told him.

"She tends to be what she thinks people want her to be. She is smart but will not show or try to be smart because no one expected much from her. So, she never even tried. She has no idea exactly how smart she is. With us it was always making sure we did things to strengthen our brotherly bond while showing us how loved and special each of us were. She still is doing it if you have not noticed. She reminds us subtly with a glance or touch and sometimes with a word. With her husband she caters to his ego and needs with her mom she hides things that will upset her but gives her just enough, so she feels needed with Shay she gives her peace and space by being a mom to her kids and taking care of her when she needs it. With her dad's family always allowing them to feel superior to her and allowing them to feel like she is grateful for their charity so that she can still be a small part of the family. With you she is afraid you will be like the other Drs and judge her instead of trying to help her so she until now stayed closed she has had enough rejection in her life that she could have filled every session dealing with self-pity and anger." Jacob sat back and closed his eyes. Dr smith just looking at him for a moment.

"It surprises me sometimes how close you three are even with so many memories still missing and years apart. How you still know so much about her and are not surprised by anything that happens." she told him.

"She is still the same underneath she is just lost right now. The only thing I wish is that I could turn back the clock and never have her leave us in the first place but then you would never get to meet her, and we would not be sitting here." Jacob smiles at her and bids her good night.

The next morning Rita meets them at breakfast. She has a picnic basket "Bob and Jess sent you some of your favorite foods for the long drive back. I hope you got a lot out of your visit as well as having some fun. It was nice to see you. "Rita hands Ki the basket and hugs Kat tightly.

"It was nice to see everyone. I had a lot of fun thank you for this wonderful visit" Kat embraces her aunt once mor before getting in the car.

CHAPTER 27

An Unexpected Detour

As they drive back to the hospital. Dr smith gets a call. "Hello. Oh, hi, how are things at the hospital? Oh, dear, well we are on our way, we will be there in a few hours. Yes, we are going straight there why?" It is the Dr on call. There has been a bad outbreak of the flu at home and every bed is taken they do not have a bed available for Kat and the ward is under quarantine. Dr smith is not sure what she should do.

"Mum Ki and Jacob, we have a problem the ward is full and under total quarantine. We cannot go there until further notice. an awfully bad strain of the flu has taken over the ward. A patient from the group home brought it in and now everyone is infected including the staff. The director says both the hospital and group home are locked down for several more days." Dr smith informs them.

"Well then I guess we just drop everyone at home instead of the hospital." Ki tells her.

"Umm what about Kat she has no bed at the hospital right now and things are to unsettle at her home to send her back. Once she leaves the hospital her family may not allow us to admit her again." Jacob tells him.

"I'm not sending her home she is still technically a patient of the hospital. I did her paperwork for the retreat as a transfer so that we could travel with her without problems. Her transfer papers were faxed this morning, which is why you got the call that the ward cannot take her. She will stay in the empty room in my private clinic. I told the director to leave one room always open for her since she was admitted. So that she would always have a place to go." Ki informed them.

Ki calls the director of the clinic "Dr faith the patient that I have been keeping the 3rd floor for will be arriving tonight. The hospital ward is under lockdown to a flu outbreak, so she cannot go there for few days. Get everything ready for her please."

"They're taken care of. Her mini apartment will be fully equipped and waiting for her when we arrive."

"Ki why did you not tell me about this in all these months. I would have let her go there months ago I kept her in the hospital thinking it was the only choice other than to send her home. I didn't send her to the group home because her husband knew where it was, and I did not want problems with him there." Dry smith asks him.

"I knew that, but I live on the 3rd floor of my clinic. The apartment next to mine is only used in extreme cases. I did not want there to be bigger problems. I figured that it could be used only in emergencies and as a backup plan. Not as a solution." Ki explained.

"Oh, I did not know you lived in your clinic. Yes, I can see where her husband could misunderstand the situation if it came to light that you would be sharing the same floor and since this is kind of an emergency it cannot be avoided since she is still a patient, she still needs to be in a clinic setting" Dr smith sighs wondering how Kat was going to feel about being at Ki clinic.

When we arrived at the clinic, I was awoken by Ki shaking my shoulder. "Angel we are here at my clinic the hospital is under quarantine for the flu. They cannot take you. We brought you here instead." I look up at a beautiful building it looks familiar, but I really cannot place it. I got out of the car and went to get my bags. There is an older gentleman already taking things out and setting them on a rolling cart. "it's ok miss I have them." He tells me.

"I could have just gone to my aunt and uncles you did not need to bring me here." I told him.

", since we never discharged you from the hospital, we can't transfer your care to your aunt's clinic and then back again. Since the ward cannot take you now, we transferred you to my clinic instead. I set it up as transferred care so that we would not have to worry about you having a bed or not it's all been taken care of." He told me I still am not sure if I believe him or not, but the three Drs have gone through a lot of trouble to help me. So, I follow him inside and upstairs.

The room he takes me to is like a small apartment. It has a bedroom, kitchen and breakfast nook, bathroom, and a small sitting room. It is very pretty with ocean landscapes on the walls. There is a picture on the wall above the bed, I cannot seem to take my eyes off it. It is a group of 5 people on the beach, they are dressed formally. Their backs to the artist they are standing in surf shoes in hand staring out into the vast ocean watching the sunset. I stare at the picture then I notice the signature it is one of Ki paintings I look at him "is this one of us together?"

"Yes, all of the paintings in this room are mine they all are a memory of ours that we share look at them and see if you can remember anything." He says as he walks to the door. "Good night, Dr smith and Jacob will be here in the morning for your session its back to work starting tomorrow." And closes the door.

I looked around the room looking at the different paintings and sketches. There was one day in the snow. It was of a young girl getting a piggyback ride from an older gentleman. Behind them were 4 younger men smiling at them. In the sketch beside it was of a very young-looking Ki standing under a tree holding a young girl's face smiling as the snow falls around them. There were a lot of snow sketches of the same girl riding on the back of one of the guys going down a large hill. Others of snowball fights. All of them were smiling looking as if it was the happiest day. I went to bed feeling very content and happy looking at their happiness. I fell asleep with a sketch of a young couple kissing under a snowy tree when I first looked at it, I felt such warmth and love coming from that picture. That night my mind was swirling with images of a large house and heavy snow falling outside. I smell hot chocolate and snickerdoodles. I feel like I am watching a movie. I see a very loving and happy family in the living room playing a board game. A fire in the fireplace and loud laughter. I can feel the warmth of the love from the people in my dream. I am at peace sleeping for the first time in years. I never want to wake up and leave this place.

I wake to a knock at the door. I stretch like a cat. I am so relaxed and content I do not want to get up. I look at the picture by the bedside and smile. Get up and go to open the door. Standing there is Dr smith holding my breakfast tray.

"Oh, come in Dr Smith. You didn't need to bring me my breakfast I could have gotten it on my own." I take the tray from her and move inside so that she can enter. I walk over and place the tray on the dining table. "Would you like to sit with me and have breakfast?" I motion for her to sit.

"Yes, I would love to that is why I brought the tray so that we could talk before the Dr parks get here." She helps me arrange the dishes at the table so that both of us can share the meal together. We sat and started to eat.

"How did you sleep last night?" She asks.

"I slept very well even though my mind was filled with images all through the night. They were warm happy images not nightmares." I told her.

"That is good I was concerned since every time we change your environment you seem to have unpleasant dreams." She smiles and continues to eat and chat about small stuff. She notices the artwork in the room.

"Ki drew them I used to love to watch him draw. He could draw even without looking at the paper. Depending on what he was drawing. He said that a lot of them are of special moments.

Dr Smith walks around the room looking at the décor and pictures. As I was watching her, I began to look at the room more closely. I notice that the room is painted in various shades of blue with white accents. That the lace curtains are snowflakes. The carpet is in the shade of tan that mimics the color of the sand on a beach. The kitchen area has a greenish blue hue that looks like the water of a flowing river. The counter tops are marbled brown and green with a tree lined tile back drop. The dining area has pink and white cherry blossoms falling like rain on the wall with a crystal cherry blossom light above the table. As I look through the rooms, I realize he decorated the rooms on memories. The kitchen is by the riverside, the living room area the beach, the bedroom, a snowy wonderland. The dining area is the tidal basin during the cherry blossom festival. In every room small change that flow into each other as if telling a story without words. Anyone walking in here would be able to see the love and tenderness given to each detail. They would feel the warmth of the summer, the tranquility of fall, the renewal of spring and the coziness of winter. In every space he has painted or sketched scenes from his life relating to each space. I go to take a closer look in the bathroom I want to see what it has if he did the same there. I open the door and I smell gardenias. I look at the walls and it is painted as if it is a gardenia bush. The colors of the bathroom give the sensation of being in a garden. On the wall is a cabinet that is carved as if it is part of the bush. I open it inside is all kinds of soaps and oils in the fragrance of gardenias, roses, and jasmine. Tears come to my eyes the moment I realize what he has done. He made a place just for me. Of all the memories he had of me. I walk back into the sitting room. I noticed Dr Smith was sitting there in very deep thought.

"Dr Smith what do you feel in this place?" I ask her I need to know I am not crazy. That I am not seeing more than there is.

"I feel at peace in these rooms. Dr Park took great care in making this space. He took great care in every room. I will show you the rest of the building after our session today. "

I look at her a little disheartened. I was thinking this place was special, so I guess I was wrong. Just then there is a knock on the door. The brothers have arrived to start my session.

"How did you sleep." Ki asks.

"I had my mind racing last night. It was not a bad thought. Just a lot of them." I told him.

CHAPTER 28

Getting back to work.

Jae looks around the room. He noticed all the little things to invoke memories. He smirks and wonders which memories she remembered.

"let's get started." Jae motions for everyone to sit. The lights were lowered, and Dr Smith started to hypnotize Kat.

I am standing in front of a door as always. This one is blue with snowflakes and a snowy tree on it. I open the door without hesitation. I see a group of people on a hill. They are sledding and playing. I just sit and smile watching them. I can see the love and happiness in their faces. It is the same scene as my dream but different. In my dream I could only get glimpses of their true feelings for them. Here I feel the love that is overwhelming. I see a young Ki standing under a branch of a tree with a young girl. He is wiping snow from her face, and he leans down and kisses her. For a moment, a wave of sheer jealousy washes over me. Then I see that it is a young me. Just then they are covered in snow. I laughed when Jae doused them in snow by shaking the tree branch. Laughter and a snowball fight ensued. I hear Dr Smith voice telling me it is time to come back. I do not want to leave this time. I want to stay and bask in these wonderful memories. Reluctantly I got up and walked back up the staircase. I open my eyes and see them. Without saying anything. I get up and give Ki a tight hug.

"Thank you for such wonderful memories." I look at him with tears of happiness.

I then turn to Jae and hug him as well. "Thank you for always being around and making me laugh. I love you both and am so happy that I have you in my life again."

I look at the three of them and start to tell them my feelings. I am pacing the floor excited to feel happiness for the first time in years. I cannot stop talking about all the wonderful memories that have begun to flood my mind. I look at the two brothers and ask them "are these memories real or are they my wishful thinking?"

"They are real. I have more letters to give you now that you have remembered everyone." Jacob leaves the room. I look at Dr Smith and ask her" so when do I get to start working on my marriage and re bonding with my family?" She looks at me and smiles.

"When we open the other doors that hold your most frightening memories and see how you handle them. I want you to enjoy these peaceful memories first at least for a few days before we send you back into the darkness again." She pats my hand and motions me to sit down.

When Jacob returns, he has several envelopes in his hands. He gave them to me. I look at them, I cannot wait to read them. I open the first one. It is from papa I look at the three of them and begin to read.

My darling girl

I hope when you finally get to read these letters that you take pity on this old man and not tease me too much for writing to you not knowing when you may get to read them. I am finding that I am thinking of you more and more and missing you so much more lately. Today it is snowing our first real snow. I came home from work today because I could not stand watching the snow fall outside without wishing you were here with us. I remember the last time it snowed when you were with us. You conned this old man into playing with you in the snow like a small child, but I had the best day that day. I was so mad and incredibly happy at the same time because you and Kris iced down all the cars the night before so that I could not take you to your grandmother's and you had to stay the night. I knew that when the boys wanted to talk to me and kept trying to distract me that you and Kris were up to one of your tricks, but I would have never guessed that you had iced down every car so that they could not move. I was happy because I got to have you in the house for just one more night and then the next day when you made me chocolate chip pancakes with cream and made a big pot of hot chocolate with cinnamon that something was up. I should have known you were going to want me to do something that I normally would not do. As usual when you looked at me with those big eyes and asked me to take you sledding with the boys, I could not refuse you anything. I could not believe which hill you wanted to go down, the steepest one of course little did I know that you go down one twice that size at your house, so you were not even phased by it. It was so much fun watching James's fuss about you getting hurt or too cold trying to get you to be careful as if you knew how. Kris of course would run and push you as fast as he could so that he could hear you scream and lauhala he was the funniest because he didn't like the snow but if he wanted any hot chocolate he had to play with you so he threw the first snow ball at you after you winked at Kris and tipped him off the sled with you and you two landed in a heap and the sled kept going and you made him chase after it I laughed so hard at his expression because he reminded me of a character off of the looney tunes cartoons you liked to watch with me in the study (which you still have to keep that a secret or else my stern uptight image will be shot and I won't have any credibility left) Then the battle began and of course you and I won. The sweetest moments of the day was when Ki shook the tree limb and dumped snow on you just so he could hear you giggle and smile at him while he cleaned the snow from your hair and face and it was the first time I saw my son kiss you it was the gentlest and sweetest kiss I believed I ever saw in my life I never knew my quiet son who could beat anyone in a fight who loved to box and do martial arts more than anything could be that gentle it was like I was seeing someone else for a moment it was also the first time that I understood what my mother was saying about the two of you being soul mates and being meant for each other I knew then at that moment that you would be married to him and I would have a house full of grandchildren in no time and I couldn't wait .Of course Jae had to ruin the moment by starting another snowball fight and you and I beat the boys soundly and then I got to give you a short piggyback ride until Ki and Kris decided to get revenge and plummet us with snowballs until we fell in a heap and then Ki informed me that only he was allowed to give you a piggyback that day and that he did not want to fight with his father over his girl he had to share you enough with his brothers .I personally think it was just an excuse because he knew that my leg was beginning to hurt from the cold and wanted to let me save face. When we got back to the house we were just finishing our hot chocolate when your grandmother came and that was the day that my wife informed everyone that she could not let the situation go on any longer after she saw how hard it was for Ki and the boys to let you go home and that would be the last day that any of us would see you until you turned 17 when I would be able to go and talk to your father and she told the boys that she already withdrew them from your vo- tech school so they could not even see you then and they would be resuming their college classes the following semester .It was the saddest day of our lives I was so angry that I could not even speak to her I asked her why couldn't she have waited till after Christmas she informed me that the longer we waited the harder it would be and she could see Ki was having a harder time keeping his distance and it was getting harder for him to let you go after each visit and if we were not careful those grandchildren I had been dreaming about were going to come to soon and that this was better than waiting for something bad happened. so, we have been trying our best to live with her wishes but if must tell you my baby girl it has not been easy, I thought our house was a cold place before now it has an iceberg around here worse than a tomb, but we are more than halfway there so soon it will be over, and the sunshine can come again and breathe life into this house again.

I love you my darling child and cannot wait for you to come home where you belong my darling this old man misses his darling daughter and is counting the days till you bring the warmth and love back into this cold dark house and make the sunshine again.

I was crying by the time I finished reading this letter. I did not realize that he loved me so much. I look at the pile of letters there are several from halimane and mama Clara I decide I want to read them alone. So, I ask the three of them if it is ok if I have the rest of the day to myself. They agreed and told me they will be back at dinnertime. For the next few hours, I read and reread their letters crying the whole day. I never knew that I was so loved or that I made such an impact on anyone's life before. I always felt like I was disposable. Those people would easily move on with their lives if I were not around.

In the afternoon Dr smith took me around the clinic. I notice that Ki has decorated the entire clinic in different seasons just as the room I am staying in. He has used nature as the basis for every room to evoke peace and tranquility throughout. On the walls he has used a combination of paintings and sketches to decorate. He comes out of his office and sees Dr smith and I sitting in the common room. He leans against the wall watching us talking to one of his patients.

"Hi, I'm Kat how are you doing?" I asked the young girl sitting next to the window.

"I'm fine I'm crystal." She replies.

"If you don't mind, can you tell me why you are here?" Kat asks.

Crystal pulls her sleeves up. On both wrists she has bandages. Kat can see that she has tried to kill herself.

"Oh, wow I did that too before. More than once. It does not solve anything though. You know if you kill yourself then you never have a chance to start over. You never get to see what new things are waiting for you. If we are living, then each day gives us a chance to make changes and start a new life." Kat takes her hand in hers as she is telling her this.

"that's easy to say, but you have no idea what it feels like to be nothing." Crystal looks at her with anger in her eyes.

", more than you can imagine. I have felt like I was nothing for as long as I can remember. I have been told by so many people that I am worthless. Waste of space, waste of air, something that even the worms would not eat. I have been told I am all those things. You know people who are sad, miserable or just like to make themselves look and feel better and say these things. We that believe that way are easy targets for them to spew their poison on." Kat tells her.

Crystal looks at her for a moment. "Why are you here then?"

"I'm here because the hospital psych unit is under quarantine because of the flu." Kat answers her.

"Why are you supposed to be in the psych unit?" Crystal puts her hands under her chin looking at her intently.

"I was put there for my safety because my husband hurt me. I am under Dr care because I have been having severe nightmares. The nightmares are caused by memories from a very scary time in my life. I tend to try to kill myself or just to disappear when that happens." Kat replies very quietly.

"Oh, so you don't really believe what you said." Crystal crosses her arms looking at her.

", I do very much so. I believe it with everything inside me. I need to get better, so I can show my kids that life is always worth living. No matter how bleak it may look at times. Sometimes my sadness becomes overwhelming, and I lose my way. You know the moment that I realize that I am at the point that I am about to lose my way. I look into my kid's eyes and remind myself that if I die who will love them more than me. No one will. A mother's love is the purest deepest love there is. "Kat tells her, her voice sounding so quiet and sad.

"How many kids do you have?" Crystal is now listening very closely.

"I have 5 children. I have 2 that are mine and 3 that I am raising with my sister." Kat smiles at her waiting to see how she reacts.

"Wow 5 kids that's a lot. It must be hard to be away from them." Crystal gets more comfortable on the couch.

"It can be, but it's more fun than anything because I get to play video games, go roller skating, take them to do a lot of fun things. It is not always easy to be a mom because you cannot always just be the one, they have fun with. You also must correct them and teach them right from wrong." Kat tells her.

"It sounds like you love your kids but why are you still having such a hard time.?" Crystal asks her.

"I have more than just depression. I have ptsd and a disassociation disorder as well. I have forgotten a lot of things that happened because of it, and it has been causing problems. These problems are the reason that I cannot be with them right now. I plan on being with them as soon as I can. "Kat lets her know.

"What would you do if you were pregnant, and that baby was conceived because he raped you?" Crystal has tears in her eyes.

Kat walks over and sits beside her on the couch. She puts her arms around her and places her head on her shoulder.

"2 of my children is by the man who raped me. One was born when I was 15 and when my sister brought him home. She gave him to me to love and take care of while she went to work. I did everything I could to protect that baby from his father. Later, after everyone knew what happened, my sister stayed with her husband and became pregnant for the second time by him. No one believed me about what happened. Then he was arrested. He was caught in the act of raping a neighbor because he was interrupted before he could rape me again. Then everyone believed me about what he did. My sister told me she was pregnant a month later. I took care of her through both pregnancy and I took care of her child. When the new baby was born, I was not allowed at the hospital because her husband was going to be there. I cannot tell you what to do, but I can tell you this. I would not trade a signal Day that I have had with my two babies. They are the most precious loving children. The baby you are carrying is innocent of any wrongdoing. All children are a gift from God. That baby is also a part of you. If I did not have those two babies to focus on, I would not be alive today. I would not be a mother or even remotely what you could call human. You must decide for yourself if you can see the love and goodness in this child. If you cannot then you have options. You can carry the baby to terms and give it up for adoption to someone who desperately wants a child to love. If it is too hard for you. Even though I am very much against it go get an abortion. You do not have to decide anything right away. I do know that if you abort your baby, you will always wonder if you did the right thing and you will wonder about what they would be like. Think hard and carefully before you decide because it will be a decision you have to live with for the rest of your life. "Kat gently rocks her as she talks to her not even realizing that they have been watching for the last hour. The three Drs have been waiting to start the group session. Though they did not want to interrupt. Kat looks at Crystal and wipes the tears from her face. She gently kisses her forehead as if she were a small child.

"no one will ever understand the depth of your pain. No one will ever walk the same path that you have to walk. Only you can decide which path you will take. Only you can define who you will be. Only you can decide if you will freeze your heart in this moment. A heart frozen in pain and hate. Only you can decide if you will love and grow instead of living with sorrow. For sorrow and pain are a part of life. Just as love and joy are. If you choose the path of sorrow and pain it will be a very lonely path. If you choose the path of love and hope you will always have someone to hold your hand to help you through the pain and sorrow. "Kat tells her.

"Are you sure you belong here? That is not something I was expecting. I thought for sure you would say either kill your baby or preach to me about what a sin it is." Crystal says while still resting her head on her shoulder.

"Personally, I believe that abortion is a sin because that baby is a living soul. children are a gift from God, but it is not my place to judge or condemn anyone. Only you can decide if you are strong enough to carry your baby to term. Many people do not understand the lasting pain that rape leaves. You can move past it and still have a good life, but it never leaves you. Every time my husband comes up behind me without saying something I get scared even to this day. I cannot touch a buck knife without my hands shaking. There are even some positions that I cannot do when my husband and I are having sex. Each person is different in how they deal with trauma. Do not let the person who hurt you win. You know forgiveness is not just for the person who is in the wrong. Forgiveness is for the victims by forgiving you are releasing your heart of hate and anger. Where hate and pain are living, love cannot abide. So, release your heart and forgive that person you do not even have to tell him that you forgive him. All you must do is say aloud that you forgive him and that you are on your way to healing your life." Kat closes her eyes as she holds this child in her arms. Tears are falling down her face. Her heart is aching for this young girl. While they are still quiet Kat has an overwhelming urge to pray for this child.

"Heavenly Father, I thank you for this child in my arms. I thank you that she is alive. I ask your father to give her strength and wisdom for the struggle that she is going through. Father God, I ask that you bring peace to her and send her someone who will love her unconditionally. Amen" Kat wipes her eyes, and she looks down and realizes Crystal is asleep. She lays her gently against the couch pillows and covers her with a throw blanket. As she is leaving the room, she notices the three Drs sitting and waiting for her.

"Oh, I'm sorry if I made you wait." She bows her head in apology.

"you're not late we didn't have a session this morning. We were supposed to have a group session, but you rocked the other patient to sleep." Jae ruffles her hair smiling.

"Oh, I'm sorry." Kat wonders how much they heard.

"it's ok you got her to open and to talk. We were not told her parents as to why she wanted to commit suicide. Now we know without even having to ask her. Not only that, but this is also the first time she has slept in two days. "Dr smith informs her.

This whole time Ki is just looking at her. He is not sure what to say to her. He has never seen this side of her. He always knew she would be a good mother. Is this how she treated Jae when they were in the hospital. Is this why Jae has always cared so much about her. He knows it is strange that he has not said anything, but he needs to talk to Jae.

"Think you deserve a day off today you may go anywhere you want on clinic grounds. Just make sure that one of the nurses is close by please." He turns to Jae and motions him to follow him.

Once they get to his office Ki turns to him" tell me about how she was when you were with her in the hospital that first time?"

"Why do you want to hear that now?" Jae looks at his brother puzzled as to what he wants to know.

"I never saw her this way. I know she has always put others first. I saw a different side of her and am curious if she was always this way and I just didn't notice." Ki sits on the sofa waiting for Jae to tell him.

"When she looked at me and said you came back, you're here. I was lost, I did not know what she meant. I had never met her before, so I knew she mistook me for someone. I fell for her the moment she looked at me. She was so white and so weak. I felt helpless but knew I wanted her to live. When she woke up the next day. She was still weak, but she was different. I almost thought that I imagined the night before. When later that morning when we were playing video games. She asked me why I was there. She became terribly upset with me because she said that doing drugs was a stupid thing to do. Then she got this far away look in her eyes. When she started talking it was like I was talking to grandma. She was so soft spoken and was telling me about her cousin who was killed by being high and drunk. He was wasted and was hit by a car. They did not find his body for a few days. He had been knocked into a ditch and the driver thought he hit a deer. She said that he stayed wasted and that the loving sweet boy who she loved became a stranger. A person unrecognizable. She was crying telling me that I should be ashamed of not loving my family enough to live. She put her arms around me and patted my back as if I were a child instead of her. I do not ever remember crying before that day. She made me not only cry but look inside myself. I never really knew why I let her so close. She just made me feel warm and loved. That was when I called you all to come visit. I never guessed that she was your angel. She made me want to not only live but to become someone that would make our family proud." Ki was shocked at the emotion in his brother's voice.

"How is it that I love her so much still and never knew that side of her. I always knew she was loving, kind and playful. I never knew that she could do that and get someone to tell everything, and they would not even realize it. That she could wrap them in such warmth like a blanket. Why did she never show me this side?"

Jae looks at his brother and busts out laughing" she never showed you that side because you never needed her to. She was always a little mother but with you she was a soulmate, she was your love who you always took care of. The only time you needed her to take care of you was when you had a fever. She stayed up with you all night. She bathed you with cool water and spoke softly to you all night till your fever broke. Mama tried to get her to leave because you were only in your boxers, but she said you were her responsibility. That you were her husband and that she needed to take care of you. Please ask the manager if you have any questions regarding breaks. You never realized that she stayed with you the whole night. She was such an adorable adult that night bossing everyone around and telling us when to leave. When I went to check on you her grandmother called to say that she was coming to get her. The two of you were completely wrapped around each other, your head on her chest and she was stroking your hair. If it were not for her being completely clothed, I would have thought, you two had sex that night.in fact when you woke up you couldn't understand why you only had your boxers on and why you slept so well."

"You mean I literally slept through having her with me all night?" Ki sank into the coach and closed his eyes.

"Yep, you did but it was that night Mama started thinking that we should be separated till she was older. She saw how attached she was and how even in your feverish state you only looked for her. It was also the same night that we all truly realized that you were the one she loved more than a brother. She always showed concern for us and gave us love but you were her everything. That night she cried and prayed for your fever to go down. She did everything humanly possible to comfort you and to break your fever. Dad said that there was no way she was so young for the first time he saw her as an adult. "Jae just watched his brother as he processed this information.

"We missed so much. That bastard took so much from us when he hurt her. For the first time in my life, I want to truly torture and kill someone.

Now it is too late she is married and has children. She will never leave them, and I don't even know if she still loves me." Ki puts his head in his hands grieving over a life that was lost. Jae slips out of the room leaving his brother to his grief and thoughts.

Kat wanders around the clinic looking at the beautiful and peaceful décor of each space. She notices each room is filled with the nuances of nature and the 4 seasons. She comes to a sunroom it is the most beautiful space she has ever seen. The room is like a garden, in the center of the room is a large tree. The room looks like it was built around a garden. The tree is a cherry tree. Throughout the room there are gardenias, orchids, roses, holly bushes, some are in bloom while others are waiting for spring, she looks in awe throughout the room touching every plant. Wondering how amazing it will be when the plants are in full bloom. She sits on the bench by the waterfall and pond. While staring at the water Kat begins to pray.

Lord thank you so much for your blessings and for the people you have brought into my life. I thank you for the chance to talk to Crystal and hope that I was able to give her some peace. Thank you for letting me be here at this point in my life. I do not know where you are leading me or what it is you want me to do. I just ask that you give me the strength and patience to do your will. While remembering everything it makes my heart ache for the things that might have been. Even still I cannot imagine my life without my husband and children. I love them dearly and miss them so much. I ask that you help my husband with his temper. He used to not be this way. He was always a little gruff but never violent till now. I do not want my children to grow up thinking its ok to be abused or to abuse others. As far as Jae and Ki go, I have been so grateful to have them back. I just do not know what my feelings for them are. I know I loved them before and still do. The problem is that a made a vow before you to love honor and never forsake my husband. Show me the path I am to be on. Show me what I am to do. Amen

Jae finds Kat sitting in the sunroom her head is bowed and she is crying. As he gets closer, he hears her softly whispering. He knows she is praying so he sits quietly under the cherry tree just listening to her pray. He remembers how much he used to love listening to her talk to God. She always talked to him as if he were a person sitting beside her. The first time he heard her he thought she was talking to a ghost or was crazy. Then when he heard her say "say thank you God for listening" he understood what she was doing. She was always so worried about what others thought and felt. She never did what she wanted to do. Thinking back, she never asked to do anything that she enjoyed just because she wanted to. She always picked things that she knew they enjoyed and went along for the ride. I bet her husband does not even realize how much she has done this for him as well.

CHAPTER 29

Kat reveals a secret.

Kat turns around and sees Jae sitting under the cherry tree. He sat there and fell asleep. she smiles to herself as she picks up a bowl beside the small pond. Quietly she walks over to him and begins to flick water on his face. Watching him wipe his face and stirring she begins to giggle.

Jae wakes with water dripping on his face and he hears Kat giggling. He smiles and before she can react, he grabs her and pulls her to his lap.

"I got you now. You are an in-trouble angel. I'm not letting you go till you answer my questions," he says while grinning at her.

"Ya, you let me go it's not proper for me to be on your lap. "She replies.

"Then I guess you should make a point to answer my questions quickly." He tells her seriously this time as he shifts her more comfortably in his lap.

"Ok what do you want to know?" she asks quietly while she lays her head on his shoulder.

"Why did you not tell anyone you were being hurt? If you had let us know we would have taken you away before it got worse."

"I couldn't he told me that if I got you all involved, he would hunt you like you were deer. He used to target practice every time he thought I had even thought of saying anything. He even shot at my dad while hunting a few times. If he had killed one of you, I do not think I could have lived with the guilt. I had to protect everyone. He would beat my sister. He would tie up his infant son in front of me and even cut him to prove that he would kill anyone that he chose to. If he had me to torture, he left everyone else alone." Kat confesses to him he could hear the terror in her voice as if it were still happening. He holds her tighter and starts to rock her to calm her a little.

"Did he ever tell you why he chose you to torture?" jae asks while stroking her hair.

"He said that he loved my sister and knew he could have her. On the other hand, he has been obsessed with wanting to take and consume my innocence and light. He said that no one was ever going to have me but him and that I would be ruined when he was done with me." Kat whispers.

"I don't understand something why your dad didn't do anything to him when he found out?" jae looks at her puzzled.

"My mom didn't want to make a fuss and didn't believe me because my sister told her that I had been flirting and trying to take him away from her for months. This was the lie he told my sister the day that he knew he made a mistake taking our friend's daughter with us. he raped me with her watching using her as leverage to remind me he oversaw my life." Kat buries her head in his shoulder hiding her face.

"How old was she." He whispers.

"6 years old she was someone I loved a lot and used to stay close with. I felt so sick that he exposed her to such dirtiness at such a young age. This was something that she was not able to forget. She asked me before she got married. What happened that day and I told her everything? I thought for sure she would hate me." Kat looks at him with imploring eyes.

"Exactly what happened that day?" Jae asks.

"It was my nephew's birthday he was 2 and we had a lot of people at the house. My mom asked me to go to the store and pick up a few things. Since she was sending me with him, I vehemently refused and argued with her in front of everyone that I did not want to go. Everyone started telling me I was being ridiculous that I should not be so selfish as to expect my sister to leave her guests. He grabbed me as I was going to my room to hide away. He told me that if I did not go, he would take someone else and give them a taste of pain. He looked towards her. He called my mom and told her it was ok he would just take one of the kids. I told him OK if he leaves her alone, I will go. He then made a point of asking her to go with us. He stopped at his house on the way and told me to go inside and get some extra clothes for the baby. I was terrified to leave her in the car with him, so I took her with me inside. He follows us and corners me in the bathroom. He grabbed me by the neck and squeezed it. I cannot breathe. He then utters to me. "I was testing you to see if you trusted me. to see if you would leave her with me. You failed now you must pay." he slams my head against the mirror and breaks it. I cry out in pain. I did not even notice that he had brought her into the bathroom with him. I heard her cries and stopped struggling. I looked at him I could see he was even more turned on by the fact that she was there crying and watching him. I beg him to please send her out and do not let her see. He just laughed and told me to do as I was told, and he would not touch her. So, I did everything he wanted so that he would not touch her. After he was done, we went to the store and got what my mom wanted as if nothing happened. Later that night when her dad went to hug her good night she began to scream and cry telling him what she saw. He called my dad. I left and went to my uncle's house in the middle of the party so that I could hide from everyone. My dad called my uncle and told him that he was coming to get me. When he asked why my dad told him that he needed to find out what was done to me on that day. My uncle was furious that someone dared to touch me and wanted to kill whoever it was. My dad listened to my mom and let it drop." Kat tells him to try to see his reaction without him noticing.

"I don't understand how your dad could just let it drop as if nothing happened to you. How can the man that my mother was terrified would send us to jail for even being around you let someone hurt you so badly?" Jae asks her.

"My mom stopped him. She saw only my sister's anger at me and thought I was lying. She felt like I was trying to get attention from them. You know they found out not long before my graduation. I had to attend graduation with them there and act as if nothing happened. I was not allowed to say anything to anyone. My Dads mother and sisters came down and I was not even allowed to spend more than a few minutes with them. I was sent home after graduation and sent to my room while everyone in the house went to my aunts to visit with them. They came to see me, but I only got to see them for a few minutes. Then a few weeks later my mom sent me away because my dad would not let my brother-in-law in the house. She missed my nephew and sister too much. So, while dad was at work they would come and spend the day with mom, and she would make sure they had food and money. When I went to stay with my mom's friend, she asked me about my nightmares that were keeping me awake at night. I told her the truth about what happened. She called my mom, and my mom then sent me away to my dad's family. She told them not to believe me about anything and that I was just trying to get some attention. My Aunt Bob and Rita knew better after the first night. They knew that something had happened. I still could not say anything about what was going on because he told me before I left that it was not over that he would still hunt everyone I loved and kill them. He just needed for people to get used to him being around again and believe that I was a slut and liar. Then things would go back to the way they should be like before. So, for the next year I was still living in terror over being hurt and having to protect my family. "Kat explained.

"it's getting dark we should take you to your room for dinner now. My brother is looking for us." Jae says as he lifts her up as he stands. He begins to carry her to the door.

"I can walk you know." Kat tells him trying to wiggle out of his arms.

"Stay still or you're going to make us both fall. It has been a long time since I got to hold you or carry you so just be still. Just pretend you're sleeping, and no one will say anything. "He tells her sternly to make sure she understands he is not ready to put her down.

They meet up with Dr. Smith on the way back to get dinner. She is surprised to see Jae carrying Kat.

"Is something wrong with Kat?" she inquires while looking very closely at Kat. She can tell she is not really sleeping. She switches her gaze to Jae. She knows something is up since he cannot look her in the eye. Dr. Smith crosses her arms across her chest and demands. "Kat, I know you are not asleep why is Dr. Park carrying you,"

"It's my fault I saw her in the sunroom, and we were talking, and I just picked her up and refused to put her down. This was one of the few times I was able to have her to myself in a long time. I just didn't want the moment to end yet." Jae explains.

Just then Ki walks out of the elevator and sees them. He looks closely at Kat and Jae without even being told he knows what happened. He smiles and decides to embarrass his brother a little bit.

"Kat did you fall for Jae's trick again. You know you may not remember this, but he used to carry you around like you were a sack of potatoes when you were younger. He would trick you into sitting on his lap and then refuse to let you go. He either would make you pretend to be sleeping or hurt just so he could carry you around. It got so bad that Mama and Grandma called Uncle to make sure that you were healthy. They would make you all kinds of Korean soups and drinks to make you stronger. Which was it this time?"

Kat tries to wiggle out of his arms, but he still is holding her tightly.

"Sleeping actually, I woke him up by flinging water on him and he is getting even." She reply's

Ki busts out laughing remembering all the water fights these two had. He cannot help himself. Kat stares at him mesmerized by his beauty. She cannot remember the last time she saw him looking so carefree and happy. A picture of them together flashes into her mind. He is laughing up at her with his arms out to her. He looked so young and happy in this moment. She taps Jae on the shoulder, and he finally puts her down. She walks over to him not taking her eyes off his face. She takes his hands in hers. He stares at her this is the first time since meeting again that she has on her own came to him. She reaches out her hand to touch his face. Touching every line. Smiling up at him she reaches up and pulls his head close to hers. Placing his forehead on hers. He hears her whisper.

"I'm sorry that I have caused you so much pain. That you have not been able to laugh and be happy for so long. The only thing I ever wanted was for you to be happy and safe. I never thought that because you met me that your life became so full of pain. As much as I love you. I wish I could go back and make sure you never met me so that you could be happy." By this time tears were streaming down her face unchecked. He reaches out and gently wipes them away.

"Don't ever say that again. You changed my life and that of my family for the better. If I had not met, you, Jae would have become an addict and dead by now carrying out nothing in his life. I would be dead or in prison. Kris and James both were cruel and cold before they met you. They may have died but they knew love and was happy before they died. My parents were so closed off they barely spoke until you walked into our lives. You are the reason any of us knew happiness and love. Do you know that after you came to our house? My parents not only got closer they even showed each other affection. Before you came, they never even touched each other. Each of us were products of my father's drunken mating with our mother, not once did they care for each other. After you came to our house, they began to love each other and even moved into the same room. Yes, our life was hell after you left. Yes, we were unhappy but not because we met you. We were unhappy because you were in pain and not safe. My mother loved you so much that she cried for months because you were not beside her. Yes, she was angry when my brothers died and said somethings in anger, but she regretted them the second that she said them. She used to go and watch you from a distance. She even used to send your grandmother money to make sure that you had pretty things. She knew that you did without so that your siblings got what they wanted. You were and always will be our family no matter what the situation is. That is what you taught us. That love doesn't go away it just sometimes changes." He pulls her into his arms and cradles her like a child. Dr. Smith clears her throat reminding them that they have an audience.

"I think that it's time for dinner and even though we did not plan a session today between our talk in the sunroom and now I think that is enough for today." Jae touches his brother's shoulder letting him know that they need to talk later. The 4 of them start to walk back to the dining room to have dinner when they notice crystal standing in the doorway.

"Kat are you the girl in all the pictures in my room? I was told that Dr. Ki drew them of his angel. Are you her?' she asks?

"Yes, crystal she is the girl in all the pictures in the clinic. They are different ages of her life. She is the inspiration for everything in this clinic. Every room is a different side of her personality. Her likes and feelings. I designed the clinic to bring balance comfort, joy, peace and love. All the things she brought to me. I would not be who I am without her. she is my angel and always will be." Ki answers her.

"I love my room. Would you like to see it Kat I think it will show you exactly why these two Dr, s love you so much? "Crystal asks her.

"Yes, I would love to. would you like to have dinner with us?" Kat asks crystal.

The 5 of them head into dinner. That night dinner was filled with laughter and playing. Crystal opened to the dr. s about her home life and about the man who hurt her. She laughed and played as if she were a child. They were having so much fun you could hear the laughter throughout the entire clinic. The night guard was smiling most of the night because he had never heard of the clinic so full of life and the mood so light and fun. He wonders if the dr. s will tell her who he is or not. Kat has worked her magic again without even trying.

CHAPTER 30

Secret room

The next morning Kat had breakfast in Crystals room. Crystal was overly excited to show her all the different sketches and paintings in her room. When she walked in, she noticed on one wall a series of paintings. They were of a small child angel. She was feeding and grooming different horses in two. The next one was a young boy sitting on one side of wall sleeping with her on the other side sleeping. the 4th was of the angel reading on a branch of a cherry tree in full bloom. The last was the young boy cradling the angel in a corn field,

"These are of when Ki first met me. He was visiting his grandmother who was my neighbor. The first 3 were of me in his grandmother's stables. The next one was when he caught me hiding in the cherry tree reading. The last one is when he saved my life. I overdosed and hid in the corn field by our house. I was 7 at That time. It was the last time I saw him until I was 13." I explained to her. While looking at the pictures I realize how talented Ki really is. He has enough sketches and paintings to have a gallery show. He could have been a world renown artist.

"Wow I find it so amazing that he can draw and paint so beautifully. He is so talented as well as an amazing doctor. The paintings throughout my room are so wonderful. There is one that is my favorite come to the bedroom with me please." Crystal shows Kat to the bedroom. There on the walls are sketches of the girl as a young adult. She is dressed in a long evening gown. In each one she dances with a different partner. In all of them the look on their faces is pure happiness. Kat walks over and touches each one. She begins to cry as she touches them. She looks at the large one over the bed. There is a family portrait. There is everyone together. Without realizing it she climbed onto the bed standing face to face with the painting. Crystal tries to get her attention but no use she is lost in her own world. Crystal slips out and goes to get the doctors.

The three doctors slip quietly into Crystals room. They watch her for a while to make sure that she is ok. Finally, Ki speaks to her." Angels are you ok.?"

"Yes, I'm fine I'm just remembering them. I have remembered so many things today. I miss them so much. I keep thinking about how disappointed Appa would be in me. I have not done anything that I promised him I would do. I did not go to university or do anything with my life. All I have done is exist. I am not the good daughter that he thought I was. Why did you put such personal things in the clinic? Why not keep them at your home.?" She turns to look at him.

"I know you don't recognize this place it is our old home I just turned it into a clinic. The room you are in is your old room. I still live here I have never moved. The rooms are just everyone old bedrooms converted into mini apartment type living quarters." He informed her.

"How about we go down for lunch now. I'm sure we have invaded Crystal's privacy long enough." Dr. Smith touched Kat's arm to get her out of bed. Kat looks around and then she walks out to the hallway. Counting doors, she walks to one door, opening it she walks in. The three Dr's looks at each other wondering what she is looking for. The room she goes into is their grandmother's old room. They follow her. When they walk in, they see her over in the corner where their grandmothers' closet is. She closes her eyes and opens the door. Inside it is empty since no one is using the room. She gets on her knees and starts feeling around the wall. She pushes the corner of the back wall, and it slides open. Standing up she pulls the door completely open. Behind the closet is another room. She goes inside. They hear her laugh loudly, looking inside the closet the two brothers are in shock. They never knew there was another room behind this one. Following her inside they see that inside there are trunks and antique furniture.

"What is this place and how did you know it was here?" Jae asks Kat.

"Grandma showed me this place when I stayed here. This is where I used to hide when we played hide n seek. That is why you never could find me. These are all her treasures from Korea. Everything she brought from there is here. All your family's pictures are here. She brought me here to show me her hairpins and old dresses. Oh, wait let me show you something. Kat excitedly goes over to another door and opens it as a walk-in closet. Inside are garment bags hanging. She brings out two bags and opens them. Inside is a traditional Korean wedding dress. In the other is a man's suit. She smiles and gently touches them. These were grandma and grandpa wedding clothes. She wanted us to be married to them. She has a suit for each of the husbands in the closet. They each were grandpa's suits. She used to dress me up in here in traditional Korean clothes and tell me about grandpa." Kat tells them.

"Why did we not know about this place?" Ki asks.

"Grandma said you all were not interested in the past or your ancestors. Did you know that you get your talent for drawing from him? In Korea he was a well-known artist. She said he was very much sought after. Even by nobility. She told me about everyone and who each of you took after.

She spent hours telling me about them. She said James took after her brother. The one who raised your father. She said he was very meticulous and precise in everything he did. He was very cold and stern. He took duty and honor very seriously. Kris took after her younger brother. He was very free and mischievous. He was always in trouble with your great grandfather and his older brother. He loved to play and sing. Jae, she said was the most like her. He always had a soft heart. He just was never shown how to express his emotions properly. She said that Appa was a mixture of everyone. And because of this he felt conflicted at times." Kat told them she walked over to the wardrobe and took out a stack of books, some were paper that was bound with string while others were leather. She places them carefully on the table. "These are the annuals of her family; she says they go back as far as the Joseon period. The first ancestor started them when he learned to read and write. It tells your family history up to her. Though I do not know if you will be able to read them, they are written in Korean and none of you learned to read Korean as far as I remember. Some are too delicate to even be opened they go back more than 100 years." Absent mindedly tells them as she continues to walk around the room taking things out and telling them what they are as if she is giving a guided tour. Ki is watching her closely. She has extraordinarily little expression. He realizes that she is lost in a memory. Telling them word for word as if his grandmother was standing there telling her what to say. He looks at the other two doctors to see if they have noticed. How is this possible? She is not under hypnosis or in pain why is she like this? Jae nods at him when their eyes meet. He has noticed it also. They continue to watch her as she goes through everything and suddenly, she walks over to the small chaise against the wall and lays down. within seconds she is asleep. The three doctors go to the outer room. Dr. smith looks at the brothers wondering what they are feeling and thinking.

"Ok how did she do that? How could she be like that? Nothing traumatic happened here at the house so why was she like that." Dr. Smith asked them.

"I have no clue. Crystal said that she was mesmerized by your paintings, especially the family one with her in it. Could that be it? She said she had been remembering so many things while looking at it. What I do not understand is how come no one ever told us about that room and she knew exactly where and how to get inside it. Why did we not know it was there even after you remolded the house." Jae asks Ki.

"I never allowed them to touch grandmother's room. She hated anyone going in there. She hated having anything touched. So, it felt wrong to change anything other than to pack her things up per her instructions. Even in her will she never mentioned the hidden room or what was in it. "Ki says while running his fingers through his hair in frustration.

"Maybe all the memories and emotions were just too much for her to process at once." Dr smith says as she turns to go back inside the room to check on Kat. She goes inside and looks around the main bedroom. It is so interesting. a mixture of Korean and American antiques. After a while she hears her talking to someone. She peaks inside the hidden room. There Kat is sitting on the chaise talking to a photo.

"Grandma I have kept your secret. I hope that you are well in heaven and enjoying your afterlife. I hope they do not hate me for not telling them everything. I told them exactly as you told me to. I hope that you get what you wanted. I do not think I can take much more heart ache. You know they loved you so much I am sure they will understand why you kept everything secret. I just hope they do not become hurt by this. I feel like I have lied to them about why this room exists. You know that if they ask me, I will have to tell them. That I cannot lie to them. I hope that as they go through these treasures of yours that they will figure it out. this way I will not have to break my promise to you or lie to them." She gently kisses the photo and holds it to her heart. Tears coming down her face as if her heart was broken. The Dr gets the feeling that this room holds a lot of secrets that have nothing to do with Kat except that she was entrusted with them. She wonders why she was the one to keep the secrets. Dr Smith decides to sit on the bed outside of the secret room and wait for Kat to come out.

Kat, thinking that no one is around goes over to the chest in the corner of the hidden room. She opens it to unpack it. Inside of the chest is a small casket looking box. She picks it up and walks out of the room. Surprised, when she walks back into the bedroom, she sees Dr Smith sitting there waiting for her.

"Kat, can we talk for a moment please?' she asks patting the space beside her.

Walking over to the bed she sits down. Wondering what she is going to say now.

"The hospital called and says that it's safe to go back now. I want to ask you if you want to go back there, or do you want to stay here?" looking at her closely to see if she can gage her response.

"I will go wherever you tell me is the best place for me to be. I am comfortable here away from all the sneers and gossip. I also know that the longer I stay here the harder it will be for me to leave. I want to go home to my kids, but we both know that is not going to happen. I miss taking care of them and having them with me. I really wish I knew what I am to do. You know when I used to come here, I was always happy and safe.

No one teased me or yelled at me. No one ever spoke harshly or down to me. I never wanted to be apart from them. Then my world was destroyed, and everything went black. Now I have some light again in my life and I keep waiting for the other shoe to drop. I feel like my life is nothing but a pawn to other people." She tells me quietly.

"Why do you say that?" Dr smith says as she pulls Kat's hair out of her face.

"When I was a kid nothing, I did was right. I felt like no one wanted me. As I got older, I found out that I was useful. Then people would want me around. My grandmothers and aunts used me to help do chores. My cousins used me to take the blame and punishment for everything. My sister and brother never wanted me around except when I had money or to do things for them. I have never felt like my life is mine. Even now I do not feel like it is my life. I feel like it will not matter what my decisions are they will be wrong. I don't know what to do" Kat covers her face with her hands and begins to cry. Her whole body is shaking from the force of her tears. The agony and the depth of her pain shocks Dr Smith. She had heard her wake up screaming and crying. She has seen her breakdown in her sessions but never this raw hopelessness. before she realizes that they are not alone. Ki is sitting in front of Kat holding her and speaking softly to her. She does not understand what he is saying, but it is calming her down. Their bond is so close that it is not hard to see why he is fighting so hard for her. Ki picks Kat up and carries her out of the room. Dr Smith follows them to Kats room. He gently lays her on the bed. that when Dr Smith realizes that her patient has cried herself into a deep sleep. Ki shoos her out of the room. once outside motions for her to follow him. He takes her up a set of stairs that looks like it is going to the attic. Once inside he asks her to sit down. It is the attic but has a large skylight in the center of the room flooding it with moonlight. he turns on the lights and she see its and office.

"Before you say anything I know that I should not keep coddling her. She has had so much emotional trauma since we started, I just want to comfort her a little when she becomes hysterical. when she is in that state is when she does stupid things like trying to kill herself. I don't want to sedate her, and I don't want to have her become suicidal either." He clarifies for her before she can even scold her.

"I brought you up here because I wanted to show you a few things that no one else has seen." He walks over to the bookshelf and behind a false panel opens a safe. He pulls out a large photo album and hands it to her. Inside are photographs of Kat as a teenager. Some were of her smiling happily. Then she turns to the next series of photos. They are of her bloodied and beaten. in various stages of undressing. You could tell that they were taken at different times. More than 20 pages of photos of her looking like she had been used as a punching bag. Then the next pages were of her looking like she was just a zombie with dirty hair and clothes. Eventually she looked normal again smiling and clean.

Dr Smith looks up at him and asks" What is all this how did you get these?"

"The first ones were taken when we would see her and at school. The next ones were taken when she would go to my uncle to get patched up. He would take pictures of her before he could clean her up so that if she ever decided to allow him to call the police, she would have the evidence she needed. The next ones I took when I would go to watch her from afar at school and such. The last ones are of her when she started dating her husband. I quit watching her then because I thought she would be ok again." He explained.

"Why are you showing me these now?" holding her breath not sure if she wants an answer or not.

"I wanted you to see firsthand with real proof of what she is hiding from. The memories that are behind those doors are there in front of you. I do not know when or how she will ever be able to open them and face what happened to her. She will be very fragile when she does. Therefore, we have been so gentle and protective of her and reluctant to let her go back. I wanted you to see these so that you will understand that it is not selfishness on our part. It is for her survival. I want to show these to her husband, but I know she will never agree. I want him to understand for her survival as well as the wellbeing of their family she needs to continue treatment and get support from home." She can see by the expression on his face he is being honest with her. All her doubts are gone about the real reasons behind their obsession with helping her.

"I will contact her husband and see what he wants to do." She tells him as she gets up to go to her room.

After some time sitting at his desk ki makes his way back downstairs. He notices that the door to his grandmother's room is open, and a light is on. He looks inside and there sitting on the bed is Jae, he has a small box in his hand.

"What have you got there?" he asks as he sits down beside his brother on the bed.

"I was sitting on the bed when I came back. I have been sitting here wondering if I should open it. Kat must have taken it after we left. "He hands him the box. Ki looks at it and it is a black casket shape with beautiful mother of pearl designs on it.

"Well since there are only two of us left it's up to us to unravel that room and its secrets. So here is for the first one." He opens the box and inside is a key, a ring and a letter, the letter says.

My dears

If you are reading this, then it means you have found my secret room. The only person who knows about this room is your father, Kat and I. Inside this room are all the treasures from Korea. It has all the information on our family as well as a few things that have been passed down from generation to generation. You will find journals that have a full listing of my family side since the beginning of time. Inside these journals are also stories of our families lives in different time periods. You are going to find old clothes some you will recognize others are so old they may just fall apart when you touch them. This key and ring will unlock a special box that is hidden in the house. Inside that box is a secret that part of me wants you to know and part hopes you never know. It is up to you if you want to find it and find out the secret. Kat knows where the box is and what it holds inside. Telling you this I know will not help since she has forgotten all about us. If you do not want anything from this room or need help translating the journals here is a card of a man at the museum that can help you.

Your loving grandmother

"I wonder if we can get Kat to show us where the box is. "Jae asks.

"I'm wondering why she was taking this box and not telling us." Ki answers

"I guess that is for us to find out tomorrow. I'm off to bed goodnight." Jae pats his brother on the shoulder and goes back to his room.

CHAPTER 31

Treasure hunt

The next morning the clinic is filled with tension as the brothers wait for Kat to wake up. Dr smith walks into the room and looks at them looking very perplexed.

"Good morning, what is on the agenda today?" she asks as she takes her seat at the table.

"We are going on a treasure hunt if Kat ever wakes up. We found this box on the bed last night after we put her to bed in her room. I want to know why she was taking it without telling us," Ki says staring at the box.

"I heard her talking to a photo yesterday after everyone left the room. She was saying that she would keep her promise to keep your grandmother's secret. That she hoped that you two would forgive her for not telling you everything. I was thinking about its last night. You know she was very precise in what she was showing you and telling you. like a script. I wonder if that is why she was so emotionless when telling you about the things in the room for fear of giving away your grandmother's secret." Dr smith explained to them.

"Good morning, I'm sorry I overslept and kept everyone waiting." Kat walks in with Crystal. Ki quickly took the box out of sight from Kat.

"Shall we start the day. We have a lot to go over today." Jae starts the group.

Over the next few hours, the patient's day goes as planned. Between group therapy and individual tasks. It was midafternoon before anyone really had a break. Kat went back to grandma's room to look for the box she had left. She could not find it, so she slipped into the secret room to look. Still no box. While she was in the secret room, she could not help herself, she had to look for her dress. She begins rummaging through the old trunks in the bottom of the closet. She was so lost in her task she never heard Jae come in.

"What are you looking for and how did you move these heavy chests?" Kat jumps at the sound of his voice "looking for a box I forgot and when I couldn't find it, I wanted to see if I could find my dress." She offhand answers him. Not even looking up from her task. Ki has joined them now and sees the mess she has made.

"WHAT ARE YOU DOING?" he yells at her.

"I am looking for a small black box and my dress. So, stop yelling and help me find it please." She glares at him."

"Is this the box. /" he shows her the box. She squeals and wades through the big mess she made and walks over and takes it from him.

"Grandma entrusted me with this, and I will keep it thank you." She haughtily tells him.

", she wrote us a letter that was placed in this box, and she wants us to find the one that the key goes to. Will you tell us where it is?" Ki holds up the letter for her to see. She grabs it and reads it verifying that it is ok to take them to find the box.

"Ok then let us go get your coats on it could be chilly unless you changed the wine cellar." She tells them as she begins to walk out of the room.

"What about this mess?" Jae yells as he follows them.

"I will clean it up after I find my dress." Kat tells him.

"What dress are you looking for?" They both ask at the same time.

"The one that she brought for me to wear that last night I never got to see it. I was hoping she kept it. I know it sound crazy looking for something that I do not even know what it looks like, she said that James designed it and she had it special made. I wanted to see it so much. The jewelry was in the room I saw yesterday. All the clothes so far are things I remember" she explains as she walks down the stairs of the wine cellar. She walks over to the oldest part of the cellar and looks for a panel. She starts moving some sheets from the old paintings on that wall.

"You know I never knew why she had these large painting on the walls between the cabinets." Jae says as he helps take the sheets down.

"They are hidden closets. Your grandmother was always afraid after coming here from Korea after the war. She had cabinets made the doors are the painting and you must have a special key to open them." Kat looks at the painting in the center. She opens the box, takes the key and the ring out. with the two she opens the closet. When the door opened, she reached in and turned on the light. She looks at in this one is all her darkest secrets things she never even told your dad. I must ask you to please remember that she loved you all more than her life. What was in here was something she always wanted to stay hidden. She told me about it because she thought that if we did get married. We would have children and she wanted me to know why you look different from your brothers." She looks at them.

Inside the small room no bigger than a walk-in closet are stacks of journals. They are written during the war. The two men take them out so that they can read them on another shelf is stacks of cedar boxes. Looking inside they see beautiful silk gowns ornately embroidered. With beautiful jade hair pieces. There is a photo hanging on the wall of their grandmother. She is in a kimono not a Korean dress. Their uncle and father stand there with her in her arms. She is holding a smaller child for no more than a few months.

"Kat do you know her secret without us having to read these journals?" Jae asks her.

"Yes, I know it. Are you sure you don't want to read her story instead of me just telling you/" she asks?

"I want to know before I read her story so that I will know if I need to read it," Jae answers.

"I will tell you only if you both agree." She looks to KI to see what he wants her to do.

Ki nods his head at her to tell them.

"Grandmother was taken as a comfort woman after your grandfather was killed. The general who took her wanted her from the moment her first saw her, he is the reason your grandfather was killed. He knew that she came from a wealthy important family. He had done business with your great-grandfather before the war started. Unlike some he treated her more like a wife than a comfort woman. She was someone he cared for and respected, even though in front of others he treated her just like they would any other comfort woman as if she were no better than a sex slave. In private however he read to her taught her to read in Japanese .in her one journal she describes the abuse she faced at his hands. She told me when she heard what happened to me. that she understood what I was going through. She told me that she suffered and often wanted to die. But she had to survive to get back to her sons. She said she was lucky compared to the other comfort women. She only had one-man rape and beat her. The others had many every day. Many did not survive or became barren after the abuse. Many were killed if they did not miscarry after taking the abortion herbs and some died from their bodies giving out from disease and abuse. others were killed just because they were not needed any longer. When She became pregnant with his child a few months after being sent to Japan. He would not let anyone give her the herbs that could cause miscarriages. He wanted their child. She gave birth to a little girl. That little girl was Ki mother. She died in childbirth. Your father was nowhere to be found. Your mother came home from college and was already 6 months pregnant. When she went into labor she started hemorrhaging. By the time the ambulance came she had already passed. When she died mama, Claire had just miscarried a child and became attached to you. So, Appa and mama Claire registered you as their child. They said you had been born at home and Dr P filled out the paperwork. They swore to never let anyone know so that you would never feel different. They later found out that your father was a Japanese man that was a married man here on business. He fell in love with your mom. They lived together until his visa expired and he had to leave. She never told him about you, and no one even knows his name. Grandmother told me that this was her shame to bear no one else's. She was worried that our children could have more Japanese features than Korean. Inside one of the journals are a few pictures of your mom. Now you must understand after the war. Koreans hated the Japanese and to have been in a relationship with one was considered as betrayal. For your mom and grandmother to go back to Korea would have been met with cruelty and shame. That is why your uncle had to bring your family here to live where people did not know the difference in Asian features. This way no one would know that she had ever been a comfort woman or that her daughter was part Japanese. This is also why she was afraid to go back, it is also why she never wanted you all to go to Japan. She was afraid someone would comment on your looks." She explains to them. Watching them wondering what they are thinking. Wondering what they are feeling.

"So, I'm more Japanese than Korean and my mother and father are not my mother and father. I have a family that I know nothing about." KI slides to the floor sitting there with his head in his hands. "If we had married, would you still have kept these secrets?" he asks, looking at Kat. She walks over to him and sits beside him pulling him into her arms with his head on her chest.

"I honestly don't know because it was not my secrets to tell. You where their child from the moment mama Claire held you in her arms. I know this because she told me so. She told me that you saved her life. Without your care she would never have been able to go on. To me none of this is shameful or needed to be kept secret. To them they were more worried that you would feel different and alone. I had already told mama Claire that she needed to tell you that I would not be able to keep secrets from you. Then everything got messed up and I was sent away from you. for the longest time I thought she sent me away because she was afraid, I would tell you and she would lose you. I never realized that was my last day to see you for so many years. "Kat sees the tears in his eyes. She wipes them gently.

"You know these secrets changes nothing. You are still you. You are still who you are. It does not matter who gave birth to you. It only matters who loved you. The people in this house loved you beyond any measure. You were their blood; you were their child. Your brothers loved you and cherished you so much. They were always so protective of you because you were so much smaller than them. More delicate like a flower. That is what James used to say. He used to tell me that we had better have nothing but girls because our children would be too pretty to ever be boys. Do not ever doubt their love for you. That brother of yours standing right there. He has always looked up to you and loved you. When he was in the hospital you were the one, he talked to me about most. You were the one he called. He always told me that the two of you had to stick together because Kris and James were already a pair. Nothing has changed by knowing these things. Do not reject their love and devotion because of these secrets. you were and always will be their son."

Jae looking and listening to her tell his brother the very words he wanted to say. Reminded him that she always knew what he was thinking and feeling. He sits on the other side of his brother and claps him on the shoulder.

"You know what she says is true because I was just going to say the same thing. You know we could always read each other's minds. Jae smiles at his brother. "You know you were just complaining that you have never needed her to comfort you. So how does it feel to be comforted by an angel? "

"Go away I want to have her to myself for a while. It is so nice to be this close to her again. For the three of us to be this close again. "He always pushes his brother playfully.

"Oh, but we are not done yet. Would you like to open the other closets?" Kat held up the key.

"Yes, lets open the rest of them to see what's behind them" jae helps Kat up and the three of them go out and open the other three closets. In one they found Mama Clare's collectables. Things she did not want anyone to touch. Her old dolls from her childhood and the boy's old infant clothes. In a chest in the corner were clothes and on top a note.

My darling son Ki

If you have found this chest, then that means you have found mother's hidden room. Forgive us for never telling you about your birth. I was terrified you would not love me if you knew. In this chest are your birth mother's belongings. Some of her clothes and treasures. I am sorry, but we never found out anything about who your birth father was. I want you to know you were my son the moment you were born. I loved you as much as all my sons. You were my little miracle. When you came into my life you saved me. I know that we're a cold family but do not ever doubt my or your father's love for you. Mikki loved you from the moment she found out she was pregnant. She would read and sing to you every day. She would talk to you about everything she wanted you to do. So, as you grew up, we made a point of having you do everything she wanted you to do. I hope you have felt how much we loved you. how much we cherished the gift that was you. I am sorry that we kept such secrets from you. Kat knows them, but I have promised her to tell you, it is my secret to tell not hers. I hope that you can forgive me, but I was such a coward. I was afraid after she left and what happened was that everyone would hate me even more. After you woke up from the accident. I could not tell you because you were so angry that she was not with you. You became so withdrawn and cold that I was too afraid to tell you. No matter what you are my son forever. You are mine Mikki gave you to me before she died. She wanted you to have a family, which was why she came home to have you.

Your loving mother

In the next one they found it lined with old military uniforms and such. The third one was a surprise to all three of them. Inside was dress mannequins. Three of them had tuxedoes and one had a traditional Korean male marriage costume. The other four had three different wedding dresses and a traditional Korean wedding dress.

"My dress it was here. She locked it in here." Kat says as she walks over to stand in front of a dress with a rose pattern on it.

"How did you know that one was James's dress?" jae asked.

"He always gave me roses and he liked seeing my legs so only he would make it so that you could see them." She answered him.

"Ok so which one did I design?" jae prompts her.

"You chose the traditional one with snowflakes, Kris's is the lace with butterflies and Ki is the Korean one." She answers him sticking her tongue out at him.

Ki looks at her and puts his face close to hers.

"Are there any more secret rooms in this house that you know about?"

"I don't know do you know about the one in the study and the one in mama Clara closet." She smiles up at him.

"Yes, we know about the two safe rooms there." He answers.

"Then in this house that should be all. At least that is all I know about. Why do you think the adults never told you about these rooms? I mean I was gone. Surely, they should have told you about them before they died. "She asks him.

"You know she is right I wonder why they never said anything," jae asks.

"Maybe because they never found the key after grandma died. So, they figured they would never be unlocked. Maybe because they never wanted me to find out about my birth." Ki answered in a profoundly serious tone.

"Well, it's getting late we should go to bed. See you in the morning. Oh, I am leaving. I have decided to go home to my aunts, so I can see my kids. I do not need to be in a hospital anymore. And I cannot stay here, or I may never want to leave. I think it's time for me to go back to reality." She walks out before either of them can say anything.

CHAPTER 32

Going home.

After she leaves, they look at each other. They know that it is time for her to go home. They just do not want her to. The two of them sit in the cellar talking into the early hours of the morning. Processing all that they have learned over the last few days and talking about how to continue to help Kat finish her treatment.

Dr Smith calls Kats Aunt to meet them at the hospital. When they arrive, Kat says her goodbyes and thanks to the hospital staff. She apologizes once again for all the trouble she caused while there. She notices that the security guard from the clinic is there. She goes over and says goodbye to him.

"MS. Kat you do not remember me, do you?' he asks.

"You're the security guard from Ki clinic right." She looks at him puzzled.

"Yes, I am but I am also someone from your past. We went to school together. You used to bake the most wonderful sweets and give them to us on the bus.' He looks at her wondering if she will remember now.

"Did you used to sit in the next to last seat on the bus. You always had earphones on. "Looking at him wondering if she is right.

"Yep, that was me. I used to watch you for the guys to make sure that you were not bothered at school. Several of us did. I did it because I always had a crush on you. So, did a few of the others. You know you were always so much fun on the bus and full of life. I always thought you withdrew because you missed them. I am sorry that none of us knew to keep your brother-in-law away from you. If we had known, we would have tried to." He was looking at the ground. Not wanting to look her in the eyes. Kat takes his hand.

"There was nothing you or anyone else could have done. My own family did nothing so how could I expect help from someone who did not know what was happening? It is not your fault it is not anyone's fault except my brother-in-law. Everyone is accountable for only their own actions. They cannot control what others do. Thank you though for watching out for me. I'm sorry it's taken me so long to say that to you." Kat stands on her tip toes and kisses him on the cheek then turns to go to her aunt's car.

The drive home was an incredibly quiet one. Not knowing what to say Kat just sat and looked out the window. When she arrived at her aunt's house the kids were just getting off the bus. She was so excited to see them, and they heard her. The 6 of them sat on the porch and talked till Kat's sister came to pick them up. Then her husband came. Kat's aunt came out on the porch and looked at him." There will be no trouble here. You may sit and talk but if you raise your voice or try to lay a hand on her I will call the police officers." She takes the children inside so that the two can talk.

"How are you?" Kat asks.

"I am doing ok. So, when are you coming home? I am not saying I will let everything go but the kids want you to be there at night when they go to sleep." Stands there leaning against the wall of the house not even looking at her. Kat wonders what to tell him. She wants to go home but she does not want to be abused anymore.

"I sent my mother back. I am sorry that you had to live with her being that way. I did not even notice that she was making things so hard on you. I am also sorry for the way I have been behaving I can't promise that it won't happen again, but I will try to have it not." He tells her.

"I want to come home but not until I feel safe with you. I want us to get marriage counselling. I want us to try to work things out." She tells him.

"Ok then we will go to marriage counselling and then see what happens." He tells her as he goes inside to get the kids.

That night Kat could not believe that he was so quick to agree to marriage counselling. He has already changed from before. He did not even put up a fight or even tell her to stop getting help. She wonders what is going to happen next.

When she wakes up in the morning the kids are there for school. She fixes breakfast and cleans the kitchen. Her uncle comes in and hands her a set of keys.

"Here are your keys to your truck. Joe dropped it off this morning before work. he said that this way you can go to your treatments and then take the kids home in the afternoon."

"Thank you." She is so surprised. She does not know what to say.

When she arrives at the center for her day treatment program, she tells Dr. Smith what has happened. Dr smith informs her that she already knew. That she talked to her husband before calling her aunt. She also referred him to a marriage counselor. The rest of the day was normal for the first time in months. Kat was feeling very content when she got back home to her aunt's house. That night when she took the kids to her house. It was like she never left, she got them bathed and helped with their homework. I made them dinner. They were getting ready for bed when her husband came in.

"I will be going now. Everything is done for them." She informs him.

"Are you not going to clean the house when you come?" he asks.

"No, I do not live here remember, you told me I was not welcome and left me homeless. I do not have a home to clean." She says as she is moving towards the door. She is terrified he is going to lash out at her. She knows if she gives in now though nothing will change. He will always only see her as someone to clean, cook and boss around. Waiting for him to hit her she closes her eyes and turns her face away. She is shaking inside not knowing what to expect.

"I also told you that you could come back. I am working on being a better man." He tells her.

"I know but until I am no longer afraid of you it will be this way," she walks out of the house and leaves.

Over the next few weeks things went the same way. She would get the kids off the bus and get them ready for bed. Each day things became more and more comfortable between her and joe as well. She started staying later to talk to him about small things. Then one night he asked her about her treatment. She was surprised he never wanted to know about that. So, looking at him closely she asks him.

"Why all of sudden do you want to know?"

"Dr Park, the one with the clinic called me at work and wants to see me. He says he wants to talk to me and to show me something. I want to know if he is going to talk to me about your treatment, or if this is going to be a man-to-man confrontation. I know he is the boyfriend you thought died. The one you had deep feelings for." He tells her quietly.

"I do have feelings for both. They are my family. They were meant to be my family. I want them to stay in my life just as that. You are my husband and I love you as such you have been beside me through so many things. I cannot imagine my life without you in it. I do not know what he wants to talk to you about but do not forget you are the one I am married to, and nothing has happened or changed that. Will you meet with him?" She tells him with such deep sincerity and warmth that he can't help but believe her.

"Yes, I already decided to meet with him. I will go to his office at his clinic tomorrow. "He tells her as he walks her to the door to say good night.

The next day was a free day from day treatment. Kat spent the day alone at her home. She cleaned and aired out the house. Sorted through the kid's clothes to take to the donation bins. It felt nice doing the housework and caring for her home. She did not realize just how much she missed doing it. She fixed a nice dinner for the kids and joe. Throughout the day she wondered what it was that Ki wanted to show and talk to Joe about.

Gentleman's agreement

When Joe got off work, he went straight to the address that Ki gave him. He was surprised when he pulled up. It was not the normal clinic style building. It was a mansion. As he walked up the front porch, he saw a young girl on the swing. She looked frightened of him.

"don't worry I won't hurt you. I know I look dirty and rough. I just got off work and had no time to change. Do you know where Dr Park is?" he asks her?

"Yes, he is inside if you go inside, he should be in the room to the right." She says as she runs down the stairs.

Joe walks in and is in awe of the interior of the clinic. It is amazingly beautiful. He notices a picture on the wall beside the entryway to the right. It is of an angel in a grove of cherry trees in bloom. She looks familiar, but the face is covered by her hair as she is sleeping beneath one of the trees. As he is looking at the painting, he hears Dr Park clear his throat.

"Sorry to keep you waiting. Would you like to come with me for a moment?" He motions for him to follow him up the stairs. "My private office is in the attic and what I want to show you I keep there it is not for anyone to chance upon."

Joe follows him through the clinic to the attic noticing all the angel pictures throughout the clinic.

"You know Kat loves angels. We have so many throughout house that you would almost think it was a church instead of a small house." He tells Ki.

"Yes, I know she has always loved unicorns and angels. They were her favorites growing up. I painted and drew all the pictures in the clinic. They are what kept me going after the accident that killed my brothers. they may look familiar they are of the Kat I remember." Tell him as he opens the attic door. "Please come in no one will interrupt us up here. Take a seat. I will get right to the point. I want to show you a photo album. I do not want to hear you say anything until you look through it, please. I won't even tell you what it is until you do." He hands him the album. Joe takes it and he smiles lovingly at the first few pages as he sees the girl in the photos. They are of his wife as a young girl. then he feels like he has been suckered punched. There in front of him is his wife, barely a teenager, her stomach bruised and bleeding. She looked like someone used her for a punching bag to practice boxing on. Her face not a bruise but her legs and stomach looked like she had been beaten to death. As he turned through the pages the pictures were more gruesome than the last. His stomach was churning with nausea and his head was ready to explode from anger. Ki was watching him very carefully to see how he reacted as he looked at the pictures. When he turned to the ones of her dirty and trying to hide, he saw his eyes look like he wanted to cry the sadness was noticeably clear on his face. He closed the album.

"Why did you show these to me and how did you get them?" His voice is exceptionally low. you could feel his emotions coming from his body this man was incredibly angry.

"My uncle took them when he would treat her after her brother-in-law hurt her in case, she ever wanted to press charges and needed evidence. The first ones are my photos of her when we were dating and the ones of her dirty and depressed were when she would be at school or forced to be out in public, the last ones of her coming back to being happy are when she met you. I wanted you to see these because these photos tell a little bit of what is locked behind the doors of her mind. These show you where her nightmares come from and why they are so violent. This is not something that is going to go away. She needs to deal with these events and emotions if she is going to survive and have a life. The life she wants is to be a good mother and wife. She wants to show everyone that she is stronger than they think. If she does not face this, she will forever be in danger of hurting herself and never being the person, she truly is. I wanted to show you these so that you could understand how important it is for her to continue to get help. She will stop if she thinks she will lose her family if she continues to get help. Angel is one of the most loving and compassionate people I have ever known. She forgives everything if you show her that you really are sorry and are willing to try to understand her. Before you ask yes, I love her very much. I love the girl in those first photos and maybe if we had never been separated, we would still be together. That is not what happened. She gave you her heart as an adult. She wants things to work out with you, but she needs us to help her get through the trauma of her past. so that she can have a future with you and your children. My promise to you is that if you let her get the help, she needs without having to choose between her family and treatment. I will do everything I can to help her return to you as a whole person. I cannot change who I am or our past together. I can tell you that yes, we are soul mates but because of her past when she was 13, we never got beyond anything more than holding hands and a few stolen kisses. I never wanted to hurt her in any way and neither did my brothers, so we treated her as a fragile flower. We babied her and took the utmost care of her. We were never given a chance to let our relationship grow. With you though she has been able to have a loving relationship in every aspect. It is one she wants to make work. With us her feelings are those still in the past. I am ok with that and so is my brother. All we want is to help her be her again and feel confident and safe. Will you help us help your wife?' KI pleaded with joe hoping that he will agree.

"I don't understand something. How could my father-in-law allow anyone to hurt her this badly and not notice? I have seen him pull a gun on a man for beating his own child and tell him you touch her again and I will kill you. That child was no relation to him and yet my wife has been raped and beaten repeatedly and he never done anything. I do not know how he could ever even say that it is my baby girl. I only must hear the terror in her voice at night and want to kill that bastard. I see the pictures and they make me sick and angry. I have always had to ignore her past so that I could love her. She has never felt worthy of anyone's love. It took me a long time to get her to let me close enough to know she even cared for me. I do not understand her, not even a clue how she feels. I already decided to not give her a hard time about getting treatment if she does not try to kill herself again. I have even agreed to marriage counseling to help me to understand her better. So, no I will not stop her from getting help. But with that said I do not need to know the details of her trauma. I do not need to know what was done to her or when. I am happy being in that dark about those details. What few I know just makes me want to kill someone. I also do not want her locked away in the hospital anymore, I do not think it will help her to be away from her kids for that long again. "Joe tells Ki his feelings on this matter.

Ki looks at him in confusion. This is the same man who beat her in the hospital and who strangled her. Which is why she was put there in the first place for her protection.

"Who I don't understand is you. You claim to love her and yet you abuse her. I understand that you have had some issues since the accident. You seem to not have any real remorse or even think it is wrong to hurt her. Why is that?" Ki asks him.

"it's not that I don't have remorse or feel that its right. I hate myself at times because of how quick my temper has become since the accident. In my culture we are taught that the man of the house has the only say in the house. Women do not talk back or even call out their husbands when they are wrong. She has always been very unmovable over certain things, and I knew that before we married. I have always been ok with those. Here lately I have not been able to control myself. Before I would blow up and throw a few things and she never would say anything. In fact, we even have argued because she refuses to confront me over certain things. I love my wife and normally we never argue. Here lately we cannot seem to see eye to eye on anything. I don't know if it's because of her depression or if it's my temper." Joe tells him.

"You may not know this, but her nightmares began when you were hurt. She was under a great deal of stress and having your family criticizing everything she was doing. Did you know she was ready to kick them out of the hospital because of their verbal abuse? If you had not woken up when you did, she was ready to have no visitors except her rule put in place. Your mother was accusing her of trying to kill you and they were telling the doctors what they thought they should do as if she had no say in your care."

"I didn't know most of that till recently I explained when I woke up to my mom and the others. That she was doing what we had always decided to do in case of an emergency. She would not call my mom until she needed to know anything. That she always needed to take care of my kids first. I did not know how badly they mistreated her until a few weeks ago. "Joe explained to Ki.

"You know unless you get your temper under control you will lose her. I will do everything I can to keep her safe. You also need to stand up to your family where she is concerned as well. It is not fair that she must be mistreated on all sides. "Ki lets him know not just by his words but also by his body language that he is profoundly serious about this.

Joe stares back at him with intensity." Just do not forget that she is my wife and I do love her. I may not always know how to properly go about things. I do know one thing and that is that she knows that I love her. I also know that I have a way to go to win back her trust and heart. I will do that no matter what. Just promise me not to lock her away from us again." Joe tells him.

"We agree on that at least about the hospital. Now I want her to get involved in charity and leadership groups that will help her. they will help her help others in a structured environment. This will also help her when she is ready to get a job, later when she is better. This group will have a few overnight trips with her peers, and it will be supervised by the day treatment program not by me. If you agree to let her do this, I think it will give her the much-needed confidence boost she will need. She will only see my brother and I in passing except in her private sessions that are with us and Dr smith. We will only be having them twice a week now. If she has an especially bad session, we can let you know to give you heads up so that you are not blindsided. If you wish." Ki explains their course of treatment for her. Joe listens intently so that he knows what to expect from them.

"That sounds ok I can agree with that. Just do not try to get me to sit in or hear about how she suffered. I do not need to know the details I already know she has been to hell. I just need her to be able to handle it. I know you may think that I am cold and selfish. Truthfully, if I know the details, I will not be able to love her the way she needs to be. I will never be able to get past the anger at what was done to her to even see her if I do, I will only feel anger if I know anything else. I do not need to know for her sake as well as mine. How can you love her and know what she has been through? How can you not let it change how you feel? I want to love my wife not only see a broken person." Joe tells KI.

"It has changed how I feel about her. The first time I met her she almost died in my arms from taking to many pills at 7 years old. The next time I saw her she was 13 with almost dying in the presence of my brother from cutting her wrist. After being raped by her mother's friend's husband. I was so afraid to even think about what he did to her because I only saw blood. I wanted to draw blood. she never told us what he did to her, we did not know till a few months ago after we opened that door, even after all these years I still wanted to hunt him down and kill him. I am forever changed because of her. She showed my family what a family was and what love was. If not for her I would have never even known anything about love or anger. Do I wish I could turn back the clock and take all her pain away absolutely but that is not possible? What I can do is help her face the nightmares and demons locked inside of her. So that they can no longer hurt her. That is how I can repay her for loving my family and giving us hope and reasons to live. As far as what will happen with our relationship, I can only promise you that I will keep it as professional as possible." Ki tells him hoping he understands that none of them want to hear what hell she went through but that he was willing to be there to help her any way possible.

Joe stands up and reaches his hand out to Ki.

"Thank you and I will put my wife and my trust in you. You know she told me last night that you were her family and that I would just have to get used to it."

"She told us the same thing that she was a married woman, and she has never cheated as wasn't about to start so we just are family nothing more/" with that they shook hands and joe went home to see his children and his wife. He just hopes he can see her for who she is now and not what she looked like in those photos.

When joe arrived home, dinner was ready. The house was spotless and smelling wonderful from the dinner she made. The kids were already in their night clothes and sitting watching tv. He could hear Kat cleaning the bathroom after giving the kids their baths. He goes in and leans against the door frames watching her. Why he wonders did he never notice how much she did for everyone. She constantly takes care of her sister's household as well as theirs. She never has had much time for herself or by herself. She never asks to go out with any friends, while he goes out every weekend. She has never asked for money from him except for what the house needed or the kids. Joe thinks about all the guys at work complaining about their wives. How they want money to go get their nails done or their hair. Not once has she ever even been to a nail shop. in fact, she has never even had a manicure or a pedicure. She gets her hair done 2 times a year. She never buys herself new clothes unless there is a special occasion. He wonders if these are even things she thinks about. He realizes that he really does not know her that well. He has never taken the time to even know if she has friends outside of her family. These last few months without her have been lonely and hard. Everything that he thought he knew about her. He realizes he knows nothing. She has managed so much even with the turmoil inside of her.

Kat turns around and notices him just standing there lost in thought. She says his name a couple of times before he even notices she has finished and was talking to him.

"Dinner is ready, and the kids are ready for bed. What did Ki want?" she asks.

"He wanted to talk to me about your treatment. He wanted to explain to me his role in it and to ask me to not to make you choose between your family and treatment." He explains to her.

"oh "she looks at her hands her face downcast as if waiting for him to give her a lecture.

"I told him OK that I am willing to let you have all the time you need and to do whatever is needed for you to get better but, he must not lock you away in the hospital again. If you need some more structured environment again you can go to his clinic or to the group home that the center runs. No more hospitals deal." Joe puts out his hand for her to seal the deal. He wants her to know that he is not going to keep her from treatment or make her try to do this without support. He just hopes that Ki will back him up if she asks him about the clinic or group home and not tell her he made that part up. She takes his hand and smiles up at him. He can see he made her happy by this. He shoves her out of the bathroom telling her to go now he needs a shower. That he will see her the next day after work. She goes and kisses the kid's good night and heads back to her aunt's house with a big smile and a relieved heart.

CHAPTER 34

A day at the cherry blossom's

The next day Kat wakes with a much lighter heart. Her anxiety is exceptionally low this morning. She is even humming in the shower. When she gets to the center everyone is ready for their trip. They are going on an outing to the museum of natural history. This is so that patients who have panic attacks and have a hard time in large crowds can get more comfortable going out. When they go on these types of trips everyone in the center goes so that way, they all get to enjoy a nice day away from their worries and help those who have anxiety over being in public. Kat is most excited about going to see the cherry blossoms. It is her favorite time. After the 1 ½ hour drive on the van they arrive at the museum. They divide into groups of 4. Kat gets to be with Dr smith Mary and Helen this time. She is relieved because that means she can enjoy the day and take lots of pictures. As they are walking through the museum Dr smith begins to ask the three of them about what they find most interesting in the museum.

"I like the gem's rooms I love stones and crystals. I like how they can just calm you by looking at them. Did you know that many of them have healing properties?' Kat asks her.

"No, I didn't realize that. what about you Helen and Mary did you know?" she asks

"I know some about them. Just like Kat they are my favorite. I love how just looking at certain ones can calm you down at once. I have rose quartz for heart healing it is to help soothe a broken heart. It's a calming stone." Mary replies

"I come from South Korea, and we use stones for balance and healing the Chakra in the body. I have a clear crystal or master healer stone. Amethyst is an all-purpose stone. rose quartz for calming. citrines for abundance and prosperity. Black tourmaline for protection and blocking negativity. "Helen says as she pulls her necklace from inside her shirt to show everyone.

"it's beautiful. I did not realize you three knew so much about stones or that you had that in common. "Dr smith smiles at them as they are admiring the necklace.

"Oh, we have lots in common that's why we are always put together. Kat helps me out by staying close by, so I do not panic. With anyone else I would be going crazy right now. Did you know Kat knows a lot about Korea and can cook Korean food? She comes over and helps me cook sometimes and we watch Korean tv. I get afraid in large crowds because when I first came here, I could not understand English. Many people would treat me like I was stupid, so I just closed myself off and eventually refused to leave my house for any reason. It was not until I was put in the hospital and placed in this program that I started leaving my house. When I met Kat, she was so kind and even greeted me in Korean to help put me at ease. Her aunt is from South Korea also and she is always so sweet to me." Helen tells Dr Smith.

"Yes, I know about her cooking and knowing some Korean. I found out when she was in the hospital." Dr Smith explained to Helen.

She notices that Kat seems self-conscious about her and Helen discussing her. So, she changes the subject.

"Is there any other part of the museum you want to see?" she asks.

"I personally have seen the museum too many times. I have been here twice or even three times a year for the last 4 years. I am the designated chaperone for the kids. So, I come every year with at least 3 of them on their field trips. I was going to ask if we could play hooky from the museum and walk over or take the trolley over to see the cherry blossoms.? "Kat looks at the three of them pleadingly.

"I'm for that it will be like back home in Korea to walk under them." Helen speaks up.

"I'm game I never liked museums anyway." Mary smiles and raises her hand in agreement.

"Ok then I guess the 4 of us are going on a different field trip. I just must let the others know where we are going so that no one worries." Dr smith says as she pulls out her phone to call terry.

The three friends squeal with excitement because what Dr Smith does not know is that it's cherry blossom festival time. which means the place is going to be filled with all kinds of activities and music. not to mention just the sheer beauty of the trees in bloom. As the four of them walk around the Tidal Basin they are doing a wedding photo shoot it looks like. They hear music coming from around the corner. Walking around the cherry blossoms is amazingly beautiful and tranquil. They stop at a bench and sit down.

"Wow you ladies were right. This is amazing. Kat why didn't you suggest coming here instead of the museum to the whole group?" Dr. Smith looks at her.

"This trip was planned when we were at the plantation house. I would have if I had been here during the planning. We can come next year, and we can invite the two DR. Parks. I used to come here with them when I was younger and then I would come with my husband even if it is just a drive by, he brings me down to see them. He knows how much I love them, so he always does his best to bring me to see them." Kat tells her. The four of them spend the whole day just talking and walking around the festival when they get to the food tents Dr. Smith gets excited. She wonders if the food Kat made was the same as here.

"Now Dr smith this is food from Japan. Japan is the country that gifted the cherry trees to the United States. So today you are going to try their food. "Helen tells her. After they eat, they continue to walk around when they realize it is time to catch up with the others. As they walk back to the van Dr Smith thanks them for a very lovely and educational day. The three ladies smile at her.

"Thank you, Dr. Smith, for spending the day with us and letting yourself relax. Oh, can you take me somewhere in the next few days hopefully before my next session?" Kat pats her hand as they get on the bus. Just then she realized why the ladies asked her to take them away from the others they wanted her to relax and not fuss around making sure everyone was doing ok. Those sneaks she smiles to herself as she gets on the van. On the way back to the center most everyone falls asleep except Jonathan, the driver Terry, and Dr Smith.

"Did you enjoy your day with the ladies?" Johnathan asks Dr Smith.

"Yes, I did they are particularly good friends, they were very chatty today and I got to know them a little better today. Did you know they were going to ask to go outside the museum?" she asks them?

"I knew they wanted to see the cherry blossoms. Kat loves them, and Helen says they remind her of home, which is why we try to do a trip to DC when they are in bloom. We cannot take all the clients to see them, it would be too hard for us to keep some of them safe. Many of them have anxiety of being in large crowds at the museum we can control the situation better since they are not in such a wide-open space. So, we discuss who is going to be paired up with them before we come. I got to go last year, and it was amazing. I can see why they love going. "Terry explains to her.

"Are there other clients who may have wanted to go? We could have taken them also." Dr smith asks them.

"There are but the ones who would have gone are not the kind that we could let go. As you know several of our clients are addicts and alcoholics. There is always the chance of them finding a dealer or getting a drink while we are out. So, we go to places that we know that there is little or no chance of that happening. When the various festivals are here, they always have alcohol and if you look closely, you can see several dealers. So, to keep them safe we just do not give them a choice. "Terry explains.

"I can understand that, but you know they are adults, and their choices are their responsibility." Dr Smith is prodding Terry to see if she is being protective or just trying to control the clients by not giving them options.

"Yes, I know they are adults. I am the one who the care takers call when something goes wrong. Take the gentleman sitting beside you. You would never know that he is an addict. One day we went bowling and he went to the restroom. While in the restroom he met a dealer. Within 2 hrs. he was in the hospital almost dead. He had been cleaning for more than 15 years and all that went down the tubes in 2 hrs. He had been dealing with a loss at the time and when the dealer approached him, he just could not resist. I felt responsible because he obtained the drugs while in my care. I decided that day. I would never let that happen again. That is why we go to the rest room in groups and go to places where we can stay in small groups with no chance of wandering from the group. I understand they are not children, but I also do not want to lose one of them while in my care." Terry explains.

"I can see why you are so protective now. I am sorry if you thought I was criticizing you. I just have not gotten to know all the clients very well yet. I was always told not to get involved with the clients and to stay cold to them. to only be their therapist and not to get to know them outside of their sessions. That would be a conflict of interest. I have found it lacking not knowing their interest, family life, or triggers. I have always in the past been able to do that. Since coming to this center, I have found that to treat them I need to get to know them outside of the therapy room. I am a good Dr and, in the past, have never had a problem getting clients to open. Since coming to the center 2 years ago I have had a hard time getting some of the clients to open and show me their true self. "Terry looks at Dr smith as she is explaining how she is feeling. She thinks for a second and realizes that her assumptions of the Dr were off. She thought she was indifferent and cold only looking down on the clients. Now she realizes she was having a hard time trying to find the balance between the center atmosphere and what she was told her role was to be.

"It's good to be reserved with the clients but with the ones here in the center you must work hard to earn their trust. Many of them have been in the system for years and no longer trust anyone. I must remind myself all the time that I am not their friend, I am their lifeline in many ways. Outside of central events I will not see a client if I do happen to see them, I just politely greet them and ask normal pleasantries. This way I can keep my objectivity and have a separation between my home life and work life. There are a few that if they had never come to the center, we would have been friends but that is not an option. Having compassion and empathy is always a good thing. "Terry explains to Dr Smith.

"I personally have the hardest time keeping the boundaries from becoming blurred." Johnathan interjects "I enjoy my work and have grown to care a great deal for several of the clients and it would break my heart if something happened to any one of them. I sometimes must take a step back to remind myself to look at things more objectively. We are human also and even though I do not have a relationship outside of work with any of the clients. There are a few that I would go out and have fun with after work if they were not clients. Thankfully, the center allows us to be able to do many things with our clients and so we can do many things with them that I would enjoy outside as well.so even though it may always be work it is still fun and rewarding."

"I am glad you all asked me to tag along today. I learned a lot. I also got to know more about my team and as well as my clients. I also learned that I could show concern and compassion without going outside the professional boundaries that this field enforces. You know these last few months treating Kat and getting to know Dr Parks have been a big eye opener for me. Kat has asked me to go someplace with her in the next few days and I was debating about going. Now I know I can go without any fear of it being unprofessional. "Dr Smith thanks them for helping her understand more about the center life verses the hospital, private practice and clinic life.

"Oh, wow she always shies away from doing anything outside of the center. Several clients have invited her to events, and she has always refused. She seems ashamed that she needs help. Sometimes I think that's why she tries to support and help others so much." Johnathan looks in the rear-view mirror shocked.

"It's not that she is ashamed it's that her family gives her a hard time over needing help. She is naturally a caregiver. It would be extremely hard for her to see someone in need and not give that support or help in some way. I bet she even tries to help you all out when she thinks you need it. I learned a lot about her while treating her in the hospital. She has been to hell and back. It surprises me how together she is for the trauma she has endured. "Dr Smith tells him. They realize that they have made it back to the center and that all the clients are still sleeping. Johnathan shuts the van off and gets out looking at Terry he asks" Who is driving the van tonight to take the guy's home?"

"I'm not sure I forgot to ask anyone to work late to take them?" terry responds.

"I will take them if you have someone give me the route and directions." Dr Smith replies.

"It's ok I will do it it's a long route and some of the houses are hard to find if you haven't been there before. Maybe if you want you can ride the van a few times to get to know the route so that if you ever need to drive you will know it." Terry tells her as she takes the keys from Johnathan.

On the way home Kat thinks about how nice the day was. She cannot wait to tell the kids about the festival. She will ask Joe if they can take the kids on the weekend.

That evening when joe gets home Kat has everything done for him just like when she lived here. Their time apart is coming to an end. He really has missed his wife in so many ways. He wonders if she would like to go on a family day trip with him and the kids. The cherry blossom festival is going on and it is her favorite time of the year. He should ask her if she wants to go.

As they sit down to eat dinner, they both start to talk at the same time Kat tells Joe to go first." I was wondering if you would like to go to DC with the kids and I this weekend. The cherry blossoms are in bloom and the festival is going on." Joe looks at her hopefully.

"I was about to ask you the same thing. The center went to DC today and I was thinking about how much fun it would be to take the kids and Maria for her birthday "Kat begins to laugh because they were thinking the same thing.

"Ok I will call compadre after dinner and see if we can get Maria this weekend." Joe smiles and finishes his dinner. That night he goes to bed feeling happier than he had in a while. though they will have a full car since they will have 6 kids with just the two of them, but he knows it will be lots of fun. They should take the metro instead so that no one is cramped. Joe falls asleep for the first time in months with no anger or resentment. He feels like a very heavy weight is lifting from his life.

When Kat gets home to her aunt's house, she gives her aunt a big hug "Thank you so much for loving me and opening your home to me. No one else would have been ok with having me in their house. Thank you for trusting me to stay here."

"You know that I have always loved you and felt like you were one of my kids. We all go through hard times and need a little extra care. You're no different. You are someone who I love dearly, and I could not have you not be in a safe place. How are things going with you and Joe?" she asks?

"We are doing better we are taking the kids this weekend to the cherry blossom festival. We are taking Maria as well for her birthday. I am excited this will be our first outing as a family in such a long time. "Kat tells her about her day and about how relaxed and comfortable dinner was tonight. It had been such a long time since they could agree on anything.

"That's wonderful. I am happy that things are starting to work out for you two. You know you can stay here if you like, but I think it won't be too long before you are home." Her aunt gives her a hug and says good night.

When Kat gets settled to say her nightly prayers

Heavenly father, it is me your burdensome child. I want to thank you for the amazing day that I had today. Thank you for the progress, Joe and I have made in our marriage. Thank you for the support that I have in my family and at the center. Thank you for all the blessings and provisions you have made in my life. Heavenly father I come to you not to ask for anything but to thank you for all that you have given me. I come to you with a heart filled with thanksgiving and praise. amen

Sharing Memories

The next day as Kat gets ready to go to the center she wonders if Dr Smith will go with her today.

When Kat gets to the center. Dr Smith is waiting for her.

"Kat is today a good day for you to take me where you want to go.?" She asks.

"I was going to ask you the same thing do you mind driving in my old truck. where I am taking you, your car will get dirty if we take it." Kat motions her to get into the passenger side of the truck.

As they are driving, they are just making small talk. Dr Smith is taking in the beautiful scenery that is passing by the window and she realizes that they are heading towards a secluded place on the river.

When they arrive Kat hands her a pair of sneakers. "I brought an extra pair just in case you had heals on. I remembered we have the same size foot." Kat smiles as the Dr puts the shoes on as she walks towards the riverbank. Dr smith smiles at the beauty of the river. Kat begins to walk across a hidden path.

They get to a small cove on the river where they can walk on a few rocks to get to a large one in the center of the river. Once on the rock in the center of the river Kat motions her to sit.

"This is our spot. This is where the husbands and I used to come. We would spend entire days here just playing and talking. I would pack a picnic and we would sit there and just hang out. Jae, Kris and I would swim out to the raft and play around or jump in by swinging on that rope over there. James and ki would sit here and watch us being silly. They would talk about lord know what. Sometimes Ki would sit and sketch all day. This is where Jae says they spread their ashes. I have come here so often over the years with my kids and Joe. I have always felt at peace here. I always had this feeling that there was something special about this place. You see that tree over there.it has a heart carved with my and ki initials. The one next to it has Kris James and jae in it. I cannot believe that I could forget them. They were my entire life at one time. You know I have not told you much about Kris or James. I have been feeling that if I talk about them that I will make the park brothers unhappy." Kat pulls out a set of envelopes the ones that jae had given her.

"You know James was always so cold and serious. To get him to do anything silly was a miracle. the very idea that jae convinced him to write a letter to me was amazing. I did not want to share it because I was worried it would make them unhappy. James would have been an amazing attorney. He was so smart and could keep everything in its proper place. He was a lot like you in many ways. He also was SOOO cute and easy to get riled up. "At some point while Kat was taking the tears of her heart ache began to flow down her face. She could not keep the sadness from her voice.

"You know he would have made a wonderful husband for the right woman. I loved having him always keeping me in line. He was always there to check my homework and to make sure that I did not fall behind. He was so protective and stern I could see him as a strict father as well, but he had the softest heart. He would cry every time something happened to me. If

I got into trouble, he would always volunteer to take my punishment. If I got hurt, he would cry with me and then be ready to take anyone apart that caused it. I loved him so much and wanted him too always be proud of me. Out of all the husbands he made no excuses about how he felt he did not compete with them for my attention. He was always there in the background waiting for me to need him. He was such a strong person both physically and mentally. I am so ashamed of times that I did nothing he wanted me to. "I want to read you one of his letters.

Hey my girl.

How is life going without me around to keep you out of trouble? You know I think this is the silliest thing in the world. To write to you knowing that you may never get to read it. I miss you so much. I got so used to you being around to get into things. Now life is so boring without you. I have no one to fuss at and no one to take up my free time. In fact, I feel empty inside right now. It is much worse than before, you came into our lives, I only had my studies and my goals. I did not care what my brothers were up to, not even Kris, I only thought of my own accomplishments. When you came into our lives I looked forward to your visits and our lazy days at the river. I was the one to suggest that we go to your vocational school so that we could see you more often. You should have seen the face of everyone when I made that suggestion. You would have thought the world came to an end. All except grandma knew that I had found something that was more important to me than myself. Even though I knew that Ki was your soul mate I wanted to be your protector, the one who you depended on who you could come to when you needed anything. For the first time I had a real reason for my goals. I wanted to become the best lawyer so that if anyone hurts you again, I could protect you with the law as well as kick their butt. I love you girl and I hope that someday soon you will be a part of our family legally since you are already embattled in our hearts.

Know this though when I become a lawyer, I am going to make you sign this contract.

I Kat will adhere to all the rules that James has put into place to secure my safety and future. If I break this contract James and only James has the right to punish me, as he sees fit. The rules are followed.

I Kat will not do anything that will put my physical wellbeing in danger.

I Kat will not go along with every hairbrained scheme that Kris and Jae come up with. I will make sure that I am not in danger before going ahead.

I Kat will not ever be separated from my husband's again once we are reunited.

I Kat will always only smile and be happy. If something happens that makes me cry, I will go to James for him to fix it.

The following are my rules for myself towards you.

I James will protect Kat even if it means my life is give up.

I James will make sure she has financial security for the rest of her life. I will make sure that she and whichever husband she chooses will always have stability by setting up a financial plan that will give them a life free of financial worries.

I James will be there as a shoulder for Kat to lean on always no matter when or where.

I James will love Kat for the rest of her life.

Your loving husband

James

Kat finishes reading the letter and looks at me, the tears flowing uncontrollably. "How could I share this with them, and it not cause them hurt. He asked God to take him and let me live. He and Kris both asked God to take them instead of me. How can I ever forgive myself for the pain that I caused them? James should be married right now with children. He should be a brilliant lawyer with an amazing career. He used to tease me that I would be the death of him because I used to worry him so much. No matter how I look at it I was the death of him. "

"Umm Kat I must tell you that you are not at fault and that I told the two Dr parks that you were taking me someplace today. They are here, and they have been listening. You were so wrapped up in your own little bubble telling me about James that you never noticed them arriving. I did not tell them that we would be here. I just told them that I was going somewhere with you. they took a guess and wound up here." Dr Smith tells her.

Kat looks over and on the smaller rocks behind her sat Jae and Ki. They both have tears-stained faces. Jae wipes the tears from his eyes. Ki just sitting there not caring that she can see that he is crying.

"I'm sorry so sorry. I never wanted to hurt you. I did not want to tell you what he wrote because I did not want you to be hurt. I loved him so much and have been afraid of remembering him because I never showed him how much I cared for him or thanked him for always protecting me. He was always so aloof except for me. He would hug me every time I passed him. how could I remember that this strong strait-laced man who had incredibly special sense of humor died because of me? When I found out that this was the place you spread their ashes, I was so ashamed. I have brought my husband and my children here to play. Not knowing how special this place was. How sad it must have made them to have me come here with someone other than one of the husbands." Kat bows her head and begins to cry even harder.

Ki, unable to bear her crying jumps over to the big rock and picks her up into his arms. He sits back down on the rock with her.

"I bet to him and Kris the laughter and happiness you had when you had here brought them a lot of joy. They got to hear your laughter and see your children. They were able to see your smiling face. Where Jae and I on the other hand were not. We were only able to know that you were alive, we never got to hear your laughter or see your smiling face. We never got to see your children play with you here. Even though you could not remember them I am sure James was here protecting you and looking out for you each time you came. I am sure Kris took great delight in watching your children play and laugh. Loving you had nothing to do with who you were with. It was always just because it was you. You are the one they loved, it had nothing to do with us, only you. If they had lived and you had not, I do not even want to imagine how they would have been. James felt like he was your protector and that he was the one who let you down when we found out what had been happening to you. He found your file at our uncle's place when he was there one day doing some work. He never told us what was happening until we were on our way to get you. He was like a mad man the weeks before that arguing with my father and begging my mother to let you come back early. He was going out at night and not coming home till the early hours of the morning. We did not know what was going on with him. Until after everything was done. He was following you around trying to find out who was hurting you. Then he found out who it was. He insisted that my parents let you come back. He knew that there was no way he could protect you if he was around, and you were still in that house." Ki told her.

"don't think that they would ever be disappointed in you. they always were proud of you. You remember when we all first met you. You were in the hospital after being raped and trying g to kill yourself. They already knew that you had problems with intimacy and trust. For the first time in any of our lives we had something to protect we had you. James told me one time that he used to wonder what his purpose in life was. When he met you, he found that purpose he said that protecting people like you was going to be his purpose that helping others in the same situation that you were in. he wanted to represent them and make sure that the people hurting them would know they did wrong and were punished. "Jae told her.

"You never asked us for anything not once. Not even when you were hurting. You always put on a brave face and pretended that nothing was wrong. Therefore, James made those rules of his. He used to lecture Kris and I every time we were going to see you. what we could or could not do. he used to tell us that if any of our pranks or schemes put you in any kind of danger or trouble that he would be beating us to a pulp once you were home." Jae busted out laughing at the memory of his big brother.

"Do you really think that James as strait laced and rule toting guy, he would ever do anything that would make you sad. Never not in a million years. He would be immensely proud of how strong you are. He would be incredibly happy to know you got to be a mom. So, do not be afraid to remember him. "Ki told her as he wipes her tears.

"Now I on the other hand I am terribly upset with you. How could you bring her here and read her James letter without us? When she told us, you were taking her somewhere today this was the only place I could think of. I am glad I was right. How could you have a session without us? Especially when it involves us. "Jae scowls at her

Dr smith sitting there listening to their exchanges with a therapist mind set she notices that when the two Dr were comforting Kat, they kept the boundaries that was set early on except for the fact that Kat was sitting on ki lap. She also notices that it became easier for Kat to talk to her this time about them without being self-conscience over their relationship. The entire situation is so complicated that she wonders how many rules are being broken. Jae notices her expression.

"No rules are being broken. You are her Dr, and we are her friends and family. When we do her joint sessions, it is no different than doing a family session. Her husband has agreed to these sessions and our role in them. If the decisions that are being made are by you and Kat, no rules are broken. I checked it out with a lawyer as soon as I realized who she was. Her husband and Ki have set up boundaries to follow and if we do not cross them, we are ok. Now we can go have lunch. I am starving, and my legs are getting cramped. Besides, Ki needs to put her down soon or she will fall asleep. "Jae complains.

"Why do you say that? Dr smith asks.

"She always falls asleep when Ki holds her in his lap. It never fails within a few minutes she is sleeping." He says as he stands up from his rock and starts to make his way across the river to the bank. Dr. smith looks down and sure enough Ki is standing with Kat in his arms sound asleep. They make their way across the rocks to the riverbank and back up the path. Dr Smith stops at the trees that Kat mentioned and sure enough there were all their initials in the trees just like she said. When they get back to the cars Ki tells Jae to take Dr Smith to lunch and he takes Kat's truck and follows them to the restaurant. He reaches under the wheel and pulls out a small box inside is a set of spare keys. He opens the door and sets Kat down gently to not wake her.

On the way to the restaurant Dr smith asks Jae about James.

"James was most like our father in terms of detachment. He was very much a loner and stern with everyone. I do not ever remember him cracking a smile, not even in pictures. Not until he met Kat. The first day we brought her to the house it was pouring down rain and she looked like a drowned cat. She is standing in the kitchen shivering and dipping water all over the kitchen. He walks in and yells at me. Jae, how dare you drag her out in this storm and then leave her in here freezing. Go upstairs right now and draw her a warm bath. He never would have cared if it had not been Kat. He ran up the stairs and straight to Ki's room to get her a t shirt and then to mama room to see if she had any under garments that might fit. By the time I got upstairs to draw her bath he had towels and clothes already there for her. When Kat got settled into the bathroom I came back downstairs, and grandma was mopping up the floor and there was James scowling at me. He was making her tea and asking grandma if there were any sweets to go with the tea. He never did anything for anyone. Grandma was just humming and smiling while watching him. When Kat came back downstairs, he took her wet clothes to wash and dry them. She was so afraid of him at first. You could see it on her face. When he came back upstairs, we were sitting at the table talking and laughing. He walked over and put his hand on her forehead to make sure she had no fever. He then did the most shocking thing. He bent down, kissed her forehead and sat at the table with us. He never sat with us, and he never touched anyone. That day sitting at the kitchen table we did so many things we never did. James was laughing and smiling with us. Just being in the kitchen was something new. We never hung out in the kitchen. We always waited for grandma to bring us snacks or our meals to either our rooms or the dining room. That was a day full of first. And the beginning of a new life for us brothers. "Jae explains to her. Dr smith notices that his voice became incredibly soft while remembering his brother.

"you 4 must have been very close." She says she hopes he will tell her more about them.

"No not since we were kids. Even as kids we treated James more as an adult than a kid. He was always so levelheaded and adult like. When we started hanging out with Kat that is when we all got so close. She refused to do anything without all of us. I think she felt like she needed to fix us. She could not stand the fact that we were family and did nothing together. Within the first month of us knowing her we 4 became inseparable. We even started hanging out at home and having meals together. She even had us start a band with the 4 of us. You should have seen how hard it was to get James in jeans and a leather coat, but she did it. "He told her chuckling at the memory.

They arrived at the restaurant and the 4 of them had a very lively lunch recalling many memories of James and their time with him.

"Kat you told me that James had a sense of humor. Every story that you all have told has only been about how stern he was. I can't imagine him with a sense of humor." Dr Smith looks at her.

"Oh, he had one just few people could get it. One time we were skating, and he knew that I loved this one song. every weekend I would wait for the DJ to play it. He decided to pull a prank. He paid the DJ not to play it until he gave him the signal. It was when he saw my dad walk in. This song was one of the songs we had the most fun with, my cousins and me. We would get vulgar and playful with it. We were so into the song I never saw my dad walk in. The look on my dad's face was priceless, especially since when I was younger there was no difference between the dance floor and skates for me. I come around the corner and I see James laughing and pointing. I look over and see my dad standing there. I go to say hi and expect a lecture for dancing to suggestively. Instead, my dad has skates on and asks me to skate with him. I never even knew my dad could skate. James asked the DJ to play the twist after that song and here I am with my dad and all 4 of the husbands on the floor dancing the twist. He set this up because he wanted to see who my dad was and if he had any sense of fun. He had the guy at the door tell my dad that I paid for him to skate to a fun song. To James that was a prank, to me it was the most fun. My dad never actually got to meet the 4 of them but he skated with them. James enjoyed pranking people and would have fun when they looked silly, he would even laugh at himself. Everyone always assumed a lot of the pranks pulled was Kris or Jae. A good number of them were also James. I just let him keep his secret so that he would not lose his reputation as the only nervous brother. He was so much like his dad in so many ways he never wanted anyone to know he had feelings or a soft spot. He thought if they knew they would think it was a weakness. He would watch cartoons, color, and even just stare at the stars with me. He really was a kind gentle dictator." Kat laughingly tells her.

"I get the dictator part. But I still don't get the sense of humor part." She tells her.

"He was one of a kind and he would wait until he thought things would be too serious and then pull something just to shake things up. And look so innocent and let Kris or Jae take the blame. You all remember when your great uncle came from Korea to visit. It was James who gave him Kris's dribble glass. It was James who woke the whole house up with the Korean national anthem the day he was leaving. It was also James who told him to leave and go back to Korea when he said I was not fit for anything more than a passing fancy. that your grandmother and father should have put their foot down and got rid of me before I turned you 4 into nothing more than degenerates with no future. I guess he had a point with that one since I caused you all so much pain. Your dad came to see me once and he told me not to take anything seriously that his uncle had to say, that he knew nothing about family the only thing he knew was honor and the military. He also told me that James took a beating from him because James told him that he was no longer welcome in your home. That I was a part of your family and that he had no say in it. James disrespected an elder, something he would never have done before he met me. Mama Clara said she was so proud of him. I was so sad for him. He should never have gone against grandma's brother. He should have just kept quiet until he left. Then things would have been ok. Instead, he got beaten by your great uncle. Just because he was protecting me." Kat bowed her head and was looking at her plate. Not really wanting to look at those around the table. The silence was deafening. Dr Smith was thinking about all she had learned today. Her heart ached for this young man who she did not know. His life was cut short with so much promise. It is no wonder these 3 cherish the memories so much. She hopes she can get them to open about other family members soon. She wants to learn so much about them.

"Hey that old man knew nothing about us. He came to visit because he wanted grandma to go back with him. He wanted her to take care of him since he never married. Grandma went back for a short visit and set him up with one of her old friends who was a widow looking for someone to take care of her. So, since he had money and needed someone to take care of him, they made for a good match. she even had a son that he could boss around and leave everything to when he died. He grew to love his family that grandma set him up with. So, no harm done, and James deserved a beating since he was pulling pranks that kept Kris and I in so much trouble all the time. I could never convince the adults that I had nothing to do with those pranks." Jae was laughing now thinking about all the things James got away with.

"KI you have been so quiet these last few minutes what you are thinking about." Kat asks him.

"I'm thinking that James was a particularly good actor to have been able to fool all of us except you. I miss him, and I wonder what kind of woman you would have picked out for him." Smiling at her

"Oh, I don't know you know I hated to share you all, but if I had to say. She would have to be smart to be able to talk to him and have good conversations with him. Someone on the same level of genius as him. She would have to be kind and sweet, someone who could put up with his dictatorship all the while pulling out his fun side. someone who had their own hobbies that could compliment his workaholic side. Someone who could stand up to him when he would go across the line but give him hugs and love to remind him, he is human. "She replies.

"Oh yeah so who would you hook me up with." Jae asks jokingly not really wanting to know the answer.

"Oh, boo I already have someone picked out for you. I am just not ready to make my move yet to get you together. It will take some time to get that person to get a clue as to your amazing self." Kat quips back at him. all the while being completely serious.

"What about me could you bring yourself to set me up with anyone other than yourself?" ki asks.

"That's not a fair question and you know it. I thought you had died. Even though I could not remember you my heart remembered the love and the connection we had. I looked for that connection with every man I met. To see if I could even let them get close to me. I could not understand what I was looking for. The only person who came even close was Joe. That is why I married him because my heart was yearning for that connection. If I had to pick anyone, they would not have any trauma like mine. I would want you to be with someone you could freely touch and hold without worrying if they will become scared, they would have to be a good cook and be kind and loving. They would have to have a temperament that could deal with your moodiness. They would need to be positive and encouraging. Smart and carried out. someone you would not feel you needed to baby and coddle. "Kat replies looking into Ki's eyes showing him how much she still loves him.

"So, you without any baggage ok. I guess I will forever be alone. "Ki looks at her. His stare shows her the depth of his feeling. Dr Smith and Jae just stare at them.

"No not someone like me. I am not any of those things anymore. I have done nothing with my life. You need someone who is your equal and who you can be proud of. Someone who can give you children. I cannot do any of those things for you. I am someone who you will become ashamed of. Not someone you can be proud of. I am someone who will only bring you sorrow. So, no, not someone like me. You deserve someone who is far better than me." she tells him very quietly. Kat looks at Jae and asks him if he and Ki take Dr Smith back to the center. She gets her purse and takes out enough money to cover her meal and tip. Holds out her hand to Ki for the extra set of keys. As she walks out, she makes sure that no one can see that she is crying. Instead of going home Kat goes back to the river. Once there she goes back to sit on the rock and cries, her heart is so torn. She truly does not know what to do. Without realizing it she begins talking to James and Kris.

"I came to see you today.to remember your smiles and laughter. As I gaze at the reflection on the surface of the water. I see your faces I hear your voices in the breeze. Rustling through the trees I let the tears flow. As the water flows inside the rocks flows inside all I want to do is scream. Please tell me this is only a dream. How could you go somewhere that I cannot follow? I felt myself wanting to sink beneath its calm shallows. to let the icy water embrace me. to lay my head on your shoulder once more. To sleep in your embrace for evermore. "

After hours of crying and talking I fall asleep in the warm sun. Thank goodness that it's mid spring. not too hot but perfect for being outside without getting sunburned. I woke up and it was dark outside. I am laying on the rock in the middle of the river. The tide has brought the water to the edges of the rock, my pants and shoes are wet. I am stuck here till morning since I cannot see to cross safely. I am just glad that there are no mosquitoes, yet I hope it does not get too cold tonight.

Joe gets home, and the kids are home Shay brought them home. He asks where his wife is.

"I don't know. She had to go someplace with Dr Smith today. She has not gotten back yet. I'm sure she will be fine." she tells him.

She gets the kids ready to go. while Joe sits to eat. "At least she made sure that dinner and everything was done and in the refrigerator this morning before leaving."

"Yeah, she always makes sure there is plenty to eat." Shay tells him goodbye and that she will see him tomorrow.

During the night Kat lays on the rock staring at the stars and wondering what everyone is doing. If anyone even knows that she is missing. Oh well at least it is quiet here and she can think. sometime in the middle of the night she falls back to sleep in the cool night air. The next morning watching the sunrise on the water was beautiful. She wakes up and stretches out her legs when a shadow looms over her. Looking up she stares straight into the angry face of KI.

"What the hell are you doing?" he asks her through clenched teeth.

"Oh, hi I came here after leaving you all yesterday and cried myself to sleep. And when I woke up it was dark, and the tide had risen the water so that I could not cross. So, I camped out here with the stars. Why are you here?" she asks him as she stands up. He grabs her and pulls her into his arms. She goes to push him away.

"If you struggle, we both will wind up in the water. So be still. How could you be so stupid to come here alone and to stay all night. Do you know how worried I have been? I called your husband to see how you were. He had no idea you were not where you should have been. "He tells her.

"I didn't think I just wanted to be by myself and here is the only place I can do that, it's where I always come when I'm upset or have a lot of thinking to do. "She tells him as she moves to go.

"You're not going anywhere yet. We need to talk. "KI sits down and pats the rock for her to sit back down.

"I thought we talked yesterday" she tells him sitting back down.

"We did but I have something to say to you. "He tells her.

"I don't want you to think that we are not equal. I do not like that you still think that you are not worthy of love. You are strong and loving. You are everything any man would want in a woman. Even with all your baggage.

I do not want to have anyone but you. I never have. For you to think that you are not worth loving means that Joe and I both are not worth loving as well. Please let me be your family again. To be worthy of your love. I am not asking for you to leave Joe or give up on your marriage, I am just asking you to let me love you and to have my angel. "Ki looks at her she is staring at him looking at him trying to see if he is serious or just trying to make her feel guilty. She sees the sadness in his eyes and notices that he has dark circles under his eyes.

Ki stood up and held out his hand. She takes it, so he can help her across the rocks to the riverbank.

'I guess I should go get showered and get ready to go to the center our session is in two hours. Are you feeling ok and how did you find me?" Kat looks at him wondering if she really heard right.

"When your husband thought you were with Dr Smith, I figured with your emotional state that you may have come back. So, I came to find you. I saw your truck, but I could not see you in the dark out there. So, I sat here sleeping in the car waiting for you to come back for the truck. Then when the sun rose, and you were sitting out in the middle of the river I just became angry." Ki explains to her.

You know when we were at the clinic, and you showed us grandma journals and the hidden rooms. You know why I could not get angry that I was not Jae real brother." He asks her.

"I wondered about it, but I figured knowing you that it didn't matter. that you always knew how much your brothers and your parents loved you. They could not have loved you more if you were their child. They always treated you the same. I always told you that love has no boundaries. it has no limits or reason. Love is the ultimate gift that anyone can give. It is to be shared and given freely. They gave you their love unconditionally always. "Kat tells him searching his face to see if she answered correctly.

"That was part of it. Do not get me wrong, I was shocked and upset those first few minutes. I was still concerned that it would affect how Jae and you would look at me. What made it bearable and easy for me to accept was Jae. He did not change how he talked to me or treated me. He did not stare at me or try to reassure me. He only hugged me and told me I love you brother. Since it made no difference to him how could I allow it to make a difference to me? I want to enjoy having my brother look at me as he always has for as long as I can. Those months after the accident if you had seen how shaken he was and how he babied me you would have thought I was his child instead of his brother. I never want him to look at me with sad pitiful eyes again. So exactly who do you have in mind for him? Maybe I can help you with it." He smiles at her as he closes the door of the truck.

"it's Dr Smith I want him to marry her. I think she is perfect for him, and I have seen some good sparks between them. I think she is aware that she may like him, but he has no clue. we need to work together to let them have more opportunities alone and to get to know each other." She waves at him and puts the truck in gear. She goes to her house instead of her aunts to shower and change because she knows no one is home and she does not want to answer anyone's questions. After a quick shower she puts some beef in the crock pot and quickly heads to the center for her morning session. As they get settled into the room. Dr Smith decides that she wants to know Kris now.

CHAPTER 36

Remembering Kris

"Yesterday we talked a lot about James and how you felt about him. What role he played in your life, and I hope you were able to find a little peace and let go of some of the grief you feel over his loss. Now I think before we open any more doors, we will give you a chance to remember Kris and say your goodbye to him. I Know at the clinic you got a chance to talk about their grandmother and what she meant to you, but I think that before you go any farther in remembering any more trauma that is hiding behind those doors. It's important that you have closure from the trauma of losing those you loved so deeply including coming to terms with the sudden loss of your father and grandmother."

"Yesterday I shared a letter that James wrote. It's not the only one he wrote but it was the one he liked most. Today I will read one of Kris's letters. Now Kris was my partner in crime we were the most alike. He used to tease me about everything. We were most like siblings. Grandma used to say that if he and James had not been twins then he and I would be. We were always getting into things together. We did so much together from taking care of the green house to pulling pranks on papa. I remember one-time papa and I was watching the roadrunner in the study. Kris slipped in when papa was not looking. He had a horn that made a loud noise like the coyote did when something exploded. He waited until papa was almost asleep and let off that horn. Papa jumped at least two feet off the couch. We burst out laughing. Papa would chase him around the room threatening him with a month of no allowance if he told anyone that we were watching cartoons. He would just laugh and tell him if you make it double and let me hang out here with you, I will keep your secret. Papa doubled his allowance but refused to let him hang out with us. He said it was his time with me and he was not sharing. We always knew what the other was feeling. We always seemed to want to eat the same things at the same time. The others would just shake their heads at the dinner table because we always reached for the same things at the same time and then fight over it. Mama Clara would always get frustrated and just serve both of us, so we would quieten down. Kris was me but as a boy." Kat tells them very quietly, wondering if the other two remember his wonderful playful smile. How easy it was to get him to laugh and smile, one that showed through his eyes with the most mischievous glint.

"Yes, you two were a handful. Man could you two always get in so much trouble and be laughing about it so hard that the adults would just throw up their hand in exasperation. You know he always laughed and played but he was the saddest out of all of us. Before you came around, he would sit in his room for days and we would never see him. Grandma used to swear one day she was going to find him dead in his room. He was the darkest of us all. "Jae told Dr Smith.

"Yes, I know he was me. We both used pranks and laughter to hide behind. We both had a lot of darkness locked up. I knew he was just as sad as I was most days. That he wanted to die as much as I did. I asked him one day if he knew why he was like me. He told me he did not know he just felt so alone and that he was so different from the rest of you. He felt like he could never measure up. So, if he got into trouble and seemed happy then he had papa's attention. That getting into trouble was his talent. I told him I knew how he felt. From my earliest memories I was always told I could never be as good as any of my cousins on any side. I was just a waste of space. I was not as smart as my sister, and I was not a boy who deserved everything like my brother. I could never measure up to being worth anything. So, we made a pact we would be each other's partners, we would always be equal and together in everything. And we did until he left me. I even found a girl that loved him and would have been perfect for him. She would have made him her world. And I knew he would have loved her if given the chance. She was kind and playful but would have let him know how amazingly smart he was. He was a math genius and could play any instrument that he picked up. That was why I goaded you all to be a band so that Kris could show off his talents. He would have been an amazing music teacher. That was his dream, he wanted to study to be a music teacher to write songs and make music. We used to spend hours making up songs in the greenhouse and singing them to the plants. He was the gentlest, most musically gifted person. "Kat told them crying thinking of her best friend and the bond they had.

"I never knew that about him. I knew I could never trust the two of you together for more than a few minutes alone before there was trouble. I knew that before you came, he was all but a hermit. After that it was a different story. you brought him out of his shell and lord could that man perform on stage he was a born actor and musician." Ki told them.

"Now for his letter" Kat tells them.

Hey my bonnie lass.

Well, I am not missing you as much as the others. Ki has not stopped drinking since the day you left. Grandma thinks that she is going to have to send him to rehab if this keeps up. He has spent every day doing nothing but drinking and sleeping. James is bellowing every 5 minutes barking orders at everyone acting like he owns the place, and we are his servants. Papa is not talking to anyone. He just comes home and goes straight to the study. Jae is staying clean though he made you a promise, so he is doing everything he can to keep it. Now I am spending all my time in the greenhouse talking to your plants. I think that is why I do not miss you quite as much as they do because I have all these plants and flowers that you left me to take care of. When I miss you or feel sad, I come in here and tell them all my worries. So, it is like I am talking to you. I miss getting into trouble with you and hearing you argue with me about everything. It is at night when I miss you the most. I close my eyes and I dream about all the things that we used to do together and the things I want to do with you. I need you to come back soon because I am afraid that the darkness inside of me may take over before you come back. If it does, I will not be here for you like I promised. So please hurry back to me so that I can see the sun again and feel its warmth. I love you my bonnie and cannot wait to see you again soon.

Forever your

Clyde

"He didn't write a lot, but I knew what he was feeling. He felt abandoned. He had gotten so close to you all when I was around that when you all started to fall apart, he felt abandoned by you. He felt that even though I was not given a choice that I had abandoned him. How I wish I could have let him know that I was feeling the same way at that time. That as always, we were feeling the same way." Kat buries her head in her hands and cries. cries that have come from her heart at the fact that her best friend felt abandoned and alone. The three DR. s let her cry for a few minutes to let out all the hurt she felt. after about twenty minutes Kat crying slowed down. she blew her nose and sniffled. "I'm sorry I should not be the one crying. Therefore, I did not want to talk about him. He was such a sweetheart, and it was so sad that he was battling the darkness so much of the time. He tried so hard to hide it. He told me once he had no right to be sad that no one ever hurt him. He never was without anything he wanted. He was always supported and given affection. I told him that even though we hide our feelings. They are still there. I broke every promise I made to him. I promised him I would always be close to holding his hand so that he would not give into the darkness. I was not I let him down. "Kat looks at Jae and KI wondering what they are feeling and thinking.

"Kat you know that he died in an accident that he did not hurt himself or anyone else. You also know that he had gone back to school and was studying to become a music teacher. He was not giving in to the darkness. He was fighting it and was winning. From what I heard in his letter was that he was with you in spirit every day when he would tend to your flowers. He found you with him when he was in the greenhouse. So, he knew you did not abandon him. He knew you were still thinking of him and cheering him on even if the two of you were not together." Dr Smith told her how she felt hoping that her take on his letter would show her the positive of it.

"Kat he is the one who pulled us all back together. He kept reminding us that you would be ashamed of us for going back to be the way we were before. That is why mama made us go back to school. It was at Kris's urging. He knew that you would be upset with us. He knew how you felt. Granma used to say that boy and kitten are to close they feel each other's emotions too much. even when they are apart, they seem to still be connected by their emotions." Jae told Kat.

Kat is still just looking at Ki waiting to see what he is going to say. Waiting to see what he is feeling.

"He came into my room one night and opened all the windows. He stripped the covers off me and told me to get up. That you were in pain and needed us to be strong and stable for when you came back. He said that he could feel your pain in his chest. And that we cannot be ready to help you if we cannot even get out of bed. Every few nights you could hear him in the greenhouse crying and begging God to take your pain away to bring you back to us whole. He seemed to know that something was wrong long before James found out what was happening. You two were truly connected on a level that none of us could understand or even compete with." Ki looked at her sadly. She knew what he was talking about because she would go to the river and pray for them every chance she got.

"I'm sorry for yesterday and today I didn't want to make you all sad, so I didn't want to talk about them. It must have been hard for you all to lose them. "Kat lays her head back on the chair and closes her eyes. She is so tired today after yesterday and this morning's session and it is not over yet.

"You told me that you found someone for Kris. Someone you wanted him to date." Ki Prompts her.

"Yes, she was one of my close friends in school. She always saw the positive in everyone. She loved music and wanted to be a science teacher. She asked me one time to introduce her to him. She thought he was the most handsome guy she had ever seen. She was soft-hearted and spoke softly and kindly. She was beautiful. She reminded me of the cheerleader he had a poster of in his room. So, I knew he would think she was pretty. "Kat told them.

"You really were going to get each of them a wife of your choosing?" Dr smith asked in shock.

: Yep, I was. Since I could not have all of them to myself, I was going to choose girls that I liked and got along with. that way I could still be close to them without being worried that they were being mistreated." Kat replied.

"That is a little to controlling and selfish don't you think." Dr Smith tells her.

"Yes, the only time I let myself be selfish was with them. I could not have anything that was just mine growing up. Then these amazing handsome guys entered my life. They were mine and only mine. I was not going to let them go to anyone that I thought was not just as amazing as they were. Still won't." Kat replies hoping that it does not sound too selfish and arrogant.

"That is fine by me I have always swore I would never marry unless you approved. Every woman I have dated since you left us, I have always asked myself. Would angel approve of her?" Jae quips

"I've never even looked or dated anyone. My only girl has always been angel." He says very sternly and seriously. As he gets up and walks out of the room ending the day's session.

The room becomes very heavy in silence. Each wondering what the other was thinking. Kat wondering how she is going to respond to Ki. Jae is curious who Kat has in mind for him. Dr Smith wondering what is going to happen next.

CHAPTER 37

Finding a new purpose.

The rest of the week was the normal day treatment activities. Then on the weekend Kat is going on her first leadership conference. She is going to Charleston. When she gets all packed and meets up with the rest of the group. Terry and Liz are the ones driving the center van this time. They all get in Liz Asks Kat to sit up front with her to talk to her to keep her awake for the 8hr drive. Dr Smith tells her she may need to ask someone else to do that. Kat falls asleep normally as soon as the car moves if she is not driving. Liz laughs and tells her its ok she will keep Kat awake by talking to her. Out of everyone Kat tells the funniest stories about her kids and family.

On the drive Kat looks back and notices that everyone is sleeping.

"You know I normally fall asleep by now. I don't know why I am still awake." Kat tells her.

"it's because you know I need you to stay awake." Liz tells her.

"Can I ask you something?" Kat asks her.

"Sure, you know you can always talk to me about anything." Liz answers

"Has anyone said anything about the fact that I have 3 Drs. Now not just Dr Smith." Kat looks at her wondering about the gossip around the center.

"No one thinks anything about it. They know that the other two Dr. s are there for consultation and that they are there to help you with your memories. Though the biggest gossip is about the 2 Drs. All the ladies at the center think they are so handsome and are very curious about them." Liz tells her, waiting for her reaction.

"Uh no they are off limits for everyone at the center. They are mine and only mine. Until I say otherwise. It has always been that way." Kat snorts at her

"Hahahaha that is funny coming from a married woman. You know you cannot own a person. I think that Ki Park is dreamy and have wanted to ask him out to dinner. He never sticks around long enough for me to ask." Liz tells her.

"He will just tell you no. he doesn't see anyone outside of work. He is very private, and he is my soulmate. He is the one person that I can honestly say that I love more than anyone ever. After him it would be my kids and Joe." Kat tells her.

"You know that isn't very fair that you have both him and joe." Liz tells her.

"I know but it's the way it is. The only reason we are not together is because of circumstances that we had no control over when I was still a teen. If things had been different back, then we would be together now. I know I sound childish and selfish. He is not someone that can be loved just by anyone. He is not for someone to just have a light romance with either. He is someone who needs and deserves to be cherished and loved completely." Kat tells her quietly.

"So, you would rather him have no one than give him up?" she questions her.

"He has already told me he wants no one else. Our connection is overly complicated, but it is strong. "Kat tells her" We do not have a physical relationship if that is what you are asking. I will not cheat on my husband. We are awfully close though closer than my husband and I have ever been. Because of that it's hard to explain."

"I see so there really is no chance for anyone of us to be with him. What about the other one?" she asks

"Nope not him either. He is already taken by someone else. They just have not realized it yet" Kat tells her.

"Oh ok. You know we will be there soon. What are you most excited to learn?" Liz asks her.

"I want to learn more about being a positive leader and to be more productive. I want to learn to stand up for myself." She tells her.

After they arrive and get settled everyone goes down to dinner. They meet the board of directors of the clinic that is sponsoring the academy. At dinner Liz introduces Kat to a gentleman who oversees the leadership program

"Mr. Delaney this is Kat she is in your workshop tomorrow on how to change the misconceptions of those with brain disorders."

"it's nice to meet you Kat. "He says as he reaches out to take her hand. Kat just looks at him and speaks.

"it's nice to meet you." But she refuses to shake his hand. Liz does not understand this. Kat is never rude, why will she not shake his hand? Just then another lady comes over to chat with them and she just watches the exchanges between them. She sees Kat has withdrawn and has become extremely quiet.

Liz is very confused by this. She has become so different since meeting the leader of the workshop. Kat excuses herself and goes to sit next to terry.

"Kat what's wrong?" Terry asks her.

"Nothing I just get a bad feeling from that guy. I am not sure why. So, it is simply better for me to sit here with you. Which workshop did you sign up for tomorrow?" Kat asks terry. She knows that the counselors must sign up for classes as well as the clients. She is hoping that she will be in the same one as her.

"I am in the changing the misconceptions of brain disorders class." She informs her.

"Oh, can I sit with you tomorrow. I really do not want to sit with anyone I do not know. Maybe I am being rude, but I am not ready to sit near any of them yet. "She tells her.

"It's fine you can sit with me. This is not like you though you usually warm up to people easily. "Terry tells her she notices that Kat is just looking around the room. She sees a few of her friends from the main center and the group home. She waves but stays glued beside her. One of the speakers notices that she is not mixing with the others. she walks over to Kat and Terry.

"Hi, don't you wish they would give you a dress code for these dinners. I always feel underdressed. "She says causally.

"I wish I had better clothes to wear as well but I only wear pants I don't like dresses. "Kat tells her.

"Same here I don't like talking and not know if they are looking at my legs or my face." She laughs.

Terry notices that Kat is warming up to this person and excuses herself so that they can talk a little freer.

"I am Mrs. McDonald I am one of the speakers tomorrow I hope you will be in my class. "She asks.

"Which one are you doing?" Kat asks her.

"I am helping out with the one for suicide and the aftereffects." She tells her.

"I am in that one and the misconceptions of brain disorders. Your class is first I think." Kat tells her.

"Oh, good I hope to see you bright and early in the morning." She says waving to her good night.

After a couple of hours, they decide to go back to their room and call it a night, so they can get up early. During the night Kat has a nightmare and wakes terry up with her cries in her sleep. Liz and Nancy from the adjoining door hear her and knock on the door.

"What do I do? I have never heard her in the throes of a nightmare its terrifying to listen to her cry and scream." Terry asks Liz. She notices that Liz is on the phone.

"Dr Smith what do we do Kat is in a nightmare and we can't get near her. she is thrashing about." Liz tells her.

"Put the phone where she can hear me, please." Dr Smith asks her.

Liz walks over to the bed close to Kat and puts the phone earpiece close to her. She hears Dr Smith speaking in a language that she does not know, and once Kat registers this sound coming from the phone she begins to calm down. And within a few minutes Kat is sleeping peacefully without ever waking up.

"What did you do?" terry takes the phone from Liz to talk to Dr smith.

"I had Dr Park teach me the lullaby he sings to Kat when she has a nightmare so that if I am around and he is not I can calm her." Dr Smith tells them "It seems to work miracles for her. Why I am not sure. Has she calm down and gone back to sleep?" she asks them?

"Yes, she seems fine now. Sound to sleep just like a baby." Liz tells her "

"How loud or violent was her nightmare?" Dr smith asks.

"Only those of us in the room and adjoining room could hear her. She did not hurt anyone or herself. she just thrashed about some. "Liz explained.

"Ok good don't tell her about the nightmare she may be embarrassed and become withdrawn if she thinks she did something to anyone." Dr smith tells her.

"Umm Dr Smith she did something very not like her tonight." Liz tells her.

"What was it?" Dr smith asks.

"She refused to shake a gentleman's hand and withdrew from everyone for the longest time. I mean she literally refused to look or speak to anyone until one of the presenters went over to talk to her.' She told her.

"Was there any drinking going on?" Dr smith asks her.

"Yes, he had been drinking and had a drink in his hand." Liz tells her.

"that's why Kat removes herself from any kind of situation when there is drinking. She has had some awfully bad memories where drinking is involved. It's not anything to worry about." she tells her.

"Ok good I was in shock I had never seen her be so rude to someone before. I am sorry we called and woke you up, but I am happy that we were able to clarify something and get her some rest. Thank you for answering so quickly." Liz tells her.

"it's no problem the clients you took with you are my patients and I need to be of help to them at all times no worries." Dr smith tells her good night and hangs up the phone to go back to sleep. She finds she cannot sleep. So, she picks up the phone and calls jae.

"hello "he answers on the first ring.

"Hello Jae, its Sarah I couldn't sleep after getting a call from the retreat that a few of the clients are on. Did I wake you?" she asks?

"No, I couldn't sleep I was wondering if angel was doing ok and debating whether I should call her or not." He tells her.

"Really that's who I got a call about." she tells him.

"What is she ok? is she having a problem?" he asks.

"Nothing serious she had a nightmare and they called me to help so I sung her the lullaby that you all taught me. She never even woke up. One of the workers was concerned because she was rude to one of the gentlemen at the retreat. He had been drinking so I told them not to worry, she just does not mix well with people when drinking is going on. "She explains.

"Oh, ok good I'm happy that you were able to take care of it you know you could have called me before and I would have taken care of it for you." he tells her.

"It's fine she is my patient, and I was happy that I can finally help her in more ways than just when she is in session." She tells him hoping that they can talk about something other than Kat.

"What are you doing tomorrow?" he asks.

"it's Saturday nothing really." She answers.

"Will you go somewhere with me tomorrow? It is someplace I have wanted to show you for a while. "He asks her to hope she will tell him yes.

"Sure, how should I dress." She prompts him.

"Jeans tee shirt and sneakers" he tells her "I will pick you up at 9 am be prepared to be gone into the evening. "He tells her.

"Ok I will be ready." She smiles as she hangs up the phone.

Jae calls Ki. He is excited that she said yes now if only he can get through the day not making it all about angel.

"Hello Jae, what did she say?" Ki asks him before he can even say hello.

"She said yes and how did you know that I actually asked her.?" Jae demands of his brother.

"Because angel asked you to take her out on a date. You do everything she asks. Also, I know you like her you were just waiting for angel to tell you it was ok." He tells him.

"How do you always know these things.?" He laughs at his brother.

"Angel told me she has chosen Dr Smith for you. She thinks that you both like each other and that she is perfect for you. Where are you taking her too tomorrow? "He asks his brother.

"I thought I would take her to the festival that they are having. You know the lallapaloosa at the old track they are going to have an all day and into the evening concerts. I think she may enjoy it. You know angel used to love it when we took her to concerts and festivals. I am hoping Sarah will enjoy it." Jae tells him.

"I'm sure she will just don't talk work the entire day and don't compare her to angel all day. Remember they are quite different." He tells his brother before he hangs up.

The next morning Kat and the others get up and quickly get ready for the day's events. Kat is excited to attend her class with the lady she met the night before. So, she hurries through breakfast and rushes to the hall to get a front row seat.

She sees they are not set up yet. "Can I help with anything?" she asks.

"Oh, if you could put a pack of handouts and put them on every. It looks like we have a full house today. "The girl asks her while handing her a stack of handouts.

Kat helps them get the room set up and finds her seat. The lady from the night before steps up to the podium.

"Hello, I am Mrs. McDonald, and I am here to talk to you about the effects of suicide. Many of you in this room have either tried to commit suicide or have lost someone to suicide. I lost my daughter a few years back.

During her life, my daughter suffered greatly from a brain disorder. She had schizophrenia and depression. We had her on medications and were incredibly involved in her treatment and care. As a mother it broke my heart to see my child struggle and suffer. Knowing that I was doing all I could do to help her. To this day I do not understand why my child wanted to die but I do understand the brain disorders she suffered from. What she did not understand was that it was not her fault that she had these brain disorders. I call mental illness a brain disorder because when you say mental illness people automatically think crazy. that is not true by any means. My child was smart and artistic. She had an extremely outgoing and sunny personality when her illness was controlled. Mental illness is no different than any other illness you have in your body. It is just that people do not understand or want to understand it. It is treatable. It is controllable. You can work with it. You can function in society and unless you tell someone many times, they will not know that there is a problem. My daughter got excellent grades and had many friends in school and college. When she decided to commit suicide, it was after a really hard time with her illness. When I found her, I thought my life was over? Until I decided that I was not going to let her die in vain. I decided that I wanted to help those who were in pain like her, and comfort families like me. So that is why I am here today. There are a few steps that need to be taken to help ensure that you that are think of committing suicide can take to prevent you from taking that step.

1 know your illness. Know all that you can about it so that you can learn your triggers. By knowing your triggers, you can avoid situations that will cause you problems. If you know that stress at work is a trigger you can fill out a form that needs your employer to give concessions to you. This may be as simple as a shorter workday or a strict break schedule that may be needed for you.to keep up with your meds and meals. Under the law they need to accommodate reasonable requests

2 do not use your illness as an excuse to check out on life. Life is exciting, fun, and yes at times hard. Not everyone is going to embrace you with open arms. do not let that keep you from living the best life you can. When you make mistakes, you will. do not use your illness as the reason. If you have a good handle on number one, then you can function and be able to work and interact within a reasonable manner with others. Allow yourself to become used to your environment and have your support systems in place both at work and at home.

3 have a support system. Have people around you that understand your illness and know what your triggers are so that they can notice when changes for good or bad happen. This way they can help you through the hard times and celebrate the good with you. This will also help with working in the world outside of your home. Many jobs will and can partner you up with someone who can help you with anything you need. Under the law they need to accommodate any reasonable request if you communicate your needs.

4 know your medications and their side effects. Often medications can become addictive. Know what they are and the side effects so that you can make informed and good choices with your doctors. Knowing your medications and their side effects will help you decide how well you can perform a job and what kind of job you can do.

5 be in control of your treatment and your life. Do not let others tell you that something you want is wrong unless it harms you.

6 take responsibility and accountability for your actions. Regardless of your illness you own your actions. Do not make excuses for your lack of control. If you are following the earlier steps, then you should never be out of control to the point you are not aware of.

When you decide to take your own life, you are not making the world better. You are not making life easier for those around you. You are causing them more pain and causing them to wonder what more they could have done. When you feel that you are falling into this dark place; go to your support system. There is no shame in needing help. There is no shame in sometimes having to start over. For if you stay and fight for your life. There is always a chance of a better tomorrow. We all who are here. Are human we make mistakes and have weak moments. Take courage and pick yourself up from those weak moments and lean on those who love you. Who is there to help you? Every day that you are on this earth be an inspiration to those who need it. Show the world that just because you have a brain disorder does not mean you are any less than anyone else. In fact, you are not weaker, you are stronger. You're stronger because you are not just surviving you are living to be the best you. Always be honest with yourself and show everyone that you are more than just a survivor. When I lost my daughter, I read her journals. Even though I was always there for her. I missed the signs that she was sinking and losing her way. I never knew that she felt that she was a burden to me. I never knew that when the voices would feed her depression she would cry because she felt sorry for me. Not until I read for myself how she felt in the months before she died. I did not know that she was having trouble at work and was giving in to the pressures of working longer hours and skipping meals and medication because she felt ashamed to tell her new her boss that she had documented concessions for accommodations to be met. That she would not work past a certain time. That she would have a structured break schedule. For over 6 years she worked at this company, and no one ever asked her to change her concessions. The hr. department never had any complaints about her work and her attendance was better than the majority. What changed was that she was given a new supervisor who did not care that she needed to accommodate her illness. She wanted her to do what she was told. This supervisor was informed that she needed to accommodate her needs and that it was documented. So, my daughter, out of fear for her job, gave in and stopped doing what was needed for her well-being. It was my daughter's responsibility to stand up for herself and not allow herself to get stressed out and worn down. It was her place to make sure that this person understood what was needed. I failed her. Why? Because I stopped looking and listening. I got comfortable with her routine and forgot to look for signs that she was not herself. I am not saying this to cast blame on myself. It is and always will be my daughters' fault for committing suicide. It is my fault for not making the time to check on her daily and for not following the plan that we set up. Both sides have a responsibility. The person who is the caretaker handles always being supportive and to be open to the person who has the illness. Just like with any other illness. The person with the illness handles communicating their needs and changes in their life so that the other people in their life not only understand what is happening but are prepared for changes. Be willing to be there for the people in your life not just be a bystander. Be willing to ask for help, do not be ashamed of your weakness. Be brave and strong, admit when something is no longer working and get help to fix it. I lost my daughter because she did not want to be a bother. Be a bother and communicate your needs and listen to your support system to know their needs as well. I urge you to surround yourself with people who are honest and positive. People who are willing to accept you as you are but at the same time urge you to be the best you. Someone who will hold you when you need to cry but will let you go when you need to soar to new heights. Someone who will hold your hand and soar with you to celebrate every milestone and let you shine. If someone is not cheering, you on and helping you to be the best you all the while being there for you when you hit bottom. Then do not rely on them for your help. Do not ever give up on living. Surround yourself with a tribe who will walk with you all the way. There is a saying that it takes a village to raise a child. There is no truer statement. It takes a village to survive and to thrive. Look who is in your village and those who do not meet up to what you need let them go. Those who do embrace them and thrive. If my daughter had embraced her village, she would still be alive today. If she had the courage to speak up and communicate her needs. She would be standing here instead of me. To commit suicide is a very selfish thing to do. It steals the joy of having you in this world. It steals the hope and love you bring to this world away. It leaves an emptiness that can never be filled behind. It hurts more than all the problems you could ever cause. Focus on the positive in your life and the darkness will grow smaller. I hope that by sharing my pain of losing my daughter and some of her struggles. That those of you who must struggle everyday with sadness will know that you are worth loving. Your life is worth living. "By the time she finished speaking you could hear the emotion welling up in her voice. You could hear the tears that she was holding back. Kat had tears welling up in her eyes and the sound of the pain she was sharing. You could tell that she meant every word and that she was literally begging them to listen and have the courage to live.

"Are you ok." Terry asks Kat.

"Yes, I'm ok I just feel so sad for her. I never thought about how my mom or kids would feel if I died by my own hand. Even though none of them really understand why I am the way I am. They do try to." Kat tells her.

They leave the hall for lunch and to get ready for the next speaker. Kat is wondering if Jae took Dr Smith to the lollapalooza.

Sarah is ready and waiting for Jae to get to her house. She is excited to be seeing him without it being about work. Jae pulls up and beeps the horn for her. He gets out and opens the door for her.

"Good morning, Sarah, I hope you enjoy today it's going to be hot but it's going to be fun." He tells her as she gets in the car. They start driving and Sarah is surprised they have turned into the old racetrack. Wondering what they are doing here as he parks the car. She sees a large group of students at the entrance wondering what they are doing. Jae shows the person at the gate his passes. He takes her hand, and they head for the stage. She cannot believe how large the crowd is. There are booths and food stands set up. Suddenly Jae pulls her into his arms close to his side. So that the group trying to get passed them does not crush her. Sarah feels a flutter curling in her stomach. She knows that she is attracted to him. Though she is not sure that she is ready to be in such proximity to him. Jae smells her perfume. It's intoxicating to him and yet awfully familiar. He looks at her.

"What perfume are you wearing." He asks her.

"It's a mixture of different oils that Kat gave me to use in my hair to moisturize it and help it stay smelling nice." She tells him.

He smiles at her and tells her "It smells genuinely nice. I knew it was familiar but different at the same time."

"Yes, she gave it to me when we were at Ki's clinic. She said my hair was too dry and wanted to mix something up for me. I love it my hair is so soft now." She smiles up at him.

His heart skips a beat. At her smile he tells her they need to make their way to the stage area, so they can get the best view of the entertainment. When they get to the pit Metallica is taking the stage. Jae gets a look of pure joy on his face. "I love Metallica the last time I saw them live it was with my brothers and Kat. I hope today you enjoy its nonstop music and food." He tells her.

"I love them also and yes; I love live music the best. Though I am not a true metal head I do love Metallica. "She tells him.

Throughout the day they enjoy the different bands. Sarah was enjoying herself so much. She had never actually been to see an actual concert live. To be at a festival where there were so many at one time was pure pleasure. Jae was so much fun and to see him smile so much made it even more special. They got to see Metallica, Sound Garden, Ramones, rancid, cheap trick, rage against the machines, Waylon Jennings. And a few she had never heard of before. By the end of the night, she was exhausted from dancing and standing so much all day. When Jae drops her back home, he did not want the day to end.

"I hope you had fun today. Thank you for not making me go by myself. "He tells her.

"Oh, you're welcome. I enjoyed the day so much. I cannot remember the last time I had so much fun." She tells him "But be honest you already had two passes you were going to take Kat if she had not gone to the retreat." She asks him.

", Kat got the passes for me and told me to ask you to go. I am so happy she did now. I got to see you completely relaxed and free today. We will have to do this more often." He tells her.

"Seriously you asked me out because Kat told you to?" She looks annoyed.

"Don't be mad about it please. It was a perfect day and Kat wanted to do something to thank us for all our help. She went through a lot to get these passes. She had to call in a favor from an old school mate for them. She did not have enough to buy them and did not want me to pay for them.so she asked for a favor from an old friend. She was worried you would not like the music but remembered how much I loved going to live concerts and wanted us to have fun." He tells her.

"Really I was hoping you were asking me out because you wanted to not because Kat told you to." She turns to go into the house very annoyed at him now.

He grabs her hand and pulls her into his arms. "I do not do anything that I do not want to even if an angel wants me to. She may have suggested it, but I had the most fun I have had in years. When she suggested it, I became incredibly happy, and my heart flipped a little with excitement. Wondering if you were going to say yes or not. I have wanted to ask you out but did not have the courage. Since she presented me with the passes, I had no excuse anymore not to ask you. I have a feeling that she wants us to get to know each other better. Which I have no objections with." He tells her sternly so that she knows that her jealousy is not called for.

"You always talk about how much you love her, and you are always rushing to her side. I just think that there is no one for you or Ki except her." She tells him quietly.

"Yes, I love her she is one of the most precious people in my life, but I know I have no future with her I never had. She is and always will be my sister. We have a connection that cannot be broken. Even after all these years we still have that connection. That does not stop me from having feelings for anyone else. Or enjoying someone else's company. Yes, I love her and will always rush to her side as her friend and brother only. If you are wondering Kat has never given me even a proper kiss it has always only been on the cheek just like any sister would. "Jae tells her as he bends his head to hers. He brings his lips to hers and kisses her softly. Sarah opens her mouth slightly to deepen the kiss. After a few moments. They say good night and Sarah goes into her house.

Jae walks away smiling his heart racing he cannot wait to ask her out again.

Sarah closes the door when she sees him drive away. She smiles at the warmth she is feeling. "Thank you, Kat," she whispered to the universe.

She decides to call Liz to check on the group.

"Hello "Liz answers

"Hi Liz, it's Dr Smith I wanted to see how everyone is doing. How did today go." She asks.

"Today went well. Everyone enjoyed their workshops and learned a lot. "She tells her.

"Good what are you guys doing now?" She wonders if Kat is still up.

"They are giving a dance tonight, so everyone can enjoy their last night of the retreat. I came back to the room exhausted. Kat and Terry are still out dancing. "She yawns as she is talking.

"Oh, I am glad that they are having some fun as well as learning a few things. I will let you get some sleep see you all in a few days." Dr Smith hangs up smiling to herself thinking of the perfect day that she had.

At the dance Kat and Terry are taking a break from dancing. Terry is curious how Kat liked the second speaker since he was the one, she was rude too.

"Kat how did you like your second workshop today?" she asks her.

Before she could answer the gentleman, who was speaking at the workshop came over to talk to her.

"Your Mrs. Sanchez, right?" he asks, reaching out his hand for her to shake.

"Yes I am. why do you ask." She replies.

"I have been looking forward to meeting you. I know your aunt. I sponsored a retreat at her facility a few months ago. She told me that she hoped you would join us. That she thinks you have a lot to offer our group. Is there a reason you will not shake my hand?" he asks her to look at her curiously.

"I'm sorry but I get uncomfortable around people when they drink, especially men. It is not you it is something that I have always had a problem with. 'She explains.

"Oh no I understand I will not drink anymore if I can join you two and you can tell me what you thought of my workshop." He tells her.

She gives him a weak smile and agrees.

"I liked it. You gave a lot of information in your workshop, but you gave no real-life experiences to show examples, only facts. It was hard to see if you related to us or not. For example, you when you were talking about how most people associate mental illness or brain disorders with people who are violent. Here was a perfect place where you could have used an example of someone who is not violent and is a productive part of society. Like you could have listed people in history or the present day. celebrities or prominent educators. People need to understand that brain disorders are a wide spectrum. That it is not something that just happens, but it involves chemical reactions and occurs because of these reactions. That mental illness is not just because someone had a bad childhood or suffered abuse. That is how media portrays people with mental illness. It is important that people understand that we are not crazy or lazy. That we can still do everything that those who do not suffer can do. Most people think that those who have depression just need to suck it up and get over it. They do not understand that the depth of the emptiness and hopelessness is caused by multiple factors. Yes, life experience, serotonin levels, stress, all play a role in this. Yet those who have heart disease and diabetes also have the same stressors and people just feel empathy for them and yet are afraid of someone who has depression. These are things that need to change. In your workshop you could show where the illnesses of the physical body such as heart diabetes auto immune and others have remarkably similar triggers. When people see that mental illness or brain disorders are all the same, they are an illness not something to be feared. Yes, people who have mental illness when not treated and are predisposed to an abusive nature are scary and give those of us who are not an awfully bad rep because we are all blocked in the same category. When people see someone with autism, they forget that it is a brain disorder or mental illness. They do not fear them, they have empathy. It is the way that our society has portrayed so many mental illnesses that people can accept some as an illness and others as something that someone is just too lazy to change. "Kat looks at them when she has finished talking wondering if maybe she went too far while standing on her soap box. She thinks to herself oh lord I am in trouble.

"Wow you were really paying attention. That is what this academy is about. It is to try to change the face of mental illness and give consumers the power to change their lives and roles in society. You're right, just by giving facts is not enough we need to have real people's stories out there as well. I hope you will continue to come to these retreats and workshops. I look forward to hearing more of your views. I am a person who deals with facts and statistics. I will also start to look for successful and some ordinary examples of those with brain disorders to highlight also in my future workshops. Thank you for your feedback." He excuses himself and goes to mingle with some other consumer.

"Wow Kat I didn't think you would say anything to him let alone be so passionate about his talk. I think you scared him a little and chased him away" Terry tells her.

"I live with my family who believes like so many others do. that I can help how I feel. That I am just not strong enough to get past the past. That I am just too lazy to do anything about my illness that I use it as an excuse to get away with things. I have even had Dr, s tells my family that I am pretending to be sick, so I do not have to face their anger or take responsibility for my actions. This is so far from the truth and sometimes I want to scream at them and try being me just for a day. See how well you handle my illness, my nightmares, my fear, my feelings. Instead of criticizing maybe you should put yourself in my shoes and see how well you would do. Then I think about it, and I would not wish this illness on my worst enemy. No one should have to live every day with a void of darkness and overwhelming sadness, one that if you do not fight it, you will take your own life. No one should have to live in fear of just waking up in the morning. "Kat tells her.

"I work with you all and even though I do not suffer myself I still can see how you all work hard to control your illness. To others it may not be a lot but we at the center do understand and know that you are working hard." Terry tells her.

"I think I am ready for bed its after midnight and we have a long day tomorrow." Kat tells her as she stands up to go to her room.

"I will go with you as well. Maybe next time we can share a room, so we can have more chances to talk." Terry tells her.

A New beginning

*A*fter they get home the van drops everyone off at their homes. Kat asks them to drop her off at her home not at their aunts' because she wants to see her kids. When they arrive the 5 kids are on the trampoline in the front yard. They all come running to get Kats bags and give her hugs. Joe came out on the porch.

"Your just in time I am grilling some steaks and burgers do you want to make some salsa and maybe some salad. "He asks her as he walks over to give her a kiss on the cheek. Kat looks at him surprised. He just smiles at her. And tells the kids to take her stuff inside.

"Sure, I can do that let me get changed into something more comfortable and wash up." She says as she waves bye to Liz.

The afternoon was a very pleasant one. They laughed and played. Kat made salad and salsa while Joe grilled. The kids were beaming with happiness to see them getting along. when it came time for Kat to leave to go to her aunt's house.

"Why don't you come home now. It has been such a long time and we have made a lot of progress. I think that for you to stay gone much longer is not going to do anyone any good. We need to try to see if we can make this work." Joe tells her.

"I agree I think it's time for us to start over. I am not ready to sleep with you yet, but I am ready to see if we can go back to be a full-time family." She tells him.

"It's ok I understand you can sleep in the living room on the roll out bed for now. And we can see how things go from there." He agrees with her and gets up to fix the roll out bed for her.

Kat is wondering if this is going to work or not. Hoping for the best. After getting everyone down to sleep the house is incredibly quiet. Kat is lying in bed staring at the ceiling. The tension in the house is very thick. It is not the kind of tension from anger or hurt. It's sexual tension. She cannot sleep because she can feel joe in their room, she knows he is awake feeling it also. She thinks to herself I do not know if I can do this. I want to go and lay in bed with him. I just want to feel him close.

Joe is laying in their bed thinking oh God this is a mistake. How am I supposed to sleep with her just in the next room? My body is aching with need for her. How am I going to survive this every day? I do not think I can do this after all. I get so short tempered when I am frustrated, and this is so frustrating. How am I going to keep it together and become short tempered with her?

Kat gets up to go take a shower, she cannot sleep and tossing on the uncomfortable bed is not helping.

"Joe, are you sleeping?" she asks at the door.

"No, I am not how can I when you are in the next room and not in here with me." He tells her.

"Can I come in just for a few minutes?" she asks.

"If you come in here, you know what is going to happen. So, the choice is yours." He tells her hoping that she will come in.

Kat opens the door and walks over to their bed. She leans down and kisses him. He cannot help himself she puts his arms around her and crushes her to him. giving her a deep longing kiss. Within minutes they are in the throes of a passionate kiss. One that shows how long they have been separated. The night takes a quite different turn they wind up staying up all night between talking and making love. For the first time in months, they talked about their fears and their desires.

"I was so afraid that you would lose your temper. I was always scared you would hurt me or one of the kids. If it were me you were hurting, I could take it but if you had ever hurt one of the kids, I think I would have lost it." Kat tells him.

"I am so sorry for hurting you. I just had no control over my temper after the fire. Between waking up in fear and feeling my body burn from the burns and hearing the words she tried to kill you. I know I belittle you sometimes think you are so weak. I know you are not weak. I know that you have been to hell and back. I also now know that sometimes you cannot control what you are feeling and your reactions. I have experienced this lack of control myself. I am working on controlling my temper more. I know I may still lose it at times and yell the house down cursing but now once I have finished venting my anger by yelling it seems to just go away. It does not linger anymore like before. "Joe tells her.

"I am glad, I can handle your cursing and yelling even if you're belittling when you're angry I just can't handle you laying angry hand on me or the throwing and kicking things around. If you can control that we will be ok." She tells him.

He hugs her close and kisses her forehead I can do that. I also want you to be the best you. You need to tell me when things are too much for you to handle. You need to talk to me about when you have way too much going on. I will take overpaying the bills and not complain about you not doing anything. I promise. I know you are working hard on getting better so that you can be the best mom you can be." He tells her sincerely.

"Thank you and I promise that I will get up every day and do my best so that hopefully once I am better, I can go back to work and help you that way too. Oh, do not forget I need you to send your mom money. Her bills will be coming due soon and she cannot be down there with no utilities. You are going to find we have a lot more responsibilities than you think we do once you start having to write those checks. And see for yourself how much we need." She tells him snuggling closer to him smiling at how nice it feels to be in his arms, and to feel his love and not his anger.

The next morning everyone gets up and goes to church, including Joe. They are all smiling and playing around. Once at church they sit at the back. Kat's cousins get up to sing and insist that she join them. She gets up and they sing Holy Holy, Holy. Joe sits back and watches his wife sing with a smile. He can see her happiness this morning and you can hear it in her voice. He wonders how often she has come to church and put a happy face on instead of letting her family see her pain. He is lost in his thoughts when she comes back and sits next to him. She takes his hand in hers while she prays. She prays silently so that he does not hear her, but he can feel her emotions through how tight she is holding his hand. He does not like coming to church much he is catholic, and her church is far too noisy with the music and the preaching is loud. Though he enjoys her uncle's preaching. He just wishes they could go back home but he knows that every person in this building will want to speak with her and hug her before they leave. He sneaks out as soon as her uncle makes the alter call so that way, she will try to get out faster. Her cousin comes out a few minutes after he does.

"Yeah, I see I am not the only one who slips out before the hug fest starts." He jokes with joe.

"Yes, I know I do not mind getting hugs, but you all just have too many who love to talk and hug. I mean it takes an hour to get out of church after it's over." He laughs with him.

"You know most of us have no clue what has been going on with her. Though I talked to my mom and told her she should not have allowed Kat to stay with her. That Kat was wrong for all the things she has put you through and you had every right to kick her out. I know we don't talk much at work, but I just don't understand that cousin of mine sometimes." He tells him.

Joe is in shock. How could he think that everything was just his wife's fault? He is her family and instead of taking up for her he is telling him: that he would rather her be homeless than stay with his parents.

"You really don't know anything do you? Joe tells him through clenched teeth "I was taking my anger and frustration out on my wife because I believed that she tried to hurt me because of my family's misunderstanding. I hit her, I kicked her, I tried to strangle her. Why because of a misunderstanding? You have no idea what kind of hell my wife has been through and not just by my hand but also at the hands of her family and others. She still forgives and acts as if none of you have ever done her wrong. You are her cousin, yes, we may be friends and may work together but you should still have her back not mine. She and I are starting over, and I pray to God that we will, be ok and that I will be a better husband. She is not how you think she is. I know that a lot of things make her look like a witch. she is not a witch far from it. I know that as soon as I start drinking, that she is going to tell me she is ready to leave and if I do not go with her and the kids, she is going to leave without me. Why? Because she does not want our children to see their father and uncles get into fights and arguments. She never thinks of herself. She always gives every ounce of her energy to those around her. giving them her love and helping them however she can. That is your cousin. I am thankful to your mom and dad for allowing her to stay with them. They have been true to what they believe that God loves all of us and intended for us to take care of each other." Joe tells him sincerely.

"Oh, I didn't know you abused her. I just thought she was being childish and using mom and dad to make others feel sorry for her. I'm sorry dude if I over stepped." He tells him.

"I'm not the one you need to be sorry too she is." Joe tells him and smiles when he sees Kat come out from the church holding the two youngest hands with the other three following.

She walks over and gives the youngest to Joe and gives her cousin Abe hug." You know we need to get together sometime for a night of cards. It been a long time since we had you over." She tells him. As she is getting the kids in the car. Shay walks over and asks her kids if they want to come home today or not. They tell her now that auntie Kat is having a cookout today and they want to go eat at her house. Shay looks at her.

"Are you sure you don't want me to take them?" shay asks.

"Oh no its fine we are going to go to the river for a little while and then I'm going to make them some hot dogs on the grill with some mac &cheese and watermelon. They are fine. You will need to be at home before work tomorrow though. they need clothes for school, and I have an early session in the morning so if you could stop by and pick up mom and bring her so that way, I can have her help me get them ready I would appreciate it." Kat tells her.

"How about I come down this afternoon for dinner and help you get them bathed and bring their school clothes this afternoon." Shay answers her.

"That's fine if that's what you want to do." Kat replies

Their mom comes out of church and comes over. She gives Joe a hug and asks what are "they are doing the rest of the day. "

 We are going to go play at the river for a bit then back to my house for a cookout." Kat replies

"How about I come home with you all and if you do not mind, I will stay the night. I do not have anything going on tomorrow and was thinking of coming down to get a head start on sorting the kid's clothes. It's gotten too hot for them to wear jeans to school, and you need to see what they are going to need for summer."

"That works out perfectly because I have an early session in the morning and Shay was going to stop and get you in the morning. This way you are already there, and I won't have to worry about it." Kat replies.

Joe looks at them in amusement. Not one time did any of them think to ask him what he wanted or thought. He just shakes his head and gets in the car. On the way back to the house the kids are getting excited to be going to the river. He knows his mother-in-law will most likely go home and lay down on the couch and sleep for a while. so much for any alone time with his wife today. At least they had last night and hopefully many more nights to come.

The day was a perfect day and there was no arguing. Joe would just randomly hold Kat's hand and kiss her wrist. Throughout the day. He felt like he was dating his wife again. He noticed that she was sitting on the big rock in the center of the river. Wondering what she is thinking he goes over to sit with her.

"What are you thinking about?" he asks.

"I am not sure what I want to tell you. I am afraid it will spoil the mood and today is such a happy day." She tells him.

"It will be ok I promise nothing is going to spoil the mood." He takes her hand as he tells her this.

"This is where the twin's ashes were spread. You know I always told you that this was a special place. I found out not long ago that this is where they spread their ashes. I was thinking how much you would have liked Kris and James, and that I wish that I could tell you about them. Without you getting upset." She tells him.

"You know I have never been jealous of you. You have never given me a reason to. So why can't you tell me about them? Personally, I do not need to know about them because they are gone. But if you want to tell me about them it will be ok." He tells her.

"We used to spend a lot of days here the 5 of us. James was like a bossy big brother. Always reminding me to be careful not to climb too far into the tree. He used to get so mad when I would jump out of the tree into the water. Kris was a joker he would have loved the kids" she says as she is watching the kids climb the tree to jump out of.

"Oh, do you want to leave. Are you ok being here?' he asks her?

"Yes, I'm very content. I think that knowing they are here watching over us with my dad and grandma makes me incredibly happy. I know that everything will be ok now. "She lays her head on his shoulder watching the kids play.

After a while they head home to get everyone cleaned up and ready for dinner. It was another perfect day.

Time to get back to work.

*I*t is back to the normal routine things have been going well at home for Kat and her family. Dr smith sees her smiling more and joking with her friends more. She has become such a ray of sunshine that she almost hates having to possibly cause her pain. But today she needs to make some progress in her therapy. She is still having nightmares and at times you can see a sadness in her eyes, other times fear. Though now it is not from her husband it is linked to the memories she is hiding.

"In today's session with Kat I want to help her bring closure to her grandmothers' death. She has a lot of anger over his death, and no one really knows why." Dr smith tells the 2 Dr parks.

"She was close with her grandmother. She felt that she was the only one who accepted her no matter what she did. She also depended on her a lot. "Jae tells her.

"She worshiped her. "Ki tells them.

"Then why does she have such anger inside at her?" Dr smith asks them.

"Don't know but maybe we will find out soon I think that finding out about grandma and her dad is the last obstacle we have before we unlock the doors that have to do with the abuse she suffered at the hands of her brother-in-law." Jae says. He does not want to dredge up those memories, but he knows they will need to be dealt with.

Kat knocks on the door so that Dr smith knows she is here. She hears Dr smith call come in. Kat goes in

"Good morning, everyone. So, what are we doing today? I think I need to do more than talk about our memories or talk about my home life. I want to move forward. I had a horrible nightmare last night and kept Joe up all night, so I think instead of just going over what we have already figured out that we need to put me back under hypnosis for me to open another door." She tells them. Not knowing how they are going to react. She knows they have been taking it slow because of her coming of the antianxiety medication and changing her antidepressants.

"We were just talking about that very thing. We think that you are stable enough with the new methods to move forward. so, since we all agree then I think today we will restart with the hypnotherapy." Dr smith tells her.

Jae gets up to dim the lights. And retakes his seat. Dr smith tells Kat to concentrate on the light. As she waves the light at a steady pace, she tells Kat that she is standing on the top of the staircase. She is slowly walking down it she sees the doors that she has opened and walks past them. She sees the light about the door. She asks Kat to describe this door.

"It's black with crosses and hearts on it. It is cold and sad. The handle is broken, there is just enough of it for me to open it. "She is very emotionless as she is talking.

"Ok I want you to open this door. I want you to remember that nothing can hurt you in here and that it will be like a movie. Remember to tell us what is happening." Dr smith tells her.

"We are at my grandmother's house. My parents have moved in to help them keep their house and to take care of my grandmother. She has developed a problem with her heart. She needs us to help take care of her. My daily routine has changed again. I bring the kids to my grandmother's house in the mornings and help my mom with anything that she needs. I am standing outside of my grandmother's door, and I hear my grandfather complaining about her being sick and always having all of us underfoot. My grandmother is telling him that he just needs to suck it up. That she wants to spend every moment possible with all of us, especially the great grandchildren. She wants them there every moment possible. She wants them to remember her. I am angry at my grandfather because he knows that my grandmother is dying and wants her family with her. I know he is tired of taking care of her. I walk into the kitchen to do the dishes for my mom. I turn the oven on so that I can bake a cake on its Friday and every Friday I bake for them. I go about my day. Until it is time for me to go home to get dinner ready for Joe. My grandmother calls me into her room. Call Joe at work and ask him to come here for dinner tonight. I want to see him. I nodded ok and went to call him. I left a message with the scale office for him. I go back and clean the kitchen. I asked my mom what she would like me to fix for dinner. After dinner that night we get the kitchen clean and get the kids home to bed. I am telling joe what my grandfather said. He tells me not to worry, we will have time with my grandmother. I feel it inside that I am not going to see her again. No one will believe me. It is after midnight, and I wake up screaming in my sleep. I woke Joe up screaming. The phone rang, it was my aunt. She is telling him that my grandmother just passed, and that the ambulance is on its way. I rush to my grandmother's house to check on my mom. Everyone has gone to the hospital. I will stay there till my parents and grandfather get home. My mom sees me and collapses on the sofa with me. I just rock her as if she is a child. "

Ok can you tell me about the funeral of your grandmother." The voice asks me.

"My mom and her siblings with their spouses make all the arrangements. My dad calls and lets us know where and when we are to be. They allow us to have a private viewing for the great grandchildren so all of us go to the funeral home together. Then she is laying in this beautiful casket with the name mother embroidered on the lid of the coffin. My aunt tells us that we need to give her money for the grandchildren and great-grandchildren flowers. I will give her the money right away. I pull out pictures of my grandmother with the kids. There are a few snapshots of her with them over the past summer before the fire. After explaining to the kids what is happening, I take them up to see her. The 5 of them are crying because they know that she is gone. I show them which flowers are from them. It is a small pillow with 3 white roses and two red ones for each of them. I place their pictures beside her so that she will have them with her. My uncle comes in and pins his green beret pin on her lapel. She was always so proud of him for what he accomplished in the military. He hugs me and tells me he loves me. His wife comes and gets the kids to take them outside. The family starts to come in within minutes the funeral home is so full that even the sidewalk outside is barely standing space. I hear a couple of my grandmother's cousins making a remark about how tacky it is that people think its ok to put things in the casket with the dead body. My mom sister hears them and goes over to take out the photos and mementos that people have left. I look at her. in a very cruel voice, I tell her. Leave them. She loved them more than anyone in this room. It is not their place to say what is ok and what is not." My aunt looks at me in utter shock. I have never spoken to her in any way but respect. she gives me an angry look.

"It doesn't matter who or why they were put there, I will not have anyone say anything bad about my mother's funeral." She tells me that she places them inside of the jacket my grandmother is wearing, placing them right over her heart. "I will let you get away with speaking to me this way today but don't think that you are ever old enough to disrespect me." She tells me as she walks away.

I go and walk around. I hear some telling funny stories of my grandmother, I hear some crying and saying how much they are going to miss her. I see the two old buddies who wanted the pictures taken out of the coffin. They are talking badly about my grandmother and how she was a mean person. I look at them and in a very loud cruel voice making sure that everyone in the room can hear me. I say to them.

." Hi, I am Kat, which is my grandmother laying up there and you are no longer welcome here. Did not great grand ma or even great -great gran by the looks of how old you are; ever tell you that if you got nothing nice to say then keep your mouth shut. I know us kids have heard that from every single aunt and grandmother, so I am sure you were not neglected to be taught manners. I do not care if you think we are tacky or if you think she was mean. She at least was honest. She never spoke about anyone that she did not tell them to her face. What happened was she got a little too honest about how rude and disrespectful you two are. It is not your place or anyone else's to say what is tacky and what is not this is her. The things she loved and wanted are what is going to happen. If you do not like it, then make sure your family knows what you want before your cold carcasses are placed in the ground. So please if you have no respect for my grandmother and her siblings and children, I ask you to leave your poison at the door or you may never know what will happen to you" I turn to my mom's sister and look at her." I do not care wo they are in this family no one has the right to talk bad about my family. Once they disrespect them, I no longer must show respect to them. My grandmother entire life was her siblings her children and her grandchildren she cared not on cent for what anyone thought in life I will not let anyone belittle or disrespect her in death. So, since I do not know who these two biddies are I do not care about what they have to say or how they feel. I only care about those who I consider family and they are not." With that I get the kids and go up to the casket and say goodnight to my grandmother and walk out. My mom is calling for me, my mom's brothers are applauding, my mom's sister is yelling out my name, the one I hate. My grandmother's sisters remind people that I have issues and cannot always control my actions. My dad is just laughing. I hear my one of my grandfather's sisters say." You go girl just like your grand ma."

I hate that everyone thinks they must virtually live at my grandmother's house right now. It is so crowded that there is not a single place to stand. everyone talking and retelling stories of her. My mom acting as if she is the host instead of others waiting on her she is waiting on them. My aunts and uncles all being comforted but not my mom. I try to get her to go rest but she refuses. One of my grandmother's sisters refuses to leave my grandfather's side, she is constantly holding his hand and giving him comfort. I slip off to my mom and dad's room. I lay on the floor behind the bed so anyone looking in would think the room is empty. I just need to cry and talk to my grandmother. I do not know how long I was there before I felt a pair of arms around me. I wake startled.

"Shh its ok. I was going to move you to bed. "I look up and it's an older Asian man I don't know why but I give him a very tight hug and cry for the longest time. When I am done, he wipes my tears and tells me its ok to cry and to let it all out. He is so kind. My dad opens his door and sees me there.

"Hey baby girl everyone is leaving you need to come say your goodbyes." He nods to the gentleman and walks over to take my hand. I go with him to say goodbye to all the people in the house. My aunt reminds me that the funeral is the next day that I cannot be sulking and hiding I need to be there for my mom. I got angry at her all she did was hold my grandfather's hand all day. What does she know about what I need to do?

"What happens at the funeral?" the voice asks me.

"I decided that I am going to dress the way my grandmother liked. I did not care what anyone else thought. I was going to say goodbye to her as the person she liked. I am dressing in a black mini dress with black stockings and shoes. My hair is curled, and I have makeup on. I look more like someone going out to a party than someone going to a funeral. I saw all my aunts giving me some very dirty looks. I did not care. I went to sit up front with my mom and my aunt tells me you are in the back of the church these seats are for us grandchildren are in the back. I looked at my mom. She just tells me its ok that they were her siblings that is just the way it is. I look at my dad and he give me a big hug and kisses my forehead. And whispers just do as they wish. Do not make any drama today. So, all my cousins and I get sent to the back and must wait for everyone to leave the church before we even get to pay our last respects. I refuse to go to the grave side. I cannot be there and see them lower her into the ground. It is so scary to think of her in the cold ground. I go to the dinner hall and start setting up the meal for everyone afterwards. I stop by my grandmother's house first. My uncle's wife stayed at the house while everyone was at the funeral to watch over it. We sit and talk for a couple of minutes. She tells me it will be ok. That soon everyone will leave, and it will be like before they will call to check on everyone, but they will not be here constantly like the last two days.

My dad comes to me after everyone leaves. He asks me if I will give him the money in the bank that he is holding for us. I asked him why? He tells me they do not have the money to pay for the funeral and that he needs it. He says he will replace it somehow. I tell him without thinking about what I am going to say to Joe. Sure, no problem. He said he knew I would say that, so he already used it. I look at him without saying anything. I knew he always needed me to help him with money since I was young, always giving me an allowance from my earnings and having me take out loans to help him get things that he wanted. I always had to pay him back when I borrowed anything from him, but he never paid back any of the loans or what he borrowed from me. He and my grandfather both always wanted money from me. I get angry but do not say anything.

"Ok I think that is enough for this day I want you to leave this place and begin walking back up the stairwell when you reach the top you will hear three snaps and be fully awake and be yourself." I hear the voice tell me.

I look at them when I open my eyes. I feel embarrassed because I let them see a side of my family that no one knows. I wait to see who will speak up first. I keep my head bowed waiting for someone to break the silence.

"Did you know the Asian gentleman that comforted you?" Ki asks.

"I do know it was Appa he and mama came to pay their respects to my grandmother. No one at the house knew who they were. I did not remember them at the time, but I felt their warmth and love. They sat with my Korean aunt most of the time, so everyone thought that they were related to her and did not question who they were. Why didn't you all come?" Kat asks them.

"We came to the actual funeral and slipped out before everyone else. We were also at the first night of the viewing. We just stayed to the back to not risk you any problems. "Ki informs her.

"I must tell you though when you ripped into those two old ladies, I could not help but laugh. You had sparks flashing in those eyes. I thought you were going to drag them out." Jae tells her chuckling.

"I don't think her disrespect at her grandmother's funeral is what is causing her to not be able to get past her grandmothers passing." Dr Smith tells them.

"Oh, but it was the most interesting funeral I had ever been to. I thought her great grandmothers were big, it was nothing compared to her grandmothers. Just the stories about her were amazing. She was strong, mouthy, and honest. She was also kind and very independent. She was truly one of a kind." Jae tells her.

 "I'm sure if she was. It still doesn't explain why Kat can't get passed it."

"I know now why I have a hard time with my grandmother death. It is because my grandfather started dating her sister almost at once after she died even before she was buried, he started making moves on her younger sister. I felt sorry for my grandmother, my mom, and her siblings. I felt that he must not have loved her if he could move on before she was even buried. I resented him and my great aunt. I still cannot understand how they could be that way and still say that they never betrayed her before she died. That is the only thing that makes me have such a hard time over my grandmother." Kat tells them.

"Then I guess we can move on from your grandmother's death. I guess your next session will be to try to help you overcome your dads. "Dr Smith tells her.

"Ok but I want to know what you two thought of my over large family I didn't notice either of you or I have no idea what those people said to you." Kat looks at them.

"Well, we still have 15minuites so if you guys want to just reminisce, I am willing I personally would like to hear more about your family dynamics." Dr Smith tells them.

"Well for starters my great grandmother was one of 16 so my grandmother already had a large family. My great- great grandmother was a Cherokee Indian and her husband was a Spanish trapper from Casteel Spain. I do not know much from that except that they had 8 children. Their daughter my great gran married a man from Ireland. They had 5 children before he died. She had two more with her second husband. one of the boys passed a small child so it was 5 girls and one boy all of which I grew up with. My grandmother and grandfather had 4 children, 2 girls and two boys. My mom was the oldest and her sister was the youngest. My grandmother and her mother were having children at the same time. So, my mom was awfully close to her aunts. They were more like siblings than aunts. One of which is the one who let me live with her when I was discharged from the hospital." Kat tells her to put things in perspective.

"Ahh just thinking how large of a family you have is mind boggling. "Dr smith says as she shakes her head.

"You have no idea you could fill the high school football stadium if you put her total family together between both sides and that's not counting the ones that are not accounted for. You know the ones that no one talks about the ones from the wrong side of the marriage bed." Jae tells her.

"Truly an interesting family. "Dr smith says.

"I remember that when we would meet up with her and her grandmother that we would see a different family member. It didn't matter where we went, her grandmother always saw a family member somewhere. "Ki told her.

"She was a force to be reckoned with that is for sure. I remember when your uncle called her to make sure that she knew about us. He was terrified of her and did not question anything she said. If she said to keep your mouth shut, you did." Jae told her.

"She was a very strong-willed woman and didn't take any flak from anyone. She also did not like weakness in any of her children. She may have catered to Kat, but she never allowed her to give in or give up." Ki told her.

"I know out of everyone in my family she is the one I tried to never let down. She not only believed in me she made sure that I always finished what I started." Kat told her looking at the clock Kat notices it is time for her session to be over, she excuses herself and goes to join the rest of the day treatment group.

That night Kat is talking to Joe about her grandmother. She tells him that they talked about her death and what it meant for her to lose her.

"I know you became withdrawn and angry after she died. it just seemed to get worse after your father died. "He tells her.

'Yes, I know. I remembered why I was so angry today. it became crystal clear during today's session. I was angry because I felt like my grandfather betrayed my grandmother. He did not even wait for her body to be buried before hitting on my aunt. It was like this sick twisted man could not be my grandfather how could he do that. I was so angry at him but because he was my grandfather, I could do nothing or say anything. It would have been too disrespectful. "I told him "If I die before you, you better not be chasing any skirts during the wake and funeral. At least wait until I am buried, please." Kat acts like she is playing with him, but he knows there is some truth in what she is saying she does not want their children to ever think he did not love their mom. Not like what her grandfather did to his children and grandchildren.

"As long as you do the same you better wait until you have spread my ashes first also." He hugs her and kisses her forehead. He knows she loves him and that it will be hard for her if something happens to him. Kat looks at him and kisses him on the cheek "it's a deal "she tells him.

CHAPTER 40

The shoe drops

Over the next few weeks Joe is amazed at the changes in his wife. She is so cheerful and busy. She is so much more like the girl he met and married. He wonders when the other shoe is going to drop and shatter this happiness she is feeling. He decides instead of dwelling on that he is going to enjoy this peace they are in the middle of for as long as it lasts. He just hopes that the park brothers and Dr smith can get her through whatever is going to happen next.

KI notices how happy Kat is, and his thinking is awfully close to how Joe is thinking. He notices she is naturally smiling easily now, and the smile reaches her eyes. He sees her as his angel for the first time in so many years. It makes his heart ache that she is with someone else. He wonders how long they can let her be in this bubble before it bursts.

Kats next session DR Smith calls her mom in. she wants her mom to help her deal with her dad's death. She thinks it will be helpful if she can hear her side along with Kats. So, the 5 of them sit down to begin her session.

"Now Mrs. Tayler I need you to understand that I am going to put Kat under hypnosis and that we are going to guide her through a series of events. You must remain quiet and not interrupt her in any way. You also need to understand that she cannot lie while she is under hypnosis. So, everything she says is a fact. I want you here only so that you can help her understand why she is so angry about her father's death and not accepting of it. You cannot contradict her here. What she remembers will be the truth and no matter what you will have to accept it. If you cannot do that then I will need you to step out and not be a part of this. Can you do this?" Dr smith asks her.

"I can try you have to realize she sometimes has a distorted view of what is reality. And it's not always as she remembers." Her mom tells her.

"That is why we are using hypnosis. Truthfully, I do not think that Kat is the only one who has a distorted view. then we can begin" she gets ready to dim the lights

"Can I ask why they are here?" Kat's mom asks.

"They are here because they are helping me and because I want them here. They help calm me down when I need it. If you do not want to do this, we do not have to you can leave. It is not like you have ever gone to my doctor's appointment before. You always left it to grandma to take me. You can leave if you like, there is the door, I do not need you here for me to do this. the Dr thought it might be helpful in case I needed any explanations from you for anything." Kat tells her mother with absolutely no emotions in the voice. The three Dr's look at each other wondering if they need to rethink this.

"It's fine I will stay I can't have you telling and half-truths and making these people think that we are something we are not." Her mother snaps back at her

The lights are dimmed, and they begin the journey into Kat's memories they come to the door that holds her memories of her father's death.

"Can you describe this door to us." Dr Smith asks.

"It's grey and green. With black a black cross in the center. Its handle is a money clip and there is grass at the front of it." She tells them.

"Can you open it and go inside." Dr smith asks.

"I see my grandmother's house I am bringing the kids here so that my sister can pick them up. Dad just left my house after having his tea and cookies. I walk in and mom is cooking dinner. I asked her whatcha making?

"Just some dinner Tai is coming over." she tells her.

"Oh, can we stay for dinner then.?" Kat asks.

"I know that your sister is staying I am not sure if I made enough how about if you come by after you have dinner at your house." Her mom answers.

Kats voice changes after she is talking about her mom fixing dinner for everyone. She becomes monotoned. Like she is trying to hide her feelings.

"What happens next" the voice asks.

I go home to have dinner, but I do not want to go back out. So, I just ignore the fact that I am left out again. It's late at night and my aunt calls me and tells me I need to go get Shay and come to the hospital at once. So, I wake up Joe we get the kids and go to Shay house. Shay husband stays with the kids while Joe takes us to the hospital. When we arrived my mom, my aunts and uncle and a friend of my aunt was there. They tell us that my dad is in the ER and that he has had a heart attack. I heard my aunt on the phone with the red cross giving them my brother's information so that he could come home. I heard my uncle telling the nurse that they were all at my mother's house for dinner when he was complaining of heartburn and went to lay down. I look at my mom she had everyone but us at the house for dinner. Joe sees my face and grabs my hand so that I do not say anything. I am so angry I want to tear my mom apart. The doctor comes out and tells us there was nothing they could do and that they notice that he is an organ donor. My aunt automatically reaches for the form to sign it. I tell her no it is not right. She thinks I am saying it is not right for his organs to be donated. It is not that I knew that. It is not right that she signs the papers she is not his wife or his child. I sink to the floor crying Joe just sits and holds me. The doctor comes back out and asks my sister and I to come back so we can see him and say goodbye before he gets a cold. We go back to see him. He looks like he is just asleep. I laid my head on his chest and told goodbye to him. I asked him why you told me what I need to do, did you know? Shay and I are crying so much finally the nurse comes and tells us it is time to go.

"What happens next "the voice prompts.

"We go home and tell the kids. Joe has an appointment with the lung specialist the next day I tell him to go. That my dad had been pushing for him to see the specialist. to make sure his lungs were ok after the fire.so Shay and I with our mom and aunt go to the funeral home to make the arrangements. My aunt tries to tell us what to pick but we know what we want. My uncle goes to the airport to get my brother. After everything is done, we head back to the house. It's already overrun with people. My dad's sisters and his mom will be here tonight. As usual it is like a mob, there is no room to walk or to hear yourself think. I am so busy waiting on people making sure that everyone has what they need. One of my aunts I notice is giving my mom medicine. I asked her what it is, and she tells me it is just a valium to help her sleep. Over the next day every time I turn around someone is giving my mom a valium. I get even more angry my mom does not need to be doped up to get through this. I hide away in their room. waiting for everyone to leave. My brother is always commanding everyone's attention. everyone is treating my mom as if she is a China doll. Shay is Shay everyone is worried about how she will manage without my dad. Joe comes and finds me." You are doing ok" he asks." I guess everyone acts like they are afraid to talk to me. So, I am just here. I do not know what to do. Dad gave me a list of everything that needs to be done, but mom and the others do not want to hear it. So, I will just stay out of the way and let them take care of it. The next day is the viewing Joe must go get suit. After we got him a suit. We headed to the funeral home. The place is over full, every room of the funeral home is over full of my family and my dad's friends. They have the street lined up from the post office to past the funeral home. The directors tell us we must get some people to go outside they are above ability, So I go and talk to a few people telling them what the funeral directors have told us. When the night is over, and we go to say good night to dad, mom tells me that the funeral will have to take place at my aunt's church and there is not enough room at our family church. As usual I am the last to know anything."

"What about the day of the funeral." The voice asks me.

"We get up early and I get everyone dressed. I'm going to get dressed. I stare at my closet and see my black and gold silk shirt. I grabbed it with my black leather miniskirt. I put it on with my black hooker boots. I go fix my hair and put my make up on. This was my dad's favorite out fit and so I am wearing it. When I arrive at the church I see several of my family shaking their heads at me; I can feel their disapproval. I do not care if my dad liked this outfit and besides, it is black. I go to sit next to my mom and there is no room her brothers are on each side. So, I sat in the next aisle. All my aunts sing for my dad and my uncles and cousins preach his funeral. I am told that I must go to the grave side I have no choice. The kids are staying with a few of my cousins. The grave side is so gloomy everyone is standing around us. We put some flowers on the casket. As they get ready to lower it. Joe comes over and holds me up. He does not want me to collapse in front of everyone.

"Ok tell me about what happens over the next few weeks. "The voice asks.

"Nothing really my mom, sister and aunt become inseparable, they go to dad's job and to the courthouse and bank. They act as if I do not exist except to take care of the house and kids. I tell them to be back in time for Shay to take her kids to get their physicals for school. Of course, they cannot. They are late. I am just getting them back when they pull in., they went to have lunch after finding out how much money mom is going to get. I have had it I meet them at the car I cannot hold it in any longer. I started screaming at my mom and Shay and asking my aunt what right she had to take my mom to do any of this, she was not my dad's child or his wife. I am beginning to hate my mother. She is getting rid of things that belong to my dad to people who have no right to them. She is acting as if she only has one child not three. I wish it were her not my dad who died. They tell me that they felt like they could not depend on me. They never even tried I knew every bill every account my dad had; I was the one he depended on to take care of things. the one he asked for money every year to pay for his property and for anything my mom wanted, or Shay and her kids needed. If my brother wanted money, he expected me to give it to him, so he could get whatever my brother needed or wanted. I guess at least I am good for that. And they go off and act as if I know nothing. I really hate them right now. "

"You are going to leave this room and start back up the stairwell. When you reach the top, you will hear a snap and wake up. Nothing in this room can hurt you. When you are awake you will be calm, and you will be yourself "the voice tells her. When Kat hears the snap, she wakes up. She looks at her mom.

"I am sorry for being so selfish when dad died. I hated you and was Shay so much and have been so angry and resentful with the two of you. You never let me do what dad asked of me. You let your sister do it instead. You did what you always do, you tell me you love me, but you cut me out of everything. But that is no excuse for hating the two of you. will you forgive me." Kat is crying and asking her mom for forgiveness.

"I need to ask you for forgiveness also. It had not been that long since you disappeared on us and wound up a thousand miles away. With no idea who you were. Even the police officer said he had not seen someone look so angry before. He told your dad he did not know what happened but that you had some serious anger building and if it ever exploded anything could happen. Your dad took what the Dr back then, and when he was told you were pretending so that you would not have to face consequences. He believed him. Your dad and Joe worked hard to clear your debts and to put things right. So, when things were going good again your dad slipped back into the habit of expecting you to take care of everything. I told him it was too soon. Then the fire happened, and your nightmares were back. And only four months later your grandmother dies. You were like a lost child. You were so withdrawn that I was afraid to ask you to do anything but take care of the kids. That is the one thing I could always count on you for. I was not trying to cut you out I was trying to protect you. It had only been four months from the time your grandmother died till your father died. I do not remember you not being at the house for dinner that night. I thought for sure you were there also. I am sorry for making you think you were not needed or that you could not do what your dad wanted." Kat's mom hugs her. They both are crying and at this point the three Drs. Slip out to give them some privacy.

"See I told you. Her family loves her, they just do not understand when to protect her and when to let her do what needs to be done. "Jae tells Dr Smith.

"I think that she is going to need a few days before we do any hypnosis and open anymore doors. I am confused about a few things though. Why did her dad rely on her so much for money.?" She asks.

"Ever since she was the legal age to babysit, she did. She used to make hundreds of dollars a week babysitting. Her dad relied on her money to pay for his habits and for the extra things the other two wanted and needed. Even after she got married, knowing her, she still was paying her dad every chance she got whether it was for her mom babysitting or was any other excuse he used, the other two were always asking for money and she was always giving it. If she needed money, he would give it to her but then he would double the amount the next time he told her he needed money. When her brother graduated, she paid for most of the graduation party for him and his cousin. They rented a car for each of them she was not even allowed to ride in one. but she was expected to cook and give her dad whatever he wanted. "Ki told her.

"How do you know that?" Kat's mother asks him when she comes out of the office, she has an incredibly angry look on her face." Is that more tales my daughter is carrying about to make her father look like a beggar?" She asks.

"Nope I heard it from your mother. She told my grandmother and I about the last time they met. Not to send her any more money because her father was using it and Kat never saw a dime of it. That he made sure your eldest and youngest got everything they wanted. that even with the money Kat was giving him he never seemed to have enough. Of course, it was because of the money Kat was giving him he was able to get his hunting property and to have the money to save your parents from foreclosure. Why do you think she was given the land they live on when he died? Why do you think he never got angry with her when she maxed out his cards or took a little extra when she went to the bank? He knew he owed her more than she ever took. I bet that was also part of the reason he did not want her to go into the military. He was afraid she would become independent and no longer blindly give him money. If you do not believe me, ask Joe. Oh, and fyi after your husband died. It never mattered that she paid for that property he would tell her how much he needed. If someone did not have it, she paid for it. When they paid your husband back, she never saw a dime of it either. Your son-in-law was told he either had to pay up or not come back that he was not welcome anymore. Nice family you got there." Ki tells her you can hear the anger in his voice. He never understood how they could take such advantage of her always. He turns and walks away without even saying goodbye.

That night Kats mom calls Joe and tells him she wants to see him. When he arrives at Kats uncles house, he is confronted by not just his mother-in-law but her brother his wife and her sister.

"Tell me did you two really pay for my mother's funeral?" Kat's mom asks.

"Yes, I didn't know about that until after it was done. He never asked me he just did it." He tells her.

"Did he really ask Kat for money to pay for things all the time?" her sister asks.

"Yes, you want to see the bank statements. She took out 3 loans a year for your husband and she was the one who paid them back, not him. Every time he needed gas money or anything he would be at my doorstep waiting for me to pay him. She paid back every loan herself for more than 6 years. he may not have used the money she gave him to pay that property directly, but he used it to pay your household bills with it so that he had the money for it. I know he was always helping everyone in the family out but still he could have cut her some slack too instead of always making her feel guilty if she did not give him money every time she turned around. When we went bankrupt yes, we had a huge medical debt from our son. But she had so many signature loans that it was staggering. I know that some of those loans were for my family as well. That is why I have never said anything. Joe goes out to the truck and brings in a box inside are their bankruptcy papers and their bank and loan papers up to 6 months after his father inaws death. "Look for yourselves." He tells them he then turns to her uncle's wife." She paid for the property we live on. You need to keep your nose off it. She more than paid for it over the years. I do not ever want you or anyone else to say anything to her about it again. She does not care about these things. The only thing she ever cared about was that she was helping her father. She was always so worried because he was always working and barely had time to sleep. To keep up with all that was being asked of hm. he asked a lot of her because she never asked anything of him. It was only when depression and anger took over that she ever did anything to hurt anyone. He never blamed her or got angry. Because he knew he was at fault. He never judged her like you all have. Maybe you should remember every time you point your finger at someone. there are three others pointing back at you." With this Joe turn and leaves them to sort through the papers for themselves. And goes home to comfort his wife and try to not say where he was tonight. He does not want her to know about the conversation he had with her family tonight. It would just cause her worry and embarrassment.

The four of them look through the papers that Joe gave them. Kat's mom is in shock she never realized that Kat was paying so much out to them she was looking at the memos on the checks written to her husband and for cash. The reasons were always babysitting, grandma groceries, grandma electric. Dad's property payment due, or just labeled dad. There was also money every month for Joe's family. How was she able to keep up with all of this? Why did anyone not ever tell her that this was going on? Her sister hands her a couple. Kat gave her dad money every time someone borrowed money from him to keep their house going. The four of them realized that she was helping her dad support the entire family and no one knew it. Not even her husband until he started paying the bills himself.

"No wonder she has always felt like she was being cut out. Here she is helping her dad support everyone. All we did was criticize her and act as if she were too weak to handle anything. "Kat's mom tells them.

"She is a lot stronger than we think but I don't understand something. How was she able to get all this money at a drop of a hat?" Her aunt asks.

"She has worked two jobs for as long as I can remember. It has only been these last few years that she has not worked outside of the house. Only because her depression has pretty much taken over her life. "Kat's mom answers her.

"Oh, wait I saw something in one of mom's bank statements" her uncle pulls it out. On the bank statement it shows monthly direct deposits from a law firm.

"They seem to have stopped after Kats first child was born. I always thought it was from the car accident mom was in. I assumed she took the annuity instead of a lump payment." He tells them.

"No, she did take the lump payment. That was how they could afford to buy the property that they had before they died. That is why until they put the house on, they had no mortgage. "Kat's mom tells them.

"Who is this from then. "Her sister asks.

"I think I know the answer to that." Kat's aunt tells them "My ex-husband was friends with the senior attorney at this law firm. He told me once that mom had an agreement with them but would not tell me any details. He said that she and the attorney mother were friends. I think she even helped take care of his mom at one point. Maybe these deposits were her pay?" she says a little confused.

Kat's mom takes the statement and looks at the name of the law firm. She now knows that this is what Dr Park was talking about.

"The secret your ex was keeping was that yes, they were friends. They also were the family that mom used to take Kat to visit. They considered her one of their children. They had hopes that someday she would marry one of their sons. They were rich and thought that they could make her life easier. so, they sent her an allowance. I never knew about it till today. It has moms and my husband's names. Look up until 7 years ago they sent it every month. I guess that is when she told them not to send it anymore. That is also when Kat started having to work and juggle with all the responsibility, we placed on her. "Kat's mom puts her head down there was so much she never knew. She never asked. No wonder her mom would get so angry when Kat's boss would ask her why her dad was only giving her an allowance from her paychecks. It makes so much sense now. Everyone, even strangers, knew that she was giving her father way too much money. Yet she knew nothing.

"Why would mom allow anyone to give her money she did not earn. I know mom doted on Kat and would take her everywhere with her. I cannot imagine she would take money from anyone. "Kat's aunt says.

"They were more than friends. Kat was dating one of the sons. She was underage while he was an adult. They were incredibly careful with her.

And never did anything inappropriate with her. Mom liked them a lot from what I understand. When the boys were in an accident the family lost 2of their sons and almost the one Kat was dating. Their mother made Kat stop visiting a while before the accident. She was afraid that something would happen. so, she wanted them to spend time apart. If they still felt the same after the separation. Then she was going to have her husband talk to Kat's dad about letting them date and possibly get married. All that changed after the accident. "Kat's mom tells them. It still does not make a lot of sense to her, but she will need to talk to Dr Park to fill in the blanks.

"From now on no one is to let her know when we need anything. If we need something, we will go straight to Joe. If he has it to give, then fine if not oh well we will need to figure it out. We will also make sure if we need to get anything from him from now on, we will pay it back." Kat's mom tells them all she is not having anyone take advantage of her child financially again. Her child is not going to work herself to death when she is better to give to them. They call it night and put things back in boxes to give back to Joe. She needs to make this up to her daughter somehow. She calls the hospital's off duty phone and asks for Dr Park.

Within a few minutes he called back.

"Hello this is Dr Park how can I help you" he answers.

"Hello Dr Park, this is Kat's mother." She tells him.

"Is she ok, has something happened?" he asks, his voice frantic.

"She is fine. I have a few questions that need answering. Many things that I did not know about. "She tells him.

"If I can answer you honestly?" he tells her.

"Why did your fathers law firm give my mother money until Kat had her first child?" she asked him.

"Your mother would come and sit with me at the hospital after the accident. She would read to me and tell me about how Kat was doing. It is because of her visits I was working hard to get better. She would also visit and take care of my grandmother when she would get sick on occasion. My mother hated the fact that Kat was not around to go shopping and just to hang out. So, my dad and your mom agreed that he would give her an allowance to get Kat a few pretties and help with things she may need. Your grandmother came to my dad to ask his forgiveness because things had gotten hard for her and your father. She told him that she had to use the money for other things and had stopped using it on Kat. He told her just to consider it payment for all the care she had given to me and my grandmother. She felt guilty about it and asked him to please stop sending the money. That Kat was pregnant and getting married. That it was past time for us to give up the dream of our families ever being united. That even though we were family at heart we could not be family. Your mom loved Kat more than anyone. She never wanted to have her hurt, not even a little. She gave me the drive to not only recover but to follow my dream to be a Dr. She was truly a wonderful woman. Strong and loving. So, my father gave into her wishes and stopped the allowance. You know it was not that much money. My mom would spend that much on just a few items when her and Kat went shopping. She was happy thinking that Kat had pretty clothes and was able to go and have fun. She would have been terribly upset to know that was not what was happening." He told her.

"So, the money my mom received she actually did basically work for it she didn't actually steal it from Kat.?" She asks.

"Yeah, I guess if you want to look at it that way." He tells her "You know that Kat loves you all very much and there is nothing she would not do for you. If she had known about the money, she would have given it to your mom and husband without ever asking for it back. My father knew that. He knew that even if your mom had told her, she would have just told her to use it for what they needed." Ki tells her.

"Thank you for taking my call and for answering my questions. Thank you also for helping my daughter. "She tells him.

"No thanks' needed Kat is still my family and my soulmate. Even if we don't have a future together." He tells her good night and hangs up.

That night Kats mom has a very rough night's sleep. She thinks about all the times her mom would just randomly go and visit her brother and aunts with Kat. I guess all those times were to visit this family. Oh, why was she so oblivious to everything? She thinks before she falls asleep.

Kat was sleeping by the time Joe got back. He knew she had a hard day today. Whenever she remembers or thinks of her grandmother and dad, she has a hard time. He knows these next few days she will be withdrawn and moody. He pulls her into his arms and breathes in the sweet smell of her hair. She has no idea how intoxicating she is at times. Just being able to hold her close gives him the most happiness. He wonders how he got so lucky to have woman who can put up with him. She is truly one of a kind. He just hopes her mom will understand just how much she does for her family. It is not always easy for her to balance everything. Sometimes he thinks that she is too much like her dad. She keeps things to herself too much and never tells anyone now. She does not tell anyone when she is having a hard time. He wonders if anyone would listen even if she did. It is going to be hard getting to sleep tonight. He stares at the wall while he holds his wife. He just wishes all this were over and she was better already. So that she could be out of all this turmoil every day. It must be harder on her than she is letting on.

Kat wakes and it is daylight outside. She overslept. Oh no, what is she going to do? She did not get up and fix Joe breakfast and lunch. The kids are late for school. She rushes out of bed and runs to their room. Their beds are empty. She rushes to the kitchen there on the refrigerator is a note.

Good morning, Kat.

Yes, you overslept but do not worry. I took off work today. I got the kids ready for school and went to town. Enjoy a relaxing cup of tea and I will be home soon, and we can have breakfast together. Think about what you want to do today. I called the center and told them you were tired, and I was home today so you would not be in. not to worry I spoke to Dr Park he knows everything is ok. See you around 10.

Love you.

Joe.

Kat looks at the clock, it's 9:45. She rushes to cook breakfast and have everything ready for when he gets home. She makes him a typical Mexican breakfast and goes to jump in the shower. When Joe comes in, he smells that breakfast is ready. And he hears the shower. He slips into the bathroom and strips off. Slips inside the shower and whispers in her ear." May I join you.?" He kisses her neck.

"Looks like you already have" she giggles and turns into his arms. Putting her arms around his neck pulling his mouth close to hers. After they shower, they go to eat breakfast, there is a large bouquet of roses on the table.

"Why did you get me flowers it not a special occasion?" she asks him as she fixes his plate to put in the microwave.

"I got them just because it's been a while since I have given you flowers. Did you think about what you want to do today?" He asks her.

"Yes, and I don't know truthfully, I would just enjoy lazing around the house watching movies and snuggling all day. It's been a long time since we just spent a lazy day together." She tells him.

"That sounds particularly good to me. He tells her as he puts his arms around her from behind. He moves her hair and begins kissing her neck. She sighs." Are you sure you're ready for this you haven't eaten yet?"

"HMM who needs food when I have you "he tells her as he takes her hand and pulls her towards the bedroom. After some time, they make their way back to the kitchen Kat heats up his breakfast. As they are eating, they talk about the kids and what movie they want to watch. Joe smiles at her seeing how relaxed and happy she looks. He hopes he can give her a perfect day.

CHAPTER 41

Jae asks Sarah out.

Sarah looks across the room at Jae. He seems troubled by something.

"Jae what seems to be the matter? You have read that same page for the last 20 minutes." She asks him to wonder what is going on.

"I am just working up the courage to ask you if you will go to the movies with me this weekend. The only problem is I have no clue as to what kind of movie you like. "He tells her looking sheepily at her with a little smile.

"I like romantic comedies and sci fi movies. I love Star Wars and those type of things." She tells him hoping he does not think her too much of a geek.

"Really, I love Star Wars. We used to binge watch them. I have all of them would you like to have dinner and watch them with me." he asks her his heart skipping a beat.

"I would love it but only if you let me cook your dinner. What kind of food do you like? I must warn you I am not a cook like Kat. I only know a few things. "She tells him.

"Hmm do you want to watch them at your house or mine?" he asks.

"Mine that way I can cook in a familiar place. Besides, I do not know where you live remember. You have always brought me home. "She smiles at him.

"This is true, but I do want you to come over to my place sometime. So that it can become familiar to you." He says as he walks across the office. He leans in to kiss her when she puts her hand up in front of his face.

"Stop right there we are in the office. no personal contact in the office." She tells him.

"Sorry doc but I did not ever agree to that "he takes her hand and quickly kisses her pulling her fully into his arms and sitting with her in his lap. He deepens the kiss as soon as he has her straddled across him. Opening the buttons on her top so that he can feel her heart beating. She breaks free only slightly to breathe and to tell him she has a patient coming in a couple of minutes. Straightening herself up she goes to get off his lap. He pulls her back to a sitting position on his lap and cradles her head against his chest so that she can hear his heart racing.

"Can we just stay like this for just a few more minutes." he asks her.

"Hmm ok only until my secretary announces my patient.' She tells him. The sit cuddled together softly talking about their upcoming date so that both of their breathing could slow back to normal. Jae leaves as soon as the patient is announced. He calls his brother to ask him where the Star Wars movies are.

"Yo bro does you remember where the Star Wars movies are at" He asks Ki.

"They are in the great room at the hospital. I left them here the last time we had movie night for the patients last week. I am on my way out for the day do you want me to grab them and drop them by your house.?" He asks him.

"Sure do. I need them for Saturday. I went on a date with Sarah. We are going to binge watch them. "He tells him.

"Oh, so things are going well then?" he teases his brother.

"Yes, they are in fact so well that I think she is the one for me." He tells him.

"Whoa hold on this is what your second date.?" He stops dead in his tracks at that comment.

"Yes, but I have known for a while that I liked her. You know when we were at the plantation. We got to talk and then angel told me at the clinic that she thought we were perfect for each other. everything has just clicked for us. "He tells him." Hey, let's have a guy's night tonight when you stop by." He asks him as he hangs up the phone.

Ki smiles at his phone and shakes his head. Wondering if Kat is right being Jae and Dr Smith right for each other. He would like a few nieces or nephews running around and neither of them are getting any younger. He heads to the great room and picks up the movie's waves at the nurses and he heads to his car.

When he gets to Jae house, he is trying to think of an excuse to just go home. He really is not in the mood the hear his brother gushing over the new woman in his life. He goes up and lets himself in. He hears Jae yell I am in the kitchen. Once in the kitchen Jae has the limes and tequila ready for some shots.

"I thought you were happy why are we drinking. You know I gave up drinking of any kind years ago." He reminds him.

"Yes, and so did I but I think you need to forget a few things and let go so we are going to have a responsible night of drinking. Neither of us are going anywhere tonight and neither of us must work tomorrow. So, I figure we take a few shots, eat some dinner, and just talk." Jae pushes the seat out for him as he places the takeout in front of him.

They sit and begin to eat. Ki is the first to pour himself a shot. He no sooner finishes that one and takes another. Jae is watching his brother he knows he may get drunk tonight, but it will only be tonight. He knows he will not allow himself to get lost in that haze again. At least he hopes not.

"So little brother does you think that Dr smith feels the same as you?" ki prompts his brother.

"I think so I should say I hope so. You know she got so jealous of Kat when we went on our first date. She thought I only asked her because Kat told me to. Of course, I set her straight. I let her know that she may have goaded me into it, but it was still my choice. She is fine now. I am really looking forward to Saturday. I have not been this excited in years to see someone. "He tells him.

"That is good." He takes another shot.

"So, are you going to drink the entire bottle or are you sharing tonight?' Jae holds out his glass for a shot.

Ki fills his glass and then pours himself another one.

"What is going on that you are so willing to drink tonight?" Jae asks ki.

"I think Kat has gone back with her husband and that they are you know." He tells him.

"Ok you knew that was the possibility and you have known for a long time that she had no plans to leave him for good." He reminds him.

"I know but I had hoped. It does not change anything. I just want to drown my sorrows tonight and pass out ok." He tells him.

"Have you thought about maybe dating someone. you haven't gone out with anyone since she left us." Jae prompts his brother.

"No, I haven't, and I won't. I will be the doting uncle to your children, but I don't feel anything when I look at anyone other than her." He tells Jae.

"Oh, so I guess then unless someone makes your heart race, and they send you into the atmosphere you're not even going to try." He looks at his brother wondering if he really is derived to be alone for his entire life.

"Yes, I know what you are thinking and yes, I intend to be completely alone my entire life. So do not try to fix me up or throw women in my path. I am ok with that. I just may need to have a night occasionally, to drown my sorrows. When she is better maybe I will give you the clinic and take over the house in Boston. Make a fresh start somewhere else." He tells him as he takes another drink.

They chatted and drank until the early hours of the morning. Finally, the bottle was gone, and Ki passed out. Jae goes up to his room after Ki settled into the guest room. As he lays there staring at the ceiling he wonders if his brother will ever find happiness. He wishes that Kat could find the perfect women for her soulmate like she has for him.

CHAPTER 42

Kat has a heart to heart with Dr. Smith.

*D*r Smith sees Kat at the grocery store. She tries to go down a different isle to avoid her. She needs to separate herself from her some. She is becoming too close to her and if it continues, she will need to hand her to another Dr and she does not want that to happen. She has invested so much in her recovery that to have to withdraw would be detrimental to Kat. Kat saw her and waves.

"Dr Smith how are you?" she asks.

"I am fine Kat how are things going?" She replies.

"Things are going well thank you for helping my husband find a good Dr and for all you have done." She tells her. "Would you go for a cup of coffee with me? I need to talk to you and before you ask it is about my treatment, so it won't be a problem with anything." Kat tells her.

"Yes, I will how about we go to the café here in the store before we finish shopping." DR Smith suggests.

"That sounds great let's go." They push their carts in silence as they stroll towards the shop's café. Once the coffees are ordered they sit. It's awkward at first. Kat does not really know where to start.

"Dr smith I know all about conflict of interest between Drs and patient. I know that our professional relationship is the most important. I want us to be family more than anything else, but I know that right now we can only have a professional relationship. I do not want to have to change Drs. I only want you for my Dr right now. So, if I do not speak to you outside of the clinic, please do not think I am mad at you. I just do not think I could deal with a Dr change. I really like you and have made more progress than I have ever before. I do not want to jeopardize that in any way. I know that so far, all our interactions have been working related to date. I am glad about that, but my fear is that I will get too close to you before my treatment is over and will have to start over. So please do not get mad if I seem rude to you, I'm sorry if I have spoken out of turn. I mean I have no idea if I am the kind of person you see as a friend or if I am just a patient, nothing more. I just know that I want us to be more, but I know we can't. "Kat tells her. She can hear the emotions in her voice like she was struggling to even bring up the subject. Dr smith understands her completely since she has been struggling with the same question.

"It's fine I understand. Most people do not understand that the role of therapist is to make a patient feel comfortable enough to speak about their inner most and often emotional thoughts. That sometimes these emotions can become blurred. I have had a few thoughts along these lines as well. That is why I was trying to avoid you just now. I do not want our relationship to change either. So, I think you're right that we need to be careful to keep everything professional until the end. "Dr smith reassures her that they both want the same thing. As she gets up to leave, she smiles at Kat." This is on a personal note though. Thank you for encouraging Jae to ask me out. Also thank you for the festival passes, it was a perfect day. "She waves bye to her.

Kat is so excited and happy that her plan for the two of them worked. She cannot wait till the next time she sees him.

That night Dr smith tells Jae about her conversation with Kat when they sat down to dinner.

"Kat is very smart. Most patients do not understand that their therapist cannot be their friend. She gets it. She told me not to be upset about her being rude outside of the center. I wonder sometimes if she had applied herself where she would be.? "She tells him.

"I know she is smart and talented. You know she loves to do so many things.it would have been hard for her to choose a profession. So, does this mean you're going to go back to being cold to her?" he asks.

"No not cold. I do not think that can ever happen again. You know since treating her I have become a better dr. I look at my patients with more compassion now. before I was detached and cold like you said. I have found that you can be compassionate without becoming involved in the patient's life. I have a few patients who have had similar situations as Kat and since I have been able to be more compassionate with them, they have made strides in their treatment. Now I do not feel I could ever be friends with them and do not feel like I even need to embrace them in any way. They are just my patients and I have a professional concern for them only. With Kat I need to be careful because I have that pull with her and neither of us want our relationship to change right now so we have agreed that we will not speak of anything personal outside of what's is beneficial to her recovery." She tells him.

"Good luck with that. I will help you as much as I can don't worry." He laughs at her confused face.

"You know my brother got so drunk last night he passed out. He has not been drunk like that since Kat first left us. So do not be surprised if he is a little surly and moody for a while. "Jae tells her.

"It must be hard for him to see Kat happy again with her husband." She tells him.

"It's not that; he is always happy if she is. He knows that their time passed years ago. He is just grieving over the lost future they could have had. He will be ok in time. I wish she could find someone for him, so he won't spend his life alone." Jae tells her.

"Maybe she will when everything is over. maybe she won't have to maybe he will find someone on his own." She tells him.

"I don't know he seems pretty bent on being alone if he can't be with her. She is the only one for him." He tells her.

"I think in many ways she feels the same. She told one of the counselors that he was off limits to everyone. That they better back off and leave him alone. She said it politely but that was the basic message." They finished dinner a went to the living room.to turn on the movie. Jae puts his arm around her and pulls her close to his side. They snuggle and watch movies until the early hours of the morning. finally, to fall asleep in each other's arms.

CHAPTER 43

The Beginning of Hell

Monday comes too quickly, and it is time for Kat's session with the three Drs. The lights are dimmed, and I am concentrating on the pen light. Today Ki is the one putting me under. He is not saying what Jae and Dr Smith done is saying a poem the same one he said when I was so upset the one when he kissed me, I feel my cheeks get warm at the memory. I then hear him say "no need to worry I am not going to kiss you I just want to have the door open for you so listen just to my voice and when you are ready, we will go down the stairwell. I close my eyes. I see the stairs well its different today its lined in glowing cherry trees filled with cherry blossoms and there is a cool breeze blowing I can hear water running like from a waterfall. In the middle of the garden is a door surrounded by dead trees and thorns. I smell an awful stench. Like something dead and rotting. The door's lock is broken. This door is black with angry red gouges and the handle is a knife and a hook covered with blood. There is broken glass imbedded in the door with blood dripping from it. I kneel in front of it and cry" please don't make me open this one it's too scary I can't touch it! "

I hear Ki soft voice. "Angels blossom its ok I am with you. I will be here to hold your hand. Nothing inside can hurt you anymore it's just going to be a bad movie I will not leave you I promise."

He touches my hands I can feel him close. I got up and went towards the door. I hesitated again, but he had my hand, so I opened it.

"I see my sister myself and her husband we are in a fast-food place picking up food. He comes up behind me and puts his hands around my waist and pulls me against him. I pulled away and gave him an angry look. We get our food and leave. He drops my sister off at their trailer first then takes me home. As soon as we got into the driveway I quickly got out of the car and ran into the house. No one is home. I turn around in the living room when I hear him behind me. He puts his arms around me from behind I struggle to move away but he pins me down on my belly on the floor he strips my pants off and I hear him undoing his. He pulls me by the hair to make my face meet his.

" You think you can get away from me. You will die before I let you get away. You do not have the gooks around to protect you anymore. "He whispers in my ear. I scream and beg him to stop. I promise not to say anything if he stops. I struggle to be free from him.

But he is using his body to keep me from moving. He pulls out a knife from his pocket right before he gets his pants down so that he is naked from his waist to his ankles. I feel the knife at my throat as his other hand finds my vagina. He puts his fingers inside me. I am cringing and crying, please do not. "Damn you slut you gave your cherry away already. Did you give it to those gooks? It was to be mine." He hisses angrily.

"No, they never touch me like that I'm not yours why are you doing this? "I cry.

"You are mine I have watched you since I got out of prison, I have wanted to ram my dick into you since that first day. Now I am going to show you how a real man takes his woman not like those weak gooks. He pulls me up on my knees with him over me from behind his one hand twisted in my hair pulling it hard to make me arch my back he rams into me while pulling my hair with one hand his teeth biting me on my shoulder to keep me still. I am begging him to stop. He is my sister's husband he should not do this.

He laughs at me" Don't worry no one will ever know if you want to keep your family alive." When he is spent and has his pants back on the kneels and spreads my legs again, he takes this sharpened hook looking thing and inserts it inside me. He rakes my insides out with it until it is covered in blood. "I can't have you getting pregnant, can I? "See you tomorrow he says as he laughingly walks out the door.

I crawl to the bathroom and sit in the tub with the hot shower running; I see blood flowing down the drain. I cried so hard. My whole body shakes when the water gets cold, I get out and go to put my night clothes on. I see bite marks on my shoulders and bruises on my inner thighs. I still have blood trailing down my legs from my vagina. I got a pad and put it on. I get dressed and it is like I am in a daze. I am me but not me. I go to bed and cry myself to sleep wondering how I am going to face my sister in the morning.

I hear Ki softly telling me that I can leave here, that I am safe and that nothing or no-one can bother me anymore. That I will close this door and will come back to him. I will not feel shame or embarrassment. I will not be angry or depressed, I will be ok and will be able to face this. I will be myself when I return. I take his hand and start walking back up the stairwell and the trees begin to fade as I get to the top, I hear 1 2 3 snap I look up and I am on the floor in front of Ki he is holding my hand and wiping my tears.

Dr. smith and Jae just look on holding their breath to see if it is me or my other side. I look at Ki and ask him "Why did you do that? Why did it have to be that door.?"

"I didn't know what door would show up. I only wanted you to feel safe before opening any door that might show up. I have a feeling that that one has all your memories of the abuse that you suffered at his hands and that is why it is so mutilated and scary. We will take it one memory at a time, and we will always be here with you through all of them. I promise."

"You promise you three won't leave me or send me to someone else." She looks at them with desperation in her eyes. They can tell she is having an extremely hard time holding her fear. She is ringing her hands and physically shaking.

"Kat would you like me to call Joe and ask him if someone can pick you up today, I do not want you to drive." Dr smith tells her.

"I can't go home I can't let this touch my kids or Joe. I'm sorry but I must go." Kat jumps up and runs out of the room before anyone can stop her. They all three jumps up to go after her. They were not able to stop her. By the time they were able to get to the parking lot she was speeding out of it. Jae runs to his car to try to follow her. Ki runs back inside. he goes straight to receptionist desk and picks up the phone. He calls Joe at work.

CHAPTER 44

Kat runs away.

*P*acing at the receptionist's desk waiting for Joe to call him back he became so angry with himself. Why did he not predict that she would run away? Joe finally calls him back.

"Hello Dr Park, what has happened?" he asks if you can hear the concern in his voice.

"We opened a door in Kat's session today she became very agitated and ran away. We asked her if she wanted us to call you so that she wouldn't have to drive. She ran out before anyone could stop her. Do you know where she might go?" he asks him?

"No, I don't. The last time she got like this she wound up in Florida completely lost. not even knowing her name." he tells him.

"If she comes home, please call us immediately I truthfully don't know what is going to happen." He tells him.

"Is there no way of knowing what doors she will open could you have avoided this one until she was in a more secure place like your clinic." Joe asks him.

"No, we never know what door she is going to open I too wish it would have been something less traumatic so that we could have been more prepared. I am sorry that this happened my brother followed her out to try to follow her so hopefully he will catch up to her." He tells him.

"If she is in a bad place, she will not want to be around the kids. She has always tried to keep this from touching them. I know she has failed in that but the worst of what she has done. She has been able to hide from them. If you find her, can she stay at your clinic for a few days to compose herself and get things under control? I know her well enough to know that no one will be able to come close to her or reason with her until she gets passed whatever she is feeling. She gets like this when she becomes afraid. When she disappeared on us it was because that bastard got in touch with her and told her he was going to finish what he started. This time though it would be worse. The next thing we knew she was gone for over a week. We had to go to get her and bring her back. I have never seen her be so angry or afraid in my life, it is scary when she gets like that. Call me and let me know if you find her and please take her someplace safe that she cannot run away from. I am afraid if she runs away this time, we may never find her, and she may lose herself forever. I know that I cannot help her when she is this way. I can only helplessly watch until she is ready for me to be there again. When she became like this before it took months to get her to even look at me. I don't know if it was from fear or if she was ashamed because of what was happening." Joe tells him.

You can hear sadness and concern in his voice. He wants to be there for her but knows he cannot do anything. Ki realizes that until his accident they must have had a very accepting and loving relationship. That for any man to be able to accept his wife so completely and ask another man for help. It took a very deep love. He sees Joe differently now. He sees that Joe loves her beyond measure. Just like him.

"Of course, I will call you and tell you everything as soon as I can." Ki hangs up and asks if anyone has heard from Jae.

"No not yet "the receptionist replies.

"Ok I am going to go to Dr Smith office and plan. Let me know if anyone calls about Kat." KI tells her.

He paces the office like a caged lion. He does not know how long he can just sit here waiting for word from Kat. It has been two hours now, where is she? he asks himself. the receptionist knocks on the door.

"Dr Park there is a phone call for you. "She tells him.

He quickly picks up the phone.

"Hello this is Dr Park." He answers.

"Hey bro it's me. I have Kat she is in a bad way can you come to the pond?" he asks.

"I am on my way." He quickly hung up the phone. He does not understand why she would be at her uncle's old hang out. Why didn't she go to their spot or home? He thinks to himself as he drives to the pond. It is still the same, an old shack right beside the pond with lots of trees surrounding the area so no one would even know it was there unless they looked for it. He sees Jae waving to him. He sees Both vehicles. What he is not seeing is Kat. He gets a sinking feeling in the pit of his stomach. he sees the panic on jae's face he knows something is wrong. He quickly parks his car and jumps out. Running towards Jae

"Where is she?" he asks Jae.

"Inside she put her hand through the window and cut it up badly. I had a suture kit and a first aid kit in the car, so I patched her up. She just keeps sitting in the corner under the table rocking and staring. I can't get her to respond or come out." He tells him.

Ki goes in and he sees her in the corner she is sitting there rocking back and forth mumbling to herself. He goes over to try to get her to come out.

"Kat, can I look at your hand?' he asks. She puts her hand towards him. He looks around and sees the blood and used bandages jae used to clean her wounds and to bandage her hand. He tries to pull her to him, and she jerks her hand away.

"Kat why are you here?" he asks.

"Here he can't find me. He does not know about this place. It's where my uncles and their friends used to come to have parties. They used to take us here to swim. My uncle's friend owns this place. She lives far away no one will look for me here. He can't find me if I am here." She tells them.

"Kat you know he is in jail and cannot get to you anymore right." Ki tells her.

"He said he will kill everyone when he gets out. He told me that it will be my fault because he got caught and that he will kill everyone. If I am not where he can find me, he will look for me and leave them alone. He likes to torture people in front of me so that I will not fight him. If he cannot find me, it will not be fun for him to torture them. So, if I disappear then it won't be fun for him.so he will leave them alone." She tells them in a toneless and distant sounding voice.

"Is this why you disappeared before, when your dad was still alive?" Ki sits beside her on the floor leaning against the wall watching her. She has such a faraway look in her eyes.

"Yes, I they were trying to get him out of prison, and he was coming for the kids. He was going to hurt them. I had to protect them. If I were far away, he would not be able to find me. If I go inside and the door, he can't find me." She tells him.

"What door are you talking about?" he asks her.

"I have a special door I can hide behind. When I am in there, he cannot find me. it is not there anymore though. I cannot find it. I am trying to go there but I cannot find it.it has disappeared. If I could find it, I could go inside and hide. He will not be able to find me or hurt me or anyone else. It was always there before now it's gone." She covers her face and begins to cry. Ki puts his arms around her. He begins to rock her as she cries.

"Do you think when we started opening her memories from behind the doors that the one, she used to disassociate to disappeared, because her mind no longer needed it to hide her from what was happening to her. "Jae asks ki.

"Maybe since we have been opening them and resolving her fears once they were closed again, she no longer needed protection from them. This I am afraid has a much bigger hold on her than the others. We will have to take it more slowly and take her where she can feel like she is hidden from him." Ki tells him.

"Kat would you like to go back to grandmother's old house and stay in her room. You know the one with the secret room. You can stay there if anyone comes to hurt you. You can hide in her secret room that no one knows about. Would you like that?" she looks up at him?

"Will it really be ok for me to go there to hide from him?" she asks, looking at him with a tear-streaked face and her hair covering most of it.

"Yes of course you can go there and stay as long as you like, no one will bother you." Ki tells her.

When they finally got her out of the shack and into Ki's car, almost as soon as the car began to move, she fell asleep. Ki wonders what more they are going to find behind that door. He looks at her as she sleeps. He thought she forgot all of this because of being put under hypnosis to help her cope. It seems that she would disappear from herself whenever things would be too hard for her. All his uncle did was help her lock them up tighter. He wonders how many times she has dissociated over the years and what she has done while in that state. She heard Dr smith say she shoplifted while in a dissociated state. He knows that she wound up in Florida while in a dissociated state. What else has she done that no one knows? He wonders if she will remember as they uncover more of her memories. He knows the memories they have uncovered so far have been truth because of the evidence from other sources.

When they reach the clinic, he settles Kat in his grandmother's room as promised. She was always happy when she would stay with his grandmother. She falls asleep almost at once. He goes to his office in the attic to call Joe and Dr Smith to tell them where she is and that she is safe.

"Joe this is Ki I wanted you to know that she is safe and here at the clinic. What can you tell me about her as far as her disassociating events?" he asks him?

"Mostly she would be forgetful or would not remember what she is doing. She would meet people and not remember seeing them. When she went to Florida, she had no money and to this day we do not know how she got there or how she was able to survive. She had a job within a day of being there. She would do dangerous things like walk on the beach at night. The hostel owner told us that she would have an emotionless face like a blank stare and talk in mono tones completely emotionless. He said he was worried for her because he was afraid that someone would hurt her. He said that she would walk and bump into things and not even notice that she cut herself. Once a guy tried to grab her hand and as soon as he grabbed her, she sat on the ground and curled up in a ball. I know this one because sometimes if I touch her, she will back away, and I will find her in the closet curled up in a ball hiding. I know that every time they bring up the possibility of that bastard is up for parole, I must watch her close because that is when she has the most problems. She steals money and hides it from me. As if she may need it for a quick getaway. I am not sure but most times these things only go on for a few minutes to a few hours. The only time she was in that state for longer was when she was in Florida, she stayed that way for almost two weeks give or take a day. It did not stop just because we found her. She came back some she recognized her dad when she opened the door. But she was still completely withdrawn from everyone and incredibly angry. To this day we don't know why she was so angry at that time except that they were trying to get him out of prison." joe tells him

"Has she ever been mean to the kids or tried to hurt them?"

"Oh, never not once. She has always done her best to protect her children. I know she lost time when with them, but they were never in any danger. "Joe tells him slightly annoyed.

"So, you do not worry about them when she has them?" ki asks him.

"Not ever she has never allowed anything to happen to them." Joe tells him before hanging up the phone. Ki is relieved that she seems to know not to allow harm to come to the kids. That will make it easier. He was worried that she had no sense of self at all when in that state. At least at times she knows enough to not allow harm to come to the kids. He wonders if there is more, they can do to help her. to keep her from going inside of herself. He calls Nurse Henderson he wants to know more about what happened to her in the hospital. Even though he was there he was not able to be with her every second. He wants to know what to expect.

"Hello this is Nurse Henderson how can I direct your call?" she answers the ward's phone.

"Hello, Nurse Henderson, its Dr KI I am calling because Kat Sanchez is having a hard time and I need some information." He tells her.

"Sure, think Dr Ki. What do you want to know.?" She asks.

"When she was brought in when she was 13, she was in a dissociative state how did she behave?" he asks.

"Umm she was mostly unconscious at that time she had lost a lot of blood and was close to death by the time she woke up she was cheerful and playful. I remember because it was like a ray of sunshine. We all knew that she was trying to show us only her happy cheerful side. That she was hiding the sad and broken side. At night though when she was sleeping you could hear her pain in the cries and whimpering, she did in her sleep. We would lose her at times and not know where to find her. Suddenly she would just show up in the hall like a ghost. Her hair covering her face as if she were hiding. The Dr at first thought she was sleeping walking because she would not respond, she would only give you hateful looks. Looks like it could chill your blood. She would curl up in the corner of the room where it was the darkest, so no one could find her. This last time at the hospital it was much the same way except she was more violent. If we tried to touch her or reach for her, she would spit at us and try to bite us. She would scream and hiss at us in warning before she would try to take a bite out of us. You could see the anger and fear in her face. We all knew she was not herself. When she is herself, she is bright and cheerful. When she is lost, she is like a scared animal. That is the only way to describe it. How is she behaving right now? "She explains to him.

"She is lost." He tells her" She is not violent, but she is lost and full of fear."

"Oh, the poor girl. It must be hard to have such striking differences in your personality. The extremes must be so stressful for her." She tells him.

"Yes, I can't imagine not having a balance within myself. I mean we all have different sides of our personality. Though the majority have a balance that they can flow without it causing problems. Hers seem to be disconnected and it makes it extreme." He tells her.

"Do you all think you can help her reconnect herself so that she can be like most of us. Able to have them be intermingled so they don't seem so extreme." She inquires.

"That is my hope that we can alleviate the pain and fear so that she can be a person who does not have to hide behind the emotionless shell she becomes sometimes or the over angry person who wants to hurt those around her." He tells her.

He hears a noise coming from downstairs and he tells Nurse Henderson thank you, but he needs to go. He makes his way downstairs towards his grandmother's room. There sitting on the floor is Kat, she has one of her old dolls that grandmother gave her. She is talking to it.

"You know that it's been such a long time since I got to play with you. A lifetime. I wonder if Ki will let me keep you. Grandma gave you to me, so I could tell you, my secrets. so that I would not have nightmares. I have a secret that no one can know. You know I have two of his children and when I see them, I only see love. You know I was relieved when the Dr told me I could not have any children. Because then I would not have to worry about hating one of my children. then God gave me another chance I had a child, but I lost it I was so sad. I did not even know I was pregnant when I had lost it. I cried so hard over that baby. Then I got pregnant with my daughter. I was so happy and relieved to have her. You know she is perfect in every way. Then there is my son. He is not extremely healthy; he has problems with his breathing and such. I pray that God will let him be ok. My only wish when I was younger was to give Ki a big family, then he was gone. It was like my other half was missing. I looked for him in every man who showed even the slightest interest in me. The only one that came close was Joe. I grew to love him so much. You know with Ki I used to dream about our life together with Joe. I got to live the life I wanted with Ki. They are so much alike. Both are kind and caring. Both have terrible tempers. Both have the most adorable smiles. I found Ki in Joe. I fell in love with him because he is so much like him. I mean he is not a talented artist or a doctor like Ki. His personality is like Ki. I still love Ki so much, but I love Joe so deeply that I cannot ever be without him. I hope that I do not hurt Ki because of my love for Joe. I can never hurt either of them. "She is talking to the doll as if it is a person telling it her secrets knowing that it can never divulge them to anyone.

Ki listens to the sound of her voice. It is clear and sad. It is no longer laced with fear. She is back to clear thinking. He feels sorry for Joe. He had to deal with these different sides of Kat. while he only got the sweet loving cheerful side. He knows she loves both. He knows that she loves Joe as a wife should. He is simply happy to be able to help her and to be here for her. Ki loves her more now than he did before. He has gotten to know just how complex she is. He knocks on the door to let her know he is there. She turns and sees him.

"Hey, I'm sorry to be such a bother again." She tells him.

"You are never a bother." he tells her.

"Yes, I am you are just too nice to say so." She tells him 'Umm I have a question?" She looks at him a little nervously.

"What is it?" He looks at her with his arms crossed over his chest.

"How am I paying to stay here. I know that the center and hospital are covered between my husband's insurance and the state medical insurance that I qualified for. But I do not think private clinics are covered. "She asks him.

"You are here as my guest for now. This room I never made as a patient room. So therefore, there is no charge you are here because your family and I need your help. "He tells her.

"Oh, with what?" she asks.

"I was looking through grandmother's journals and she talks about a special person she met in Florida. I know it was you but what I truly do not understand is how you got there and were able to find her. She also wants Jae and I to have a few experts look at her things and tell us if they have any value of any kind. I do not know where to start and I have no time in which to do anything about it. Would you like the job of sorting through the hidden rooms and figure out what we should do with them? I know you can do this. "He looks at her. Hoping she will say yes.

"Ok I can help you out since you are letting me stay for free. But you must tell Joe the agreement. He may not believe me. "She tells him.

"Then let us shake on it. I will call him after dinner. "He tells her as they shake hands. "Oh, and your family can visit you here anytime and that includes Joe." He tells her.

They bid each other good night and Kat goes into the secret room. She sits on the chaise and falls asleep holding the doll that grandma gave her.

Ki goes back up to his office to call Joe back.

"Hey, Joe, it's my Ki again. Kat wanted me to tell you a few things. First, she is almost back to herself. At least she is talking and not shaking in fear. Second, I am not going to charge her for staying here. I did not last time either. She was worried about it not being covered by your insurance. It is not needed. She will be staying in my grandmother's old room. It was never refurbished for the clinic. Third is that I need her help to organize some things for my grandmothers. She says she wants to do it as payment for staying here. That is not necessary of course I will place some money in an account for any work she does. This money I will use for whatever she needs. unless you want it." He explains what is going on.

"No, I don't want it. I mean could we use it for the kids and their unpaid bills yes, but I will not take it from her. I bet you she will not take your money. So do not bother setting it aside. That is ok with me if she is in a safe place and will not disappear again. "Joe tells him.

"Oh, and I also told her that you all can visit anytime you want. on one condition. You cannot fight with her or ask her to come home until we are sure that she will be stable at home." He tells him.

"Ok that is fine I will bring the kids to visit on the weekends." Joe tells him.

They hang up again and Ki decides he needs to sleep. So, he goes down to his room. On the way he stops at his grandmother's room he does not see her. He checks the secret room, and she is sound asleep with his grandmother's blanket and her doll. She looks like a child laying there. So much like the last time he saw her in this house before they were separated. He wonders if he will be able to hear her if she has a nightmare in this room. He decides that he will leave his door open tonight and the other two doors open so he can hear her if she wakes up.

CHAPTER 45

Kat is back.

The next morning, he wakes up to an amazing smell. He hurries and jumps in the shower. After getting dressed he runs down the stairs. In the kitchen he walks into the most hilarious sight. Kat is dancing around the kitchen oblivious that she has an audience. Cooking bacon, sausage gravy and pancakes with biscuits and eggs. She has flour in her hair on her clothes and even a few smudges on her face. He notices that the three patients he has in the clinic are watching her from the sun deck. The two guys are smiling, and the girl looks annoyed. He cannot help but smile broadly. He cannot believe even as an adult she still dances around when she cooks. The music changes from an upbeat pop song to a sexy Spanish song. His mouth drops. she is dancing like a stripper in his kitchen he decides to let her know he is there before the guys outside get too much of a show.

"Umm something smells good "he says from close behind her. Kat jumps and splatters pancake batter on his face. He busts out laughing.

"Oh, I'm sorry I wanted to make breakfast for you, and I saw your counselor and she told me there were 3 other patients. So, I made enough for everyone, staff, and patients, I just need to fry a few eggs for everyone." She is saying in a hurried voice as she is wiping his face. Not even realizing they are standing super close. When she gets him cleaned up, she turns back to the stove to fry the eggs.

Ki puts his arms around her to give her a hug. He whispers in her ear." Its ok no worries. I do not care how much of a mess you make or how loud you play music. Just no more sexy dancing where others can see you, please. "He hugs her tight, so she can feel his reaction to watching her dance and being so close to him. She draws in her breath and closes her eyes as the heat of having him so close overcomes her. Her reaction to him is still the same. She does not know how she can still want him so much, and at the same time love her husband so much.

She is so confused now about how she feels again. "Oh god help me" she prays to herself. Ki reluctantly lets her go and asks her if he can help in any way.

"Can you set the table for however many people who will eat breakfast?" She asks him. He smiles and goes to the cabinet and starts to set the table. He motions for the 3 still watching from the sun deck to come inside.

"Good morning what smells so good?' a good-natured young man asks.

Kat turns and smiles at him and says good morning to everyone. Motioning for them to sit down. By the time she has all the eggs fried and the food on the table everyone is seated and ready to eat. She asks who would like to say the blessing. KI tells her that he lets us everyone say their own silently so as not to upset anyone or have them think he is forcing his religion on them. She bows her head and says a silent prayer for the meal. Everyone enjoyed the large breakfast, there was nothing left. The three patients volunteer to clean the kitchen. The girl goes over and turns the music back on and the three of them start cleaning the kitchen. As Ki and Kat leave, they hear laughter coming from the kitchen. Ki assistant. Meets up with them in the hallway. She hears the laughter coming from the kitchen. She looks at Kat.

"Is this your doing?" she asks.

"I'm not sure I just made breakfast. "Kat answers her.

"You know you may be Dr Parks special patient, but you should know your place. We have someone who comes and cooks all the patient's meals and does so without all this commotion." She haughtily tells Kat to look down her nose at her. Ki gets an angry look on his face.

"My office now." He growls at his assistant. As he strides towards his office. He looks back at Kat he sees is almost in tears." Kat I will see you in your room when I am done don't worry or be upset you are not at fault." He tells her as he walks with his assistant towards his office.

"What do you think you are doing. How dare you speak to any patient that way? Is this how you treat my patients when I am at the hospital? All these years I have entrusted you with the wellbeing of my patients in my absence. That woman downstairs is incredibly special to me she is the reason for this clinic. Her images are all over this clinic. You have no right to be so unprofessional to anyone. I am and will always be the boss here. Kat has done nothing to be sorry for or ashamed of. What she did do was make a delightful breakfast and we had a wonderful meal laughing and talking with those three who were in the kitchen. They are enjoying themselves. It is good for them to have fun also. It will make it more comfortable in group sessions. With that said do not ever talk to her in that tone or manner again. If you do you will find yourself, put on notice. I have let you for the most part have run of the clinic because of my shifts at the hospital. That does not mean you are or ever have overseen the decision making of the clinic. I am sorry if you feel slighted or think she overstepped. That is not for you to decide. Do you understand?" Ki tells her.

"You know that you are too close to her, and you are not objective when it comes to this patient. She needs to know her place." She tells him angrily.

"Yes, I am close to her, and I will not, or have I ever allowed anyone to talk down to her in my presence. I also am not her physician I am her family. Her physician is Dr Smith not me. I am just helping in her treatment as a friend. I am not stupid. I would not do anything to jeopardize my medical license or my clinic. I not only have Dr smith permission but also her families for her to stay here. You need to apologize to her at once. Do not ever make the mistake of speaking to any patient in that manner again. especially not her if you want to keep working here. You may go now. make sure you apologize and think of how you talk to people." He tells her to turn his back on her, so she knows he is done talking and listening to anything she may want to say.

She quietly lets herself out of the office. And walks back downstairs. She stops by the room Kat is using, she hears her weeping. Reluctantly she knocks on the door. Kat opens the door thinking it is Ki. Instead, it is his assistant.

"May I come in for a moment?" She asks Kat to move aside so she can enter the room.

"I am sorry if I upset you. I just wanted to make breakfast for everyone. I left you and the cook a plate in the oven. "Kat tells her.

"I was not upset that you cooked breakfast. I was angry because you are here again. You are too close to Dr Park, and he could get into trouble if anyone thinks he is your Dr. "she tells her.

"He isn't my Dr yes, he is helping my Dr and me, but he is not my DR. He is my family. It is no different when he is in my sessions with me than if someone else in my family was sitting there as well. I know enough to know that we have done nothing to put his practice or clinic in jeopardy. I am not stupid any more than he is. I may have a lot of problems, but I am far from the stupid person you think I am. I would never put him in jeopardy ever again, you of all people should know that he is a wonderful caring Dr who would never cause any harm to anyone. "Kat tells her. her voice getting louder and louder with each word. Ki is standing outside of the door listening. He smiles at Kat defending him and standing up for herself also. He is waiting for his assistant to apologize before he interrupts them.

"I came to apologize to you. I let my anger get the better of me. The thought of our clinic could possibly get into trouble made me angry. I did not know that Dr Park was not your Dr. I honestly thought he was." she tells Kat.

"Your forgiveness. Please do not talk to patients that way. You know those of us who have brain disorders have so many people who talk down to us and assume we are beneath them because we have this illness, we are not. Do you know that there are people who have brain disorders that are professionals? They are lawyers, doctors, firefighter, scientist, police officers, and even a few presidents. You might want to consider that. You know our illness is not that much different to most physical illnesses. They have many of the same triggers. Yes, I have several but that does not make me a lesser person. So, try to have some compassion for your patients. Know that they often have it harder than you do." Kat tells her as she walks over to the door to let her out. Just as Ki decides to knock on the door.

"I wanted to apologize on behalf of my assistant. She was out of line." He tells Kat. She pats his cheek and tells him.

"It's ok she is forgiven. Can we go down and see if the others have finished the kitchen?" she asks as she walks past him and out the door.

Ki looks at his assistant "Get ready its almost time for group. I will be conducting it this morning you can sit and take the notes today." He tells her as he follows Kat down to the kitchen.

When they reach the kitchen, the cook is there the kitchen is clean. She and the three patients are having coffee while cooks enjoy her breakfast.

"Dr parks thank you for such a wonderful treat this morning." She tells him.

"Oh, don't thank me thank Kat she cooked breakfast and these three cleaned up." He tells her.

"You know maybe we should implement a group cooking class when we have patients it may help them bond. These three was laughing so much when I came in that I just had to smile." The cook tells him.

"If you want to do that then we can try it. you will oversee it making sure that no sharp utensils go missing after each session. It will only be for those who are not suicidal and have earned privileges." He tells her.

"I can do that if you will let me try it." She tells him.

"Ok good." He looks at the three patients and asks them "You guys ready for group? Kat you're joining us, right?"

They all nodded and headed for the group room. After they all get seated in the group room one of the young men raises his hand. He looks to be in his late teens and seems kind of shy.

"Yes, Clarence what is it?" Ki asks him.

"I want to thank Kat for breakfast. It is the type of breakfast I have at home. I was missing home this morning a lot. Thanks to you I got a taste of home this morning and am feeling much happier." He tells her.

"Oh, you're welcome I am glad you liked it. I love to cook so if you tell me what food you like. If I cook will allow me to. While I am here, I would like to cook for everyone." She tells him.

Kat looks around the room at the assistant. Waiting to see if she is going to say anything. She just rolls her eyes and looks away. Kat figures she is still upset from the incident this morning.

"Ok then let get started." Ki tells them "What subject would you like to discuss today?" he asks.

"I want to know why we even have group discussions when no one ever says anything." The girl patient replies.

"Jessica, we have them so that if there is something that is bothering you. You can discuss it with the group. It helps you to know that you are not in this alone. It sometimes can give you a different perspective and it also gives you a chance to possibly support and help someone else. it is a great way to express your feelings with someone other than myself in individual therapy." Ki explains.

The other male patient raises his hand.

"Yes Terrence?" ki asks.

"Do we have to discuss our problems, or can we discuss things we enjoy. Things we like to do?" he asks Ki.

"We can discuss anything you like at any time. The aim of group therapy and activities is so that you can connect to other people. To find support and to support others. It also is to make you more comfortable in a safe environment to share your problems. One without judgment or anyone looking down their noses at you so to speak." He tells them without realizing it they all three turn and look at the assistant. And nod their heads ok.

"So can we talk about some of our likes today to see if we have anything in common with each other?' Jessica asks.

"Of course, that would be great. First why don't we reintroduce ourselves by a brief description of who we think each of us are." Ki prompts them Jessica raises her hand and says she wants to go first.

"Hi, I am Jessica. I am 16 years old. I like music, drawing and love to give makeovers. I like watching all kinds of sports. I don't have a clue what I want to be when I get older, I only know I want to be successful at it." She laughs the young man sitting on her right. Raises his hand.

"Hi, I am Clarence I like playing the guitar and singing. I also like mountain climbing and water sports. I love amusement parks. I am 19. I love to eat "tells them.

The next young man speaks up.

"Hi, I am Terrence, and I don't like much of anything except gaming and animae. I don't like talking much and really find being here a waist of my time." He tells them.

Kat raises her hand.

"Hi, I am Kat I am the oldest here besides the doctor of course. I am a mom and I love cooking, crocheting, doodling, animae, video games, writing, music, and dancing. I think that finding new things to do is an adventure. I also don't like to talk about myself much but love listening to other talk."

"I am Dr Ki and I like drawing, music, dancing and eating. My favorite thing is seeing my patients grow and learn about themselves. to watch them become confident in who they are so that they can manage their illness and go on to do great things." He smiles at them. They all look at his assistant.

"Hi, I am Alice, and I don't share my personal information with anyone. So, I think I am going to excuse myself and go do a few of my other duties." She says as she stands up to leave. Ki stands up and excuses himself from the group for just a moment. Once outside of the room. He is called Alice.

"Alice why do you work here if it is such a burden to you?" he asks.

"I started working here after I got my degree because I needed work experience and since it was a small clinic, I didn't think I would have to work hard at it." She tells him.

"So, you thought I would be an easy ride." He prompts her.

"Yes basically. I do not conduct a group in this manner. I pick the subject based on why the patients are here. I tell them they must take part, or they do not get privilege points. It is a structure that works. I do not understand why suddenly you are coming in here after 5 years and deciding to change things. I have run this clinic successfully for you." She tells him.

"No, you have not. You have run this clinic the way you think it should be done. If you look at the mission statement above the reception area what you just described is not what this clinic is about. I know it is my fault that I was too busy with my work at the hospital. to watch over how you handle things, but I think that it is time that you looked for a new job. I will not have anyone working here who cannot respect the patients and treat them as equals when it comes to their own recovery." He tells her.

"What you're firing me just because I don't agree with you. after all the work I did here." she spats out the words at him.

"Yes, you are fired I would like your desk cleaned out by the end of the day. I will give you two weeks' severance pay in your next check. I never realized that we saw patient care so differently before; for that I am sorry. Being a counselor is all about connecting with your patients and having empathy for their struggle. If you do not have compassion, they will never trust you. "He tells her as he turns to go back into the group room. The three young patients were glued to the door listening. When they hear him coming back, they rush back to their seats.

Ki walks in and apologizes to the group.

"So, where were we?" he asks them.

"Dr Ki did you really mean what you said. That you want us to learn and become confident. You know I have no confidence in myself and am always afraid of failing." Jessica tells him.

"We all fail but instead of looking at it as a failure think of it as a learning experience. For every time we fail, we also learn. When we fail at something it gives us a chance to start over. A fresh start with a new perspective. Let me give you an example. Say you bake a cake, and it does not turn out the way you want. What do you do? You look at the recipe and see if you missed any steps. Then you try again. If you have the courage to keep trying, then you will not fail. You have only learned a lesson. Terrance is it ok if I use you as an example?" Ki asks him.

"Sure, I don't care." He tells him.

"Take Terrence for example this is his second time here for the same problem. I do not consider him a failure, because he is back. You want to know why. He took what he learned last time and used it to help him stay on track with his life. He just had a setback recently when something he could not control happened. He already is making progress towards getting back on his feet. So therefore, he is not a failure. The only time you are a failure is if you give up trying to grow and move forward. You all have struggles in your life, things that only you know how hard it is to move past. With support and understanding you can achieve great things in your life. Never compare yourself to those around you. They each have their own struggles. they are no better than you in anyway. We each have our own special talents. We just must find them and learn the proper way to use them. "He tells them.

"Wow doc that was deep I never thought you were such a deep person." Terrence tells him.

"You would be surprised at how deep I am at times." He tells him with a smile.

"Doc did you really fire mis Alice?" Clarence asked him.

"Yes, I did. It is mostly my fault because I have spent too much time at the hospital except when I am needed here for your individual therapy sessions. I did not keep a check on how she was performing her job. Since no one was complaining I thought she was doing ok. So, you could say I learned a lesson from my own failure. My failure to make sure that I had the right employee in the right job." He tells them.

"I never liked group sessions because I always felt I was being judged and had to tell everyone my problems. I like this kind of group sessions doc. "Terrence tells him.

"Really, I'm glad you like the change. I will keep that in mind when I start interviewing new counselors." He tells him.

"I know we did not make much progress today. I think it was still a good session. You all learned that you all are artistic and enjoy music. Terrence, I know you did not mention your love of music, but I hear you playing it constantly in your room. "Ki tells them as he dismisses group therapy. He heads to his office to call the accountant to make the arrangements for Alice's last paycheck. After taking care of that he heads to the kitchen to have lunch. He stands just outside the door of the kitchen he hears Alice talking to the cook.

"How can he do this to me after all I have done for this place. I have half a mind to call and lodge a complaint to have his license revoked. He has no idea how much I did around here so that he only had to worry about his precious one on one sessions. If only that woman was not around, he would not have changed." She is ranting, and the cook is just sitting there letting her vent. The cook notices him, he puts his finger over his lips to let her know not to say anything. She nods at Alice.

"You know I only stayed here after my first year because I had full run of this place and was hoping someday, he would notice me and maybe we could get married, and nothing would change. Not anymore since she arrived. You must know dirt on him or his family that I can use to get him to see reason. that he is throwing his clinic away by my leaving. 'She asks her.

"Sorry Alice, I have worked in this house since Dr Ki was a teenager. He has never done anything to cause others pain. He has always been a good man. It was you who was wrong. You just assumed that you were in charge and doing things the right way. I told you many times over the years that if any of the patients complained about how you would act above them and treat them as if they had no choice. that Dr ki would be angry. You just got lucky that since none of them ever said anything to him directly. This has nothing to do with Angel, it has only to do with you and your attitude towards patients. He just was never able to be here when you showed your true colors because you were always so careful to hide it. Now if you go to try to make trouble for him you will only get hurt more. You just need to do as he says and find yourself a place that sees things the same as you." The cook tells her. Ki walks into the kitchen.

"You're still here I thought you would have left by now. Oh, and I had a talk with the accountant, and you will receive your check on time, and it will include all your vacation sick and personal leave that you have. It will also have two weeks' severance pay. Also do not forget that you signed a confidentiality agreement every year that you worked here. If you say anything about anyone of the patients that have been treated here, you will be sued and your license to practice will be revoked. That includes Kat, since the last time she was here she was a regular patient. Also, I never had any interest in you outside of work. You are not my type. I do not like people who pretend to be one thing and are something else. The only thing I ever asked you to do was to show respect and compassion to our patients. This clinic is supposed to be a safe place for people to get their lives back on track. If you want to run it like an institution, then you should go work at one. "He tells her "Now your day is almost over if you are not gone by the time you are supposed to leave, I will ask security to escort you out. "With saying that he turns and walks out of the kitchen to round up the 4 others in the clinic to see who would like to go work in the green house. After cleaning the greenhouse everyone was exhausted. the kids thanked ki for letting them have such a fun day. As they were going to their rooms. Ki walked Kat to her room.

"Good night, keep your door open, so I can hear you if you have a nightmare, please." He asks her.

"I will and thank you for today it was fun working in the green house. I felt like Kris was there with us today." She tells him.

Ki goes up to his office. He wants to make sure that everything is in order and to post a job opening on the hospital's website. It is going to be exhausting until he can find a replacement for Alice. She was right about one thing. She did take care of a lot of the daily responsibilities around here, so he could focus on the patient's individual treatment and his work at the hospital. He calls Jae.

"Hey bro "Jae answers

"Hey, can I ask you for a favor. I had to fire Alice today. Now I have no one to cover the clinic while I am taking care of individual patients and my shifts at the hospital. how does your schedule look for tomorrow.?" He asks him.

"I am free all day. I do not have a lot of patients since I am just starting my practice since leaving Boston. In fact, I was going to ask you if I could meet my patients at the clinic for now and give up my office space since I am never there. "He tells him.

"That would be perfect. That way you can oversee things here for me until I find a replacement for Alice." He tells him.

"Also, this way I can hang out with Kat when she isn't at the center or in her sessions." He laughs. He knows this is going to irritate him.

"Since I know your dating Sarah its fine. it does not bother me." he tells him "I will see you in the morning. Thank you, Jae, I owe you." He hangs up the phone and heads down to his room to sleep. He stops by each patient room and all the kids are sleeping. He walks by Kats room she is not in bed. He goes in and slips into the secret room. Just as the night before she is sleeping with her doll and grandmother's blanket. He wonders if she is still afraid from the previous day. He slips out and goes to his room to sleep.

CHAPTER 46

Jae joins the clinic.

The next morning Jae is in the kitchen having breakfast with everyone. When Ki arrives.

"Morning bro I'm going to stay in my old room for a few nights so that way I can get used to the routine here if you don't mind." He tells him.

"That is fine I have night shift tonight at the hospital, so it works out. "He tells him.

"Ok great I'm going to go unpack and get settled in then." Jae walks past him grabbing another biscuit as he heads out the door.

"Kat are you going to the center today or do you want to stay here. You know except for your individual therapy you basically have day treatment right here. So, you don't need to go out if you don't want to." He tells her.

"I need to go and pick up my truck. if I leave it there much longer someone may decide to have it towed." She tells him.

"I already took care of it. it should be delivered sometime today." He tells her as he sits for breakfast. The rest of the day was not much different than most days at the center. They had group therapy and individual activities as well as life skills classes. The kids seemed to enjoy having Jae as their counselor. Even Terrence opened a little today about what he is struggling with. Dr smith arrives for dinner and is introduced to the kids. They have a very lively game night planned before bed. Dr smith seems to be enjoying herself. That makes Kat smile as she watches how affectionate she is with Jae. Ki leaves for his shift at the hospital. Kat tells everyone good night that she will see them in the morning.

"Don't forget I need you to come to the center tomorrow Jae and KI for your session." Dr smith reminds her.

CHAPTER 47

Going back to Hell.

The next morning, they arrive at the center. Kat's truck is in the parking lot. The receptionist goes to hand her the keys. when Jae takes them instead.

"Not taking any chances today." he tells her.

They go in and take their seats. Dr Smith tells ki she wants him to guide Kat again today. They get started. The lights are dimmed, and Ki recites the poem. Kat is standing at the top of the staircase. She is descending into the darkness of the stairwell. She comes to the door that was opened last time. She hesitates, she does not want to open it. She hears a distant voice. "Nothing can hurt you here remember."

"I don't want to open it. Do I really have to.?" She feels so much fear she cannot move.

"We will be with you I promise." The voice tells her.

She opens the door. Inside the door is a hallway lined with doors.

"There are more doors here. I do not know what to do. Its dark here." she tells them.

"Just go to one and tell us what you see. open" the voice tells her.

"It is baby blue. It has rattles and pacifiers on it, and it has a knife through a rope for the handle." She tells them.

"Can you open it?" the voice asks.

She reaches out and opens the door. She walks in as always; she can see herself and everything inside the room.

"We are at my sister's trailer. It is the day we are moving in here. My dad and her husband got into a fight over his cruel mouth to my sister. So, he made them move out. Everyone is coming and going I and rocking the baby to sleep. My dad, sister and mom went back to our trailer to get some more of my sister's things. They left me with him. since I am getting the baby down for his nap. After they leave, I am sitting in the chair with the baby, and he comes over and yanks him by the arm. Wrenching him away from me. I scream at him asking him what he thinks he is doing. Her voice is terrified. You can hear that she is on the verge of crying. her voice is so heart breaking that Dr Smith looks towards Jae. He has tears in his eyes and clinching the edge of his seat. KI has his head buried in his hands. She is trying her best to stay calm. As a woman it is hard to hear another woman in such agony.

"I don't like him laying on your breast he needs to learn to go to sleep without you. You are not his mother you are his aunt. He is to attach to you. "The baby is screaming I can see he is in a lot of pain. I get up and try to take him from him. He will not let me near him. He takes him to the bedroom and slams the door. He is standing there blocking it. pushing me away each time I try to move him. I cannot get to the baby. I am on my knees begging him to please let me get him and make sure he is ok. He grabs my hair and pulls my head up to his crotch where he has his pants down. You want to get him and put him to sleep. Make me cum and I will think about it. You must hurry though everyone will be back soon. you do not want them to think you are a whore do you. He rams his dick in my mouth and uses his hand in my hair to push my head the way he wants. I close my eyes so that I do not see anything. I feel my self-separating from her, I am no longer there I am not feeling the pain. I see myself in the room with the baby. Softly singing to him to try to calm he, I can hear the noises outside the room, but I can't see what is happening." Her voice becomes devoid of emotion, it is cold and quiet. They know she has disassociated from what is happening to her. just like before.

"Can you go back out to where you are with him. can you tell us what is happening?" The voice asks.

"I don't want to."

"Remember nothing can hurt you here. try "the voice tells her.

"He has my hair pulling it as hard as he can with both hands. I am crying and have my eyes closed. His body starts to shake as he shoves my face tighter to his body. He flings me away from him and smacks my head against the wall. He pulls his pants back up and zips them. I am curled up in a ball crying. I hear myself ask if I can please check on the baby now. He kicks me and tells me to go ahead. We need to make sure he is asleep before they get back. He snickers and tells me I am a good little whore. I go to the bathroom and throw up. Wash my mouth. I went into the bedroom and the baby was still screaming, he broke out in a sweat. I go over and lay beside him on the bed and make sure he is ok. I sing to him to calm him down to go to sleep. By the time, my parents are back both me and the baby is sleeping." She tells the voice.

"You can leave this place now you will never have to open the blue door again. Nothing here can hurt you. You will be yourself once you close this door. You will know that he cannot hurt you and that this memory cannot hurt you again. When you leave the second door you will start to walk up the stairwell. As you get closer to the top it will become lighter. When you reach the top, you will be awake on my snap. 123snap." Kat is awake. The Dr's are holding their breath. not sure as to how she is going to react to this door.

"Kat how do you feel" Ki asks her.

"I am angry. How can a father mistreat a baby when he isn't even a year old? how could he be so cruel." She asks them in a whisper.

"That I do not know. "Dr smith tells her" More importantly how are you feeling right now. Besides anger." She asks.

"I am tired I feel like I just fought a war. Do you think I could see if Shay can bring the 5 kids over to the clinic for dinner? I just need to hold them right now. I feel dirty and need to shower and brush my teeth. "She asks them. She keeps wiping her mouth as if she can still feel him there.

"I will call her and if she says yes, I will call cook to add extra plates." Ki tells her. 'Jae, will you drive her back to the clinic in her truck I have to go to the hospital for my shift" Ki asks his brother.

"Of course, no problem." They all stand and end the day's session with the unspoken reminder to keep an awfully close watch on her these next few days. The moment Ki gets to the hospital he stops by Shay department.

"Hey Dr Park, what are you doing here?" she asks.

"You know that Kat is staying at the clinic. She wants to know if you can bring the kids over for dinner tonight. She really needs a visit with them today." He tells her.

"Sure, I will need to call Joe and make sure I can bring all of them if he says no then it will be just my three. "She tells him.

"Ok that is fine" he waves goodbye to her and heads for the psychiatric floor. Once in the office he calls Joe.

"Hey Dr Park, what can I do for you. "Joe asks him.

"I was wondering if you and the kids could come for dinner. Kat had a hard day today and wants to see the kids." He asks.

"I have to work late today but if someone will bring them its fine by me, they just have to be home before bedtime." He tells him.

"Ok Shay is going to call you in a few minutes and ask you if she can bring them "Ki tells him. "I am working night shift at the hospital tonight, but my brother Jae will be there taking care of the clinic. Since he and Dr smith are dating now, she will be there also." He tells him.

"Oh, ok that's fine. I told you I trust my wife. She has never given me a reason to be jealous. I know she will not cross any lines. I also know from what I have seen from you that you will not do anything to hurt her. So, I don't think I have anything to worry about." He tells him "I will be there on Saturday to visit her if you have nothing scheduled for her."

"That will be fine. Thank you, Joe, for not giving her a hard time about treatment this time around." Ki tells him.

They hang up and Ki goes to the nurse's station to get the evening report. Back at the clinic as soon as Jae and Kat arrive, she jumps out and heads for the bathroom. Jae follows her to make sure she is ok. She never spoke all the way to the clinic. He hears her vomiting inside. Jessica comes up to stand beside jae.

"What's wrong with MS. Kat is she ok?" she asks.

"She just seems to be a little under the weather "he tells her.

"I think it's something else but ok.' She knocks on the door" MS Kat are you ok do you need me to get you anything?" she asks her.

"No, I am ok. I am going to take a shower after I get some clothes from my room." she tells her through the door.

"Ok I will see you at dinner." She smiles and heads downstairs.

Kat opens the door. And collapse in front of Jae. He catches her and carries her to her room. Lays her on the bed. He takes her pulse and checks her breathing. He thinks she just passed out from the stress of the morning. Deciding to let her rest for a few minutes he sits on the chair beside the bed. Watching her closely. He wonders how much more she will be able to handle her memories; before she completely cracks. He looks at her and all he sees is the fragile girl she has always been to him. someone to protect and to love. He wonders if she will be able to keep the loving and forgiving heart after she gets through these doors. It is amazing to him that she has functioned as she has so far. Even though she has let different sides of her personality take over. She has not split into completely different personalities. She has always stayed her just disconnected. Only once did she completely lose herself. That was when she disappeared. And went to Florida. He knows subconsciously she must have been looking for them. Since they always talked about going to grandma's retirement house during the winter to visit her. He wonders if they keep going, if they will wind up losing her or will they be able to piece her back together so that she can be a whole person again. Kat opens her eyes and calls out for Ki.

"Kat are you ok now.?' He asks.

"Yes, I am sorry I got really dizzy and passed out. "She tells him.

"Here let me help you sit up. I want to have your primary doctor run some tests. To make sure your levels are ok. Do you think you can get up and shower now? Shay will be here soon with the kids for a visit." Jae asks.

Kat nods her head and gets up. she asks him if he will stay by the bathroom door in case, she feels dizzy again. He nods and stands outside of the bathroom while she showers. He closes his eyes and takes a deep breath. He always loved the smell when she was showering. The oils she used made the entire floor smell like a garden. When he hears the click of the lock, he knows she is ready. She opens the door and thanks him for staying there with her. He smiles and pats her head as if she is a child.

"I think I hear voices coming from downstairs. maybe the kids are here." he tells her.

She smiles and races down the stairs to see the 5 kids still in their school clothes, and Shay asks them to be quiet.

"It's ok, they can make as much noise as they like. They have been cooped up in school all day. "Jae tells Shay.

The kids stopped at his voice, they turned and saw Kat. All 5 of them rush her at the same time. To give her hugs and kisses. They hit her with such force that she fell to the floor to a sitting position. The 3 other patients are standing on the stairs watching them.

Jessica has a big smile on her face. "I guess she must be a great mom. I don't think I have ever had that much joy just for seeing my mom." She speaks.

"Me "both boys say at the same time.

The kids are firing a thousand questions at her at one. They notice that she still has the oldest boy's hand. She is holding it as if her life depends on it.

Jessica wonders what is wrong with Kat today. She is different from when she left in the morning. Just then Terrence taps the two of them and motions for them to go down to greet everyone. They get to the bottom of the steps and Terrence introduces the three of them to Shay and the kids.

"Hi, I'm Terrence and this is Jessica and Clarence. We are visiting the clinic with Kat." He puts his hand out to shake Shay's hand. Shay takes his hand.

"It's nice to meet you all. I hope you don't mind the noise, but the kids have missed my sister these last few days." She tells them.

"Oh no its ok I like kids and a little noise never hurts anyone. it reminds me of home." Clarence tells her.

"Are you guys staying for dinner?" Jessica asks her.

"Yes, Dr Ki said it would be ok for the kids to visit and have dinner with her.' Shay informs them.

One of the girls taps Terrence on the hand. He looks down she has such big black eyes. She is just too cute, almost like an angel.

"Hi, I am peewee would you like to go to the garden with us to play. Aunty Mama is taking us outside, so we can play before dinner." She asks him. He looks at the other two and the three of them nod in agreement. So, everyone heads to the back yard and garden to play. Jae goes to the garage and gets some old outdoor games they have stored there. He pulls out a soccer ball, some rackets, and a birdie. He finds frisbees and heads to the garden. The kids are already playing red rover. With the 3 teens. Kat and Shay are sitting at the patio table. He decides he will let them talk in private. He takes the toys over and joins the kids. He thinks to himself even though Appa and mama are already in heaven. They would be over the moon happy if they were here to see all these children playing in the garden. Appa wanted a house full of grandkids. He looks at the oldest boy. When Kat left them, she was already playing mom to this little guy. How is it that he grew so fast? When he thinks of the time, they were apart. It seemed like a lifetime dragged by so slowly. Now though time seems to be rushing by far too quickly. He hopes Sarah still comes for dinner. He secretly wants to see how she reacts to kids. As if by magic she walks through the patio door. She smiles as she sees Jae playing soccer with the kids. She goes over and sits with Kat and Shay.

"You know that I am here in the role of Jae girlfriend. So, I cannot really talk much to you." She tells Kat.

"I know so I won't talk to you tonight since you are not here as my Dr." Kat tells her.

"How are you doing after today's session?" she asks.

"I had an awfully bad time for a while. I got sick and passed out. Jae wants you to contact my primary and have a blood work up done to make sure I am ok. I think he is worried that my anemia is back." Kat tells her.

"Ok I will call your case worker and have her arrange that appointment." She tells her.

"Oh my God you two do you really think anyone here is going to say anything about you two having a conversation that is not about her treatment. I swear sometimes I think Dr, s has it the worst. They cannot ever have anything to do with their patients outside of work or it is a conflict of interest. I know the two of you have a lot in common and you could be such great friends. I hope that you get better soon. so that you two can stop being Dr and patient and start being friends. "Shay tells them as she stomps of in frustration at the two of them.

"I think your sister is probably right. But we cannot change our relationship just yet. When I am sure you are stable and handling your memories, I will then find someone else to be your doctor ok." Dr smith tells her as she gets up to join the others on the lawn.

The oldest boy of Shays comes over and sits close to Kat. He looks sad. Kat gives him a big tight hug and kisses the top of his head." You know I love you right and nothing can change that ever." She tells him.

"So how about you tell me why you are looking so sad?" she asks him.

"I miss having you home. I miss having things the way they were before. Mom is great, do not get me wrong. But I miss having you at home and cooking us dinner. Will you be home again soon? Though I like this place much better than the hospital. And the people here are much nicer." He tells her.

Kat kisses the top of his head again and just holds him until the cook comes out to tell them dinner is ready. They all go inside to wash their hands to eat. Dinner was a loud but fun time. The kids kept everyone well entertained with stories of their moms and school. They all kept telling the cook about how great of a cook Kat is. And they should let her cook for them sometime.

'She cooked us breakfast already "the three teens told them at the same time.

"She better not has made you crepes or hamburger gravy. "The oldest boy spoke up.

"No, she did make us pancakes with bacon and sausage gravy though." Jessica tells them.

"Oh well that's ok she just isn't allowed to make the other stuff without me here to eat it or I will get mad. We each have our own special dishes that she makes for us. We don't like to share." He tells them.

They all burst out laughing at that. You can see why they all love her so much. She gives them anything they want. After dinner all the girls help the cook clean up and Shay gets, the kid ready to leave. Kat gives them all a big hug and tells them she will be back soon and that she loves them. after the kids go everyone heads to their rooms and it is just jae and Dr smith left.

"I will say good night and I will call Kat's case worker to set up her blood testing and her appointment with her primary tomorrow. "She tells him.

Jae pulls her into his arms and gives her a kiss good night. He then just holds her close for a few extra minutes, so he can be close to her." Ok I will see you tomorrow." He closes the door and locks it up. It was a remarkably interesting day today. He thinks to himself as he goes up to his room for the night.

CHAPTER 48

A New Game Plan

When Ki gets home in the morning he and Jae go to his office.

"How was everything last night?" Ki asks him.

"They were good. She was much better after the kids were here. We all had a blast with them. They are wonderful kids. Even the other patients enjoyed having them here. Kat became extremely sick when she first got home so much so she passed out." He tells him "I told her to ask Sarah to have her case worker make her an appointment with her primary for some blood work." He let him know.

"Any nightmares or dissociative behavior last night?" he asks.

"No, she was present the whole night she was quiet, but she was here with us. "He tells him.

"Ok good I want you to talk to Sarah about us giving her sometime between sessions. I'm worried if we open them to soon, she will have a psychotic break and we will lose her, and she may never recover." Ki tells him.

"I was thinking along the same lines yesterday. maybe we should cut her sessions back to once a month no more than twice instead of weekly. Her weekly sessions can be just talking therapy to make sure she is doing ok with everything. That way she can be home except when we open a new door. Depending on how she is doing. So, it will not stress the family as much and she will be more comfortable. Also, this way she can make sure she will be ok with her husband as well." Jae suggests.

"I can agree with that I know this way her progress will be slower, but we must make sure she is ok before moving forward." He tells him.

"We also have another problem. With Kat staying here and Sarah and I dating it could cause some grey lines. Tonight, they would not speak to each other unless it was about her treatment. They both are worried that they will cross the line from Dr patient to friends. I know Sarah does not want her to have a different Dr yet. The only one in the area that can treat her is a male. She thinks it will make her too uncomfortable to have someone she does not trust or know. To suddenly become her Dr., she is afraid she will revert inside herself. "Jae looks at his brother wondering what he is thinking.

"I think that when Joe comes this weekend, I will tell him; she is ok to go home if she is still behaving stable. I will talk to him about this plan. You know that you need to talk to Sarah about this she is the one who makes these decisions with Kat not us." He tells him.

", I am one step ahead of you. I already talked to her. The two of us came up with this plan before she left tonight." Jae grins as he tells him as he is walking out the door to go down to breakfast. Ki smiles at his brother who is back as he leaves the room. He is really smitten with Sarah looks like Kat picked a good match for Jae. Ki decides to go down to sleep since he has night shift again tonight. He was hoping to see Kat before he went to rest. Maybe later before he leaves for the hospital.

Over the course of the next few weeks. Things went back to some semblance of normalcy. since they were only doing talk therapy on a weekly basis. Kat was still having nightmares and was still losing time on occasion. Dr Smith was concerned with her not making progress. It is almost like before they opened the doors. She has not reverted inside her shell, but she is not moving forward either. She decides to talk to Jae and KI to see if maybe they need to do a hypnotherapy session. Kat is at a standstill. She will not be able to move on with her life if she cannot move on in her therapy. She is not ready to go back to work and she has become too nervous to be around strangers. Especially men. At their last group trip, she cringed every time a man came close to her even just in passing. Today is Kat's therapy session. She will discuss it with her and see if she is ready yet. The receptionist announces that Kat is here.

"Hi Kat. how has your weeks been?" she asks Kat?

"I'm fine. How about you? Kat replies

"I'm fine. I want to discuss a matter with you. I want to know how you feel about starting hypnotherapy again. I know we talked about not doing it for a while. I was not expecting you to stop making progress. It is up to you as always. I know you are having nightmares. I know you are still having trouble being in the same room or having men even pass you on the street. I know we have uncovered many painful memories behind the doors and it's ok if you are not ready. My concern is that you will stay stuck in this place if we do not continue to move forward." She explains to her.

"I know I feel like when we have our talk therapy we are just going through the motions. Do not get me wrong. It helps me to talk to you about Joe and the kids. It relieves my stress over things. I just don't have any more to say at times because it is like I am standing at a wall that I cannot climb or find a way to get around." She tells her.

"How have you been doing without seeing or talking to the two Dr Parks.?" Dr smith asks her.

"I miss them horribly. I picked up the phone to call the clinic to see how they are. Only to put it down and not call. I was without them for so long and then had them. Now I am afraid to call them because I do not want to cause them trouble in their work. I also do not want to depend on them too much. I am afraid that I will become too dependent on them. I do not want them to feel like I only want to see them or talk to them when I have a problem and need them. I also do not want them to become disgusted by me. I love them they are my family." She tells her. You can hear the sadness in her voice. The longing to talk to them.

"it's been a month since we did a hypnotherapy session. Do you want to restart them but only once a month depending on how you are doing after the next session?" She tells her. Kat nods her head in agreement. She knows she must get rid of this fear pent up inside of her. She has not even been able to have Joe touch her much in the last month. She has gone through the motions so that he does not get short tempered or frustrated. The fear she felt after opening the big door had not left her since that day. She knows she needs to get out of this place she is stuck in. She just does not know if she is brave enough to keep going.

CHAPTER 49

Opening the next door.

Things stayed the same over this last week. Kat woke up filled with energy and excitement. Not because today, they resumed hypnotherapy but because she gets to see them today. She takes care with her appearance today. She wants them to think she has been doing well and not been depressed. She does not want to have them be concerned. They are already in the waiting room when she arrives. Kat cannot have her excitement. She goes over and hugs each of them and gives them a kiss on the cheek. They think nothing of it since that is how she greets everyone she considers family. The receptionist though is very shocked at her and just stares. Ki thinks to himself oh lord her goes the rumor mill again. Kat begins talking excitedly asking a hundred questions in one breath.

"Who slow down. Did you miss us that much?" Jae asks her smiling.

"Oh God yes. I felt like a part of me was missing without you two. You know we are having a cookout this weekend and I would love for you two to come. Do not worry I already asked Joe he is ok with it. Tommy is coming down to visit, he has a conference close by and is going to stay with us. "She tells them.

"Then are you sure you are going to be up for today. If you are going to have a lot of people over, should we maybe postpone till next week.?" Ki asks her.

"No, I don't want to if I am having a hard time, it's better that I have a lot of distractions instead of dwelling on it. At least I hope it will be ok. Besides Tommy will understand if it turns out to be a small dinner instead of the whole crew there." She tells them.

The receptionist lets them know that Dr smith is ready for them. They go in and take their seats.

"Ok Kat who would you like to guide you today. I know that each of us has taken turns doing it. I just want to know if you have a preference." Dr smith asks her.

"I don't care who does it as long as they are close by incase, I need them." She tells her.

"Ok then let us get started. I want to guide you today because I want to try something different today." Dr Smith dims the lights and turns on her penlight, she begins by guiding her down the steps and to the big door. "When you open this door, you will not merge with yourself. I want you to be on the sidelines and tell me what is happening and all that you see. Nothing can hurt you here." She tells her Kat reaches for the door and opens it. She looks to the side of the hall that the blue door was at it gone in its place is a small tree with pink flowers.

"I see a tree with pink flowers where the blue door used to be. I am looking around there is a dark blue door with bows and streamers. It has teddy bears and a car for the handle." Kat tells them.

"Go ahead open it." The voice tells her Kat opens the door instead of seeing things as if she is a part of it, she is watching it as if she is watching a movie.

"What do you see here." the voice asks.

"I am at my house our old trailer. It is filled with so many people. I see myself sitting on the floor in the far corner of the living room. I heard my mom tell my sister that we need some ice and more drinks. That someone will need to go to the store. My sister yells for her husband and gives him some money from her pocket. She tells him to get a list from my mom and go to the store. He gets an irritated look on his face. He tells her he is not going by himself and that someone needs to go with him. She tells him to take my brother. My mom tells her he cannot go, he has a date outside and not to bother him. so, she yells for me. I hear myself telling her that I am not going. that I do not want to why cannot she go with him. She gets an angry look on her face. And she is telling me how she can go when it is the baby's first birthday, and she has so many people at the house. My brother in laws mother tells me to just suck it up and go. The sooner I get back the better. My mom walks over and grabs me by the arm and tells me to get going that I am embarrassing her and my sister. I stand up and walk over to my dad and hide behind him. He puts his arm around me. He tells my mom if she does not want to go do not make her. She has her cousins here and maybe she wants to hang out with them. My mom shouts at me with an angry look. I reach up and kiss my dad on the cheek and tell him thanks.

 I start walking towards my room. As soon as I get into the hallway my brother-in-law grabs me by the hair and pushes me against my door. He is whispering in my ear I cannot hear what he is saying. He is telling me that if I do not go with him, he will take my little friend that is so attached to me. The little girl who is always following me around. I turned around and told him no he could not. He just grins at me and walks over to her. He starts smiling at her. She nods her head and walks towards the door. I raced over to him. I hear myself tell him OK I will go with him. Once in the car, he opens the back door and puts Kayla in. He gets on the driver's side and starts the car. I heard him say I need to stop and get the baby a change of clothes before we go any further. When we get to their trailer, he tells me to get out and go get the babies clothes. I get out and run inside hoping to be quick so that he cannot follow me. Kayla wants to come with me, so I take her. I come out of the baby's room, and he is there grinning. He shoves me into the bathroom and against the sink. I hear him whispering in my ear do not make a sound or what I do to you I will do to her. I am closing my eyes. I have tears coming out. He is undoing my blouse and biting me. He is leaving a trail of bite marks down my chest. a couple of them are bleeding. he is stroking his man hood when he is done, he rebuttons my shirt and cleans himself. telling us lets go. I hold Kayla's hand and tell her its ok if he does not hurt her. It does not matter what he did. She is crying so hard I sit in the back with her while he is in the store. I got her to promise not to say anything and have gotten her quiet. We are driving back to my house. "

"Do you remember how old Kayla is? I want you to walk around the party and tell me what you are doing now.?" The voice is asking.

"She is 6 I babysit for her and her brothers. I am asking my aunt if I can stay at her house tonight since my cousin is visiting. I hear her say of course but we are leaving now. I go grab my stuff and race out before anyone can say anything." Kat tells the voice.

'Is it showing you anything else?" the voice asks.

"I am at my aunt's house its late we are already for bed. My dad is walking in the house. He looks angry. He is talking to my uncle, and they are coming over to me. I heard my dad ask me to open my shirt. I am begging him no. He is telling me either I will open it, or he will. My aunt walks over and tells him to let her take me to the bathroom and look. She is holding my hand guiding me to the bathroom. She asks me to please show her under my shirt. I am begging please no. she takes my hands and tells me its ok. I slowly lifted my shirt. She sees the angry looking bite marks I hear her gasp. And asking me who did this. I told her I cannot tell her. She goes out I stay in the bathroom, and I hear them yelling. I walked out and my dad told them what Kayla told her dad when he went to kiss her good night, he said she started screaming and climbing away from him. When they finally calmed her down, she told him everything. My dad is looking at me, he has tears rolling down his face. He walks across the room and holds me crying. I had never seen my dad cry before. He is taking me home." Through this entire session Kat has been emotionless and withdrawn. Almost like she is reading a story.

"it's time to leave here you will leave this room and close both doors. You will walk back up the stairwell and be more awake with each step when you get to the top you will wake up." The voice tells her.

When she opens her eyes, they are all looking at her wondering what she is feeling.

"Are we done now?' Kat asks in a quiet voice. She is not looking up at them she is looking at her hands. They are clenched till the knuckles are white.

"Kat how are you feeling?" Dr smith asks.

"I feel nothing. I am empty inside. "She tells them.

"Why do you say you feel empty. "Dr smith asks her.

'I couldn't connect with myself. Even when I would be outside of myself, I could still connect and feel the emotions of what was happening. This time I could not connect. I could not feel anything. I always can feel something but not this time. "She tells her.

"Do you think it's because you were not seeing it through yourself as the person he is hurting. I know you kept talking about yourself as a third person." She tells her.

"You told me not to. That I needed to be separated from what was happening. so, I could not feel anything. "Kat tells her.

"Do you remember the events after this." Ki asks her.

"Yep, the next day my dad confronted him, and he denied it being him. My sister and mother told my dad surely the little girl was mistaken and that I was just trying to get attention. I remember my dad being angry at my mom for not believing what happened, especially since I had the marks to show for it. That was when my hellish life began. I was called all sorts of names and not allowed to go to visit certain family members. They said I did not deserve to be around decent people. Finally, my dad sent me to his mom's house. You heard a little about it when I took you to dinner at my aunt's home." She tells them "I know I couldn't face Kayla for a long time. I was so ashamed that she saw what happened that day. Dr smith I do not like how I am feeling now. I think I would rather feel the pain and emotions and must deal with the fall out. than to feel this void. I feel like I am not a person right now. It feels like I am doped up and on a bad trip. I am sitting here wondering if I cut myself would I even feel pain or even bleed. I am worried because this is how I feel before I lose time. And I can never remember what happens when I lose time. "Kat tells them her voice and face expressionless.

"I wanted to try to disconnect you from the pain so that you might not have such a hard time. You were feeling too much the last few times we did this. I won't ask you to do it this way again." Dr smith tells her.

"Ok is it ok if I go now. I need to get home." She tells them as she gets up and walks towards the door. Not even saying goodbye.

After she leaves the three Drs discuss the events of her session.

"I will go by the house to make sure she is ok before going to the hospital "Ki tells them.

"Do you think she is ok I mean I have never seen her like this." Jae asks.

"She will be ok. I am sorry that she is so withdrawn. I honestly thought giving the command to stay disconnected would help her not feel the pain. I guess her ability to disassociate is stronger than I thought. She has completely cut off her emotions. I will call her husband and tell him to watch her close until our regular session. I will see her the day after tomorrow. Hopefully, she will have come out of this by then." Dr smith told them.

"If anything happens to her it will be our fault." Jae tells both.

CHAPTER 50

A Rough time.

Kat walks around in a daze the rest of the day going about her duties as a robot or auto pilot. The kids come home from school and their snacks are on the table she is just sitting on the couch no tv or radio. They all say hi to her, but she does not reply. When Joe gets home, he is not sure what to expect after Dr Smith call. He walks in and she is still sitting on the couch not moving, his dinner is on the table. The kids are doing homework.

"Hey baby I'm home." He calls and she does not answer.

"Hey dad mom has been like this since we got home. Do you think they changed her medicine again? She was like this before when they put her on that other medicine." One of the kids told him.

"Yeah, I remember." Joe tells her.

Joe asks Shay if she can take all the kids home tonight and that Kat is not ok to take care of them. He also asks if her mom to come down and put them on the bus and stay with Kat tomorrow. He does not want to leave her alone and he cannot miss work.

Ki stops by the house on his way to the hospital. Joe meets him outside.

"What the hell did you guys do to her today?" Joe asks.

"We did her session as normal except Dr smith gave her the hypnotic suggestion not to merge with herself in the memory to disconnect from it and watch it as a movie instead. It always seems like a movie to Kat except she is part of the movie so to speak. This time she was disconnected from it. Dr smith wanted her to not feel anything from the memory hoping that she would have an easier time. What she didn't count on was that Kats dissociative disorder was so strong." Ki explains.

"Look my wife hasn't been like this since we brought her back from Florida when we brought her back, she was like this except she was angry. Then they put her on medication, and she had nothing. She was a zombie not even able to carry on a conversation. "Joe tells him.

"We are hoping she will bring herself out of this. Dr smith has a session with her the day after tomorrow. Hopefully, she will be herself by then if not she will put her back under and have her go back into the memory this time like she has in the past." He tells him.

"I know I have not wanted to know about her memories. Was this one a bad one/" he asks.

"It was the memory of the day that the neighbor girl told what she saw. they day everyone found out what was happening." Ki tells him.

"Oh, you mean the day that they blamed my wife for everything. saying she seduced him and wanted to take him away from her sister. The day my wife became a whore to everyone. The day that every guy who ever liked her started to harass her and make her life hell. You know she had to live her senior year having guys cornering her in the hallway and groping her and trying to get into her pants. I remember that I was dating one of her friends at the time. I used to hear the horrible things they said about her. Though all I saw was a beautiful girl with a kind heart. That was more than 3 years before we started dating. "Joe tells him you can hear the anger in his voice. Joe has some deep-seated anger at how his wife was treated. Ki bets that Kats family does not even realize that he knew some of this before they started dating. Joe is a better man than he thought.

That night Kat had a never-ending nightmare. She was not screaming or fighting like she normally does. She just cried in her sleep all night. He laid her down on the couch when he came to bed since she was not responding to anything. About 2am Kat is standing over Joe staring at him. He wakes up startled.

"Babies are you ok what is it.?" He asks her, she just smiles at him. Turns and walks back to the living room. He follows her on the blanket on the couch and he notices that there is blood on it. He turns her around and he notices she has cuts on her arms. the blood is on her hands she raises her bloody hand to his face and touches it.

"Baby what did you do. Let me clean you up. "He goes to the kitchen and gets a cloth and a bowl of warm water. He sits her down and cleans her up. After he cleans the wounds, he sees they are not that deep. He bandages her up and cleans her face. "Oh, baby why did you do this. what is wrong.?" He asks while he is holding her close rocking her back and forth. She falls back to sleep. He goes and calls Ki at the hospital.

"Hello this is Dr Park." He answers.

"Hey its Joe. Kat cried in her sleep for most of the night. She woke me up a few minutes ago. She was covered in blood. she cut her arms. She still is not talking, I cleaned her up. What am I supposed to do? How can I trust her like this?" joe asked him?

"Do you want me to pick her up in the morning and bring her back to the clinic. I can call Jae and he can come get her now. He is living at the clinic right now." Ki tells him.

"I don't want to keep putting her into the clinic or hospital it's too confusing for her and the kids. I just don't know what to do." Joe tells him.

"What is she doing right now?" Ki asks him.

"She is sleeping I need to leave for work in about 30 min and do not want to leave her alone." He tells him.

"I will call Jae to come sit with her. he will stay with her till someone comes in the mooring." Ki tells him.

"Ok I will call and tell them I might be late. "He tells him as they hang up.

Ki calls Jae as soon as he hangs up the phone with Joe. Jae goes over to the house to sit with Kat so Joe can go to work. She was still sleeping when he arrived. Joe thanks him for coming over so quickly. Jae sits in the chair just watching her sleep. Wondering what is happening to her. What is she feeling and thinking? Why did she cut her self-last night? She did not cut deep enough to cause real damage. Jae falls asleep in the chair. He wakes up startled when something touches his face. He opens his eyes and looks right into Kats big blue-green eyes. They are still expressionless. He smiles at her.

"Good morning, Kat "he tells her as he tucks her hair behind her ear.

"Good morning. why are you here?" she asks?

"You had a rough night last night and I came to sit with you." He tells her.

"Oh, did I do anything bad?" she asks.

He lifts her arms for her to see. He unwraps the bandages, so she can see her cuts.

"What do you think?" he asks her.

"I did this?" She looks at him puzzled, not understanding that she cut herself.

"Yes, you did this. can you tell me why?" he asks?

She shakes her head now. Before he can say anything, else Kat stands up and sits on his lap. She places her head on is shoulder.

"Will you hold me for just a few minutes. I'm so cold inside and scared." She asks him.

"Of course, I will hold you for as long as you like." He tells her.

They sat like that until they both fell back to sleep. Jae gets woken back up when Shay taps him on the shoulder.

CHAPTER 51

Mama gets called out.

"Hey mom is here to sit with her. So, you can go home at get some sleep." She tells him.

"Thanks, but I will wait till she wakes up. She had a real bad night last night." He tells her.

"Yes, I know joe called me from work. Why is she sitting on your lap though" shay asks him?

"When she was younger, I used to trick her into letting me hold her like this or carry her around like this. She was cold, and I think a little scared last night, so she asked if she could sit on my lap and fell asleep." He explains. Kat's mom hears this and becomes appalled at her daughter's behavior. She has never even sat on her husband's lap. Kat's mom walks over to grab her daughter to wake her up and give her a stern talking to. When Jae grabs her hand

"You will not wake her up. She is fine where she is. You will also not say a word to her about anything that has to do with her actions these last 24 hours. She is in a fragile state, she does not need your judgment or lectures on how to behave. If that is what you are going to do, I will take her with me. do you understand?' Jae tells her.

"I do not know why my mother liked you boys so much, but I do not like you being so close to my daughter. She is a married woman and should not be so close to another man other than her husband. "Kat's mom glares at Jae

"Just so you know I was her husband long before her current husband, I am not going to hurt her or let anyone else hurt her again." He tells her.

"What do you mean you were her husband. She has only ever been married once." Her mom tells him.

"Maybe legally only once. But she has had 4 husbands before this current one. She married me and my three brothers when she was 14. Grant it was just a pretend wedding and more of a way to protect her when she was younger. We took our roles very seriously. We never touched her in that way so do not get any dirty ideas. We just always made sure she was happy and felt safe. She has always felt safe with us, especially when she was in pain. If we had not been separated, she would never have fallen into the clutches of her brother-in-law. If you do not believe me, ask Shay, she will tell you. We all quit our universities to go to the vocational school she was attending because we were worried about her after the incident with your neighbor's husband. We saw her every day for over two years. Between the school skating rink and your mom bringing her to visit us. We were never far from her side. She was happiest those years. She became our whole world. If one of us is close no one will hurt, her again. "Jae informs Kat's mom. Watching the indignation on her face.

"She has a husband a real husband now she doesn't need you all hovering around her. She has done fine without you." She spats at him.

"Oh, really you think that she has done fine. Really, she has been beaten and raped in your house under your care. Her husband has beaten her. She is in such a state of shutdown that she can barely function. You call that doing fine. Her husband asked us to help her. He called in the middle of the night because of the state she was in. we will not leave her this time until she truly doing ok and does not need us. If you do not believe me, ask her husband." Jae tells her through clenched teeth trying hard to not raise his voice so that he does not wake up Kat.

Kat begins to stir in his arms. He looks down at her hoping he did not wake her. she snuggles deeper into his arms and sighs. The phone rings and Kat's mom goes and answers it. It's Joe checking on Kat. He asks her if Jae is still there. she hands the phone to Jae.

"Hey bro what's going on?" Jae asks him.

"Not much I'm too preoccupied to be here at work. How is my wife doing?" he asks?

"She woke up really frightened and confused earlier so she is curled up in my lap asleep right now. When she was a kid, she always slept peacefully like this. So, I am just keeping her till she wakes up." He says with a little smile on his face wondering how her husband is taking this news.

"Yes, I know she all but tries to crawl inside of you when she is scared. She sleeps on my chest when she is scared. At least it is you and not Ki. I know you are just her big brother, and you have a girl. So, I have no worries about you. I bet her mom is beside herself with anger at her right now. Don't let her bully her when she wakes up, please." He tells him.

Jae hands the phone back to Kat's mom.

"Joe, are you ok with him being here should I make him leave?" she asks him.

"I called him to come when I had to leave for work if he is there, she will be ok. If he tells you he needs to take her with him its ok. He knows what is best for her. Do not give him a hard time, make him a good breakfast please. "Joe tells her before he hangs up. Kat's mom shoots him an angry look. As she goes to see what they have to fix for breakfast she comes back to the living room to ask him what he would like. She sees him looking at her daughter with such love on his face she is speechless. She does not understand these three men and how they are with her daughter.

"Excuse me, what would you like to eat? Joe told me to feed you. He also said that if you need to take her with you its ok." She tells him quietly.

"I am fine for now why you don't come and sit until she wakes up. We can chat and I will answer any question you want. will you answer a few for me?" he asks her?

"Sure, why not." Kat's mom sits on the couch when she notices for the first time there is blood on the blanket and on the couch.

"What is this why being there blood on the furniture and blanket?" she stands up picking up the blanket. And heads for the laundry room

She comes back carrying a small bowl of warm water and a sponge. To clean the couch.

"We can talk while I clean this up ok "she tells him.

"That's fine. do you ever remember Kat cutting herself other than when she wanted to kill herself?" Jae asks her.

"When she was 15 almost 16, she would take a scrubber like the ones you use for the dishes. She would scrub her skin till it bled. She said she was itchy and could not get it to stop. She did that for the longest time. Her skin had so many scabs on it that she looked like she had a disease. My mom took her to the Dr, but he could not explain it. It was not until she was almost ready to graduate from high school, we found out about my son in law molesting her. She stopped after that and withdrew from people. 'Kat's mom told him.

"Can you look at the scrubber in the kitchen see if it has blood on it.?" Jae asks her.

"Oh my God its completely red. "Kat's mom tells him.

"I think that Kat was scrubbing her body with it trying to scrub away the feeling of him touching her. When she came out of her session, she was completely withdrawn emotionless. "Jae tells her.

"Yeah, she would go days without ever saying a word to anyone except the baby during that year and half as well. I had no idea he was doing anything to her. Then things got worse after everyone found out.' she tells him

"Why didn't you believe her?" he asks.

"If I had believed her, I would have lost Shay and my grandson. I cannot lose them." She told him.

"You could lose Kat instead though?" Jae asks her.

"Kat never needs me; Shay cannot survive without Kat and I. Kat can survive on her own no matter where she is at. She proved that when she disappeared and was already working. Though she was using my granddaughter's name. She still had a place to live and a job. "She tells him.

"She still needed you back then. She was a child and had lived through so much. She needed to know you at least believed her. Do you even know what she has lived through?" He asks her.

"No and I don't want to. Shay lived in hell with that man and needed me to help her break away from him. you do not know what he put her through." She told him.

"Yes, I can imagine. I know what he put the person who is sleeping in my arms through; and we have only uncovered 3 memories so far. She has been through hell. I just do not understand how you can choose one child over the other. This child was raped beaten and who knows what else and kept her mouth shut to protect you and you could not even believe her. Even when someone else told you what happened to her. You are pathetic in my eyes. How can you even call yourself her mother? Kat told us how she begged Shay not to marry him. to not have anything to do with him. She told us how worried she was for her sister. How that psycho would walk up and down the road with his gun saying he would kill himself. She tried everything to get her not to marry him. When she found out she was pregnant. She gave every cent my parents gave her as an allowance and her babysitting allowance to Shay for clothes and food. She would pack a lunch at leave it in Shay's locker for her. You all only cared about Shay and your son. You used her for your own ends. Her whole life she has always put everyone first. Yet not one person has put her first. You wonder why she could not trust you." He tells her.

"It's so easy for you to say you did not have to try to balance three children and be expected to take care of everyone else's needs as well when asked. We could not say no to them. They gave us a place to live and fed us when we had nothing, how could we tell them no when they needed us to give them money when they did not have enough to pay bills. It would have been thrown up in our faces if we had said no., we didn't have a choice but to ask her for her money as well." Kat's mom told him.

"Really, she was a child not an adult. It was not her responsibility to make sure that everyone had their needs met. I noticed your husband did not sacrifice his son's needs or ask him for anything. He only asked Kat. He only ever asked Shay for what he needed for her children. She could go out. She could do what she wanted if she worked. So why was it Kat had a curfew, was only given an allowance from her earnings. The fact is that Kat could never tell you all now, and you took advantage of it. What's worse is no one thinks it wrong for that to have happened." Jae tells her.

Kat begins to squirm in Jae's arms. She looks up at him and stretches. leans in and kisses him on the cheek.

"Thanks, booboo, for a wonderful sleep. I'm starving you want some breakfast." She tells him in her normal voice. When she stands and turns around, she comes face to face with her mom. Her mom smacks her across the face.

"Are you pretending again. you make everyone worried and here you are playing games." Kat's mom looks at her angrily.

"Mom, I don't know what you are talking about and why are you here.?" she asks.

"I am talking about you acting pathetic and pretending that you are sick so that you can dally about with these men under Joe's nose." She tells her.

"What is she talking about. Jae was here when I woke up earlier and I was scared so he let me sit with him until I was feeling better. How is that hurting anyone? How is that pretending or being pathetic?" she asks?

"You have a husband and yet you just kissed another man." Her mom yells at her

"I kiss lots of other men in front of Joe all the time. You have never said anything before when I hug and kisses joe's family or even mine. Jae is part of my family why would I not kiss him in greeting like everyone else." Kat asks her mom.

"Are you deliberately being dense are you stupid." Her mom yells at her

"No mom I'm not Jae is like my brother he is someone I love most. I will not hide my feelings for him anymore to just make someone else comfortable. Joe already knows this. I told him that I love him and Ki that they are my family, and he will need to get used to it. He has agreed to be nice to them and he has been. I know how much my husband loves me and I also know that for some they may not understand how I feel about Jae and Ki. They are my feelings and I do not have to explain them to anyone. I have given up everything that I ever wanted in my life to make those around me happy. I have swallowed my pride and given everything I am to this family; I will not give up my friends that I love more than my family. Not again ever again. do you understand me." she tells her mom? Her mom was standing there in shock her daughter had never spoken to her like this before. Except when she was out of her mind in grief over her father. She sees the determination in her eyes and knows she will not be able to get her to budge.

"Kat are you feeling better now. you were so withdrawn and emotionless yesterday that we were so worried about you?' Jae tells her.

"Yes, I am myself today thank for staying with me and for keeping me safe while I was scared. I am sorry if my mom said or did anything to hurt your feelings." She tells him as she walks to the kitchen. She starts taking things out of the freezer and refrigerator. She makes breakfast for the three of them and gets things prepped for dinner. She has the music blaring in the kitchen. To block out her mom and him as she worked in the kitchen. Jae goes and stands in the doorway of the kitchen and watches her dance around the kitchen as she cooks. He turns to her mom and smiles.

"She is still the same. She dances around when she cooks or cleans. "He tells her.

"I know it is so distracting it drives me crazy." She tells him.

"Breakfast is ready" Kat yells from the kitchen.

Jae and Kats mom go to the kitchen and sits down for breakfast. It was quiet since Kat turned the music off.

"Is your breakfast, ok?" Kat asks the two of them. They look at each other and both nods yes to her.

"Jae what time do you have to leave?" Kat's mom asks him.

"I'm not sure that depends on Kat if she is ok to stay here with you then I can go after breakfast. If she wants to go and help me at the clinic in the greenhouse that's fine as well." He tells her.

"Oh, I want to go help in the green house today if you will bring me back later, please." Kat asks him.

"Sure, either I will bring you or Ki can drop you off when he is on his way to the hospital. "Jae tells her.

"Hmm what about the kids. Who is going to be here when they get off the bus?" Kat's mom asks.

"Oh, you don't drive right so you must stay here till Shay gets off work anyway, so I just assumed you would be here for them. "Jae answer before Kat can

"I guess I can. I really don't like it, but Joe said it was ok so just made sure you come home at a reasonable time." Her mom tells her as she gets up and clears the breakfast dishes. Jae cleans Kats scratches and puts fresh bandages on before they leave. Once on the road Kat turns to him and smiles.

"Thank you for making an excuse for me not to have to stay with my mom today; and thank you for coming to stay with me during the early morning hours. You know you did not need to. "Kat tells him.

"It's ok and yes, I did it was our fault you were in that state. If we had thought this would happen, we would have taken you to the clinic instead of letting you come home. We will go back to the old way of putting you under from now on. Though I am not sure if it was that or just the memory we uncovered yesterday." He tells her.

"I knew about this memory it was talked about so much over the years. I was not expecting it to be behind a door. Though I had forgotten a lot of the details I still knew about the main events of that day." She told him.

"So, it was just because she asked you to stay detached from the memory that sent you into a tailspin." Jae notices that she is still not showing much emotion even though she is more herself.

"I have always felt so guilty for having Kayla see him do those things to me that I blocked so much of it away. I had hoped that I would never have to remember that day again. Everyone kept telling me how ashamed I should have been and how I could try to even act innocent after luring him away from my sister. No one believed me. It was not until he was arrested that my dad even took me to the police to tell them about him. If he had not been arrested, who knows how long, I would have been the bad person not worthy of living. My mom tells me that he abused Shay as well. That I should not cry so much about my pain since I do not know what she lived through." Kat tells hm.

"How can she say that. Shay was his wife she chose to live with him. I know that is no excuse or maybe even the right thing to say. She went against everyone to marry him. She brought him into your life, and he hurt you. Ok I get it he abused both of you, but as an older sister she should have protected you if she was being abused. She should have tried to make sure he was never alone with you instead of turning people against you. The day that he was exposed for what he was by your neighbor's child. She had the chance to protect you and side with you. She had the chance to get away from him. Instead, she turned everyone against you and protected him. that is unforgivable to me." He told her.

"You don't understand Shay was obsessed with him when he came out of prison. She even dated a guy to cover up the fact that she was still seeing him. He had her completely under his spell. He even had her get married as soon as she turned 18 so that my parents could not do anything to him. The only time I had a moment of happiness and peace was when I was with you all and your family. I looked forward to those days so much. My grandmother knew that. That is why she would take me to visit you all. You know my dad's sister who lives close by. She always knew when something was wrong. She would just say to me you are staying. I would be allowed to stay. That was my place of refuge when I lost you all. She would never ask me questions, she would just hold me and let me cry in the middle of the night when everyone would be sleeping. She never asked me about my nightmares or anything. She would just keep me till she thought I was ok again to go home. Sometimes it would be days, other times it would be weeks. "Kat told him by the time they had gotten to the clinic Kat was her normal self; and ready to blast the music to the plants and play in the green house. When Ki heard the music in the greenhouse, he knew Jae brought Kat home. He got up from his desk and ran down the stairs to go see her. He worked a double today, so he does not have to work tonight. He was so exhausted when he got home, he went straight to bed and slept till about an hour ago. He walks into the green house and there Kat and Jae are. Kat watering and talking to the plants while she gently sways to the music. Jae pulling heavy bags of soil out of the greenhouse shed. He just watches them for a few moments. Then Kat turns, and he sees the bandages on her arms. He rushes over to take her hands, so he can see them.

"What did you do." he asks in a whisper.

"It's not what you think. She did not try to kill herself or even intentionally hurt herself." Jae tells him he explained to Ki what Kat's mom told him.

"When she woke up last night to an emotionless and disconnected state, she tried to scrub the feeling of him touching her away. In the process she scrubbed her skin raw till it was scratched and bleeding. The cuts are superficial and will be scabbed over by tomorrow. "He tells him.

Kat looks at Ki and takes her hand from his. She puts her arms around him and hugs him. She then kisses him on the cheek.

" I'm sorry to have you worried or scared for nothing." She tells him as she goes to move her arms from him, he pulls her into his closer.

"You had me scared to death. When Joe called me, I could not leave. I had a patient that I could not leave. I am sorry I was not there. I had to work a double today. So, I do not have to work tonight. Can you stay for dinner?' ki asks her?

"Sure, I have already prepared dinner at home and Joe already told my mom I could come here if I wanted to. I still need to go home tonight, or he will be worried." She tells him.

"Ok I will take you home after I check out your scratches and clean them after dinner. "He tells her he goes over and the three of them enjoy the rest of the afternoon gardening and listening to music. It was a wonderful afternoon.

That night when Ki took Kat home Joe came out to the car to talk to him.

"So, do you know what happened yesterday?" Joe asks him.

"It seems that your mother-in-law knows more about her behavior than she let on before. Kat would scrub herself raw every time he would hurt her to try to wash away the feeling of his touch. That is what she told Jae this morning. This is something we will have to watch her with as we uncover the memories of his abuse. She is fine now though. I cleaned the scratches and put new bandages on so they should be scabbed over by tomorrow or the next day. "Ki tells him.

"Oh, good I was worried that she cut herself with a knife or something sharp. It looked bad this morning when she woke me up. You know she smiled at me when she woke me up. I don't know why but she did." Joe told him.

"She slept on Jae lap like she used to during thunderstorms when she was younger. She always felt safe with him when she was scared. It is their bond. Do not get angry with her over it please. There is nothing sexual between the two of them. She has never felt that way with Jae, I do not believe he did ether I think he just did not like sharing her attention. He was always the one she ran to when she would be afraid." Ki tells him.

"I don't worry about him. I know they are close, and I am sorry for the middle of the night call. That part of her life was over by the time I met her. She never showed me that side of her until last night. Though I have had to hold her in my lap a few times during thunderstorms. Now I know why she likes to be cradled like that. I won't call her a big baby anymore over it." He tells him.

"That one you can blame all on Jae. He used to carry her around like she was a helpless child all the time. Making any excuse he could find to just hold her." Ki told him laughing.

"Thank you both again for your help today I know it made her feel better." Joe tells him as he waves goodbye and walks back into the house. Ki thinks to himself as he pulls out of the driveway. Joe is not as bad as he thought at first. He can see that he does love Kat. If they had met under different circumstances, they most likely would have been good friends. They have a lot in common.

CHAPTER 52

Back to the old way.

The next day Dr Smith apologizes to Kat for her last session.

"I am sorry for what happened in your last session. It was completely my fault. I did not think your ability to cut off your emotions was so strong. I won't make that mistake again." She tells her.

"It's ok I really don't have control over it. Sometimes it's effective, sometimes it is not. There are days I have no control over any emotions and cry at the drop of a hat. Other days you cannot even get me to respond. So, don't worry about it." kit tells her.

"Since you seem to be yourself today how about we just do talk therapy. I am a little bit worried about putting you back under especially since the Dr Parks are not here to help me in case, we have a problem." She tells her.

"Ok that is fine what do you want to talk about today.?" Kat asks her.

"We have never talked about what your dreams were growing up. How about we talk about that." She asks her.

"Sure, what would you like to know?" Kat asks.

"What exactly was your dream. what did you want to do with your life?" she asks her?

"I wanted to be a nurse. I wanted to help people who had terminal illnesses. My cousin died in NIH from cancer at just over 18. I loved him a lot. I always felt bad because there was nothing anyone could do to make him better. I remember when I was around 12, he died. His mom and dad were devastated. He spent most of his young life in a hospital. Where he was always having experiments done on him. My family could not afford his treatments, so they had him in a hospital that did research on cancer patients. To test new drugs and such. He was such a beautiful soul. When he died it was hard for everyone. I always kept thinking if only there was someone who could have been there to give them comfort at the hospital. A nurse who looked at him as more than a research subject. I am sure there were, but I never saw them. When would we go visit? It was always such a cold heartless place. I always made a point of making him smile and laugh every time I saw him. to make sure he knew that I loved him and would miss him. To this day I can't stand to see someone need something and not try to help." Kat tells her.

"Is this possibly why you can never say no to your family. Why you always would do without so that they could have." She asks her.

"Maybe I know I have always played host and was the caregiver in our house. Many said it was because I was like my mom. Others said I did it to get attention. I do not understand how it is wrong to love people. Why has it always got to be negative? I love the people in my life. I just want them to be happy and to show them that I love them. How is that seeking attention and negative. My mom has always told me to stop begging for love. That was not what I was doing. I was just showing compassion and empathy for those I love even as a small child. I guess I am wrong about a lot of things." Kat told her.

"Tell me about going in the army?" Dr smith asks her.

"I wanted to go into the army to get away from my brother-in-law and to get my education. The plan was I would go in and volunteer for all overseas deployments. That way I would never have to meet him again, also that way if he messed with me, I could break every bone in his body. As you see that did not happen. My dad convinced me not to go. He was afraid I would put myself in danger on purpose, so he made me promise not to go. Even after I got married and was pregnant. The military was calling me to see if I still did not want to go. I really wanted to go, but I gave in to my dad. Sometimes I wonder if he did not want me to go because he was afraid for me or if it were because he no longer would be in control of me. Even after I was married, he still controlled me to a certain degree." Kat tells her.

"Do you still resent your dad for that.?" She asks Kat.

"Sometimes I wonder how different my life would be if I had gone in and if I had been able to be the kind of nurse I wanted. Though I may never know those answers. I can still make a difference in people's lives." Kat tells her.

"How so?" She asks if she is extremely interested in this answer.

"I want women to know that even though they have been abused and raped. They still have life. They can still find love and happiness. I want them to know that with the right support and help they can achieve anything they want. Even though as of right now I have not achieved anything. I will achieve something in my life. I will be the best mom I can be. The best wife I can be. I will love those around me unconditionally regardless of what problems they have. Even if people think I am putting on a show or trying to get attention. It will be because I genuinely care for those in need." Kat tells her with determination in her voice. She knows that she means what she says. She hopes that Kat can carry out what she wants to do.

"How do purpose to accomplish this?" Dr smith inquires.

"I will come here to get the skills I need to be able to go back out into the world. I will go to leadership conferences and work hard to be a positive role model to those who need one. I want people to see that just because I have a brain disorder. I am not stupid. I am not pitiful. I can think for myself. I am not someone they need to be afraid of or pity. "Kat tells her.

"I will be here to support you and to help you anyway that I can in this. I think you will show by example to your kids. That with hard work you can overcome all obstacles in life. "She tells her that their time is up and it's time for Kat to go back to the day treatment class.

Cousin Tommy's Visit.

At the weekend Kats cousin Tommy comes for a visit. He is attending a conference close by, and she is letting him stay with her. Jae and KI joined the family for the BBQ as she asked. Tommy was excited to see Jae again so soon. They decided to go out to the local bar and catch up, so the four men went out. Once at the strip club they had drinks and was shooting the breeze when a girl came over and asked if any of them wanted a lap dance. The two old friends smiled and got one for their Ki. He became angry because of the dance. He never had one and did not find them arousing at all. Joe began to laugh. Ki shoots him in an incredibly angry face.

"Hey, don't look at me that way. I am not the one who got it for you." He reminds him.

"Should we even be here. you are a married man and Jae you have a girlfriend." Ki reminds them.

"Kat never cares when I come here with friends. The only requirement is that I do not come home horny expecting her to take care of me. Though that never happens. I am like you this kind of stuff does not turn me on, but you let Kat lay one finger on me or even just kiss me and I am hard and ready. I have had a wife and a lot of other girlfriends before her and none of them could turn me on like her. "Joe tells them.

"Oh, so if we tell her, she won't get mad.?" Jae asks.

"Hell, she most likely already knows." Joe ells them

"How?" the three of them ask in unison

"The girl who gave you the lap dance is her cousin. Those three over there are Kats friends from school. I can almost bet you one of them has called her. My friends like to come here a lot. I found out the first time I came that she had family and a few girlfriends who worked here. They know who I am, that is why we have not had to order but one time. They already know my preferences. "Joe tells them.

"Which cousin is she. I mean which family is she from?' Tommy asks.

"Don't worry it's from her mom's side. No one on your side has shamed that precious bloodline." Joe tells him very sarcastically.

"You really don't like us much do you/" Tommy asks Joe.

"I like your aunt who lives close by and her youngest son. I do not have a problem with the one I work with even though he is an asshole at times. But no, I do not like you all much. I don't like how you all act as if she is beneath you; when she is worth more than all of you." He tells him.

"You mean she really won't be mad at you for coming here with us. I know it was my suggestion since I am visiting but I don't want to cause you all any problems." Tommy tells him.

"No, she won't be. Before I met her, I loved coming to these places and would have the most fun. I would even hook up with a few. But after meeting her. no other woman turns me on but her. I tease her a lot telling her I am going to find her replacement. There is no other woman who can replace her. "Joe tells them.

"Amen to that." Ki lifts his glass to Joes in a toast. One of the girls comes over and sits beside Joe.

"So, Joe how is my cousin doing these days." She asks him.

"She is doing better. How are you doing? Have you gotten settled in your new place?" he asks her?

"Yes, I have. It is not far from here and it is a safer place than the last one. "She tells him.

"I will let Kat know you've gotten settled. You should come over sometimes she would like to see you." He tells her.

"No, I don't think so you know that I'm don't live the kind of life that the family approves of." She reminds him.

"You also know that she doesn't care about that. Seriously you should at least call her up for lunch sometime." He tells her.

"You know I can't do that. Not after what happened. It will cause to much pain for her." She reminds him.

"What are you two talking about?" ki asks them.

"Kat blames herself because I was raped by Shay's husband. She found out that every time she was able to avoid him, he would rape someone else. He raped me and one of her friend's little sisters. Then he got caught when he was raping a neighbor after showing up at her house to get her again. When she came back from her dad's family. They did not know that the police had him on several counts of raping minors, not including her. He liked virgins, so he liked middle schoolers and early high school. Anyway, since then she has avoided me and her friends. She blames herself for my addictions that have landed me here and she feels sorry towards her friends over their little sister "she tells them.

"Oh, how come this has never come up before. Why didn't you say anything before this Joe?" Jae asks.

"It's not my story to tell and I think that it a shame that she can't get passed it. I told you all she got talked about and treated very badly after people found out and that by the time her dad decided to take her to the police, they had him dead to rights and they made a deal. If he pled guilty for the rape with a deadly weapon when they caught him in the act. They would not charge him the multi counts of rape of a minor. So, he has never been charged as a pedophile or made to pay for them. She thinks if she had just let him hurt her then no one else would have been hurt." Joe tells them.

"oh "the three of them exclaim.

"Yes, so I just keep tabs on her through Joe and he lets her know I'm ok. Which let her know my 2-year anniversary of being clean is next week and I will be graduating college in two months. When that happens, you know she may not let you come here when I am not around anymore." She tells him as she ruffles his hair. Before going to get them refills. One of the other girls comes over and sits on the arm of Joes chair.

"Hey joe. how is my girl doing?" She asks.

"She is doing better." He tells her.

"So are you two of the brothers that used to hang out with her at school/" she asks them.

"Yeah, that's us." Jae tells her.

"I used to have the biggest crush on you all especially the tall one. the one that liked music, I tried to get Kat to introduce us. She refused. She told me I was not the right kind of girl for him. That I liked to party to much and liked to sleep around too much. She was so selfish with you 4. She would not even let me talk to any of her cousins about that matter as well. She may have been my friend, and we may have had lots of fun together, but man was she a prude." she laughingly tells them.

"Really my cousin a prude. How is that she has always been the life of the party." Tommy tells her.

"Yes, she was but when it came to sex, she was a prude. She might as well have been a nun. Those of us who knew her before the rumors started knew none of that crap was true and we were ready to beat down anyone who spread them. Anyway, are you all still single? I would not mind making up for lost time. "She winks at them as she moves away before the other server comes back.

"Don't pay any attention to her. She has had sour grapes against Kat ever since the guy she liked in school told her he liked Kat. She is the one I told you about Joe. The girl who used to give head to all the boys on the bus. When she hit on one of Kats cousins and they got into an argument over it. So, she moved on to some guy on the football team and he would not have anything to do with her because he liked Kat. He followed her around everywhere. Even went to the vocational school to keep watch over her. She hits on Joe every time he comes just because she knows he is Kat's husband hoping that he will cheat on her with her. She acts like they are still close, but we all know the score. "She tells him.

"So how come we managed to spend the whole night only talking about my cousin. I wanted to come out to get drunk and have fun with my friend and get to know my cousin's husband. not talk about her all night. "Tommy complains.

"Aww sugar I can make sure you have fun the floor show is about to start." she tells Tommy just as the music comes on. The rest of the night they drank and laughed. They did not get home till the early hours of the morning. In fact, when Kat woke up Jae was on one couch, Ki on the roll out sofa and Tommy in the guest room. Joe was sleeping in the recliner. They all reeked of alcohol. She went to the kitchen to fix spicy hangover soup, put on a pot of coffee, and then turn the cd player on surround sound at full volume. The 3 of them in the living room jumped up grabbing their heads and Tommy came out of the guest room holding his. Joe shoots her an angry look, and she busts out laughing. She cannot help it, the look on their faces is just too funny. She takes pity on them and turns off the music and quietly tells them breakfast is made. They all get up on shaky legs and head for the kitchen. Joe kisses her on the cheek, and he passes her mumbling good morning. Jae and Ki followed suit. Tommy looks at her dumb founded. Shrugs his shoulders and gives her a quick kiss as well. She smiles and follows them into the kitchen.

"So, did you guys enjoy your male bonding last night?" she asks them.

"Oh, wow Kat this is good. Where did you learn to cook this? "Tommy asks.

"It's called hangover soup. She learned it from my grandmother." Jae tells him.

"No, it's a little different" Ki tells Jae.

"I mixed my aunts and your grandmothers' recipes with a touch of extra heat to make it spicy enough for Joe." She tells them.

"Will this really cure a hang over?" Tommy asks.

"Give it a few minutes and you will never know you even drank last night. How do you think I survived college with a much as we partied? "He tells him.

After breakfast, the 4 of them took turns showering Joe lent Jae some clothes and Tommy lent KI some clothes. When they were done Kat handed them a honey dew list. It was their punishment for getting wasted the night before.

"Hey why do I have to work I am a guest; you knew that I was going to want to go out with Jae." Tommy complains.

"Yes, but you involved Joe and Ki in your shenanigans so therefore you get punished as well." She informs him as she walks back to the kitchen to wash the dishes.

"Does she always do this?" Tommy asks.

"Hahaha, we got off easy. Usually, I do not even get breakfast when I get to wasted. This list is a walk in the park compared to what I normally must do." Joe tells them.

"What do you mean she has us doing all kinds of random things. Change the oil in the cars. Mow the grass, wash the outside windows. This is not fair all we did was get drunk." Tommy complains.

"No that's not all we did. She gets worried when I am not home by 2am we stay out till almost morning. She knows that we drove drunk. She hates it when I drive drunk. She does not sleep until I get home when I go out. Unless I call her to say I am staying at one of my friend's houses so not to drive drunk. We are getting off lightly trust me. I totaled our car the last time I drove drunk luckily no one else was involved and I was able to get the car home and was not hurt. She will not even talk to me when we go out and I start to get drunk. She will not even allow alcohol to be drunk in the house. Your cousin is very adamant about that. She has never told me about why she hates it so much except that the adults would get into fights when they drank." He tells them.

"It's not just that. A drunk driver killed my brothers. Her life changed because of that." Jae tells them.

"I know she has always been uncomfortable around drunks. I thought it was because she didn't drink herself." Tommy said quietly.

"No, it's more than that. Even at 13 she could out drink most adults. I remember we took her to one of Jae's frat parties and she drank so much I thought for sure she was going to be sick. She did not; in fact, other than getting quieter you would never know she even took a drink." Ki looks at Jae and remembers her and James having to drag them out of the party.

"She got mad at me in Mexico at one of my cousins' weddings. Normally she would have just gotten in the car and driven back. Since it was dark, she did not know where she was or how to get back. She drank a bottle of brandy and started on strawberry wine before the music started. She just sat there with this blank look on her face and refused to talk to anyone. My compadre was so upset that his happy and funny compadre was just sitting there. As soon as the dancing started it was over, she dragged me on the dance floor, and I had no choice but to dance with her. I wasn't sure what would have happened if I allowed her to dance with someone else." Joe laughed at the memory. Jae and KI sighed at the memories of going dancing and skating with her. how they would love those times back. Tommy just sat there staring at the three of them. not knowing what was happening. They all look like lovesick fools. He decides to go to the kitchen and see if Kat had lunch ready yet. He gets inside, and he hears music playing. There in the living room is Kat dancing to the music as she vacuums the floor. He leans against the wall and watches her. No wonder the girl last night was so jealous of her. She dances better than the stripper does. Her hips softly swaying to the beat in a very sexy way. He used to go dancing with her all the time how come he never noticed how sexy his cousin was without even trying. No wonder all his friends were always clamoring to spend time with her when she visited. When she turned off the vacuum, he pulls a dollar out of his pocket and walks over to her and sticks it in the collar of her shirt. She takes it and smacks him in the back of the head.

"Hey, give me my money back "he tells her.

"Nope you gave it to me so it's mine now. You already for lunch?" she asks as he heads towards the kitchen. She already has the table set and is taking stuff from the oven. Just then Shay comes in with the kids. They all yell they are hungry and sit down at the table. Joe and the other guys come in and she hands each of them a plate. Then makes all the kids theirs. After everyone is eating, she grabs her purse and goes out.

"Where is she going?" tommy asks.

"She must have to go back to the store. I know she is making Korean food tonight. she told me earlier that if Ki and Jae were staying for dinner tonight, she wanted to make them some food, so they could take some back." Joe tells them.

"Didn't she make Korean food for breakfast." Tommy asks.

"Yeah, but that's hangover soup that's different." Joe tells him "Tonight she will make Korean BBQ that's why she made grilled tequila and lime chicken tacos for lunch today. She wants you to have a good variety." Joe tells him to eat, and Shay cleans up the kitchen Kat starts to cook as soon as she gets back. By the time dinner is done. They guys finished the honey dew list. That evening they played cards, and the house was filled with music and the sound of laughter and kids playing. When it was time to say good night. Ki and Jae left with enough leftovers to keep them in food for at least a few days, including the patients at the clinic. Tommy thanked Joe and Kat for opening their home to him.

"Oh, please your family your welcome anytime." Kat informs him before going to bed.

"Joe, can I ask you something?" Tommy looks at him.

"Sure, what do you want to know?"

"Are you really ok with her being so close to Jae and his brother?" Tommy looks at him as if he is questioning one of his clients on the witness stand.

"Yes, I am fine with her and Jae. They are like siblings. a little to close at times and Jae lets his love for her to be too obvious but it is a brother sister thing more than anything else. Ki I am trying for her sake. I know she loves us both. I also know that if she had not loved Ki then she would never have loved me." He tells him.

"How so?" tommy is looking at him to intently.

"She told me that I am a lot like the angel in her good dreams. That she fell in love with me because I was so much like him. I always knew she had a love before me and that I reminded her a lot of him. I have a lot of respect for Ki because he is doing everything, he can help her and trying to keep his personal feelings out of it. We have an understanding. If he does not cross a certain line, I will not give him a hard time. So far, he is keeping his word." Joe tells him.

"What's the deal with all the hugs and kisses though?" Tommy asks before taking a drink of his soda.

"She is like that with everyone. That is how she greets those she loves. Have you not noticed she has kissed your cheek at least 5 times in two days? She is like that with my family as well. Lord you should be here when we have company there is a line to get her for her hugs and kisses." Joe laughs at his expression.

"I never noticed so much about her I was always just so used to it that I never thought about it. Until I saw all of you kissing her cheek this morning before breakfast." He tells him.

"Yep, that's the way it is. It took me a while to get used to every time we went to the store or out somewhere. These strangers to me were coming over and hugging her and kissing her cheek both female and male. She then would introduce me, and I would realize they were family. I must tell you. This family should stop breeding there are far too many of you between the 3 sides I have met." Joe tells him he then says good night to him and tells him he hopes he has a safe trip home that he must work in the morning.

The next morning Kat gives Tommy a small cooler with food and snacks for his long drive back home. She hugs him and kisses him on the cheek.

"Hey, you shouldn't be giving so much love away. Joe might get jealous." He tells her smiling down at her.

"He is never jealous, and I can never give too much love away. You know the more you give the warmer your heart grows. I love you and please call me when you get home. Thank you for coming to stay with us. I enjoyed having you here." she tells him as she hugs him again.

"Love you to and I will. Thank you for having me and for not getting upset over us getting drunk." He squeezes her back in a big bear hug.

"You're welcome. I know you all must blow off steam occasionally. I also know I have given those three a hard time lately. So, I went easy on you this time." She smiles and waves at him as he starts to drive away. Kat goes into the house to clean it and start dinner for the evening before heading to the clinic to work on the project that Ki had given her.

CHAPTER 54

Grandma's treasures.

Over the course of the next few weeks Kat lovingly goes through the secret room. She looks at the old pictures of their family. She calls the man at the museum to see if she can meet up with him. He tells her he would like to come to the house. He wants to see them there so that he can assess the more fragile pieces without risking them getting damaged by moving them too much. They set up a time and day for them to meet up at the clinic. She has everything organized by items since she does not know the time periods of them. As she looks through the trunks. She finds old letters. They are written in Korean, so she does not know what they say. She hopes she can do this for them to have grandma's memories put in an organized way so that the guys will be able to share them with their families when they have them. Kat spent hours in the secret room not even knowing how long she had been working.

The warm sun shining through the small window. she gets up off the floor and stretches. walks over to the chaise to sit just for a few minutes. Without realizing it she fell asleep. When she wakes up the room is pitch black. It had gotten dark since she fell asleep. It is cloudy outside so there was not even any moon light to shine in the room. Kat feels the fear rolling up inside of her. She is afraid to stand up or to even move. She hears a noise in the corner of the room and curls up in a ball on the chaise. She hears rustling and bites her lips trying not to cry out. She can feel something coming close to her. It brushes against her she cannot help it she lets out a very loud scream. The next thing she knows is the room is flooded in light and Ki is standing over her.

"I'm sorry I did not mean to scare you. I came here because I saw your truck and could not find you anywhere. I was trying to maneuver through this as to not wake you when I heard you whimpering, I turned on the light to be able to see where you were exactly." He tells her his face is so close to hers. She can smell the toothpaste he uses to brush his teeth.

"I'm sorry I sat to rest just for a few minutes and woke up to total darkness and was scared before I heard you moving around. She tells him.

"You should get home its after 9 or do you want to call Joe and just stay the night.?" Ki asks her.

"I will call Joe and explain what happened and make sure everything is ok. I don't like driving at night." she tells him as she is getting up. She asks him if she can use the phone in his office. Once there she calls Joe.

"Hey it's me. I am sorry I sat to rest after sorting a few things and fell asleep. I just woke up. Is everything ok at home.?" She asks him.

"Yes, everything is fine. I had called Ki to make sure if you were still there, but he was not home yet. "He tells her.

"Do you mind if I stay here tonight it's so dark out and I don't like to drive at night as you know." She asks him quietly wondering if he is mad.

"That is fine it is supposed to start storming and I do not want you on the road, so it will be fine. Did you get a lot done?" He asks.

"Yes, I didn't even stop eating today. I was so engrossed with what it was doing. I never left the room except to use the bathroom." She tells him feeling slightly embarrassed at that.

"Ok tell Ki to feed you and then go get some rest. I will see you when you get home tomorrow after work. "They say good night and Kat turns to see Ki stand in the door with a tray of food. She laughs and walks over to take it from him.

"Joe was just telling me to have you get me something to eat and here you are with food," she sits the tray down on the table and starts to set their plates on it.

"Cook left me a note that you had not left the room today not even to eat or drink. So, I figured you would be hungry. Since she left both of us a plate, I just brought it up here. "He tells her as they begin to eat. They talked about Kat's progress on his grandmother's treasures. She tells him that the gentleman from the museum will be coming the following week. That was why she was trying to get it all separated and organized. She only has a few days to complete it. After dinner they say good night and Kat goes down to her room while Ki stays in his office to work.

Over the next week Kat works hard to organize the annuals and journals from the vault and the secret room since she wants the gentleman from the museum to look at them first. She hopes he has someone to translate them. She really wants to read them, especially the letters. She shows Jae and Ki what she wants him to see first.

"You did all this work why you don't come tomorrow to see what he says for yourself. "Ki asks her.

"Oh no I can't. I have a leadership conference to go to tomorrow." She tells them.

"Maybe we postpone his visit till you can be here." Jae tells her.

"No, we can't it will be months before he is having any time available again. He said he may have to be here more than a day. So, he may still be here when I get back. Please do not let him stay in grandmother's room. That had become mine and I would be terribly upset if something gets misplaced. Only show him what I have in my room on the 3rd floor for starters. I want you all to be incredibly careful with her things. Nothing is to leave this house unless you get a detailed list of what he wants to take. Nothing is given to him unless you have a definite date to expect its return. I do not want anything damaged. None of grandmother's jewelry, clothing or pictures is to go anywhere. If he wants them appraised, then that person needs to come here. Where we know what is happening. Nothing is to be just given away do you understand me. Grandmother cherished these treasures for more than 90 years before she passed, I do not want anything lost. Even if we must have the translator come here to stay. While they translate them." Kat tells them about her hands on her hips as if she was talking to naughty children. Instead of grown men. They both just nod yes to her that they understand everything she just told them.

She hugs them both and tells them goodbye and that she will see them in a few days. Jae busts out laughing as soon as Ki closes the door.

"Oh my God. I almost thought mama was standing in front of us just now. She so reminded me how mama would give us a list of things we needed to do all the while scolding us before we even did anything."

"I know. She is so much like her just now. It makes me miss her right now. Are you really ok with a stranger going through grandmother's things?" Ki asks Jae.

"Yeah, as long as one of us is here I am." he tells them as they head to the kitchen for dinner.

Over the next few days Kat immersed herself in her conference. Connecting and talking to others who have PTSD. The one thing that was a common thread all the speakers had in common was the importance of living a healthy lifestyle. Just like any physical illness. They all stressed the importance of eating right and exercise. They all also focus on the importance of connecting with others. She looked over the list of support groups to find one in her area to join. She wonders if she can talk to ki or Jae about hosting one at the clinic. On the second night she decides to call to see how things are going.

Ki is in his office when the phone rings. He picks up at the same time as Jae.

"hello "they both answer at the same time.

"Oh, wow I got both of you." Kat answers

"We both just happen to be near a phone." jae answers.

"So how are you both doing?" Kat asks.

"I personally am fine and before you ask things are going very well with Sarah and me. We have been having a date every evening after work. In fact, I think I am going to ask her how she feels about getting married soon." Jae rushes to tell her almost like he cannot hold his happiness.

"Aww I am so happy for you. There is just one problem." Kat tells him.

"Oh, what's that?" Jae asks.

"I won't be able to attend your wedding. I know I am being very selfish, but I do not want another Dr other than her. if you get married soon, I can't come to your wedding." Kat tells him.

"I didn't say we were going to get married right away just that I want to start talking to her about it." Jae tells her very irritated at her.

"Hey bro don't get upset with her. You know she did not mean it that way. She just meant that she would have to not be a part of your plans for now." Ki tells him.

"Yes, I know but I must have the person who got us together not be involved at our wedding. That is not an option. It will take 6 months to a year to plan the wedding and who knows how long it will take me to get up the courage to ask her." Jae tells them.

"Hahaha, ok I get it. Anyway, how are things going at the conference." Ki asks Kat.

"They are good. I just wish I were there to meet up with the museum guy." Kat tells them.

"He is here he hasn't left your room on the third floor since this morning I have had cook take him meals and to check on him. He is taking small samples of the paper of the older books to date them. He says he knows a translator in south Korea that can come and translate the books for us. He says he can make the arrangements when he gets back. He seems to be exceptionally reliable and knowledgeable. I just wish he would tell us more about them. Maybe he is waiting for the translator to confirm what he thinks they are." Ki tells her.

"Has he said how long he will be staying?" Kat asks.

"He is leaving in the morning. He said he will get back to us about the age of the books as soon as possible and will get in touch with us when he secures the translator." Ki tells her.

"Oh, ok so I won't get to meet him this trip. Did he even go in grandmother's room?" Kat asks.

"Nope once we showed him the stack of books, he was so immersed in them he has barely moved from your room." Jae tells her.

"Ok then maybe he will come back sooner than later. Jae I am sorry for earlier. I really am happy that you love her so much. I am not upset that you want to marry or anything like that. I just do not want to try to get used to another Dr. I know I am super selfish. I'm sorry." Kat tells him.

"We have talked about how to get around your treatment more than once. I think the only solution is to open those doors and come to terms with them soon. this way you can move on and so can we." He tells her.

"I agree but would it be safe to go back to weekly sessions?" Kat asks him.

"We can take each session as they come and see how it goes." He tells her.

"Ok it's time for me to go and still need to call Joe before sleeping. Good night loves." She tells them before hanging up to call joe.

Joe answers on the first ring" Hey baby how are things going?" he asks.

"They are good how are the kids behaving?" she asks him.

"They are good as always. Will you be home tomorrow?" Joe asks?

"Yes, I should be home by the time you get home from work" she tells him. "If I get home early enough, would you like enchiladas for dinner?" she asks him.

"That's fine you know me I eat anything you fix. It is getting late, so I am going to say good night now. I love you and drive careful tomorrow." He tells her before hanging up. They both go to bed to sleep. That night Kat had a restless night's sleep. She keeps waking up not understanding why. She needs to sleep since she has a long drive tomorrow. She decides to pray maybe talking to God will help her to sleep. She gets out of bed and kneels at the side.

"Heavenly father it's me your burdensome child. I cannot stop the racing thoughts going through my mind today. I am so excited that Jae and Dr smith are together. I am worried that I will have to have a different Dr if things keep going like this. I want them to be together more than anything. I ask you to let me get better sooner. Do not let it continue to drag out so that they can be together. Thank you for how things are going. That everything in my life seems to be going in the right direction. I am so grateful for your blessing and favor in my life. God thank you for my husband and those around me who help me every day. Without you I could do nothing. Thank you for loving me despite my many flaws. I thank your heavenly father.

Amen

CHAPTER 55

Next Door

After talking to God for a while she falls asleep almost as soon as her head touches the pillow. The next day Kat arrives home early and gets the kids clothes cleaned dinner done well before they get home. She has fresh cookies waiting for them when they get off the bus. That night is the perfect night they have a fun dinner and a night of video games. She tells Joe that the next day is her session she hopes that all will be ok afterwards. He just hugs her and tells her to trust in God and reminds her that her guardian angels will be with her.

When she arrives at the center the next day. Everyone is waiting for her.

"I hear you want to step up your therapy is this true?" Dr smith asks her.

"Yes, I want you to open a door every week if necessary and even extend my time if needed to talk about it afterwards. I need to get better faster please." Kat tells her with an anxious voice.

"Why the sudden change in plans. Is something going on?" she inquires?

"No, I am only tired of everything and want to be able to go back to work and to some normalcy in my life. I am ready to be done with this part of my life." She tells her.

"Ok I am not so sure if I am ready for this to go so fast, but we will give it a try. Are you ready?" she asks as Jae gets up to dim the light as she turns on her pen light. This time when Kat gets inside the black mutilated door there are two trees blooming and a small light shining just past them, she walks towards it. She sees a door. It is grey and stormy. Looking there is duct tape holding up small hands the handle is a buck knife. She takes a deep breath and opens it.

"I am at my sister's trailer again I am in the baby's room he is sick he has a fever and is crying. I cannot get him to calm down. I told my sister that we need to go get him to the Dr.

"When he gets home, I will go get him some medicine and see if we can get his temperature down first." She tells me I tell her that is fine, but I want her to take me and the baby to my house I do not want to stay here. when he gets home. Shay grabs the keys and races out the door. She turns and tells me she will be right back. I told her not just take us to mom. I keep trying to get Shay to take me with her, but she refuses saying she does not want to take the baby out. As soon as she leaves, and he hears the car pull away he grabs me by the hair. dragging me into the bedroom. He takes the baby from me and puts duct tape over his mouth and ties his hands. He takes out his buck knife. I am begging him to please stop the baby is sick. He looks at me and gets a creepy smile on his face.

"Then I guess you need to be a good girl don't you. If you do not, I will just have to cut him." He takes the buck knife and scratches the side of the baby's neck a trickle of blood starts to flow down his neck and onto his chest. I scream and lunge for him. He grabs me and puts the knife around my neck.

'Shut up and get on your knees now or I will kill him. I will tell everyone you did it. You see this is your hunting knife. It's super sharp because it has never been used. 'He tells me with joy.

 I sink to my knees and cry. My voice cracked as the tears fell down my face. My whole body is shaking. the voice tells her.

"Remember nothing can hurt you here. These are just memories. They hold no power over you anymore."

"I am so scared he is going to kill my baby. There is blood and the baby is screaming and crying uncontrollably. I need to make sure he is ok. So, I sink to my knees. He strips his pants off and takes the knife. He cuts my shirt so that it falls off. In the process he cut my chest. He then sits in front of me. He licks the blood off my chest and turns me to my stomach. He rams his man hood into me pulling my hair with the knife pointing at my stomach. I see blood dripping on the floor. I am crying so hard now. When he is done, he gets the sharp hook and rakes my insides and licks the blood from it afterwards. He goes and grabs a shirt from my sister's dresser. Tell me to get cleaned up. He already told my dad to come get me and the baby. I go clean up and then get the baby cleaned and calm. Before my dad gets there. When my dad comes, I get the baby and run out into the storm to the car.

"Kat, I want you to leave here now. I want you to come back up the stairwell, you will never have to revisit this door again. You will never have to relive this memory again. You will be calm and yourself when you come back. You will not be afraid. "The voice tells her Kat opens her eyes when she hears a snap.

The three of them look at her waiting for her to say something. She is rubbing her chest like she is trying to feel the cut. She looks at Ki and Jae. Then at Dr smith

"How can a father be so cruel to their child. I am so relieved he was not a part of his life past being a toddler. I could not protect him. I tried to, but I could not always protect him. I tried to keep him with me at my mom's every day and night. So that he could not touch him. He always pretended to be the perfect father in front of others, but he would hurt his son at every turn to get me to give to what he wanted. I am so ashamed that I was not able to protect him better. I remember telling my mom he fell and scratched himself on the wire rack in my sister's room. To explain the cut on his neck. He was so tiny since he had been a premature baby. I could not bear for him to cry or be sick." Kat tells them her voice soft almost a whisper. You can hear the regret and that she is trying to hold back the tears from her voice. KI gets up and walks over to her. He puts his arms around her and hugs her close.

"You know there was only so much you could do. You were still just a child as well. You were not strong like him. You did what you could do to protect that child. You are still doing everything you can to protect him. By getting help to face these memories you are helping your children. To know that they can overcome everything this life has to throw at them. You are so strong to not only to have endured, but you protected that child and have made sure he and his sister knows what love and caring is. You are always on their side and there for them "Ki tells her as she is crying into his shoulder like a child. He sits there patting her back and rocking her till her tears are finally spent.

"How do you feel now?' Dr smith asks her.

"I am calm sad and angry. I am ok though. I may not be the most perky and bubbly person right now, but I am ok. "She tells them.

"I don't understand why I am opening doors out of order?" Kat asks them.

"That we don't know maybe it's just the way they are locked away. This memory was crueler than the last two. Maybe the more violent ones are buried deeper than the others. "Jae tells her.

"Do you need us to call Joe and take you to the clinic or do you want to go home." Dr smith asks her.

"I want to go home. I need to hug my kids and have them close to me tonight. I need to shower and get out of these clothes I feel dirty." She tells them.

"Just don't scrub yourself till you are raw and bleeding again. Ok "Ki tells her.

"Hmm I will try not to." She tells them.

"How about you use the herbal bath that grandmother made you before it will let you soak and wash away that dirty feeling." Jae prompts her.

"I don't remember what we used to use in it." She tells him.

"I will see if I can find the ingredient list and get it for you before tonight. I have it at the clinic I may even have some already made up in your old room." Ki tells her.

"Really, I used to love it when she used to give me a good soak and scrub. I always felt so clean and soft afterwards. I do remember warm milk after she would scrub all the dead skin away. she would rinse me with warm milk. But I just don't remember what she used to put in the water to soak in." Kat smiles at the memory. thinking she should do that for her girls sometime.

She leaves the office and heads home to start dinner and clean the house. She passes the old trailer park her sister used to live in. She breaks out in a cold sweat. She cannot breathe. Kat slams on the breaks and pulls over. Closing her eyes. Reciting the poem, she wrote for Jae. calming herself down. She sits there for the longest time. She hears the kids getting off the bus. She knows she needs to hurry home now. When she gets home the kids are sitting on the porch talking to Ki.

"Hey mom why did it take you so long to get home. "Her youngest asks her.

"I had a stop I needed to make before coming home. It just took longer than expected." She tells him to get the keys out and unlock the door. Ki hands her a bag it is the herbal soak. And the ingredient list so if she wants to make it one another time. She smiles at him and tells him thank you.

"Hey doc you are coming in I know mom has tea in the fridge. She still puts a pitcher in there every morning. I think she still expects pappy to come by. It good though cause we all love her mint tea." Her youngest invites Ki inside.

"Not this time partner maybe next time. I must work tonight and if I don't go now, I will be late." He ruffles his hair as he goes to leave.

Kat and the kids wave goodbye to him before going inside. She asks the kids to start on their homework while she gets dinner finished. After they have all finished their dinner and homework, she asks the girls if they would like a special treat. That the doctor brought a special pack of herbs to take a bath in to get rid of all the dead skin on their bodies and it will make their skin super soft. That evening as the girls takes turns getting a bath Kat gets the gloves Ki brought with the herbs and gives each of them a scrub down before warming up some milk to rinse their bodies. After each of them got done she would rub them down with lavender oil so they would sleep well that night. Now it was her turn after everyone was sleeping, she enjoyed it so much it had been so long since she had done this. She will need to remember to thank KI again the next time she sees him. when she crawls into bed. Joe turns to draw her into his arms.

"Hmm you're so soft and smell so good tonight. What did you do?" he asks?

"I had a session today. Ki and Jae were worried I would scrub myself raw like last time so Ki brought me some herbs that his grandmother used to mix up when I would stay. I would soak in them and then scrub my body. I would completely get rid of all the dead and dirty skin on my body and leave it super soft. They thought maybe if I did this and felt clean afterward then I would not scrub myself raw trying to feel clean." She explains.

"Hmm and did it work?" he asks.

"Yes, very much so" she tells him turning her head up for a kiss. Joe deepens the kiss as his hands roam over her body. He feels her stiffen a little.

"Is this ok or are you afraid?" he whispers as he holds her close.

"I don't feel dirty, and it feels nice having someone hold me lovingly. I know you do not want to know anything. Thank you for understanding that sometimes it's hard for me." She moves over top of him. taking the lead lowering her mouth to his. Joe groans with desire as she deepens the kiss. They make love tenderly and not rushed. So that Kat does not become afraid. He lets her be completely in control, moving only at her pace. Until they both are spent and falling asleep.

CHAPTER 56

Translator arrives.

Over the course of the next few weeks Kat was kept terribly busy between home, day treatment and her work at the clinic. She has not been this happy for an exceptionally long time. Everyone seems to be more relaxed and content. The gentleman from the museum informs her that a translator from south Korea will be arriving in the next week. He gave her a list of things she would need to prepare. Before hanging up the phone he asks her about why he was not able to meet her on his last visit.

"I had an important conference to go to. I hope you were not too disappointed. I will make a point of being here when you arrive with the translator. "Kat tells him.

"I look forward to it. I have heard so much about you over the years from Mrs. Park and I saw how much care you gave to the journals and annuals to make sure they were protected. I was curious if you had worked in a museum before?" he asked.

"Oh no nothing like that. I just did not want anything to happen to grandmother's things. She cherished them so much and protected them for her entire life. Even through the war she kept them safe. How could I do any less? I did call the museum to ask how to care for old brittle books so that I could be sure they would not fall apart." She informs him.

"You did a wonderful job. You made my job so much easier thank you." He tells before hanging up.

Kat goes to the therapy room to tell Jae when the curator and translator will be arriving.

"Hey angel how is things going?" he asks.

"Fine I have almost everything organized in grandmother's room. The curator and the translator will be here next Tuesday. I am curious though. Where am I supposed to put them to sleep?" she asks" I have the books that need translating already set up in my room on the third floor. The translator can stay there so that she can work at her pace and not disturb anyone. The only thing is there is only grandmothers room left or a non-patient. That is my room, and I don't feel comfortable having anyone stay there." She tells him.

"We have empty patient suites he can stay in one of them. If we do not have them in use. I am surprised you even let anyone stay in either of your rooms. "He ruffles her hair playfully as he smiles down at her.

"Ya, I know I am selfish but I'm not that bad. I just do not want anyone but family in grandmother's room. I mean Ki made my old room into a patient suite so it's ok for others to be there. Not grandmother's room. "She tells him playfully punching him on the shoulder.

"Hey that hurt no hitting. You now must pay me for hitting me." He rubs his shoulder as if it really hurts.

"Oh, booboo I am so sorry I did not mean to hurt you." Kat rubs his shoulder and is fussing over him when Sarah walks in.

"Am I interrupting something should I come back later." she asks sarcastically.

"No, I am just tormenting angel since she is being a silly goose over where to put the curator when he comes next week." Jae tells her crossing the room giving her a kiss.

Kat excuses herself so that they can have a few minutes alone before the next patient arrives. She smiles to herself at how happy he looks these days since they have started dating. She frowns wondering if she should try to set Ki up with someone. Kat shakes her head no I do not know if I can.

The next few days fly by. Kat is so immersed in getting things ready for the curator and translator that she did not even go to day treatment or have a therapy session. When joe gets home, he finds Kat sound asleep on the sofa. The kids have been fed and bathed. They are in their rooms playing video games or watching tv. Dinner is ready on the stove. He notices that Shay has not come by to pick up her kids yet it's already bedtime so that means they are here for the night. Joe wonders if she is doing too much trying to take care of everything. She gets up before he goes to work to make sure he has lunch and breakfast. She takes care of all the kids, keeps the house clean, works at the clinic and still finds time to take the kids to practice and do the shopping for both our house and Shay's. She even goes to day treatment and therapy most days. He has enough on his plate just going to work every day. All Shay does is go to work and take the kids home to put them to bed. Kat's day begins at 3am and ends around 11pm. He keeps waiting for her to collapse. The only problem is he does not know how to make things easier on her. Everyone is working. The house is empty during the day since all 5 kids are in school. If she did not have so much to do, she could sleep, then. He wonders how much longer she will have to go to treatment and therapy. He goes and eats then goes to the girl's room.

"Hey, do you guys think you can wash the dishes for mom tonight?" he asks" she has fallen asleep on the sofa, and I don't want her to be woken up." He tells them.

"Sure, we can do you want us to pack your lunch for you. Like we did when she was sick in the hospital?" the oldest asks

"That would be great thank you. Let me know when you all are done so I can shower please?" he asks him as he closes the door and goes to their room to watch tv. He hears the girls in the kitchen cleaning and smiles. They are good kids. he thinks to himself.

The next morning Kat wakes up with a start. It's daylight and the house are completely quiet. She is still in her clothes from the day before and on the sofa. She begins to panic. She jumps up quickly and goes to the bedrooms to check on the kids. Their rooms are empty. Looking at the clock she sees it's almost 9 they have already left for school. Walking into the kitchen she sees it's already clean and their cereal bowls are washed and in the drainer. The phone rings. Its Joe

"Oh, I'm so sorry I fell asleep last night and just woke up. Did you eat last night, and did you get lunch for today? She asks him hurriedly.

"Yes, and yes. Everything is fine. I was just calling because I know that the curator and the translator are coming today and did not want you to oversleep. You said you needed to be at the clinic by noon today. "He tells her.

"Oh, thank goodness. And thank you. Yes, I got up in time I was on my way to shower and change now." She tells him "Though I won't have time to put together anything to prepare dinner for today, so I hope I can get them settled before time to make dinner." she tells him.

"No worries I asked your mom to come down to watch the kids after school she said she would fix dinner tonight, so you can stay there if you want to make sure all goes well, and we can see you tomorrow if things are ok. I know how important this is to you so its ok don't stress please." Joe tells her before he says goodbye.

Kat rushes to get ready to go to the clinic. she has a few things to take care of before Jae brings their guest from the airport. Once at the clinic she cooks the night menu and asks if the rooms have been finished yet.

"You finished everything yesterday all I had to do was go back and double check your list. We have no clients for this week except individual patients, no overnight ones. The Dr. cleared the clinic so that they could have patient rooms and be in either of your rooms. Dr Ki has cleared his schedule at the hospital and taken a week's vacation so that he can be here if you need him. Dr Jae has a few clients, but they only have regular private sessions. So, the clinic is basically empty for the next week except for you all. Do not worry, you have done an amazing job getting everything ready. There is nothing out of place. Just breathe and relax. You're going to be fine I promise and if not, they will be here with you." She pats Kat's hand as she heads back to the kitchen.

 Not long after Kat hears a car in the driveway. She knows its Jae since Ki will not be back till dinner time, she goes to the door to greet their guests. Walking up the porch steps is a beautiful petite woman. She has the cutest little top and jeans on. Her hair is cut in a bob. She takes off her sunglasses and Kat notices right away she is Korean. She smiles broadly at Kat and walks over to her and puts her hand out for her to take.

"Hi I am Suzy. You must be Kat. I have heard so much about you from my conversations with Mr. Kim the curator. I have been looking forward to meeting you."

"Yes, I'm Kat and he never mentioned that you were a woman he only ever called you the translator." Kat takes her hand and shakes it warmly.

'I don't mind. This house is stunning. It so big and well kept." She says with a smile.

Just then Jae and Mr. Kim walk up on the porch.

"Mr. Kim this is Kat. She is the one who has been taking care of everything from this end for us. "Jae tells him.

"Wow Mr. Park you did not tell me that the funny and charming lady I have been talking to was also so beautiful. Mrs. Kat I am incredibly happy to finally meet you." Mr. Kim is not what Kat expected. She kept thinking he was an older pertly fellow with glasses. Here standing in front of her is a tall young well-built Korean man. He is taller than both Jae and Ki. He looks like he exercises a lot. His smile is mesmerizing as well.

"Mr. Kim it is genuinely nice to finally meet you as well. I am sorry about last time not being able to be here." she tells him nervously.

"It's fine these two explained that you had something important to take care of. I am so happy though that you were able to make it this time." He says as he puts his hand in the middle of Kats back. Jae interrupts him at once.

"Let us get these things inside and get you all settled. I know Kat has asked the cook to get dinner ready early tonight. We will have it on the terrace so that you can enjoy the outside after your flight." Jae takes the luggage inside and Kat shows them to their rooms. Suzy is looking at the paintings and décor of the room she is in. It is the room crystal hand when she stayed here.

"Oh, wow this place is so beautiful and peaceful. I love the family paintings on the wall." She says as she turns to Kat.

"Yes, I love it here it's always been my haven. The painting above the bed is of the family. grandmother is in the hanbok. It is her journals and annuals that we need translated. Where did you learn English so well?" Kat asks her.

"Oh, I was raised here in the states. My parents are Korean and came here with my grandparents before I was born. They raised me in a traditional Korean home. I was taught how to speak Korean and English before I started American schools. Then when I was in my first year of university, I got the opportunity to go to Seoul university to study ancient languages. I spent three years there then came back to the states to finish my master's degree. I have been flying between South Korea and New York for the last 5 years. That is where I met Mr. Kim. I just came back from South Korea this morning to catch the flight from New York to here. it's so beautiful here." she tells her.

"I must agree with you there. Our area is very pretty. I can take you to a few of the historical places close by while you are here if you like." Kat tells her "I will let you get unpacked and please let me know if you need anything?" Kat turns to walk out when Suzy stops her.

"Ms. Kat can you tell me something please.?"

"Sure, if I can?" Kat answers her.

"Will you be here with us this whole time, or do you live somewhere else.?" Suzy turns and looks at her this time with a profoundly serious look on her face.

"I live somewhere else, but I have rooms here also. I will be going between my house and here. though I will be staying here tonight. I can stay any night you would like. If you are worried about being here with 3 men alone, I can stay, and you can even come to visit my home as well if you like. "Kat hopes that will put her at ease. She knows she would be too afraid to stay in a strange man's home without another woman around especially if there were three of them.

Suzy smiles at her relieved." How did you know that was what was bothering me?"

"I would feel the same way. I do not like to be around strange men. That is why Jae took care of Mr. Kim for me. I do not like to be touched except by those I know well. So, you need not worry about Jae and KI, they will not bother you. I will be here most of the time. I can decide if I need to at home and just stay here till you feel comfortable if you like." Kat tells her with a smile. The two ladies smile at each other and Suzy out of impulse walks across the room and gives Kat a big hug.

"Thank you so much for that. I feel more at ease already." Suzy tells her.

"Would you like to rest for a little while since you have been on a plane since yesterday?" Kat asks her.

"Oh, thank you I may not come down till morning if I go to sleep now though." Suzy tells her.

"It will be ok no worries I stocked your mini fridge with snacks, so you can sleep if you like, and I will make your excuses to everyone." Kat tells her as she closes her door, she hears her click the lock. She makes her way downstairs to check on dinner and to inform everyone that Suzy may not be down till morning because of jet lag. After dinner Kat went to check in on Suzy. Her door was still locked so she figured she was sleeping. She went to Ki office to call Joe to check on things at home.

"Hey baby how are things going at the clinic?" he asks when he answers the phone.

"They are good, but I may need to stay here for a few days. The translator is a woman. She does not seem to be comfortable around strangers, especially men. The curator as you know is a man. I kind of promised to be around so that she feels more comfortable." She tells him worried about what he will think and if they will be ok at home.

"that's fine I know that you don't like being around strange men either. Just stay close to the docs and cook, ok? I know you have spoken to the curator a lot on the phone, but you do not know him personally. Stay close to the other girl as well. Do not be alone with anyone that you do not feel comfortable with. I'm sure if you tell the docs one of them will make sure that they are always close." He reminds her "do you need me to pack you a few things or will you come by tomorrow to pick up some?" he asks her.

"I still have a few things here but if you don't mind maybe, I will invite everyone over tomorrow night for dinner I will ask Ki which he would like. for me to cook here and you all come for dinner or to go to the house. I will call you tomorrow ok." she tells him.

"Ok I will tell the office to contact me as soon as you call so I can make sure to talk to you." Joe tells her he loves her, and they say their goodnights. When Kat hangs up the phone, she sees Ki and Jae come into the office.

"Oh, so this is where you disappeared to. Did you call Joe?" Ki asks her.

"Yes, I called him and checked on things at home. Is it ok if I stay for a few days? Suzy is a little nervous about being in a house of nothing but men. I already asked Joe he said its ok if I stick close to you two and am not alone with Mr. Kim until I get comfortable around him. I also think it will make

Suzy more comfortable. Oh, and would you all rather have a cookout at my place tomorrow night, so I can get a few more things or would you rather Joe and the Kids come here?" She explains what she wants to do.

"Hey, I'm for whatever you want you know that I love hanging out with your kids." Jae tells her "You know if we go to your place than I can't see Sarah tomorrow. If you are here, you two can have a quiet session either before or after dinner." He winks at her.

"Yes, but then I must walk on eggshells trying to keep her at arm's length so to speak. It is getting harder and harder for us to keep the boundaries in our relationship. I need to get better soon so that you all can be more relaxed when I am around. I am sorry that this last week was a bust for therapy. I promise after things go well with grandmother's things, I will work harder at getting better," she tells them.

"I have a solution. We have Joe and the kids over for dinner. This way Sarah can see how well he is doing and can feel more comfortable with you being home with him. I know she has been worried since he has all but stopped his anger management classes. You two can have a session after everyone goes to bed. That way Jae can see his girlfriend. You get your session this week even if it is just talking therapy. Suzy can see that we have other women around the house at any time. She will also see us with your husband and kids. This way she can get to know us in a more relaxed and unpredictable setting. It also will remind Mr. Kim that you are a married woman with children. That way Joe will be put at ease as well. The final thing I took was the time off for the period he would be here just for that reason. I did not want there to be an opportunity for Kim to ever be alone with you. so, I think I have all bases covered." Ki smiles at them both. It surprises Kat that he had already thought about all of this prior to their arrival. She looks at him confused.

"How is it you thought about all of this before I did. It never dawned on me to even consider that the translator may be a woman. I thought Mr. Kim was an older man since he knew grandmother. So, it never dawned on me that I would not feel comfortable around someone grandmother trusted." Kat tells him.

"I decided it when he was here last time. He was too preoccupied with the fact that he did not get to meet you, also he is the grandson of grandmother's friend. since I do not trust him completely yet. I would never leave you alone with anyone I do not trust. "Ki tells her he then looks at Jae. "Besides Sarah is just getting used to you being around Kat and not getting jealous I do not want her to start having ideas about the translator. So, the more she is around the easier it will be for you. "He then turns back to Kat "I am a little disappointed at your choice for my brother. I never expected you to choose someone so jealous."

"Hey, I didn't know she would be jealous of me. Besides Jae loves her being a little jealous. he likes the fact that she gets angry when another woman tread on her territory. He always was hurt because I was never angry unless a total skank came onto him, if a good girl came on to him, I let her be unless she crossed the line. I was not even jealous then either, just protective. He has never been one for caution and I was always afraid he would catch something from one of those sketchy girls who would come on to him. either that or they would wind up pregnant and he would have to deal with them for the rest of his life. It just made my skin crawl, so I just made sure none of them stayed around long after introductions some never even got that far. In fact, one of the girls that works at the club you all went to hated me for the longest time because I told her she was not even worthy enough for any of you to say hi to. She kept pushing me until I had all the guys on the buss jack off in a jar and poured their sperm on her head just to show her that her life choices were not worthy of you all." Kat told him.

"Waits are you telling me that you poured a jar of sperm on a girl's head. Just so that she would stay away from us. How come we never got to see this side of you." Jae has the most shocked look on his face, he cannot believe his angel would do something so evil. Ki just is staring at her as if she grew two heads both are dumbfounded that she would do something so horrible to this girl.

"Hey in my defense by the time she wanted to meet you all she had already given head to every guy on the bus and had been treated for crabs, herpes, and chlamydia. I was not going to let someone like that near you all or my favorite cousins. I made sure that she stayed with the horny dirty guys that did not care what kind of diseases she may have had to get into her pants. Now I warned her on many occasions to step away from my husbands and my cousins. She wanted someone who she thought would take her out of her life. I told her no guy was going to do that until she had some self-respect and treated her body as a temple and kept it clean. Since she did not, I had all the guys, she had sex with a or gave head jack off in a jar. They laughed so hard that she was able to see exactly how they felt about her. They only used her to get their sexual release and then went to their girlfriends for their nice dates. That until she stopped acting like she was just a hole for some guy to get off in that was the life she had. It's not my fault she didn't listen and wound up embarrassed and hurt by them." Kat lets them know her voice is filled with sadness and disgust. At first Ki felt like she was proud of what she did. but now he sees it made her sad and disgusted.

"When did you do this?" Jae asked her.

"About two weeks before I had to leave you all. She had told one of my friends that she bought a drug and at the next party that she saw you at she was going to slip it to you. That way you would be putty in her hands. She said she was going to make sure at least one of my precious husbands became hers and that I would get what was coming to me. That I deserved to be staked out and have a line of guys screw me until there was nothing left. She hated me because the guy she liked did not like her because he told her he liked me. That he wanted someone who had not been used by so many guys, he wanted someone who was pure. What she did not know was that I may not have put out. I also was not pure either. I tried talking to her so many times about not letting guys use her. She would not listen and when I heard that I only saw red I was so angry I wanted her to see that these boys did not care about her they were only using her. I wanted her to see that and wake up. I was so ashamed that I let my anger get the better of me and caused her to be the butt of so many jokes after that. Then when I was being tortured after everyone found out about my brother-in-law. I went back and told her I was sorry; that I did not understand. How it felt to be tortured like that. She told me that she chose to do those things that she was never raped or abused. She liked sex and wanted to have it all the time. If a guy was willing so was, she. She then told me that I deserved all the torture that I was getting because I didn't deserve to live." By the time Kat finishes telling them she is noticeably quiet and looking at her hands in her lap. She was worried about what they would think of her now.

"Wow angel now I know why Kris loved having you prank people. This also explains why James only showed you his twisted side as well. Who knew you could be so evil? I'm impressed." Jae tells her Ki reaches out and smacks his brother in the back of the head.

"It was inappropriate and beneath her to do something so dirty. She should have just told you about the girls' plan instead of doing something like that. It could have gotten her in trouble. It also made her look like a hypocrite later. She should have just come to us and let us handle it." Ki still cannot grasp the fact that she did something like that.

"James was ok with it. If I was not personally getting the sperm and made it look like an accident. which I did. It just looked like I tripped, and it spilled and one of the boys that she slept with on a regular basis got the sperm for one of my cousins to give me. So that way it technically wasn't me who got it from them." She tells them.

"JAMES KNEW!!!!!" they both exclaim at the same time.

Kat nods her head yes.

"How could he be ok about it." Ki asked.

"One of his frat brothers got crabs from her at a party and he slept in his bed when he passed out afterwards. So, then James got them also. "Kat tells them.

"So that's how he got them. oh my God no wonder he was ok with it he was so embarrassed and angry. I remember he went to Appa and asked him to call uncle for him. It was so embarrassing for him. "Ki understands now why it happened now it doesn't seem quite so farfetched that Kat would do something like that especially since James had already fallen victim to the girl without her even knowing. Still, it does not make it right. They decide to say good night since they have an early morning with their guest.

The next morning Kat was up at her normal time as if she were home getting Joe ready for work. She decides to go down to the kitchen. She mixes fresh bread and is dancing around the kitchen making the marinades for the meat they will be grilling tonight. She did not hear when Mr. Kim came into the kitchen. He was standing in the doorway when she turned around. Startled she lets out a small scream. Within a few minutes Ki was in the kitchen asking if she was all right.

"Yes, I am sorry I came down when I woke up to start prepping for tonight's dinner and did not hear Mr. Kim come in. I was startled and screamed." Just as Kat finished explaining what happen Jae was in the kitchen. They both looked so cute with their hair a mess and stubble on their face. Ki standing only in his robe and boxers. Jae in his pajama pants with no shirt. Kat could not help but smile at them. When Kats eyes met Ki's, her heart did a summersault. A wave of heat rushed through her body. She has not felt this way since she was a teenager before she had to leave them. Her cheeks get flushed, and Ki can see the desire in her eyes. He gives her a big smile back and crosses the room. Making a point of his bare chest through his open robe touching her arm as he reaches for a cup from the cabinet. He hears her suck in a breath. He lowers his head to whisper in her ear.

"You are not to come in here again unless someone is with you, or cook is here. "Ki takes the cup and gets a cup of coffee.

Kat looks at them and clears her throat before asking if anyone was ready for breakfast. Cook comes in and just stares at the 4 of them not understanding why the two docs are half dressed and looking like they needed to still be sleeping.

"Aww MS. Kat you didn't need to start cooking so early. I will get breakfast." She tells her as she puts her apron on. Kat goes to the refrigerator to get out the ingredients for breakfast.

"I will take my coffee up to my room to drink while I get dressed." Ki says as he walks out of the room.

"I think I will grab a cup as well. Mr. Kim, you might want to get out of here as well, these two ladies do not like their kitchen invaded unless you are invited. That is why each room has a coffee pot, microwave, and refrigerator. If there is something, you need to please let cook know and she will make sure to get it for you." Jae grabs a cup of coffee and walks out.

 With that said Mr. Kim apologizes for scaring Kat this morning and causing a commotion. He excuses himself and goes back up to his room to wait for breakfast to be announced. After Kat helps to get breakfast started, she goes up to Suzy room to check on her and to bring her a try with tea. Kat knocks on the door. Suzy opens the door a crack and sees its Kat. She opens the door and lets her in.

"Thank you so much Kat. For letting me sleep last night and for bringing me tea this morning." Suzy sits on the small sofa in the sitting area of the room.

"Did you sleep well/" Kat asks her.

"Oh yes very well. Thank you. It is so peaceful here. I love the décor of this house." She tells her.

"Is there anything special you want for breakfast. cook is preparing it now." Kat asks her.

"No, I will eat anything that is prepared. I am not fussy. "She tells her.

"Ok it will be ready in about 15 minutes "Kat tells her as she goes out of the room and closes the door. At breakfast everyone was talking about where they wanted to start.

"I got the journals and annuals a few of the most delicate ones have dated back to the mid-1400s the language is early hangul. Suzy they should be easy to translate. The annuals are in excellent condition. They just need to be handled delicately. Kat had them set up in a room for me when I was here last time. I do not know how she managed to have them stacked in chronological order. "Mr. Kim says between bites of his food.

"Oh, that was easy grandmother taught me how to recognize a few hangul numbers." she tells him as she serves more tea.

"You know some Korean then." Suzy asks.

"Very little mostly just greetings and pleasantries. She taught me before her brother came to visit one time. She wanted me to make a good impression. My aunt also taught me a few things as well when I would stay with her" she tells them.

"That is really interesting I was expecting the two docs to know Korean but not an American." Mr. Kim tells her.

"Oh, why is that. She has a truly diverse family, and she is a member of our household after all. She may not be able to carry a conversation in Korean, but she was always willing to listen to what ever grandmother and her aunt wanted her to." You can hear the irritation in Jae's voice. He is not sure if he likes this Mr. Kim.

"We did not use Korean much in our house we only spoke to it amongst ourselves or when we had family from Korea visiting. In fact, Kat's aunt is always surprised that she still remembers anything that she was taught as a child. "Ki tells them "So please refrain from talking in Korean around her and cook since it can lead to misunderstandings." Ki asks them his voice sounding like a warning.

"Oh, I am fine with that I like using my English every chance I can. Now Kat if you would like to learn more, please let me know. I would be happy to give you one on one instruction." Mr. Kim tells Kat as she starts to clear his plate to take to the kitchen.

"That won't be necessary I won't get much chance to use it and I am too busy right now to learn anything new." Kat politely tells him to cast a glance at Ki and Jae.

After breakfast Kat shows Suzy to her room on the third floor. She never moved the books from Mr. Kim's last visit.

"This is my room I put the journals and annuals in here. I wanted them to be in a safe place that no one else uses. As you see grandmother has a lot of them. She told me most of them are just the list of births and deaths of the family. There are a few though that tell of life during various time periods. Depending on which family member oversaw them. These last few here are grandmother's personal journals. She always felt most comfortable writing in Korean. I have a personal favor to ask though. When you get to the box of letters can you let me see the translations first? I know most of what is in grandmother's journals. I do not know who the letters are for or who they are from. It's something that I am most curious about." Kat tells her "Do you want me to come and get you for lunch or would you like for me to bring you something here.?" Kat asks her before leaving the room.

"You have the mini kitchen well stocked, so you don't need to bother if I get hungry, I can get me something from the snacks you have in the room. Or I will come down myself. Can you ask everyone not to disturb me please I am excited to get started? "Suzy smiles at her and Kat nods ok. Before closing the door.

She sees Ki in the hallway waiting for her.

"Remember what I said until we are sure that Mr. Kim is a man who respects women and will not bother you. you are not to be alone with him. I will not have you uncomfortable in your own home. Make no mistake, this is still your home just like the one you share with Joe. "Ki takes her hand and pulls her behind him to go downstairs to meet Mr. Kim and Jae he wants to see the vaults in the wine cellar.

Once they are at the door of the cellar Kat asks them to stay up at the top of the stairs till, she has them opened. Since she does not want Mr. Kim to see how to open the vaults. Once they are opened, she calls them to come down.

"Which would you like to see first?" she asks him.

"Which is the one that has the military memorabilia in I will be able to date them and tell you if they are worth more than sentimental value or not just by looking at them." He tells them.

Kat motions him to the center vault. Once inside he sees the uniforms of the Korean army from various periods in history. He is especially drawn to the one hanging on the wooden cross against the wall. He goes over to it and pulls a thread from the ornate embroidery. "If this dates to when I think it will you have a unique piece of history here. This is a palace guard uniform from the Joseon era. The fabric is very thin and delicate, we will have to take extra care with it. This sword is from the same period. I cannot believe you have actual armor from that time. "You can hear the excitement in his voice. "You know your grandmother promised my grandfather that she would allow the museum to preserve and display anything of historical value." He tells them.

"Yes, I know but only if we agree I am not sure that we want her things flown across the world not knowing if we will get them back. "Jae tells him "Grandmother protected these things her entire life. Even through wars and moving here she never let anyone other than Kat and her two sons see these things before she died." Jae lets him know by his tone that they will not just let him have her things.

"I understand it just is amazing that they are intact. These are from the Korean war. These uniforms here are from when Japan occupied Korea. There is even a Japanese uniform here. There is a lot of valuable memorabilia here if you wanted to make money from it, I know a few collectors who would pay top dollars especially for the older pieces. The museum would not be able to pay what they are worth. Though we would love to have them." He tells them as he points to the various uniforms. He notices the trunks against the wall beside the weapons cabinet." What are in those?" he asks?

"Only grandmother knows we don't have the keys. And Kat has not found them yet." Ki tells him.

"Have you thought about calling a lock smith to open it?" he asks.

"Yes, but he said as old as the trunks are they would be damaged. "Jae tells him.

"It would be nice to see what is inside of them. I will tell you that some of these pieces are priceless in historical value. If you ever decide to sell them, I can set it up for you. Through the museum I would not be able to pay you for them but if you were ever willing to loan them to us for an exhibit, I would have them returned to you in pristine shape." Mr. Kim tells them "What is in the other vaults?" he asks.

"In one is grandmothers clothing from when Japan occupied Korea. There are a few photos and some jewelry from that time. One has some old furniture and toys from when mama was young and through the boy's childhood. The last one is some clothing that grandmother had specially made for us. Do any of these sound like something you would be interested in looking at?" Kat hold her breath wondering if he wants to see anything else or is he simply happy with what he has found so far."

"I would love to see all of them. I like old furniture and I would like to see the clothing from Japan. If they have and of the designer tags from a certain period, they could be worth something. They went ahead to the other rooms.

Over the next few hours Ki and Jae stayed with Mr. Kim to look through their family's treasures. They had very mixed feelings about some they barely knew going through them. Especially since they did not know what was in the vaults themselves. Ki was touched by just how much their mother and father loved them. They had chests set aside for each of them, these were not locked so they were able to go through them with ease. Each of them had their first clothes and photo albums. Each had a memory book with their mother writing describing every memory that she cherished about each of them. They told Mr. Kim these trunks were off limits. They were too personal. One trunk that was off by itself was a white trunk with pink cherry blossoms painted on it. They opened it up and inside was a letter addressed to Kat. Ki puts it in his pocket to give to her after everyone leaves tonight.

"Hey docs this room has a lot of good antiques in it, but I have a feeling you're not going to want to part with them. Some are from the late 1800s early 1900s. It is mostly solid oak and cherry. They are in excellent condition. I guess since they have been here for a long time. The cradle is exquisite." He tells them.

"Yes, this was my parents vault they crammed our stuff in here things that mama wanted to keep safe. the things she cherished most. Do you want to see the other two rooms after lunch? We have been down here for 5 hours. I'm sure Kat and cook has it ready by now." Ki asks him.

"Sure, that sounds perfect. I wonder what Ms. Kat has planned for lunch today?" he asks.

"I'm not sure I know she will fix dinner tonight, so she may have just left it up to cook. You will get to meet her family tonight at dinner." Jae makes a point of letting him know that Kat has a family so if he has any ideas, he can get rid of them.

"Oh, that will be nice. She seems to be a very caring person. "Mr. Kim says as they are climbing the stairs to the main floor.

Once there they can smell lunch, they go into the dining room and there is Suzy already. She and Kat are setting the table and chatting as if they were old friends. Kat hears them and tells them over her shoulder that lunch is about done.

"I hope you don't mind but I asked Kat if we could have dinner today. She agreed and made me cheeseburgers, fresh french-fries, with all the trimmings. She even made fresh squeezed lemon aid. I am so excited I haven't had a good burger in such a long time." Suzy tells them excitedly she follows Kat into the Kitchen to help her bring in the food.

When she bites into the burger and gets a look of sheer joy on her face.

"Oh my God Kat these are better than any diner. You are such a good cook." Suzy tells her.

"Oh, thank you but it's just a burger. Tonight, though I am making you Mexican food, so I hope you like it. I will need to start making tortillas and salsa after lunch. How is the translating going?' she asks her?

"Oh, it's going well. The older books are just logging of births and deaths in the town where your family originated. Your ancestor was the person who recorded all the deaths and births in the village. There are special signs besides the ones who are members of your family. There is a description of each person's life next to their name. That is why there are so many books. Your ancestor was very meticulous. He had a different family in each section of the book. He separated each family in the village by having a blank page between them. When one family married another, he made a note of which book and section the family of that person married was in. So that if someone wanted to research their family they just had to go to that book and section. It is remarkably interesting that he did that. Most families either do not know about their ancestors beyond a few generations or are not interested. Granted there are only about 30 families listed in these books. I glanced at the others, it then became just your family tree, and more time was devoted to stories about the times and family. There was one story in one that I found so beautiful and so sad at the same time. I loved it. it told about a child being born with striking blue eyes with very white skin and red brown hair. It seems that one of your ancestors fell in love with a person who came from across the sea. They married and had a child. The father left after their child died from a fever. The parents became distant from each other due to their grief. That they began to not even speak. She told him to leave because she could not bear to see his eyes. Seeing him reminded her too much of their child. He left back across the sea. In the story they promise to meet again in another life. Hoping they will be able to be together for a lifetime in that new life. To see their child and watch her grow, marry, and have children of her own. The woman died soon after he left from a broken heart." You can hear the sadness and empathy that Suzy has for the couple in the journal. She has a distant look in her eyes like she is imagining how they looked and felt to be so in love to only become estranged from that love over grief.

"Wow that is a sad story. At least they had love even if for a short time." Jae tells her.

"Yes, please tell us more as you translate more of the books. I would love to know more about our ancestors in Korea. Since we grew up here even though grandmother was here, we really don't know much about our family there or even if we still have any there." Ki tells her.

"Oh, I will I am going to cross reference some of the newer parts of the family histories with the archives in Korea and see if I get any hits. I may find you some long lost family before I am done." She tells them." How did your treasure hunt go/" she inquires.

"The one vault is magnificent it has military uniforms and memorabilia from as far back as the Joseon era. I cannot wait to send some of the thread samples back to have a correct date for them. The other vault was family treasures." Mr. Kim tells her. They continue to talk after lunch comparing the writing from the journals to who the uniforms could belong to. The rest of the afternoon Jae and Ki continued to stay close to Mr. Kim while Suzy went back to Kats room to look more into the journals. She decides to go back and see if there is any mention of who served in the palace guard and militia. Kat goes and cleans up the kitchen and starts to prepare dinner for everyone. Knowing the kids are going to be here she makes a few more burgers so that they can have more of a choice for dinner. The 3 men go down to the cellar to look at the other two vaults.

In the cellar they decide to show him grandmothers vault with the items from her time in Japan.

"Oh, wow what a beautiful portrait. Your grandmother was an incredibly beautiful woman." Mr. Kim tells them "I can see why my grandfather admired her so much. "

"Yes, she was an incredibly beautiful person inside and out. She always had a kind heart. She is what kept our family together in so many ways. "Ki tells him.

"I can see that she cherished you all very much to have kept so much intact for you to have the history of your family. It is something that most have not only forgotten but do not care as much about anymore. What I do not understand is how Ms. Kat plays in your family. I see her in every room, and you have entrusted her with your grandmother's treasures. Who exactly is she?" Mr. Kim asks Ki.

"She is an incredibly special part of our family. One that needs no explaining to anyone outside of our family. We are not entrusting her with grandmother's treasures. Grandmother entrusted her with them years ago. She is the only one who knew about grandmother's treasures until recently. She will be treated with only love and respect. "Jae interrupts KI before he can even answer. They both give Mr. Kim a stern stare letting him know by their look that she is off limits for discussion or anything else he may have planned.

"Hey, I am simply curious that is all. I just happen to notice how big of an influence she seems to have been all." He tells them as he opens a chest in the corner. "Wow looks at these they are exquisite the embroidery is magnificent. "He says as he lifts a kimono out of the chest. Under it he finds a box. Opening it he finds hair pins in all manner of gold, silver, jewels and jade." These would be worth a fortune at auction. They are called Kogai Kanzashi. They are ornate hair decorations. "He explains to them. "May I ask why your grandmother has this room filled with more journals and only things from Japan. It's unusual for a Korean woman to have such things from a time when Korea was occupied by Japan."

"When we give Suzy the journals from this room everything will be explained. We are keeping them in here till she is done with the others. These are my grandmother's personal thoughts and are not to be confused with the other family journals." Ki tells him in an incredibly quiet voice. It hard for him to imagine his sweet grandmother ever going through any pain. He is not sure if he wants to share those thoughts with anyone other than Jae and Kat.

"Well, I can tell you that just in the two rooms that were just your grandmothers you have a fortune sitting here in these chests and on the walls. They would make a wonderful exhibit in the museum. Can we see the last room?" Mr. Kim starts to move out of the room to head towards the other room.

"There is no need to see the other room. It is just some clothing from our younger days. You can see them, but we know that they are not worth more than just sentimental. We don't even know who made them" Jae tells him as they move out of the room.

"I would still like to look you never know many things from the 70s and 80s are very in right now." He tells them.

Once in the last room he sees the wedding clothes he does not recognize the designs of the clothes. so, he walks over to check the labels. "Ralph Lauren these tuxedos are nice, but I don't remember these styles on the market they are all like those he released but not exactly. Each is unique. "He then checks the wedding dresses Priscilla of Boston. "These are the same just like the tuxedos they have been special designed. who were they made for?" he asks?

"The tuxedos were specially designed for myself and my twin brothers. The wedding dresses were made from designs that we each made.

The rose dress was designed by James, the snowflake lace was one I designed, and the butterfly Kris designed. The dresses were designed for an incredibly special girl in our lives. "Jae tells him while touching the wedding dress he designed, thinking how beautiful Sarah would look in it.

"The hanboks are pure silk and with soft cotton under skirts. The embroidery is amazing. The matching cherry blossom design is not what you normally see. Usually, the hanbok is different colors but this one is white with only pink cherry blossoms. Unique. There aren't any labels in these two why not?" he asks.

"My grandmother made them herself. They were made for me and the person I was to marry." Ki tells him.

"These could bring you a few grands nothing like the other two rooms. Only because these designs were never released to the public and are exclusive. Other than that, they are just sentimental. Thank you for showing me these 4 rooms. Now from what I understand there is one other room that has a few treasures in it? Will I get to see them while I am here?" Mr. Kim asks.

"That will be entirely up to Kat she oversees all these rooms. The other room you will not get to see. if Kat wants to show you anything from that room, she will make the arrangements for you." Ki informs him his voice is very cold and curt. Showing him by his manners that the subject is closed. The 3 men make their way back up from the cellar. They hear the kids running from the front door through the house. Jae looks at Ki and smiles.

"Yay the kids are here let's go play." Jae runs to the kitchen to find the kids. Ki not far behind him

Once in the kitchen as usual all the kids are almost knocking Kat over from trying to hug her at the same time.

"Mama are you coming home with us tonight?" the youngest boy asks.

"No not tonight the uncles have guests, and I am needed here for a few days. But you all can come for dinner while I am here ok. Now go outside to the garden to play till I get dinner finished." She kisses each other on the forehead as they walk out of the house to the garden.

"Hey kiddos wait for me I'm coming to play as well." Jae calls to them as he grabs a carrot from the counter as he follows them out the door. Kat playfully slapping his hand as he passes her. Ki walks over and reaches around her to grab one as well.

"Hey, you all stop eating before dinner. "She tells him. He quickly kisses her forehead and follows the others out.

"Now Kat you know those two men are no more that overgrown children. It is so nice when your kids come and visit. This house comes alive just like when you used to be here as a child. I miss those days. Your Appa loved to play with you all also he turned into a big kid when you would visit." Cook told her.

"Really I always just thought they were the same when I was gone as when I was here." she tells her she continues to prepare dinner.

"Oh no they were so quiet when you were not around you brought the joy and sunshine to their lives." Cook told her.

"Yeah, my wife has that effect on people." Joe says as he walks past Mr. Kim to go and give his wife a big tight hug and kiss. Making sure that this new handsome man understood that she was not to be bothered in anyway. While he has her pinned against the counter he reaches for a piece of fruit and rushes outside before she can smack him for stealing food

'Hey, you are as bad as the others go out and watch the kids make sure they don't get too dirty or get booboo too dirty like last time please. Dr. Smith is coming, and I would like him not to look like a ragamuffin when she arrives." Kat informs Joe. "Oh, we also have a guest. Mr. Kim this is my husband Joe and those loud tornados that just ran out of here are ours." She tells him. Joe walks over and shakes his hand staring him in the eye so that he knows she belongs to him.

"It's nice to meet you." Joe replies

"Same here "Mr. Kim takes his hand.

"You will meet Suzy at dinner she is still working upstairs. "Kat lets them know "why don't you join the rest on the terrace, and I will bring out some iced tea." Kat shews them all out of the kitchen praying that tonight will go well.

 When Dr. Smith arrives, she can hear the laughter and squeals of the kids in the backyard. She decides to walk around to the back instead of going through the house. She sees Kat serving iced tea. Jae is wrestling in the grass with the two boys. The girls are sitting at the table chatting up a man that she has not met. It must be the curator that Jae told her about. She smiles and it is so funny how much Kats kids fit in here with everyone. As if they were always meant to be here. she sees another young woman come out from the inside. Curious as to who she is. She decides to let everyone know she is here.

"Hello everyone. how is it going?" she greets them in a cheerful voice looking at the other girl wondering if Jae thinks she is attractive or not.

"Hey sweetheart "Jae walks over and kisses her on the cheek while giving her a big tight hug. He puts his arm around her waist and pulls her next to him. Walking her over to the table for introductions.

"Everyone this is my girlfriend Sarah or Dr. Smith whichever she wants to be addressed by. Sweetheart this is Suzy the translator and Mr. Kim the curator. "He introduces them to her, so she knows not only who they are but also that she knows that there is nothing to worry about.

"Hey Kat, is it ok if I take Sarah down to the vaults, I would like to show her something?" He turns to Kat for permission.

"of course, I have not had a chance to lock them back up yet, so they are still open. "She tells him with a small smile. She knows what he wants to do. Saying a little prayer that she will agree.

Jae asks Sarah to try a dress.

arah and Jae go to the cellar and Jae takes her to the room with the wedding dresses. You know that we all designed a dress for Kat. These are those dresses. I never knew that grandmother had them made. I also never knew that she could tell who designed each of them just by looking. Can you tell which one I designed?" he asked looking at her closely?

"Well, I think knowing you that you designed the snowflake. I remember from her sessions and from this last winter how much you love the snow. Why did you want to show me these?" she asks?

"Today when we showed Mr. Kim, I wondered how you would look in the dress I designed. I want to know if you would try it on for me so that I can see how you would look? Kat has jewelry and a train in grandmother's secret room. The shoes and under garments are in the trunk with snowflakes on it. Would you try on my dress for me?" he asks her sincerely his voice pleading with her. She can hear the worry in his voice that she will refuse.

"I don't know you designed this for Kat not me. I am not sure she would even be willing to let me. I am not sure I am even willing to wear someone else's dress. Do you not even know how hard it is for me to know that for most of your life you have loved someone you cannot have. That she is all that you have thought about for most of your life." Sarah tells him.

"Yes, I love her. I would give my life to her and yes, I wanted her to wear this dress, this dress was not to be her wedding dress. We each designed a dress to show her how much we loved her and accepted her into our family. She would have worn this as a dress at her wedding for a special part of it but not as the dress she would have worn in the marriage ceremony. That one was always going to be the hanbok that Ki designed. We all had our wishful thinking, but we also were all realistic. Yes, she loved us but only as her siblings. We each held a special part in her heart. You know when she first opened the secret room, she was looking for James's dress. Grandmother brought it for her to change into for our first meeting with her after being separated. She cried when she saw the four dresses and knew who designed each of them. Yes, these are her dresses but this one is also still mine. I already know she wants me to give it to you. She has told me so. She knows how much I love you and that I want to spend every one of the remaining minutes of my life with you. Now I will still love my sister and be there for her. Yes, always but you are the person my heart aches and longs for when I am not with you. So, will you accept my heart and my dress? I know it is a lot to ask. But will you marry me and become the most important part of my family? "Jae sinks to one knee and pulls out a special box one that he asked Kat for earlier in the day. Inside the box was a snowflake engagement ring. It has a large diamond in the center of a snowflake of smaller diamonds. He is staring up at her holding his breath hoping she would say yes. There are tears of happiness in her eyes that he would even ask her to marry him. Her heart is still torn though wondering if she can ever overcome the jealousy she feels for Kat. She nods her head yes and holds out her hand. He places the ring on it. It is a perfect fit. She smiles at him.

"How did you know my ring size?" she asks.

"I didn't, I just hoped that it would fit. "He tells her.

"This is the ring you designed for the dress. this is the one you hoped to give to Kat isn't it." She asks.

"It is the ring I designed to go with the dress. But it was never meant as an engagement ring for her. We each designed jewelry and a dress. I always imagined giving this ring to the girl I would spend the rest of my life with. I knew it would not be her. You see I am not who I am today without knowing her. So yes, she will always be a part of me that I cannot change. I cannot be who I am without having her in my heart. But I also cannot grow and continue to love without you. You are my soul mate. I am not complete without you. You are the person who completes me. She only showed me love and taught me that I could have feelings. I know it is hard for anyone to understand how she changed our lives. If it had not been for her, I would not be standing in front of you. I could not even be considered human when she came into our lives. She changed us all for the better. I know she wants us to be together. She has told me more than once. I know that she even chose you for me. She told me so. She told me to open my heart to the person beside me. The person who complements me and completes me. The day she gave me the passes she told me that she wanted me to take my future bride to the festival. I just looked at her dumbfounded. I was not sure who she was thinking of. She told me to take you that she could see my heart melting and reaching out to you. That if I were sincere and true to my heart you would come to me. She saw what the two of us could not. That we are destined to be together. That our souls are only complete with each other." By the time he is done Sarah is in tears. She can hear the love and passion in his voice. She for the first time knows that he loves her beyond everyone. She throws her arms around his neck and goes up on her tip toes and kisses him deeply. Jae pulls her fully into his arms and deepens the kiss. They stay in the cellar kissing and talking for a while and finally they hear one of the kids yelling.

"Uncle Jae where are you it's time to eat. "They look at each other and smile.

"I guess it's time for us to tell everyone you said yes. "Jae asks her. She just nods her head.

When they come upstairs Kat notices right away that Sarah is wearing the ring. She takes off running towards them without thinking and hugs the two of them tightly. She whispers to Sarah.

"Take good care of my booboos heart you know he is a big softy inside despite how cold he tries to be. Thank you for loving him. thank you for accepting his heart." Kat tells her she grabs their hands and walks them to the table. She nods to cook, and she brings out a bottle of champagne from the cellar. Sparkling cider for Kat and the kids. They all toast to the happy couple. Kat asks Sarah.

"Dr. Smith would you like to come with me after dinner I need to show you the rest of the pieces that go with your ring." She asks her.

"I would love to. you know we must have a talk after everyone leaves so after that ok." She reminds her.

"Oh yes Joe will be leaving in a few minutes to get them home, so they can get to bed. They have school tomorrow. "She tells her.

"Aww can't we stay home tomorrow and stay here instead with mama." The youngest boy asks.

"No, you cannot but I will see you tomorrow don't worry ok." Kat hugs each of the kids and kisses Joe on the cheek when she says good night to them. As soon as she closes the door, she motions for Dr. Smith to follow her to the therapy room. She also looks at Jae and Ki. They see that look on her face they know she wants to do more than talk she wants to talk to them about how fast she can get through opening the rest of those doors so that she can be done with the worst of her recovery. Once in the therapy room. She turns to them.

"I cannot have a different Dr, so we need to finish with these doors quickly. I cannot cause you all any more problems. So as soon as Mr. Kim and Suzy leave, I want to start opening those doors again. I don't know how many more there are, but I want to get them done." She tells them you can hear the urgency in her voice. They know she wants to be able to help plan the wedding.

"You know we cannot rush this it could cause you more problems than help if we go too fast and don't give you enough time to process the emotions opening these doors causes. You could have some severe problems I cannot have you try to kill yourself or run away just because Jae and I want to get married. I am your Dr. not your friend or family. Yes, we have skirted the rules a little closely, but we still have not broken any. I will continue to only be your Dr. till you are able to be able to confidently be out in the world without fear. If that means I cannot marry Jae for a little extra time, then ok. I made a promise to you, and I will keep it. Jae would be angry if I let something happen in my rush to marry him." Dr Smith tells her.

"I agree when we started this, she was overly concerned about us crossing lines. So, we will just have to wait. Just because we wait to have a wedding does not mean we are putting our lives on hold. We will continue to date and build our lives together we will just have to keep the gatherings where you two would meet outside of the center or hospital apart. I will date her outside of the clinic while you are staying here. and we will only meet during your sessions. Just like before." Jae tells her.

"Are you ok with that?" Dr Smith asks Kat.

"Yes, I am. I want to come the morning they are scheduled to leave for my next session that is 3 days from now is that ok?" Kat asks Dr Smith.

"Yes, I will make room for you and have the receptionist call you. Now how are you handling the stress of these last couple of days?" Dr Smith asks Kat.

"I am ok I am extremely nervous about showing anyone the things in grandmother's room. I like Suzy and am overly cautious around Mr. Kim. I am not sure what he is looking for. Sometimes I think he wants them to let the museum preserve and display her things other times he sounds like he wants them to sell them and for him to make a commission on those sales. I know grandmother would not want her treasures sold. She would not mind if the museum borrowed them if the family could have them back. Maybe there was a place the family owned that could be turned into a museum to display her treasures without the risk of them being damaged. I do not know I just want her to be proud of what we do. she entrusted this to me, and I do not want to disappoint her." Kat lets her know.

"I can understand that, and they are legitimate concerns. You are not feeling any different than these two guys are I assure you." She tells her they continue to talk about how Kat can ease her anxiety and be able to stay focused over the next few days. Dr Smith says good night to them all at the door. Ki hands Kat the letter from the trunk. She looks at him confused.

"It was in a trunk in the room from Appa and mama. It is addressed to you so I slipped it out before anyone could see it. I figured you would want to read it before you go to bed. Kat takes the letter and tells Jae and KI good night and goes to bed. Once in her room she opens the letter and starts to read it.

My darling girl

If you are reading this, then that means you have opened the vaults. I hope you are doing well. I am so sorry that things worked out the way they did. I so wish I could turn back the clock and take everything away. We miss you and want you to know that this is and always will be your home. You became my daughter the moment you walked into this house looking like a hooker on the corner. I know the boys dressed you that way to hide how young you were, but I still find it appalling that a sweet child was dressed in such a manner. This trunk is empty only because you were not here to help me fill it. I hope that someday you can fill it with beautiful memories and cherished mementos. I love you my darling girl and have missed you so much over the years.

Forever your loving

Mama

Kat smiled at the letter thinking of mama wondering how she was able to forgive her enough to write to her. She went to sleep dreaming of herself and all the fun they had before she had to leave. Before the night was over her peaceful dreams turned into a fierce nightmare. One where mama was screaming and yelling at her. She was blaming her for losing her sons. Telling her she was nothing more than trash to her now that she should be the one dead, not her sons. Jae could hear Kat crying out in her sleep he rushes across the hall to her room. He hears her crying for mama to please forgive her. she is thrashing in the bed. Tears ran down her face. He goes in to calm her. He goes to put his arms around her and she the digging at her clothes like she is trying to rip something from her. He goes out and runs to KI room.

"KI, I need you to get up. Kat is having a dream, and I can't get her calm enough to get close to her." Jae tells him as he shakes him awake. Ki jumps out of bed and the two of them rush to her room. When they get there. She is standing beside the bed, there is blood on her shirt. They cannot tell where she has hurt herself though. They see Mr. Kim come out of the adjoining bathroom.

"it's not what you think. I heard her crying and was concerned, when I got close, she threw that at me and hit my head. I was just in her bathroom cleaning it up. I truly did not do anything to harm her. "He tells them quickly.

"I know it's my fault I left her door open when I went to get KI, she has nightmares that can get loud and sometimes violent. I am sorry." Jae tells him.

"Ki is already standing next to Kat checking her out and talking softly to her in Korean. She looks at him and puts her hand on his face.

"You're dead why are you here. have you come to finally take me?" she asks in a dazed voice.

"No angel I'm not dead and neither are you. You are just in a nightmare. I need you to wake up now. He talks to her again in Korean and puts his arms around her. whispering softly to her while cradling her head to his shoulder. She slumps in his arms. He knows she has fallen back to sleep. He picks her up and carries her back to the bed and tucks her in. He sees the letter and reads it. He gives it to Jae to read. They both know now that she was dreaming of the night of the accident. They turn to Mr. Kim.

"Please don't say anything to her about hurting you. She has horrible nightmares and cannot remember most of them when she wakes up. Sometimes she fights and cries. Sometimes it is just horrible screams. She will be embarrassed if you mention it to her." Ki explains to him. His voice was soft and quiet. You can hear that he is trying to be understanding about this stranger being in her room. Knowing that he should be apologizing in her stead.

"I am sorry. I heard such pitiful heart-breaking cries coming from in here and when I saw the door open. I just wanted to see if I could really help. I have a sister at home I would not be able to bear it if she cried like Ms. Kat just now. Forgive me for if I caused her any harm." His voice is very sincere, and you can hear his concern.

"You had no way of knowing. I should have closed the door so that she could not have wandered out and no one could come in except one of us. It is my fault not yours. Thank you for your concern over her." Jae tells him again motioning him to leave. Ki's is sitting on the edge of the bed. holding her hand.

"I will stay in here tonight to make sure she has no other nightmares please do not worry yourself over her cries if you hear anymore tonight. She will be ok now. "He tells them as they leave the room this time Jae making a point to close her door.

Chapter 58

Saying goodbye to Mr. Kim and Suzy

Over the next few days Mr. Kim basically has a mini vacation since he has seen what is in the cellar and has made a list and taken thread samples for dating. To take back to Korea. He tells the three of them again that he would like to have the two rooms to put together a display at the museum. Suzy has only made it through about 7 of the journals. She asks if she can take a few with her to continue to translate in Korea since she needs to get back.

"Can't we make copies of the books to send with her instead of her taking the books themselves. I mean surely, she just needs to be able to make out the writing. "Kat suggests.

"I don't know since some of them are so delicate it may damage them. "Suzy tells her.

"Can we try it I don't feel comfortable having the books removed at this time. "Kat tells her.

"How about I make copies of the newer ones and save the older ones for my next visit. "Suzy suggests.

"That will be much better thank you." Kat tells her they go and get the books that can be copied and go to Ki office. They make several copies of each page so that Suzy can have several people working on them at once. Once finished they put the copies in binders and pack them for shipping.

"I will have the postman pick them up in the morning and have then sent by the fastest route." Kat tells her.

"Ok thank you. I've been curious what kind of Drs are the Park brothers?" she asks.

"They are physiatrist, and this is their clinic since we had guest this week, they closed it to patients and took vacation leave from the hospital." Kat tells her.

"And Dr. Smith Dr. Jae fiancé?" she inquires.

"The same as they are. She is a particularly good Dr as well." She asks her to wonder why so many questions.

"I was curious because when I first arrived, I had a little crush on Dr Jae. I was hoping that he was single." She tells her.

"oh" Kat exclaims wondering why she did not notice.

"You have a wonderful family it must be hard though to love two people." Suzy asks her.

"Thank you for what you said about my family. Why do you think I am in love with two people?" Kat asks her.

"It's obvious to most of us that you love your husband. We can also see how much you love Dr. Ki. It is just not clear how you love him. Sometimes it feels like siblings, other times it feels like he is your lover. "She tells her.

"We are soul mates. We were just not meant to be married ones. "Kat tells her.

"I feel sorry for whatever woman who falls in love with him. she will have a hard time not demanding him to have you out of his life." Suzy makes this remark not thinking it would really have merit. Kat begins to wonder again if she needs to try to fix him up so that he has someone." They say their goodbyes and Jae takes them to the airport and Kat heads to the center for her session.

Chapter 59

Next Door

When she arrives, Dr Smith is waiting for her.

"Both of the Dr parks are busy today do you want to have just a talk therapy session today and wait till next week. When they can be here?" she asks Kat

"No, I want to have this over with so that everyone can move on with their lives. I am so tired of living like something is going to jump out at me and send me into a tailspin." She tells her.

"Ok then let's get started." She dims the lights and takes out her light pen. Kat concentrates on the light she hears Dr smith soft voice telling her to start down the staircase. That the deeper she goes the sleepier she will get. When she is standing in front of the big mutilated black door. Kat opens it without hesitation this time. She sees the trees blooming in place of the other doors she has been through she sees a red door with water running down it on the handle is chains. I take a deep breath and open it. Kat begins to describe what is happening.

"I am in a car. I am looking around and the only other person here is my brother-in-law. My hands have chains holding them together with a lock. I ask him what is happening, where is he taking me? He laughs at me. I am taking you to see your maker today. I am struggling to get the chains loose. They will not budge. I begged him to let me go. I am sorry that someone told him that I will not say anything else if he will just let me go. He takes a long draw from his cigarette.

'It is too late for you to write a note and say that you made everything up and that you seduced me. Then you are going to be my slave for the rest of your miserable life. You will be at my beck and call. That is until I get tired of you and kill you. or you kill yourself. "He puts his cigarette out on my arm burning me.

I scream out in pain. He laughs harder. When he stops the car, we are at a secluded place by a large lake. He drags me out of the car. Throwing me down. He unlocks the chains. He tells me that he wants to play. He takes the gun out of the trunk of the car. I started to get up to run away. He kicks me in my side.

"If you run, I will just put it in your mouth and pull the trigger. You see just across that field your dad is sitting in his deer stand. I am going to shoot him if you do not do as I say. If you do not believe me watch what happens." He grabs me by my hair and drags me across the field into the forest there I can see my dad sitting in his stand; and reading his bible. He is not even hunting today. He is just here for some quiet to read. I look at my brother-in-law as he takes aim at my dad. I began to cry. I open my mouth to scream to call my dad. My brother-in-law slaps me across the face.

"If you make a sound, I will kill him in front of you. He turns and aims again. He shoots and hits the branch below my dad. There is some rustling in the bushes; a large deer rushes out and runs across the hollow. My dad looks up and sees the deer run but looks around to see who could be hunting no one is supposed to be on the property but him. He sits back down and picks up his bible. I am crying trying not to make a sound.

My dad does not know how close he just came to dying. I hope he never knows. My brother-in-law drags me back to the car. He tells me to strip. I quietly strip off my clothes. He laughs again as he puts my hands behind my back and ties them to my ankles with the chains and locks them. He then strips off his clothes.

"Time to torture you. I work so hard when you are around to pretend so everyone believes the lie. This is going to be fun today. Maybe I will even go more than once. He begins to rape me with the gun pointed at my head on the seat. He takes his little tools he uses on me and cuts my insides up they still have the blood on them from last time. After he cuts me up, he tells me sorry, but he is hard again and starts all over again. I cannot feel anything anymore. The next thing I know is he has picked me up and thrown me into the freezing lake. telling me to clean up that he cannot have blood in the car. After I get cleaned, I put my clothes back on and get back into the car. We headed home. He drops me off at the end of my grandmother's lane. I am walking to her house."

"Ok I want you to stop there for now. I want you to leave this place and start walking back up the staircase.as you climb the staircase I want you to leave all the anger and fear inside of here. Nothing from here can ever hurt you again. When you wake up you will be yourself. When I count to 3 you will wake refreshed and alert .123" snapping her fingers Kat wakes up.

"How do you feel?" Dr smith asks her.

"I am sick to my stomach. As always, I am disgusted at what I remember. I just do not know why he enjoyed hurting me so much. I never would let my dad take me hunting after that day. I could not stand touching a rifle after that day again. To this day I hate the sound of a gun firing. I hate hearing taps because of the guns firing afterwards. All I see when I hear gunfire is my father sitting in that stand. the bullet literally was only a few inches away from him if it would have hit him, he would have died. "Kat tells Dr smith she is ringing her hands and rocking back and forth. Dr smith can tell that she is still reeling from the effects of the memory uncovered. She seems to be handling it ok for the most part.

"Do you want me to call Joe and tell him that you are having a hard time?" Dr Smith asks her.

"No, he doesn't want to know the details of my memories. He says they may change how he feels about me. You know he has loved only a broken me. He has never gotten to have me in control or unbroken. I really want him to get to know me. The happy person inside. I was always pretending that I was ok with everything when I met him. I did not want my family to see just how broken I really am. Then things became too hard to pretend anymore. Everyone thinks I have changed just these last few years. I have been broken inside for so long that I cannot remember who I am. I want to be me again. I want to be able to laugh and play without fear of causing someone to see me in a way that is not good. I love to party and dance. I cannot do that because it may cause misunderstandings and jealousy. What is funny is that Joe is not a jealous person. Neither am I. He has never cared who I danced with as long as they never touched me. I love him completely, but I still have feelings of that closeness with Ki. does that make me a bad person?' Kat explains to DR Smith.

"No, it just makes you a complex person. A person who loves for a lifetime. You know love changes as we get older. It does not stay the same. It grows and becomes comfortable. I see you and Ki as family not lovers." Dr Smith tells her.

"They think that you have regrets about not being able to live your life with him and letting the course of your relationship go as it should have.

That is normal when you do not get to see something to its conclusion. Personally, I think that you have a closer relationship now than before. You have grown as a person. So has he. He can see you now as an adult, not that fragile child that needed to be protected. So, he can be more honest with you. Where before he catered to you and protected you from anything he thought would upset you. I think that if you had stayed together, you would have remained a porcelain doll and never been able to be strong enough to break out of that box the 4 of them had you in. You are an extraordinarily strong person. A lot stronger than you realize. You can handle everything that is behind those doors and still come out on top. I am sure of it. You do not realize just how much you have already faced and overcome. I have patients that will never leave an institution who have suffered less than you. You are a force to be reckoned with making no mistake about that. I think that having him here with you now gives you a chance to have a closer and a new beginning as well. It gives you a chance to tell him all the things you could never say before but also gives you the chance to let him go so that you can move forward with your life." Dr smith tells Kat how she feels about the square that is her life. She is being controlled by the regrets and shame of her past and has not been able to move past it. This is her chance to move forward to not just a better marriage and life but a more fulfilled one. She sees how she is struggling to keep Ki at arm's length and not make Joe jealous when there really is no need to. The love she has for both men are so quite different. She sees the hatred and anger she is harboring for her brother-in-law and the men in her past. She also sees the hurt and sadness she has over her father never knowing just how sick she really was before he died, and she really wanted to do the things that he wanted her to do. Dr Smith hopes she can help her tie up all these loose ends so that she can finally put all the things tying her down behind her. As their session ends Ki and Jae arrive. Only to find out that they finished already. Jae asks Kat if its ok that Dr. Smith fills them in on the details of the session.

"Of course, she recorded it as always. You can listen if you want. Did you get our visitors off ok?" she asks?

"Yes, though Suzy will be back next month alone to translate the older books. She told me to tell you thank you for everything and that she will be calling you soon." Jae tells her.

"Ok good I am just heading home. I have missed my family these past few days. I will be at the clinic later this week to finish the pictures and list grandmother's jewelry. This way you can decide what pieces you each want. "Kat tells them she hopes that Mr. Kim will have an antique jeweler get in touch with her soon so that she can get the collections put in the right order. She wants to have everything finished before Jae gets married so that Dr. Smith can choose what will go best with what she wants.

"I will see you next week. I am back at the hospital tonight and will be on schedule next week. I have 3-night shifts and 2-day shifts. So, it most likely will be Jae at the clinic most days next week." Ki tells her "I have several times available for your sessions next week, so I will share my schedule with Dr Smith so that she can pick the right time for you." Ki informs her.

They all say their goodbyes and Kat heads home. When she pulls into the driveway the kids are just getting off the bus. Thank goodness school is out. She has 21/2 months before they go back. Jae has already told her to bring them with her to the clinic when she is working that they can swim and play in the pool. They will love it. All of them love to play in water. She goes in and gets dinner and gets things ready for the first night of summer vacation.

Coming to Terms with the Past.

Over the course of the next week, they get into a routine. Kat takes the kids to the clinic in the morning while she begins working. The kids eat breakfast with the cook. Then outside to play in the pool. Around lunchtime they go to their grandmother's house while Kat attends day treatment in the afternoon. Then home. The days are very full but manageable. The next session Kat has gone off without any bad memories. She is having a hard time with the last door opening. Not knowing what to do, the three doctors are unclear as to know how to open it. This last one is extremely hard. It is a very scary door. No matter what they do it will not open.

"Kat what do you see when you come to this door.

"it's covered in dark blood I put my hand on it, and it's covered in blood. I cannot open it. It had chains and a lock on it. There is no key. The poem does not work. Uncle did not close this door. I closed this door, but I do not know how to open it. "She tells them.

"How do you know you closed this door?" Jae asks.

"It has my name written above the window of the door. It has my elephant and clips hanging on the handle. I go to try to open it and the handle disappears. "She tells them.

"Ok Kat I want you to walk back up the stairway when you get to the top you will be awake and yourself." Jae tells her he snaps his fingers, and she is awake.

"I don't understand why I can't open that door. Surely the memories behind that one can't be any worse than the ones I already have had." Kat looks at them confused.

"Kat when was the last time you had any dissociative attacks outside of opening the doors?" Ki asks her.

"Not since we opened the first door behind the black door" she tells him.

"How has your anxiety and black out been?" Ki asks her.

"I've not had any except right after sessions why?" she asks.

"Your moods have been leveled out and so has your suicidal thoughts you haven't had any for a while now." Ki tells her.

"Do you think that we can just leave this door alone and only try to open it if I start to have problems again?" she asks.

"We can if you want but I want to resolve things about your brother-in-law before you stop therapy." He tells her.

"Ok I can do that I know how cruel he really was now. I do not need to live through any more memories to know that. I want to do something for myself though. I want to forgive him. I have been carrying too much anger and shame around because of him. I think if I truly forgive him, I will be able to put all that he did to me behind me. "She tells them.

"Ok so how do purpose to do that? "Ki asks her.

"Am going to write a letter and then burn it. He does not deserve the comfort of knowing that I forgive him. I need the comfort of releasing my heart from the chains that he has placed around it. "She tells them "Can we have a ceremony at the clinic to release all the guilt, anger and shame that I have felt all these years." she asks them.

"Yes, we can do that you just tell me what you will need." Ki tells her.

"I only need the three of you and a fireplace ready to light. The rest I can do." she tells them.

"Ok when do you want to do this?" ki asks her.

"My next session will be perfect. You know I am free after this. I will be able to move forward and go to work for my family. I will be able to not have to worry about hurting anymore because of what was locked behind those doors. I am at peace with what happened now. I just must forgive and close that chapter of my life. I can talk about the things he did to me without fear of judgment or hatred. I know it was not my fault and the choices that I made were to protect someone else. So, I now have a clear conscience towards Shay. I also can have a full life with Joe. I still get a little queasy over a few things, but nothing compared to like before. I know that I am not cured but I can manage things now. Which is something I could never even think of before. I do not have the voices telling me to run away or to hide anymore. This is truly a fresh start for me, and I thank you all for it." Kat tells them.

Over the next week Kat finishes the groundwork for her next session. She writes the letters she wants to read and burn. She makes miniature replicas of each door that she will be burning. She also gets the flowerpots ready to plant the seeds she wants to stand for the trees that are now in place of the doors in her mind. She knows that these are just symbols of what she had been through but to her physically burning the doors and planting flowers in their places will help her say goodbye to them forever.

The morning of her next session arrives and instead of going to the center she heads to the clinic. Once there she goes into the living room where the fire is laid out and sets everything up. The three Dr's arrive and meet her in the living room.

"Are you ready for this?" KI asks her.

"Yes, I am ready, so this is what I want to do. If you all are willing?" she asks them the three nods their heads." I want you to put me under one last time I want to go to each door and take a flower from each tree growing there now. I want to physically in my mind bury or burn the remnants of each door under those trees. So that they can no longer come back. The one I cannot open I will then plant the flowers in front of it so that it will be overgrown with the flowers of the memories that I have already conquered so that it cannot ever be opened. That whatever secrets it holds nothing can break it open. Once I am finished inside my mind I will then come back and do the same here in the real world so that it reinforces the fact that I have conquered those memories that they can no longer hurt me." Kat tells them honestly and quietly. They can hear the determination and emotion of the weight those memories have had on her life for so long. So, they all agree. with Jae on one side and KI on the other Dr Smith starts taking her down the staircase. She stops at the first door. Takes a small branch from the blooming tree. Looking behind the tree she can still see the door, she takes a small tool from her pocket and unhinges the door. It falls at the base of the tree taking the garden shovel she dies down and buries the door beneath the rich soil at the base of the tree and plants the seeds in her pocket. Looking up from the door she sees her 7-year-old self. She reaches out her hand and the little girl takes her hand. Kat encircles her with her arms and whispers to her." You are free now you are no longer trapped inside of this place. You can laugh and love. you can come freely out into the sunshine and into the world without guilt or fear. You did nothing wrong you are now free forever "Kat's emotions are so intense you can feel them throughout the room. When she lets herself go the 7-year-old Kat moves into the sunshine and out of the shadows of the memory. Kat continues to the next door and repeats the same thing until she gets to the door of her 13-year-old self. After doing everything she takes her 13-year-old self and hugs her close. "You are a brave child you thought of your friends and even those who hurt you. You tried to protect them by warning them away from him. You may go from here now. He has no hold over you. You can walk in the light. It is time to forgive the pain from this room and be grateful for what happened because of this room. You got to be with a family that you loved and who loved you. You are no longer held to this place so go into the light and embrace it. She waves goodbye to her 13-year-old self. And moves on to stand in front of the big black door the one in which she has several doors behind it she takes the big door down. Then she walks inside and knocks the others down dragging all the doors to the one that has yet to be opened, she takes her 16 and 17-year-old selves and they bury the doors in one place. Planting seeds across the threshold of the door that will not open. The three of them stand in front of this door holding hand and Kat looks at it." I do not know what nightmare you hold but there is nothing left of these others. Nothing can hurt me or keep me prisoner to here anymore. I forgive all the pain and suffering that occurred inside these doors. I thank you for being brave to endure all the pain and suffering that you experienced. Know that you were not at fault or the cause of anything that happened to you. That all the guilt and shame that was laid at your feet were his to bare. You are now free and able to walk in the light knowing that you did all you could to protect those who you loved.

Even if they never know it, they were safe because of your sacrifice and suffering." By the time she has finished she is on her knees in front of the last door crying her tears causing the seeds to sprout and to grow by the time she is done. The darkness in her mind is filled with light and it is a beautiful garden, the door is no longer visible for the vines and flowers have completely covered it. She stands up and begins her journey back to the top of the staircase. Knowing that she will no longer be trapped by the darkness of her memories. no longer a victim but a survivor. No longer a person to be pitied or vilified but a person to be celebrated and worthy of love. When she gets to the top, she hears the finger snap that will bring her back to the present.

"How do you feel?" an emotional Ki asks

"I feel energized and ready for the next step you guys ready?" Kat asks as she walks over and lights the fireplace. She pulls out a few pieces of paper.

"To the Dr who thought it was ok to harm a 7-year-old child I forgive you and all the pain you caused. I forgive and thank you. for if you had not been such a bad person, I would never have met my soul mate, so I forgive you for all the pain you caused and release all the bad memories with burning this replica of the door you were hiding behind and this letter. "Kat wraps the letter around the replica of the memories door and throws it in the fire. She continues doing this with all the doors. When she gets to her 13-year-old memory she reads the letter.

"Dear John and Eva

I forgive you for the pain and suffering you caused, and I thank you for taking me to the hospital. Because of you I was reunited with my soul mate and met my new husbands. Whom I loved more than life itself. My forgiveness to you does not absolve you of your guilt or shame for what you did. It just releases the hold that this memory has on me. It can no longer cause me pain or anger. I forgive you and I will burn this memory with a glad heart knowing that you can no longer hurt anyone." With that she burns the letter and door. She takes out a small shoe box inside are replicas of the doors from her memories of her brother-in-law. She pulls out the letter she wrote.

"Ok jerk faces it's your turn now. I have refused to ever mention your name because I cannot associate you in any way with my baby boy. To mention your name who brings nothing but pain for him. I forgive you for ripping my life apart and causing me the worst pain I have ever experienced. I forgive you for causing a rift between my sister and me. I forgive you for almost killing my dad but most important I forgive you hurting the most precious child in the world. One that you will never get to know now. I release the anger and pain that you have caused. The pain that has kept me in fear and locked behind a shell of myself for so long. I release the pain that you caused for I won against you for not only do I have my precious boy but also 3 girls and another son as well. I will no longer allow this pain and fear to rule my life, so I forgive you so that I can move on and be the kind of person I want to be. "She has tears rolling down her face by the time she finishes you can hear the anger and pain being released with every word she utters. Kat throws the letter with the box into the fire and takes Jae and Ki's hands. The 3 of them stare at the doors and letters burn up when the last shred is gone, she walks over to the table and for every door she just burned she has a flowerpot each painted in the colors of the doors. She continues to plant a few seeds in each pot. And places them back on the tray. When she has finished, she asks them to follow her to the atrium once inside she places each pot beneath the flowering tree there. "I want these to be planted in the atrium when they get big enough so that I can see them when I visit and know that I overcame so much in these last 5 years. Wow can you believe it took us 5 years of praying, talking, and mucking about in the scary darkness of my mind for me to be able to stand here ready to face a new future. Thank you for always believing in me and loving me. Thank you for never giving up on me. I release the two of you from the promises you made to a 15-year-old girl. I want you to go and get married and have lots of nieces and nephews to love. I want you to find someone who completes you in a more adult fulfilling way than I ever could. I do not want you to be stuck back there. I want you to move on and have a beautiful future and to love someone to the fullest. I have loved you as my knight in shiny armor, my refuge and my little broken heart. I will love you for eternity. You will always be my soulmate and protector. "Kat embraces the two of them in the tightest hug possible. And cries her heart out. It is a good cleansing cry. Not one filled with sorrow or pain. The two men are crying as well. Their hearts released from all sadness, guilt and pain. years of loneliness and yearning being released. When the three of them had finally finished crying and hugging. Jae looks at Dr. Smith and smiles reaches out his hand to her. Kat looks at her and asks" So how soon do you want your wedding? My soon to be ex doctor and soon to be a sister. "Kat asks.

"Did you tell them that we found you a different Dr to take over for when you need a little help?" she asks Kat.

"I don't think I will need it anymore. If anything crops up, then I will ask for help. Until then I will do all the things we have in place and try my best to live to be the best me. "Kat tells her.

"Have you told Joe your done with everything for now?" Ki asked.

"Nope but I told him that I start on Monday at a childcare facility so that I can help him take care of our family. He was a little shocked. That I am done with daily treatment and therapy for now. He of course is ok with it. He never liked how much of my time it took up. Thank you three again for giving me my life back. "Kat gives them a hug again. When she hugs Ki, she holds him a little tighter and longer.

"Hey angel you know that I will always be close by you are never alone. Even if I were to die you would never be alone, I am always here in your heart and mind. I will never leave you. We have been connected since you were 7 years old. You are my soul mate, my love, my angel. I could never leave you. I would sacrifice everything just to make sure you are happy and safe. I like your husband and I am happy you found someone to love. This is not goodbye because I will forever be with you." Ki whispers in her ear as they hug, they both have tears in their eyes when they part. She smiles up at him and tells him.

"I have loved you my entire life. I have always looked for you in every man I saw. When I could not remember you. The only person who ever made me feel close to you was Joe. I love him so much now that I cannot imagine my life without him. Thanks to my loving you and having you as a soulmate I was able to find someone who could love the messed-up person I am. I sometimes wonder what life would have been like if we had never parted. That was not Gods plan though. The day I Jae told me what happened to you three. I felt that pain all over again. I felt that my life was over. That I could never get through life without you. Then grandmother came and told me that I had no choice but to live. That the three of you gave up your life force to me. that your last words were that I needed to live and love. That it was not my time yet. That each of you said I needed to stay to take care of Jae. I did not do anything to help Jae I could not remember anything about you all. I just knew that a part of me was missing. I know what you have told me about the day the twins died but it is still fuzzy. I do not ever want to say goodbye to you again. I also know

I do not want you to not have someone to love you. Promise me that you will open your heart to someone so that you can have a full life. It is not fair for me to be happy and not you. You are my other half and I feel sad that you are not being loved by someone in that way. "Kat reaches up and kisses him fully without thinking Ki returns her kiss. They stay wrapped in each other's arms just holding on to each other knowing that this may be the last time they can be this close. Ki lifts Kat's face to his again this time he kisses her with all the pent-up passion he has held inside. Kat returns his kiss with all the love she has for him. The heat between them is intense. Jae and Dr smith leave the room giving them privacy. Ki picks Kat up and sits down on the sofa with her straddling him. she can feel the full force of his desire between her legs. She rocks back and forth against him the heat of her desire building as they continue to kiss. Kat begins to unbutton his shirt as she kisses him down his neck. Ki grabs her hands and pulls her tightly into his arms.

"If we do not stop now, I will not be able to. I do not want to stop. I want to love you completely just once. I also do not want you to have guilt over it either. If we stop, we can still be in each other's lives. If we do not stop, I will never be able to let you go. I will never be able to not have you beside me not just in my life but also in my bed. You will have to choose either me or Joe. You also have your children to think of where I only have myself. I have loved you and only you my entire life. You are the only woman I have ever loved. You will be the only woman who will have my heart. The choice is yours to make. I will love you and accept whatever decision you make. "Ki whispers in her ear his voice breathless and filled with desire. He knows she will decide to go to her children and their father. He would never be able to live with himself if she continues and loses them. Him and joe already had a talk about if she cheated on him, he would take her children away using her illness against her. He will not let that happen. Not after she has worked so hard and been through hell reliving her memories.

"This is not fair. I have loved you for so long and now I have you in front of me and I cannot show you. I know it is wrong for me to want to do this. I want too so much. I have wanted to since before I left you. Mama knew that. That was why she sent me away. She was afraid that I would not be able to continue to resist you much longer. She was so afraid I would have wound up pregnant at 16 and our futures would be over. She did not know what was going to happen. I have always loved you and never wanted to say goodbye to you. After my brother-in-law raped me the first time. I already knew that I could never return to you. That I was nothing but trash. He told me that it would bring him the greatest pleasure to hunt you and then torture me in front of you. to make you watch him rape me and cut me up in front of you. I could never let that happen. I made my decision that day that no matter how much I longed for you, no matter how much I loved you and wanted you that I could never see you again. Then for these last year's having you with me all the time it would have been so easy for you to have taken me. You being you have been nothing but a gentleman and taking care of me and only doing what is honorable. You are the most loving and honorable person I have ever met. I love you beyond all time and reason. I know that I can never love anyone the same as I do you. I love joe and I cannot imagine my life without him. I love you I just cannot have you. Thank you for knowing me better than I know myself. Thank you for always loving me and for always doing what is best for me. I know that you always kept your brothers around us every time we met when I was younger. It was so that this would never be able to happen. You always were so considerate of my feelings and my age that you held yourself in check constantly. I am so sorry that we never got to have the life we dreamed of. That our time together was truly way too short. I so wish I could go back in time and tell you all the things that I should have said to you then. That you were my only reason for living. You were the person that I wanted to protect most. To be with most and to love most. When you were no longer there, I was lost and had nowhere to turn. It was not until my husband started loving me that I even felt like a person again. "Kat tells him.

"That is why I know this cannot happen no matter how much we want it to. You would never be able to forgive yourself it this happened." Ki tells her as he shifts her to just sitting on his lap her head on his shoulder. "I know you and this would cause you too much pain so things will go back to where they should be. You will go home to your family and tell them that you have finished with your therapy for now and are able to move on with just a few meds to help you when and only when you need them. "He kisses her forehead, and they get up to walk her to the door. Just as they are reaching the door it opens and Jae comes in.

"You are leaving already?" Jae asks her mischievously.

"Yes, I am going home to my family. Nothing happened, just FYI "Kat at tells him punching him in the shoulder.

She walks out and heads home to her family to tell them that she will no longer need to go to therapy unless she has a setback. She is not planning to have any.

The End

I want to thank you for reading my story. I made this as a fiction story so that I could say a proper goodbye to Jun Ki, Kris and James. The locked memories and what happened during therapy sessions were events that occurred. The parts that the Park brothers were my way of saying everything that was in my heart. This book not only let me release all the anger and pain I had while recovering, but it also gave me a chance to relive some of my favorite memories of people that meant so much to me. The ritual at the end I did when I ended my therapy to forever release the pain of those memories and to release myself from addiction from my medications. We are stronger than we think we just need our why and stay positive in our thoughts that everything will work out.

9 781961 438743